BEAR INTO REDEMPTION

Onoma Series Book 2

Alisa Hope Wagner

BEAR INTO REDEMPTION

Onoma Series Book 2

Alisa Hope Wagner

Bear into Redemption
Book Two of the Onoma Series
Copyright © 2015 by Alisa Hope Wagner.
All rights reserved.
Marked Writers Publishing
www.alisahopewagner.com

Scriptures taken from multiple translations of the Bible.

Author photo by Lori Stead of www.wetsilver.com
Cover images designed by Muhammad Ahsan Ayaz
Cover designed by Alisa Hope Wagner

ISBN-13: 978-0692594193
ISBN-10: 0692594191

DEDICATION

Daniel, my high school sweetheart and soul mate.

Isaac, my first-born son and prophet.

Levi, my brown-eyed boy and shepherd.

Karis Ruth, my cherished girl and graceful companion.

Christina, my amazing twin.

ACKNOWLEDGMENTS

I'm amazed by the people God brings into my life who help me with each book that I write. My husband, like always, has been my biggest supporter. He not only reads and edits my books, he also gives me the time and resources to write them. Thank you for being the best husband and dad and pouring into our kids, so I can take moments in the day to write.

My three wonderful kids—Isaac, Levi and Karis—always encourage my writing, and they are proud to call their mom a writer. I feel satisfied with my work, knowing that they will one day read all of my books.

I'm so appreciative of my twin sister, Christina, who listens while I discuss the current happenings in the lives of my characters.

I especially want to thank the people who took time to read my draft, finding all those pesky typos and offering me their valuable insight. Cynthia Faulkner, Patti Coughlin, Jennifer Smith, Shay Lee, Bernadine Zimmerman, Kerry Johnson, Faith Newton and Daniel Wagner—thank you for making time for this book. I know your efforts will be multiplied in God's Kingdom.

Finally, I am grateful to the Holy Spirit Who went above and beyond to guide my writing in this book—even going so far as to "accidentally" having me add a scene to a chapter that needed that extra touch. I appreciate Your movement in my life. I may never deserve Your guidance, but I pray I will always be sensitive and appreciative of it.

INTRODUCTION

The World Government's tactic to form two factions as a means of control has stood firm for many years, but subtle strategies are shaping a resistance that no one can foresee. Efficientists and Colonials may appear like dissimilar social classes, but they are both pawns of a higher agenda, and the infrastructure governing them is dissolving. Former Efficientist turned Colonial, Ruth, finds herself in a new environment, surrounded by family she barely knows. She quickly discovers that she is a critical contributor to the revealing of truth in her fractured world.

"All of God's people are ordinary people who have been made extraordinary by the purpose he has given them." – Oswald Chamber

CHAPTER ONE

Bear nimbly jogged through the densely wooded forest. Things had changed, and the passage to his last fight felt strange. It didn't alter his focus, though. He would fight. He would win. And he would go home. His last public bout on the fighting circuit was over five years ago, and he was a different man. He once exploited his heritage to please the crowd. He was the Shaman. He used drugs, beat on the drum, sang peyote songs and wore the Mohawk of his original ancestors, the Ka'to Indians. The people loved him, and he consumed the fame until it almost took his life.

He heard a buzz of voices in the distance. Bear stopped and listened, leaning against the long trunk of a pine tree. He looked up to the sky. The sun was almost above him. The bout would start soon. He appreciated the unseasonably warm winter day. The temperature was in the low 70s. He wondered how many people would show up for his last fight. Would they recognize him? He wore the simple leather sarong that he had always worn. It gave him the most mobility, and he was used to its presence. He tied his long black hair in a leather cord down his back. Would they notice the silver that now streaked through his midnight strands? He had chosen Enchanted Rock as the place for his bout because he knew his opponent was tall, young and too cocky for his own good. He had been challenging Bear for over a year now, and Bear finally accepted. The challenged opponent chose the spot for the bout, and Bear would take all the advantages he could get so he could win without injury.

Bear continued his brisk run, allowing the movement to warm up this body. He had parked his truck on the other side of the forest. He didn't want to linger long in the crowd, and they would try to congregate around his vehicle after the fight was over. He didn't understand why God had asked him to do one more fight. He didn't need anything. The winner's booty would be nice but unnecessary. He had arranged for his fighters to take the loot back for him. They wouldn't cross him, and he would give them each a gift for their troubles. He, on the other hand, would slip back into the woods unnoticed. He also didn't want to see the look of shame on the young man's face when he lost. Bear knew what it was like to put all your security in the fighting circuit, and he didn't want to see the young man lose face. Maybe the crowd wouldn't be big, and the young man would easily recover from this loss. The young fighter was supposed to be unbeatable, but Bear knew that he had weaknesses—every fighter did.

The crowd would be angry if Bear won quickly. He wasn't going to put on a show like he used to. When he was younger, he'd allow his opponents to take punches or bring him to the verge of submission, so the crowd would be entertained. He allowed his body to be strained and broken under the hands of his challengers, knowing the entire time he could easily win. But he learned from his father that no one wanted to see an easy win. He thought of his father—a giant man who looked otherworldly with his pale skin, white hair and translucent blue eyes. Bear was thankful he favored his mother—a full-blooded Ka'to Indian—though, at 5'11" he was taller and much stockier than his mother who was small even compared to her siblings. He thought of the day she died when he was still a young man. Before she passed, his father would visit whenever he had a break from the fighting circuit, but he had never been faithful to his mother. He got his mother addicted to the same drugs he was using, bringing her more whenever he came. Bear's childhood was filled with memories of watching his mother slowly die from drugs and a broken heart. His father eventually stopped coming home, until the day Bear came of fighting age.

Bear quickly refocused his thoughts. He needed to keep his mind on his bout. He was almost to the clearing. He was in great shape—probably better shape than he was in his last fight when he was a younger man. He ate better. He slept better. He trained with the other men from the surrounding villages. They came to learn from him, and they would bring goods in exchange for his expertise. Many of them were beginners, but a few of them challenged Bear and kept him alert and sharp. But he wasn't willing to eat punches anymore. No matter how many fights he fought, getting hurt never got easier. He was at a point in his life when he realized winning meant more than merely submitting to your opponent—it meant not getting hurt either.

He saw people standing near the tree line, and he wondered why they weren't already at the base of Enchanted Rock. As he got closer, he turned his jog into a quick march and kept his face expressionless. When he walked into the valley surrounding Enchanted Rock, he had to keep his countenance firm. He had never seen a crowd so large. People were by the tree line because there was nowhere else to stand. Thousands of people had gathered to watch his last fight. They didn't notice him at first, and he had to walk around them. Suddenly, the path gave way before him as people began to whisper and motion to him.

"It's the Shaman!" someone shouted. "Where's your Mohawk?"

"Sing Shaman!" one man yelled.

"Where is your drum?" another yelled.

Bear didn't answer the questions, and he didn't look to his left or to his right. He stared straight to where the red flag of the fighting circuit stood. He noticed the winner's booty spilling out around the fighting line. It looked to be more than double his biggest earning. Bear hoped his men had brought more than one vehicle. Each bystander at the fight had to bring something for the winner, but many times several people would pitch in to bring larger items. He saw containers of preserved food, car batteries, hand-sewn clothes and linens, vats of alcohol, carvings of wood and other treasures hidden in boxes and burlap bags. He even saw a few paintings, and from a distance he could see the signature Mohawk of the Shaman. The crowd would be severely disappointed if they came to see the fighter he once was. That man was gone.

11

Bear came to the base of the mountain and began the trek up. He could already see his opponent waiting for him at the top. He was called the Bald Eagle, and Bear noticed that the man had embraced his title. His shaved head was stained white, his chest red and his legs blue. Bear couldn't help but chuckle a little bit. Each fighter exploited some sort of theme, and this young man had chosen Old America. Didn't he know that Old American had toppled in on itself? Bear only hoped that the stain the man used to dye his skin wouldn't rub off on him. He was going to be nice and win by submission, but now he contemplated a knockout, so he wouldn't get color on his leather sarong.

Bear made it to the fighting line and noticed that his young opponent's knees were locked. Bad choice for a tall man standing on an incline. Maybe he would pass out before the bout began. Bear walked adjacent to the man's corner where another referee stood.

"Interesting place for a fight. Do you remember me? I refereed the fight when you tore Watchman's shoulder and took him out of the fighting circuit for good," the referee said.

Bear said nothing and opened his mouth, waiting for the referee to check him for illegal paraphernalia. The referee paused for a moment and got the hint. Bear didn't want to talk. The referee grabbed Bear's jaw and looked into his mouth. Bear lifted his tongue, and the referee nodded and stepped back. Bear opened both his hands palms up and the referee grabbed them and inched his way up Bear's arms to the sides of his ribs. When the referee stepped back again, Bear lifted the front of his sarong, exposing his undergarment and the muscular lines of his quadriceps. Then he turned, lifting the back of his sarong so that his angular hamstrings were barred.

The referee nodded, "He's clean."

Bear went back to his corner. He noticed some people close to the fighting line had small video cameras. Some of his fights had made their way into the LPSs of Efficientists. His fights were labeled as documentaries, which made them more acceptable in the Efficientists' world, but he knew the entertainment value of his fights were what drew people in. Bear had visited a few of the Efficientists' parties, and they paraded him around like a trophy they owned. They never cared about his heritage or about Colonials. They wanted to see a raw fight from the safety of their homes. The Efficientists were one group of people he didn't mind disappointing today. They could stick their cameras into someone else's life.

Suddenly, large generators kicked on, and the announcer stood in the middle of the fight line with a microphone. Bear noticed there were more speakers than what was normal for a fight. Bear didn't listen to the man's words as they echoed against the granite mountainside and across the surrounding fields. He recognized the announcer. He had emceed many of his earlier fights. He was good at getting the crowd pumped up for a fight, and the applause sounded like thunder. Bear kept his eyes on his opponent. He had been standing rigid for too long. Bear noticed that he started swaying from his left foot to his right foot, trying to get the blood circulating back up his large frame. He looked a lot like his own father minus 50 pounds of extra bulk. He definitely looked intimidating, but his posture revealed that his balance was poor—most tall fighters lacked stability.

Finally, the announcer asked the fighters to join him. Bear made his way to the middle of the fighting line, keeping his eyes on his opponent's face. Bald Eagle made a show of sneering down on him, which was normal for the taller fighters. Bear kept his chin up and gave no expression. The man took out his black mouth guard, obviously made from the rubber of a tire. He spat out an insult, but Bear didn't listen. He never let the words of his opponents enter his mind.

"Where is your mouthguard," the announcer asked Bear.

"I won't be needing one," Bear said without removing his gaze.

"Fine, fighters to your corners!" he yelled into the microphone and the crowd erupted.

Bear walked back to his corner. He still didn't know how he would take out his opponent—whether he would finish him standing or on the ground. He'd let the man's first mistake dictate his termination. The announcer gave a few more words, but Bear no longer noticed. His eyes were on his challenger's body, reading every move he made. Bear barely noticed a large copper disk being presented to the announcer. A moment later the loud rapping of metal was heard through all the speakers. Bald Eagle instantly started making his way toward Bear. His elbows were low, and his fist framed the bottom of his chin. Bear made his way up the side of the granite mountain, and the man snickered, thinking Bear was afraid to confront him. Bear wasn't afraid. He simply needed a shot from higher elevation.

Bear stealthily leaned into the incline, gripping the granite rock with his bare feet. He kept his body tight but his muscles loose. Once he gained the right altitude, he began treading horizontally toward his opponent's location. Bald Eagle was still about five feet further down the hill but a stone's throw across the granite expanse, trying to keep up with Bear's speed. Bear quickened his pace. He wanted to intercept his opponent where the incline flattened a bit. He thought it best to take him out in a spot where he wouldn't roll down the side of the mountain face. Bear noticed the man trying to keep his balance, and his hands dropped further away from his chin. This was the perfect time to strike.

Bear ran a few steps and planted a jab-jab-cross combination into the man's jawline, testing the fighter's pain threshold. The man flinched a little, but didn't cry out. Bear knew his opponent was taking some sort of numbing drug. His pupils were too wide for the brightness of the day. The man lunged at him, but his imbalance caused him to teeter. Bear sprang into the air. His foot landed into the man's left kneecap, and Bear felt a crack. Bear landed swiftly on his feet, and powered his torso to the right, turning his flattened toes on the rock ground to meet the force of his momentum. His shoulder slid across his tucked chin as his right arm extended like an agitated cobra. His fist—hard as rock from years of fighting—pummeled into the man's unprotected chin. The man's head snapped back, and his body fell flat on a small piece of even granite. Bear looked at his opponent's limp body, and saw his chest rise and fall with air. He was alive. He'd be okay.

The crowd roared as the referees checked Bald Eagle's pulse. The announcer came up to Bear holding the microphone to his lips.

"The winner by knockout in 1 minute and 9 seconds is the Shaman!" the announcer yelled, while grabbing Bear's right wrist and bringing his arm into the air.

Bear gave no expression.

Then the thunderous crowd quieted, the announcer looked toward Bear. "People have said that you had no more fight in you, but obviously they were wrong. In fact, you seem to have become an even better fighter in the last five years of your retirement. This is your quickest knockout or submission to date. You are notorious for winning in the final round, which is why people loved coming out to watch you. It's almost like you are a different fighter now. What has changed in the last five years?"

Bear stood for a moment. *Is this why you brought me out here, God? To show that I have changed?*

The announcer saw that Bear wasn't answering. "Don't you think the people have the right to know what happened to the Shaman they once knew? The fighter with the drum and the Mohawk who sang Indian songs with his bass voice? Do you think the people expected something more from you here today?"

The announcer put the microphone back toward Bear's face. Bear grabbed the microphone from the announcer's hands.

"Do you think I came here today to please you?" Bear asked, looking out over the crowd. "I came here today to please the Holy One. He is why I am here. I wear the blood of the Holy One's Son. I have the Holy One's Spirit inside of me. I am not the Shaman anymore. My name is *Cabena Sa Ne'aw-ze*! I am Fighting Bear, and I fight for no one's pleasure except for mine and the Holy One!"

15

Bear gave the announcer back the microphone. The announcer stood speechless for a moment, but remembered the priority he was given. "Yes, but look at the winner's booty," he said swinging his arms toward the piles of goods spread across the base of the mountain.

"Don't you think that it is deserving of a song from the Shaman?"

The crowd yelled and started chanting, "Sing! Sing! Sing!"

Bear looked over the crowd.

"Just one song, and you walk away a wealthy winner," the announcer finished and motioned for Bear to take the microphone.

Bear slowly took the microphone and waited for the crowd to quiet their chanting. "I gave you something better than a song. I gave you the Holy One and His Son. The winner's booty is for a fight not a song. It is mine by right. If anyone thinks I'm underserving of it, he can face me right here, right now!"

Bear looked around at the crowd and waited for several moments. He saw a few men approach, but they were his fighters from his village come to pick up his winnings and take them home. He put the microphone to his lips.

"This winner's booty is mine. I came out of retirement to claim it. I fought for it. I won it. My men are here to pick it up. If anyone touches it or bothers my men, I will find you, and take care of you like I did Bald Eagle."

Bear handed the microphone back to the announcer and began to make his way back down the mountain. He noticed his opponent sitting on the ground, sneering at him as he passed by. There was no shame in the man's eyes—only revenge. The crowd was silent as he walked the rock face to the mountain bottom. He marched steadily through the crowd, keeping's eyes on the tree line. He would make his way through the forest and back to his truck. He will never come back to the fighting circuit again.

16

Suddenly, one man shouted, "Fighting Bear gave us a knockout in one minute. We should honor him!"

Others began to shout. "Fighting Bear, you will always be the Shaman!"

The crowd began to clap and cheer. The sound of applause once gave Bear a high that drugs couldn't match, but now it only solidified his new existence. He would no longer chase fame—it was an empty facade that forced him to be something he was not. He was a fighter. He wasn't a showman.

CHAPTER TWO

Pilar flattened the pedals of her bike, and stretched her legs to see the large community water well inside Zach's government housing complex. The metal fence encasing the small neighborhood of Runners gaped open. She sighed with relief and slowed her speed. They hadn't closed and electrified the gate yet. Her father had seen Zach's truck heading past the filling station, and she borrowed her brother's bike without thinking. She needed to see him. She was tired of waiting.

She appreciated the coolness of the early winter season. Her perspiration only lightly misted her body, so she knew her carefully applied make-up held up. She tried to ease her breathing. The excited beating of her heart had little to do with her three-mile bike ride and more to do with her nerves. Her last encounter with Zach over two weeks ago caused her to question the ultimatum she had given him. She didn't want to lose him, but she couldn't stand by and watch him let go of everything.

His father had been dead for five years now, and she had watched Zach slowly walk away from the path that was so obvious to everyone. Zach was the spiritual leader of the area, yet he had shunned his post and joined the World Government as a Runner. A Runner of all things. The very job his father had denounced. Zach ran goods to the Efficientists—goods created by the sweat and blood of the Colonials.

Pilar had many words. She was good at speaking her mind—something she learned from her mother. She presented Zach with a smorgasbord of arguments interlaced with forced patience. For over five years she set her love aside, so he could find his peace with the death of his father. The flames that consumed Zach's father destroyed more than the walls of that small church. They devoured an entire ministry that expanded to bring power and redemption to their town. Healing evaded Zach because he would not wrestle with the pain. He avoided redemption, and his festering wound poisoned the work for which his father gave his life.

Pilar could see Zach's truck parked on the side of the street. She put her left foot to the ground and slid the bike to a stop. She wouldn't let Zach see her pedaling haphazardly on a bike obviously too small for her. She wished she could have taken her father's truck, but they needed the last of the gasoline to make their weekly deliveries. She swung her right leg over the seat and leaned into the small mirror attached to the left handlebar. She appreciated the attractive physical features that her blended family had endowed to her. She had her mother's Latin qualities—dark hair, full lips and thick eyebrows and lashes. Her father's black heritage had given her darker skin than her mother's and a taller build, but her father's white mother had passed on her green eyes to Pilar. She was the only child of her parents to have the green eyes of their grandmother, and she knew that they gave her a distinctly unique look.

Pilar had been experimenting with a few new shades of blush before finding out that Zach was in town, and she was glad she had tried the peach hue first. It had given her face a natural glow, and she needed all the advantages she could get right now. Satisfied with her appearance, she began to walk the bike toward Zach's house. She didn't know exactly what she would say to him. She needed to know that he was still on her side. She could handle his moods, his aloofness and his denial, but she couldn't allow their relationship to disintegrate—if what they had could even be classified as a relationship.

Pilar suddenly stopped the bike. Her skin became hot even as a cold gust blew across her body. She stared at Zach's porch and saw Zach's mother embracing a young woman. Pilar's grip on the bike's handlebars stiffened, as she watched Zach help the woman up and embrace her. The woman's arms clung around Zach's torso, and he gently stroked her shoulder length chestnut hair. Pilar could hear the woman crying—a soft wail of joy and relief, entwined with an emotion that Pilar couldn't place. Pilar sensed that the relationship this woman had with Zach and his mother ran deeper than mere friendship, and her conclusion felt like a slap in the face. Had she been replaced?

Pilar pushed the bike against the curb, and her clenched fists rubbed against the long stride of the rigid cadence of her thighs. The atmosphere around her blurred except for a circular parameter around Zach's porch. Zach let go of the woman, and he helped his mother to her feet. He opened the door and held it wide, allowing the woman and his mother to walk into the house. He looked down the porch, calling for his mother's missing cat. He looked past Pilar and quickly looked back. He locked eyes with her and closed the door. As Pilar stomped up the porch steps, Zach put his hands into his pocket and leaned his back on the side of the house—his face emotionless.

Pilar's 5'10" stature allowed her to stare directly into Zach's nonchalant blue eyes, as he slouched against the house siding. Her tanned skin and emotionally charged expression seemed to radiate off of Zach's white skin and calm countenance.

"Who was that?" she asked, forcing a whisper. Zach's mother had always been sickly, and Pilar didn't want to disturb her.

"My mother?" Zach asked.

"I know who your mother is, Zacchaeus Mark Daniels. I'm talking about the young woman you were embracing only a minute ago."

"Oh, you mean Eve—I mean, Ruth," Zach said, fumbling over his words.

Pilar squared her shoulders and put her hands on her hips. "Well, which is it, Zach, Eve or Ruth? And what are you covering up? I can tell you don't want to tell me what's going on."

Pilar knew that Zach had difficulty lying to her. She had seen him lie about menial things to strangers or co-workers at the Sleeper plant, but he couldn't lie to his friends. His conscience wouldn't let him deceive those he valued and loved.

Zach's countenance turned serious, and he pushed off from the wall. He took several steps down the porch stairs and sat down.

Pilar quickly followed him and stood in front of the last step. "What is going on Zach? Are you seeing her?"

"If you mean am I dating her the answer is no and never," Zach said firmly.

Pilar stared at Zach for a second before sitting down next to him on the step. She knew he was telling the truth. "But you have some emotional connection to her, Zach. I could see it. She can't only be a family friend."

Zach sat quietly.

"I've never seen her before, Zach. I know every face in this area, and hers is new."

"She came here from Trinity," Zach said.

"Does Pastor Isaacs know her? How does she know your mother? Wait. What's that?" Pilar stopped talking and looked to one of the bedroom's windows positioned over the porch. "I hear crying."

Zach turned his head and stared at the window too. The crying grew louder.

"She sounds like a little girl," Pilar whispered.

"She's dealing with an old wound," Zach said and turned his gaze to Ruth's car parked on the side of the street.

"How old is she?" Pilar asked. From a distance she thought the woman was about her age, somewhere in her mid-twenties. Now the woman sounded to be much younger.

Zach sat silently for a moment and looked at Pilar. "She's probably in her early thirties."

"Zach, what is going on? Stop avoiding it and tell me who she is!"

Zach rubbed his palms on his jeans and sighed. "You remember when I told you that I have a half-sister. My mom

21

had to leave her. You remember me saying that ever since I was little, my mom and I prayed that she would return to us?"

"You expect me to believe that your long lost sister has come home?" Pilar asked, searching Zach's eyes for sincerity. She brought forth a memory of him confessing that he had a sister. He had always been so envious of her large family. She couldn't understand why. She recalled that he had struggled not to cry when he talked about his sister. She realized now that her appearance into their world would change everything. She didn't know yet if it would be for the good or bad.

Zach looked back toward the window after hearing his mother cry out. Pilar could hear the crying of both women now.

"Whether you believe it or not, Pilar, the answer to my mother's prayer is in my house at this very moment."

"How did she get here?" Pilar asked, looking toward the window. The crying grew soft again.

"From what I have gathered, she left *Life Efficiency* and moved in with the old sisters in Trinity who used to run a foster home," Zach said.

"You mean Deborah and Esther? The foster home my dad stayed at for a few weeks when he was young?" Pilar asked with disbelief.

"Yes, that very one. Apparently, they house Efficientists now who have dropped rank," Zach said.

"My dad lost track of them long ago. They don't keep an HMS and we don't have one, but we heard they had retired," Pilar said.

"Well, it looks like they are now out of retirement," Zach said, bringing his hand across his blond hair. "And they helped my sister find her way home."

"Did you know who she was?" Pilar asked. "I remember you saying that your mom kept her identity hidden from you."

Zach looked at Pilar. "I never understand why, but Mom knew what she was doing. I'm glad she never told me."

"Did she have a high rank?" Pilar asked.

Zach got up from the step. "Look, Pilar. I really don't want to discuss all this stuff now. I'm as shocked as you are."

"You're right," Pilar said. "I'm sorry. I'm glad your sister has finally come home."

Zach said nothing.

Pilar smiled. "Can I bribe you to give me a ride home? My dad has some leftover meat pies and sweet bread that you will love."

Zach looked toward the window again. The crying had stopped. "That sounds good. I need to stop over by Bear's house anyway. I think my mom and sister can use the time alone."

Pilar began walking toward the bike she threw on the curb. "Will you bring some sweet bread to Bear's grandfather for me?"

"You spoil that old man," Zach said.

Pilar smiled. "He appreciates what I give him. It makes me want to give him more, so I can see his toothless smile."

CHAPTER THREE

Neil Elder leaned forward on his LPS desk, trying to rub away the tension stretching across his face into both his temples. The hum of the machine sounded lifeless after the voices ceased clashing through its systems only moments ago. The uproar from the nine other regional magistrates morphed into quiet discord that seeped into his mind, gnawing slowly at his compromised condition.

"You are not well," Dr. Michael Linton said as he quietly closed the door behind him.

Neil jerked his head out of his hands. "Who let you in?" he asked louder than he anticipated. He wasn't expecting Dr. Linton so early.

"Randall showed me up. You knew I was meeting you today at 10 am," Dr. Linton said, placing his bag on the couch.

Neil looked at the clock on the right corner of his LPS screen. "The meeting went longer than expected." He paused and stared past the monitor, rehearsing the array of arguments directed at him over the past two hours.

"How did the meeting go with the other World Government Magistrates? Are they having the same complications with *Life Plethoricity* in their regions?" Dr. Linton asked as he pulled out his stethoscope and portable blood pressure cuff.

"It's a disaster," Neil answered. He began to roll up his right sleeve to let Dr. Linton put the blood pressure cuff around his arm. "The STATS are finally coming in. People are not happy about the new life plan. They are labeling it a control tactic by the World Government. Many Efficientists have dropped rank and others have put their rank on hold until the World Government retracts it. The other nine magistrates do not want to back down because they fear the government will be weakened in the eyes of the people. They are demanding that I find a solution quickly before everything collapses and we usher in a sweep of civil disobedience."

Dr. Linton unwrapped the Velcro cuff from Neil's arm. "Your blood pressure is too high. How much sleep have you been getting?"

"I don't know. I think I went into my Sleeper a few days ago. I haven't been keeping track. I can't seem to keep up with everything."

"You look like you lost more weight since I saw you last week. Have you been taking your diabetic medications? Have you looked over the diabetic diet I sent to your LPS a few weeks ago?" Dr. Linton asked.

"Look, I have bigger fish to fry than watching what I eat and making sure to take my pills. *Life Efficiency* is falling apart at the seams, and you want me to look over a meal plan!"

"If you die, none of it matters," Dr. Linton said calmly and turned back to the couch and put the blood pressure cuff into his bag and grabbed the stethoscope. He put the earpieces into his ears and walked back to where Neil was sitting. He leaned over Neil and placed the bell of the stethoscope onto his chest. "Breathe deeply."

Neil took several deep breaths while Dr. Linton checked his chest and back with the stethoscope. "You know, our visits would be easier to achieve if you would simply move into the flat underneath mine. It's been vacant since I moved out of it over 30 years ago. I don't know why Arthur Pallue never leased it after I left, but I have a feeling he was trying to make some kind of statement," Neil said.

Neil noticed that Dr. Linton remained quiet. "The electrical system on this floor has been completely redone. I don't anticipate any fires occurring ever again. I assure you it is safe to live here or I wouldn't have moved in."

Dr. Linton removed the stethoscope from Neil's back and stood upright. "No, it's not that. I prefer not to live in the middle of the city. My patients are all Efficientists now, and I would like to keep my distance. Plus, I enjoy living on the outskirts of the town where I can have an unobstructed view of the horizon from my backyard," Dr. Linton said matter-of-factly.

"Yes, but it takes you fifteen minutes to drive into the city. You are wasting an exorbitant amount of time."

"I enjoy the drive. Gives me time to plan my day," Dr. Linton said, cutting off the conversation. He wrapped the stethoscope around his neck so the ends dangled over his shoulders. "Okay, let me be frank with you," he said as he walked over to the couch and sat on the armrest to face Neil. "We need to see some drastic changes in your lifestyle choices or your health will continue to deteriorate. You need to habitually take your medicine every day. You must remain on the strict diabetic diet that I have prescribed. I will contact the food preparation service for you and let them know your meal plan. I want pre-made meals to be sent to you every day. That will mean less PR outings for you, unless you are able to preorder according to your meal plan. Also, you should not consume any more alcohol, not even in social settings. Finally, I strongly urge you to get at least 3 hours of REM sleep a day. And I would prefer you do it at the same time every day, so your body can have some consistency."

Neil quietly stared at Dr. Linton for a moment. "You are asking a lot."

"I understand. I know it's a lot to change. But I care about the health of my patients, and you are one of my top priorities. In my professional opinion, I would strongly suggest that you hire more help. Your work in the World Government has increased since the ten regional magistrates were established, but you are still trying to keep up with *Life Efficiency*. You can't be expected to help run a world government properly without an infrastructure of support."

"I have Randall, and he's good at getting things done," Neil said, pausing for a moment before he continued. "But it's obvious he's getting overwhelmed with work, though, he's too proud to admit it. But I worry about *Life Efficiency*. I wouldn't want to lead anyone to believe that I've paid to cushion my rank. I have penalized many Efficientists for doing just that, sending most of them to prison. And I'm not about to drop rank. I've worked too hard to get where I am now."

"I've noticed that when the ten magistrates were organized the World Government did not give added rank to the new positions. Most of the ten were Elite Efficientists in their regions and have all taken on additional responsibilities. Why wasn't the rank system adjusted for the promotions?" Dr. Linton asked.

"We all agreed that we didn't want to cause the Efficientists to question our motives. Getting the ten magistrates established came with a lot of criticism, and we didn't want to add to the resistance being raised."

"Well, right now is the perfect time to establish a new rank system for the magistrates," Dr. Linton said.

"How's that?" Neil asked warily.

"At this moment there is a lot of disorder. People are freezing and dropping rank. They are questioning the new life plan. This is your time to slip governmental mandates into the system unseen. I guarantee no one will notice the small changes in the World Government when they are too worried about the livelihood of *Life Plethoricity*."

"Yes, but all those new mandates mean nothing if the entire system collapses," Neil said.

"That means you must find a way to save the system— maybe a distraction of sorts, but before you do, make sure to pass all the mandates you and the magistrates deem necessary. Ensure that you can have the help you need to run the government before your body decides to quit on you."

Neil felt a glimmer of hope for the first time since *Life Plethoricity* was established. "Maybe the chaos created by the transition of life plans is actually a good thing," he said with obvious excitement. "Yes, that's it! We ride the storm a little longer, making changes along the way. Then, we introduce the final puzzle piece to *Life Plethoricity* that will appease the Efficientists. We'll say we saved the best for last!"

"And what do you think that final puzzle piece might be?" Dr. Linton asked.

"I don't know yet, but I'm sure the solution is out there," Neil said, looking visibly more relaxed. "You know, Dr. Linton, I was skeptical when Randall suggested that I take you on as my personal doctor, but I have to say that you are definitely proving your worth. You do understand that silence is golden around here, and if information were to leak out, we'd have to quiet the noise."

Dr. Linton looked at his folded hands for a moment before retrieving the stethoscope from around his neck. "I think my silence is the virtue that Randall found most appealing about me."

Neil smiled. "That's what I hoped to hear."

Dr. Linton stood up and reached for his bag. He placed the stethoscope inside and zipped it up. "I'll be setting up your food delivery when I get back home. I'll try to get the deliveries started by the end of the week. Until then, just don't consume any breads, desserts or alcohol."

"But that's all the fun of dining out," Neil said in mock distress. "But I'll do my best."

"I'll see you next week unless anything changes. I'll send my work schedule to Randall's LPS," Dr. Linton said and turned towards the door.

"On your way out will you stop by Randall's door and go over what we discussed here today? Tell him to bring up a list of possible new agents that we can recruit. We'll start by taking the workload off of his shoulders, so he can help me with mine," Neil said before sitting back down at his LPS.

"I'm impressed with you, Dr. Linton. Not only are you a fine physician, but it now seems you dabble in a little Life Therapy, as well," Randall said. "I now get to hire a new team because of you."

Dr. Linton watched Randall wrap a small exercise towel across his neck, draping along his wide shoulders. He stood in the entrance of the door that he held only half open. He had just been working out, and his muscles were swollen and sweat dripped down his body. Looking at Randall with his shirt off made him even more intimidating. At least with his suit on, his strength was covered up. Dr. Linton knew that he could never cross this man. Not only was he strong, but Dr. Linton sensed that his conscience had no meter of right or wrong. He was simply guided by what would benefit him.

"I'm trying to help my patient from slowly killing himself," Dr. Linton said.

"Well, I'll need you to come by next week sometime to give my new guys their physicals. Don't want anyone not fit to handle himself working for me."

"Send me the names and the date you want to meet, and I'll clear my schedule," Dr. Linton said.

"Good. I'll send you the names by the end of the day. I already got several in mind. Go home and get some rest, Dr. Linton. You look tired," Randall said, closing the door behind him after he entered his home.

Dr. Linton looked at the door for a moment and then made his way down the corridor. He walked several paces beyond the elevator and pushed open the door to the stairwell. He would rather walk down the many flights of stairs than continue to be on Randall's surveillance for one more second. He felt drained, like all his energy had been sapped by a performance that would save his life—or end it. Randall watched him closely as they discussed the changes that Neil would be implementing into the World Government. He knew Randall kept him close to keep an eye on him.

He felt like he was slowly being strung into a dangerous circle next to Randall every time Neil confided in him, and he was quickly realizing that Randall was not what he seemed. He once thought Randall to be an honest, easygoing bodyguard, but he had since learned that Randall's laid-back demeanor hid something sinister in the shadows. From his years working in a colonial hospital, he could spot a crack of deception in an otherwise perfect façade. He had seen indirect glimpses of a darker personality underneath Randall's veneer of appeal, and he knew with all certainty that Randall could never be trusted.

Why couldn't I have just kept my mouth shut? he thought. When Neil started using him as a soundboard to release the stresses of the World Government, he should have immediately suggested a Life Therapist. Now it was too late. He was in too deep and with his latest heaping of advice, he knew he had just imprisoned himself with the actions of a madman. An image of Eve's penthouse filled his memory. After the fire, Neil kept the reconstruction of the flat to be almost identical to how Eve had it when she lived there. Neil even placed his Sleeper under the double-stacked windows in the living room—the same place Eve had hers.

What really happened to Eve Pallue? he wondered. When Randall sent for him only weeks after she left his care at the colonial hospital, she had second-degree sunburns covering much of her body. He stayed with her for two days, but he finally turned her care over to Randall. Then only weeks after that, she had burned alive in her penthouse, the very penthouse Neil Elder took over. None of it made sense. He suspected that Randall had once loved her, but now he never spoke of her. How could someone as infamous as Eve Pallue disappear so seamlessly from the scene of *Life Efficiency*? If her life could be blotted out that easily, what hope did he have?

Dr. Linton paused for a moment on the steps, leaning against the stair rail. He looked behind him to make sure no one was following his footsteps. He waited briefly, listening for any movement or sound. He inadvertently shivered from a stale draft, drifting up from the lower level. The last thing he intended on doing was to move into this high rise. He had once coveted the personal doctors who lived in one of Arthur Pallue's buildings, but the gilded veneer had been exposed, revealing a silent graveyard of secrets and conspiracy. The anticipation he had when he left his internship at the colonial hospital morphed into regret. He soon discovered that the life he had yearned for was a prank, spun by a World News that misled the masses—both Efficientists and Colonials.

By the time Dr. Linton made it to the parking garage exit, sweat trickled down his face. He knew his calf muscles would be sore the next day, but he would take an early run in the morning to stretch them out. As he walked towards his car, the oppression of the high rise began to fade. He could feel the breeze of the open parking garage fill his lungs and thoughts of his small house on the outskirts of the city hushed his fears. He would be okay. If he continued to do his work and keep out of trouble, he would be fine. He remembered the words of advice that Randall had given him when they met only a few short months ago. *"It is always better to appear to know less than you really do. Don't give people any reason to distrust you."* And that's exactly what Dr. Linton intended to do.

CHAPTER FOUR

"You had some food in your car. I hope you don't mind that I brought it in," Zach said, sitting down on the corner of the bed. "Mom is getting lunch ready in the kitchen. She wants us to join her."

Ruth tried to open her eyes, but the dried, salty tears from her night of crying had sealed her eyelids closed.

"I moved you into my room last night, so Mom could sleep," Zach's voice came again. "Are you hungry? You have some great snacks in that basket you brought."

Ruth tried to get up. Though her body felt exhausted, something inside of her had lifted. She had a peace she had never known.

"Here, let me help you."

Instantly, Ruth felt strong arms around her, lifting her against the small headrest of the bed. She blinked again, pulling apart her entwined eyelashes. When she finally opened her eyes, she saw Zach Daniels, her brother, sitting on the corner of the bed.

Ruth noticed that she was still wearing her clothes from the night before as she adjusted her weight on the bed. She tried to compose herself, but knew her dignity was lost with her recent conduct. "I apologize about my behavior last night," Ruth said visibly embarrassed. "I don't know what happened."

"Mom left you when you were almost five, so I think your inner child burst through," Zach said chuckling. "It was pretty intense, but I guess it's better to get everything out in the open quickly than let it simmer for years."

Ruth watched as Zach's demeanor grew gloomy, but he shook it off quickly. He tried to fix a carefree expression on his face, but Ruth could tell he was worried about something.

"You know, I've been praying for you all my life," Zach said, pausing to collect his thoughts. "I'm sorry about the circumstances that we first met."

"At the gas station?" Ruth asked.

"No, I'm mean at your apartment. Well, not there. I enjoyed your company after you loosened up a bit. In the city, outside that restaurant. I would like to talk with you about what happened that night before Mom wakes up. There is no excuse for what I did, but I just want to explain the full story before you judge me."

Ruth held up her hand to quiet him. "I know you didn't intend to hurt me," she began. "I know you didn't mean to kill the Elite Efficientist either. The World Government hired you to tamper with the Sleepers, but you didn't realize that it would cause death."

Zach sat speechless for a moment and looked down. "I didn't," he whispered. "They said it would cause no harm.

"In fact, before I signed on, I tampered with one of the Sleepers at the plant just to see what it would do. The person I talked to gave me specific instructions on how to manipulate the Sleeper. The only thing that happened after I went into REM was that I woke up in a paralyzed state. I don't remember how long, but it did feel like several hours, though, it could have been only a few minutes."

Ruth was intrigued. She wondered how he survived an Awakening—the same Awakening that almost killed her. "What did you do while you laid there?"

Zach thought. "It was hard at first. I was really getting antsy, and I could feel my heart rate accelerating. But I realized that I might be stuck there for a while, so I started trying to occupy my thoughts while I waited."

Ruth listened intently to Zach's words and motioned for him to continue.

"To be honest, I really struggled in the beginning. I tried to hum tunes in my mind. I thought about the books that I've read. I even tried to calculate the gas I would need to drive the entire length of Old Texas and how many stops I would have to make. But I could tell my anxiety was still really high."

"What did you finally do to stay calm?" Ruth asked. The Awakening still scared her at nights, and she needed to know that if it happened again, she would be able to save herself.

It was Zach's turn to look embarrassed. "Well, I prayed. I didn't want to pray to God. I still have a lot of hurt and anger towards Him—about letting my dad die. I knew if I unleashed the emotion of my father's death, my body couldn't handle the force of energy in my paralyzed state. So I prayed for my mom, friends and any other person that came to my mind. I prayed for you too," he said, looking at Ruth. "But honestly I didn't have the faith that I would ever meet you."

Ruth stared at her brother—the Runner who had made her laugh. She had a family once again.

"I want you to know," he continued, "that I didn't want to mess with anyone's Sleeper, but I had good reason."

"I know. You needed the money from the World Government to pay for Mom's surgery," Ruth said.

Zach looked relieved that Ruth knew the details. "Yes. It's funny. I hate the World Government for killing my father, but here I am working for them and taking their money to heal my mother. How did you know that I took the money for Mom's surgery?"

"When you were setting up my new Sleeper, I looked at your profile. Something about you seemed familiar. Now, I can see why. You look a lot like Mom did back then—at least, from what I remember. I saw that your mother was sick, and after you tried to warn me at the PR event, I knew you needed money to help her."

"The surgery hasn't helped much," Zach said, rubbing his beard. "In fact, she has been getting worse ever since. I talked to the doctors, and they think she has a secondary infection from the pacemaker. They want to redo the surgery. Even if I had the money, which I don't, I know Mom will not go back to the hospital."

"Why not?" Ruth asked.

"She wants to be in heaven with Dad. I think you were the only reason she was holding onto this life," Zach said.

Ruth didn't want to discuss her mother's condition anymore. She could tell last night that her mother was weak and had shortness of breath. She had her mother back in her life, and that's all she wanted to focus on right now. "Did you tell my bodyguard about tampering with the Sleeper?" Ruth asked. She wondered what had happened to Zach after Randall had taken him away.

Zach's eyes reflected into his memory and his jaw became stiff. "Yes, I told him that I tampered with another Elite Sleeper and the man died. I told him to warn you not to sleep in yours. I tried to explain how to undo it, but he wouldn't listen to me. He threatened me by force. Then he said if I came back or told anyone the story about what happened that he would find my family and destroy every person I loved."

"How did he hurt you?" Ruth asked. She was beginning to understand how deep Randall's brutality went.

Zach looked away. "Let's just say that Mom thinks I fell asleep on the road and ran my truck into a tree."

"I'm sorry he hurt you," Ruth said.

"I'm sorry I almost killed you in the Sleeper," Zach replied.

"If it weren't for my Awakening, I would still be in my high rise flat, plugged into my LPS. I didn't remember Mom until I woke up in my Sleeper unable to move. I'm thankful you tried to warn me. You risked a lot to save my life."

"But that's what confuses me," Zach said, shaking his head. "The World News said that you died in the fire. They found proof of your remains. When I carried you to my room last night, I could see burns on your hands and arms. How were you able to get out of the fire?"

"A friend sacrificed his life to get me out. I drove his car west until it ran out of fuel. Then I walked through the woods and fell asleep in a barn owned by two elderly sisters."

"Are you speaking of Deborah and Esther of Trinity? I heard you talking to Mom about them," Zach said.

35

"Yes, they cared for me while I recovered," Ruth said.

"Do they know who you are?" Zach asked.

Ruth smiled a bit. "They found out at my first Sunday at Trinity Church. Pastor Tom is well informed about the Efficientists."

"Does Pastor Tom know?" Zach asked, trying to shield his astonishment.

Ruth pointed her finger at her mouth. "I think he saw my missing tooth when I smiled. He put the pieces together quickly."

"Their church has gone underground. I'm really impressed with what he's doing in Trinity with the new trading center. Were you at the communion? Did you see that little boy with CP get healed?"

Ruth stared at Zach for a moment. She didn't know why, but she felt she could tell him anything. "I was watching him when he was healed."

"You were with him? What happened?" Zack asked amazed.

"God told me to pray for him and I did," Ruth said matter-of-factly.

"You mean he was healed from your touch?" Zach asked, now leanly intently towards his sister.

Ruth looked at her brother for a long moment. "God told me to hold Jason's face and pray for his healing, so that's what I did. When his mom came to get him, he could talk and run like his brothers. I don't believe my faith had anything to do with it. I think Jason's faith stretched out so wide and thick at the moment, he simply needed someone to respond."

"So no one knows that you touched him?" Zach asked.

"No one but you," Ruth replied.

"Well, that's a good start to our relationship. We already have a few secrets," Zach said smiling.

CHAPTER FIVE

"**Z**ach, will you go get some water from the well? We're all out," Naomi asked her son. Although her breathing was shallow, she couldn't help the smile that stretched the width of her face. Here in her kitchen stood her son and daughter, together. She sifted through the basket of foods that Ruth had brought with her.

"Sure, Mom. I'll be right back," Zach said, as he grabbed the large pitcher from beside the sink.

"I thought you would have a water system since Zach is a Runner for the World Government," Ruth said. She could hear Zach chuckling as the screen door shut behind him.

"No, all the Runners share the same water well. The Government doesn't give Colonials anything that would hurt their budget for the Efficientists. We do have a septic system where the waste dumps, so we don't have to shower or relieve ourselves outside," Naomi said while preparing the food that Ruth had brought with her.

"But you have air conditioning," Ruth said.

"No, we don't. In the summer, it will be hotter than an oven in here."

"But I see a refrigerator and I've already used your HMS," Ruth said, confused.

"We receive a small portion of electricity from the World Government, but it's just enough for the fridge and HMS. And many times, the electricity will go out on us, and we have to eat everything in our refrigerator or give it away before it spoils."

"How do you cook?" Ruth asked in awe.

"We have a multi-fuel stove," Naomi said, smiling at her daughter's shocked expression. "It cooks and will also heat the house when a cold front comes in."

"Where," Ruth said, walking deeper into the kitchen. "Is this it?" she pointed.

"Yes, it's not that big. We don't need a huge once since only Zach and I live here. Zach's gone most of the time, so he eats on the road. I'll make bread or roast a chicken. It will last me a while."

"And this is the fuel," Ruth said, pointing to a bag of charcoal and several neat stacks of wood.

"Did Deborah and Esther not use a multi-fuel stove?" Naomi said, wondering at her daughter's amazement.

"No, they have electricity—enough for air conditioning, an oven and a refrigerator," Ruth said.

"Did they have running water too?" Naomi asked surprised.

"No, they had a well like you, though, it was just outside the back door. They also collected rainwater for showers. The water would come from a reservoir tanks attached to the roof. They had some sort of septic system like you have where the wastewater collected. I think they pumped it into their garden somehow. I was hoping I'd be able to take a hot shower here, but I guess those days are gone," Ruth said. "My showers were hot in the summer, but they cooled down with the weather. My last shower was so cold that it took me a long time to warm back up."

"How are Deborah and Esther? Did they make this food for us? I've heard that Deborah is an amazing cook," Naomi said. She had almost given up on her daughter ever coming home, but God had promised her long ago that she would see her before she died. Little did she know that at the time she had just given up hope, her little girl was only a few hours away at the home of two renowned sisters from Trinity—Deborah, the nurse, and Esther, the school teacher.

"I tried to contact them, but I think their HMS went down again. They have difficulty sometimes working it. But I sent a message to Pastor Tom. He'll let them know that I found you. Deborah is an amazing cook. They are setting up their farm as a bed and breakfast, and they'll be using it to help the

Efficientists that drop rank," Ruth said, taking a seat at the table. "I'm sure they'll be excited to know that I made it here so quickly. All this time I've been waiting to meet you. I never realized it would be so easy."

"I see it as nothing short of God's miracle that my little girl is here, sitting at my table. Nothing easy about it, I'm sure," Naomi said. "They said you were dead, but I didn't want to believe it. God had promised me that He would bring you back to me. I lost all hope yesterday, but there you were on my doorstep—my little girl. Right when I gave up, God's promise came through."

Naomi paused for a second and looked at her daughter. "Do you know that I never once called you *Eve*?" I wanted your first name to be *Ruth*, but your father insisted on his way. I wound up calling you little pet names, which your father hated."

Naomi's eyes lingered into the past as she began to remember. "I think your father finally realized that I would never be able to hold you at a distance. A mother must love her child. I tried so hard to hide my love for you, but I couldn't. I used to get so angry at myself, but then I realized that no matter what I did, I would have lost you."

"Mom, I'm so sorry about my anger yesterday. I'm embarrassed by how I behaved. I know there was nothing you could have done to stop him from taking you away from me," Ruth said, staring down at the fading burn marks on her hands. "When I finally had you with me, it felt like something inside exploded. I told you that I hated you, but I didn't mean it."

Ruth felt uncomfortable as she spoke with her mother— as if another person were speaking through her. She realized that she was reacting to her mother like a young girl, but no matter how she tried to calculate her responses, they continued to be childlike. Ruth wanted more time to ease into her relationship with her, but instinctively she knew that her mother had very little time left. The strong woman Ruth remembered from her childhood was gone. In her place was an aged and weakened woman, and the urgency Ruth sensed overshadowed her awkwardness. No matter her inward struggle, Ruth loved her mother and knew she needed healing in their torn relationship in order to bridge an emotional chasm she had lived with since her mother was taken away.

Naomi walked over to Ruth and wrapped her little girl into her arms. "I know you didn't mean it, but I don't blame you one bit for having those emotions. Your reaction to me was much like my reaction to God when He wouldn't let me go see you. When I found out that Arthur had died, I drove to the city. I waited outside your building door for many hours. I knew I was walking a line of disobedience. God finally told me that if I didn't go home, you would never come back to me."

Ruth sat quietly for a moment, listening to her mother's soft cries fade into heaving breathing. "God knew. If you came to me right after Dad died, I would have never believed you. My bodyguard would have escorted you out of the building and probably have put you in jail. When Dad died, all I wanted to do was prove to him that I could surpass his life. No matter how hard I worked, I was never satisfied. Nothing I did was enough."

Naomi gave her daughter one last squeeze and walked back to the basket of food to prepare lunch. "To be honest, your work both horrified and amazed me. It was a torment to read your writings when you began publishing. You had become exactly what your father wanted you to be."

Ruth looked at her mother. "What was that?"

Naomi would not shield her daughter from the truth. "A tool used for control. Your father was so scared of people and their ability to create chaos, so he thought up a plan to divide and control them. The Second Civil War caused him to mistrust and hate everyone."

"But how could one man be given so much authority? We both know Arthur Pallue. He was a normal man with flaws and weaknesses," Ruth said.

"There are no accidents in this world, my sweet girl. There are two powers at play on earth and both are supernatural. We can either be pawns in the Enemy's plans or servants of the Most High God. Your father was merely a pawn who was given a lot of power."

"I'm back," Zach said as he opened the screen door. He paused and looked at his mother and sister. "Why is it that every time I leave you two alone you cry?"

Naomi finished setting out the food and sat down in the chair next to Ruth. "We have to give up our pain, so we can claim God's peace. I want to enjoy my little girl, so we will hurry up and get the hurt out of the way. Zach, will you ladle us each a cup of water? Deborah and Esther have given us a wonderful feast, and I want to celebrate. My daughter has finally come home!"

"No, Zach, you keep your room. Ruth and I will fit nicely on my bed. I've been without her for so long, and I will not waste another moment," Naomi said, averting her attention to Ruth. "You don't mind sleeping with your mama, do you, baby girl?"

"Not at all," Ruth said. "I am accustomed to sleeping in small spaces, so I do not need much room." Ruth would not admit that she felt uneasy about sharing a bed with her mother, but she had already decided to overcome her inhibitions. She sacrificed everything to find her mother, and she would not let her own petty reservations limit her experience with her.

"Good, I have two extra drawers in my dresser and ample closet space. Just unpack and make my room your room."

"Are you sure, Mom? I don't mind sleeping on the couch. You're sick, and I don't want Ruth to have to worry over you," Zach said.

Naomi stared at her son. "I know what you're thinking, young man, and you can't always keep everything perfect for everyone. Life is messy and there's no way around it. You have to allow people to walk through the mess. They'll never grow otherwise."

"I know, Mom. I just don't want Ruth to become upset by your condition," Zach said. "Plus, she only just met you again. She might feel uncomfortable."

Naomi straightened her fragile frame and placed her hands on her hips, demonstrating a strength that wasn't there a few seconds ago. "I've been praying to have my daughter back for far too long to let her slip through my fingers because of silly formalities. I will devote every last moment and every last breath I have left on this earth getting to know her and spending time with her. She was ripped from my arms when she was not even five years old, and both she and I need time to heal. But time is something that I do not have anymore. I may be leaving this world soon, and I will be leaving both my children behind to find their own way. Ruth needs healing more than I do because she still has her entire life left to live—a life where she will be expected to love and to receive love—something her father was incapable of showing her. And you, my son, are going to have to get over the small inconveniences of life and realize that there is a bigger picture that you can't control."

Ruth looked at her brother fidget under their mother's reprimand. He was a grown man, but still his mother's son. She knew she needed to ease her brother's worries. "I watched my father go through his sickness. I will be fine, Zach. I want to spend as much time with Mom as I can. I do find myself slightly uncomfortable—everything is so new and different—but I have already decided that I need to heal, like Mom said, and I believe she is right. I want to spend as much time with her as possible."

Naomi grabbed Ruth's hand and continued. "Now, Ruth, follow me. I want to show you my favorite room of the house," Naomi said, leading Ruth to a small door next to the bathroom. "It's small, but it is the heart of our home."

When Ruth walked in her mouth gaped open. "Mom, where did you get all of these books?"

"Let Zach explain how we got them. After all, they are his inheritance—though, he doesn't seem to care about them anymore."

Zach leaned against the wall next to the door and peered into the small room. "My Dad's grandfather started collecting those books before the Second Civil War. My grandfather and dad have added to his collection ever since. I've added a few until Dad died."

"What kind of books are they?" Ruth asked, not recognizing them.

"They are writings of faith from the *Bible* through church history," Zach said with obvious respect. "We have Thomas Aquinas, John Wycliffe, Martin Luther, John Calvin all the way to John and Charles Wesley, Oswald Chambers, Mother Teresa, Billy Graham and Martin Luther King, Jr. Right before the Second Civil War is when we got most of our books. So many Christian writers from so many different backgrounds— blacks, whites, Latinos, Asians, men, women, poor, rich, young, old—all wrote their own revelation of God. It was like an explosion of literature that ended with the collapse of our country."

"Makes you wonder if God was preparing His church," Naomi whispered.

Ruth walked into the small space and rubbed her fingers against the bindings of the books. Some were leather, plastic or paper. She saw other stacks of printed paper that had been hand bound. "What are these?" she asked, pointing to them.

Zach walked next to his sister. "Those are posts from Christian bloggers just before religious online writing was banned. My grandfather printed them out. Average people sharing their faith in God," he said and picked up a small pile.

"Those are Zach's favorite," Naomi said. "What was it that you told us? Oh, yes. *They reveal the hearts of a people watching the demise of their Promise Land.*"

Zach's cheeks flushed. "I said that a long time ago."

"I know, my son. You said it at the last sermon you ever gave just before the church fire. That day both the men I loved stopped preaching," Naomi said, bringing memories to her mind. "Those notebooks over there have Austin's sermons in them. He used to write them out before he spoke, so he could send them electronically through email. When the World Government banned all new electronic religious materials, he continued sending out his sermons. That's when he got into trouble."

"Austin is your late husband's name?" Ruth asked.

"Yes, he was a good husband, a wonderful father and a powerful leader. He was visiting sick people at the hospital the day he met me," she said, looking toward her son. "Zach, you know most of the story, but I never told you who the Efficientist was that had hurt me. Now I guess you can put the puzzle pieces together for yourself." Naomi looked back to her daughter. "Austin was a good fifteen years older than I was, but we fell in love instantly. When I was released from the hospital, we were married and we moved to Cedar Wood, where we started our church and Zach was born."

Ruth noticed a box of clipped photo printouts. She grabbed the first one on the top. "I remember this photo," she said, as she examined the black and white still shot. "When you came to my flat," she continued, looking up at Zach, "I entered your HMS and looked up your profile. I saw this photo. I couldn't see Mom's face, but the image saddened me. I think your presence caused me to start to remember."

Zach's eyes widened and he quickly looked at his mother.

Naomi's stare turned from the books and focused on her son. "You met Ruth in the city?"

Zach fumbled. "I did, but I did not know who she was at the time. It was only yesterday that I realized that she was my sister," Zach said.

Naomi looked from her daughter to her son. "Did you know she was Eve Pallue?"

"The day I found out was the last day that I saw her in the city," Zach said simply.

"Well, God has answered another question for me," Naomi said.

"What is that?" Ruth asked.

"He wouldn't let me tell Zach his sister's true identity. I simply said that you were an Efficientist. I've had all the secrets hidden in my heart, and I didn't know why. But now I know that if I would have spoken them, maybe my Ruth would never have made it home," Naomi said.

CHAPTER SIX

"**W**here did you get this beautiful quilt?" Naomi asked, as she unfolded the blanket. "It's the Story of Ruth! It's stunning."

"Esther made it for me," Ruth said, sitting next to her mom on the full-size bed of their shared room.

"The fact that you were safe in the home of Deborah and Esther makes me want to praise God. I've met some of their foster children through the years, and they have almost all done very well for themselves and for their community. In fact, I heard that Levi stayed with them for a few weeks when he was a young man. He is one of the founders of Levington."

"Yes, they told me briefly about him. They didn't know much because they lost track of him over the years."

"You'll love his family. In fact, Pilar is—well, she was Zach's girlfriend, but now I don't know if they are dating anymore," Naomi said. "Where did you get this?" she asked pointing to a large *Bible*.

"Deborah gave it to me," Ruth said, reaching into a box on the floor. She pulled out the great leather-bound book and handed it to her mother.

When her mother opened it, a small card fell out. "What is this?" she asked.

Ruth looked at the card that she had placed in the *Bible* when she changed clothes this morning. "It's my access key card to the World Bank. I don't know why I still have it. My account is probably frozen. I'm sure the World Government is fighting for the rights of my estate."

Naomi examined the card. "No, I think Neil Elder is trying to claim rights to your entire estate. From what I've seen, he's already taken over your building."

46

"He's not allowed. It hasn't been a year since Eve died," Ruth said, trying to navigate the anger filling her.

"From what I've read, he's only 'leasing' your home until the estate is given to him. I haven't read anything about a bank account yet, so he may be biding his time. It really doesn't matter now. Ever since he set up the ten magistrates, there is no limit to his power," Naomi said, shaking her head and putting the card back into the *Bible*.

"Pastor Isaacs told us about the ten magistrates," Ruth said. "They're not listed in the new life plan he implemented."

"Yes, *Life Plethoricity* caused such a disaster. Neil's having to institute a stronger government to keep control," Naomi said. "You know, Neil was always so jealous of you. When you were a couple of years old, your father and he got into a huge argument. Arthur kicked him out of the space under our penthouse flat. Ever since then, there was intense hatred between those two. I think Neil realized that you had replaced him as Arthur's protégé."

Ruth got up from the bed. "I'm sorry that *Life Plethoricity* has created so much trouble," Ruth said in a soft tone.

Naomi sensed something was troubling her daughter. "Don't be sorry about anything, Ruth. God allows things to happen to fulfill his purposes on this earth. Some of those things are beautiful and some are ugly, but He has to work through the choices of His children. Your brother chose to leave ministry to become a Runner, which I was strongly against. Yet, through his choices, God led him to you, and then you finally came back to me. You saw the photo of him and me at the fire, and something in your memory came through."

Ruth nodded and smiled. Both she and Zach decided to spare their mother the full story of their first meeting. Naomi didn't need to know about Zach's tampering with the Sleepers to get money to pay for her pacemaker. Or that Eve was the one who wrote *Life Plethoricity*. Naomi had a life full of heartache. They chose not to burden her with the past.

"I find it interesting, though," Naomi said, "that all I wanted was to get into that penthouse and bring you home. But instead of using me, God used Zach. It's remarkable. You know he's prayed for you ever since he was able to talk. He always prayed for his lost sister. Even now when he prays, he remembers you."

Ruth felt an awkward sense of warmth, knowing that she had family praying for her. All the years she spent isolated at her LPS with no familial connections, there were people praying and yearning for her. Ruth saw a hand-sewn pouch where she placed her pearls that morning in the box where the *Bible* was stored, and she reached down to hand it to her mom. "I have two pearls left from a trading transaction I did, Mom. I would like to give them to you to help with living expenses."

Ruth handed the pouch to her mother.

Naomi opened the drawstring, and poured the creamy white pearls into her palm. "I've never seen pearls before, Ruth. These are exquisite! They feel exactly how I imagined them to feel," she said as she rolled one along her fingertips.

Naomi put the pearls back into the fabric pouch, and handed it to Ruth. "I have everything I need. Zach takes good care of me. You keep them. God will help you use them for another reason."

Ruth took the pouch from her mother and slipped the key card in with the pearls. She placed the pouch with her folded clothes in one of the drawers. "May I hang the rest of my clothes in your closet, Mom? I don't have much."

"Of course, dear." Naomi said, as she flipped through Ruth's *Bible*.

Ruth opened the closet door and gasped. "Mother, you have a sewing machine!"

"Yes, I've done a lot of sewing in my years, but I was never very good at it. My eyes are not keen and my hands are not steady," Naomi said, placing the *Bible* back on the bed. She got up and walked toward the closet.

"How do you use it? Are you able to plug it in?" Ruth said, looking at the black metal machine.

"No, baby, it has a foot pedal," Naomi said, pointing to the base of the sewing machine.

"Can you teach me?" Ruth asked.

"I can show you what I've learned. I'm a terrible seamstress, but I did my best at making clothes for my family," Naomi said with a chuckle. "My husband and Zach never complained when my stitching was crooked or when their shirt sleeves were uneven."

"I know how to sew, Mother. Esther taught me. I sewed everything in my wardrobe."

Naomi stepped a few paces back to look at her daughter. "Really? You sewed that sweater dress? And that jacket you wore yesterday?" she asked, fingering the jacket folded over Ruth's arm. "Stunning, Ruth. I may not be able to sew, but I can definitely recognize beautiful workmanship when it's in front of me."

"I want to be able to help you and earn a living. I'm good at sewing, but I know I'll get faster with a sewing machine," Ruth said, eyeing the black machine again.

"Well, I'll tell you what. I don't have much of an inheritance to offer you, but I know Zach will share his books with you, and I will give you not only this sewing machine," Naomi said, walking over to her bed, "but also the thread wheel that I've stored under the bed."

"You have a thread wheel too?" Ruth exclaimed, setting down her clothes and getting onto the floor. She crawled under the bed skirt and pulled a large wooden wheel out from under it.

"The base of the wheel is under there too. You can tell from the dust that I haven't used it in a while. We can have Zach set it up for us, and I'll show you what I remember. I don't sew anymore, so it is a good thing that Zach and I have been the same size for many years now," Naomi said.

Ruth noticed a box that slid out from under the bed when she moved the thread wheel. She leaned down and picked it up. "Are these photos of Zach when he was a child?" Ruth asked, picking one up.

"Yes, he was such an anointed boy. He loves very deeply—almost too deeply," Naomi said, taking the photo from Ruth's hand, bringing it close to her face so she could see it.

"Who's the boy next to Zach?" Ruth asked, picking up another photo.

Naomi looked at the photo in Ruth's hands. "Oh, that's Bear. Well, his real name is *Cabena Sa Ne'aw-ze*, which means *Fighting Bear* in the Ka'to language. But everyone calls him Bear."

"Does he have a Native American heritage?" Ruth asked, mesmerized by the young boy's long black hair, tan skin and hawk-like nose.

"He's half Ka'to. The Ka'tos used to live along the Trinity River around these parts long ago. Most of them lived in what was Oklahoma before the Second Civil War."

Naomi sat on the bed and looked at the wall, reflecting on the memories in her mind. "His father was white. He fought for a living. He and his band of people would travel across the land, challenging known fighters. He was a very large man and very intimidating. He met Bear's mother when she was really young—only about sixteen or seventeen. She became pregnant with Bear, and he set her up in a small house over by our old church in Cedar Wood. Bear's father would come into town every now and then, but he never stayed for long. Sometimes he would take Bear with him on some of his fights, but only for a few weeks, and then he'd bring Bear back home."

Ruth looked at her mother. "Why are you crying, Mom?"

"Oh, don't mind me. It's the memories of life flooding my mind. Bear's mom died when he was a young man. She overdosed on something. We all knew about the situation. Zach must have overheard his dad and me talking because after church one day he asked if he could take some food and other things to Bear. We asked Bear if he wanted to live with us, but he didn't. He had been taking care of his mom for so long that he already knew how to provide for himself. But every Sunday we would take him to church, and he would come over some afternoons while I was teaching Zach."

"How did you wind up in Levington?" Ruth asked.

"We had a thriving church in Cedar Wood, but Austin knew that Levington needed a pastor. He started having meetings here on Saturday mornings. Zach was supposed to take over when he was finished with school, but when Austin died, Zach stopped everything and became a Runner. He said he wanted to provide for me, but I knew he was only running away from his pain," Naomi said and remained silent for several moments.

Naomi looked at Ruth and smiled. "You know, after you live so many years, God's hand in the lives of His children becomes clear as day. Bear barely knew how to read—even though he was already a teenager. He was on the same reading level as Zach. I wound up teaching them both how to read and write and do their numbers. I remember having so little patience during that time. I couldn't wait until my two-hour lessons were done, so the boys could play outside and I could do other things. Now I look back and wonder why I was in such a rush. All the trivial moments now seem so beautiful. I just couldn't see it."

Ruth looked through more photos. "You seem to have a lot of photos, Mom."

"One of my husband's hobbies. He loved taking photos of people. The church bought him a solar-powered generator and real nice photo printer, exclusively for his digital camera. He'd take portraits of all the church members and their families. I think that's why they didn't mind the extra expense of photo paper."

"Bear looks older in this one," Ruth said, eying a close-up shot of Bear.

"Can you hand it to me?" Naomi asked.

Ruth grasped the corner of the photo and handed it to her mother.

"He was about sixteen here. This is the day he left us. His father wanted him to be a fighter, but my husband tried everything to convince him to stay with us. As he got older, he would come back and visit us every so often. He would go to church with us and confess his sins. But as time wore on, his visits were less and less. We heard a lot of rumors, and I know Zach went to find him several times when he got older. But when my husband died five years ago, Bear came back to mourn with us. And he's been here ever since."

Ruth quickly pointed at the boy in the photo. "This boy lives here in Levington?"

"Yes, he's kind of the town's pastor," Naomi shrugged her shoulders. "I guess you can call him that. We all hoped that Zach would take over the ministry once my husband died, but Zach took it real hard. He's been ignoring God for many years now. Bear has been doing his best to be a spiritual guide. His heart is in the right place, and he's learning and growing, but when the World Government banned all religious material, he took it pretty hard. Zach told me that he threw his HMS into the Trinity River. I don't know how he's handling all the changes. I'm trying to give him space until he figures out what he's going to do next."

Ruth could hear her mother's shallow breathing. She looked at her mom's face and could see her weary expression. "Mom, would you like to take a nap?"

Naomi put the photo of Bear on her lap and stared at the wall again. "God has plans for Bear just like he has plans for Zach. Your brother is anointed. I feel it in my spirit. I see him struggling with his feelings toward God. He loves God deeply too, but his anger at losing his father runs deep too. God will reach him, but I don't think I'll be here to see it."

Naomi looked at her daughter and smiled. "Did you know that I wanted Zach's first name to be Mark?"

Ruth shook her head.

"It's interesting that both the men I loved insisted on naming my kids, but I see now why my husband wanted to name him Zacchaeus."

"Why is that?" Ruth asked. She had wondered.

"Zacchaeus in the *Bible* changed not because of guilt, but because of love. Jesus loved him and Zacchaeus gave from the overflow of that love. That love is in Zach. When he used to preach, he wasn't judgmental or critical, like my husband sometimes was. Zach preached from an enormous amount of love in him. I've never seen anything like it. Zach is blessed with a supernatural love. It is his greatest blessing, but also his heaviest burden."

CHAPTER SEVEN

"**I**t's almost winter, and I'm still sweating," Zach said as he brought a large jug of water into the kitchen. He wiped his forehead with the bottom of his shirt. "People are predicting this will be a cold winter, but if the warm weather of fall is any indicator, I don't think they're right. I brought some water. Is Mom still asleep?"

Ruth closed the book she was reading and looked up at her brother. She couldn't understand how he could be so hot when she always felt so cold. "Mom is getting sicker. She fell in the bathroom the morning after you left for work. She didn't break anything, but she's bruised her thigh and hip area."

Zach set down the jug on the table. "Why didn't you call the factory? They would have contacted me. That was four days ago!"

"Don't yell or you will wake her. She wouldn't let me contact you," Ruth whispered, looking toward her bedroom door to make sure her mother was still asleep. "She wouldn't let me take her to the colonial hospital. She wouldn't let me call Deborah or Pastor Tom. She's gotten so thin in the past two weeks. I didn't think I would be able to help her up after her fall, but she was so light. Why won't she see a doctor?"

Zach sat down next to his sister. "I've already argued with her about going to the hospital, but it doesn't matter what I say, she won't go. I've never seen her so adamant. She doesn't want another surgery." Zach stopped and looked at Ruth. "It looks like you've lost weight too, Ruth. You look more like the Eve I remember."

Ruth felt her eyes sting with tears and she lifted her head to stop the flow. She had been so emotional since she came home almost three weeks ago. Her heart was worn out and she missed the physical activity of the farm. "I used to work in

Esther's garden, and harvesting in the fall kept me outdoors for hours," Ruth said. "Deborah always gave me a steady supply of food and sweets to eat. I didn't realize how much muscle and fat I put on until I had to take in the waist of my slacks yesterday. I made them before I left the farm. But it doesn't matter. I want to stay with Mom as long as I can."

"I'm sorry we don't have anything to keep you occupied. It must be hard being cooped up in here all day. Mom used to keep a garden, but she let it go when her health declined. She still tries to cook every now and then, but I make sure to bring home premade soups from work. They're easy to make."

"Reading and taking care of Mom, and I'm glad you have the soups. They're actually easy for me to make. I can't crack an egg, but I can handle boiling water," Ruth said. "I'm trying not to worry. I know I'm supposed to give my worries to God, but applying the truth is so much harder than knowing it. I keep reading your books, and—"

"What books?" Zach interrupted, noticing for the first time the book Ruth had closed.

"Your books in the small room. I hope you don't mind. Mom said that you would share them with me," Ruth answered, wondering why her brother seemed agitated.

"How many have you read?" he asked, trying to appear nonchalant.

"I started reading the blog printouts you talked about. I was intrigued about what you said about all the Christians from different backgrounds writing about their faith. I see why you like them. I can see their struggle in their writings. In many cases, when I read their work chronologically, I could see their spiritual growth. It was really profound to watch their journey unfold before me."

"Now you are reading *City of God* by Saint Augustine," Zach said, eyeing the book. "Why did you choose that one first?"

"Actually, I noticed that you had the books in semi-chronological order. I've already read several books before this one. You seem agitated, Zach. Do you not want me to read your books?"

"No, I—I'm sorry. I want you to read them," Zach said, looking back down at the table. "I think I'm dealing with old feelings that I thought had died. I had put those books in order, and I've read about a third of them. I was determined to read them all before I finished graduate school. But here I am, almost twenty-eight, and I'm still where I was five years ago."

"If you don't mind," Ruth said feeling uncomfortable. "I used to discuss my thoughts with Deborah and Esther. They were both keen listeners, and I miss hearing the revelations the Holy Spirit showed them personally. They gave me exactly what I needed at the time of my spiritual birth, but I wonder if you wouldn't mind discussing some other topics and questions that I've been pondering."

Zach quickly got up from the table. "Look, Ruth. You heard Mom. That side of me died five years ago with my dad."

"But we don't have to talk about your faith," Ruth said. "I only want to hear your thoughts about these books."

"Ruth, you are probably the smartest person living today. Why on earth do you need my insight?" Zach asked.

"I have knowledge, Zach. I have a lot of knowledge stored in my mind, and as I read these books," Ruth said, picking up the large book on the table, "I fill my mind with more knowledge. But—it's hard to explain. I feel like I'm so ignorant in other ways. I read all of Paul's letters, over and over again in the *Bible*. And I sense something in him that I don't have. I sense it in you too, and I know I can't get it from reading a book," she said, placing the book carefully on the table.

Zach exhaled and thought for a moment. He walked back to the table and sat facing Ruth. "God says to love Him with all of our heart, soul, strength and mind. These are four aspects of our spiritual life. Our heart is our emotions. Our soul is our personality. Our strength is our free will. And our mind is our knowledge. And God wants us to love Him with all four equally. The only problem is that we are each designed differently, and we each have our own strengths and weakness. For example, it's very easy for me to love God with my heart. By nature I've always had a deep sense of emotional love for God and others. But loving God with my mind was a choice. I had to really work hard to read books about Him, so I could learn more about His character. But as I read more, my emotional love for Him grew stronger."

"So God must know I'm weak in certain areas," Ruth said, thinking over Zach's words. "I keep reading books, and they are not satisfying the hunger I feel inside. You know where I'm weak, don't you?" Ruth asked.

"Yes, your emotional development has been severely halted—probably from when Mom was taken from you. I don't know much about your home life, but I've studied your father, and I suspect he didn't adequately fulfill your emotional needs," Zach said.

Ruth looked away slightly embarrassed. "No, I guess not."

Zach leaned closer to Ruth. "And I know where my weaknesses lie."

"Where?" Ruth asked. She wondered why he had suddenly become comfortable in revealing his weakness, but she suspected that her own embarrassment prompted his compassion somehow.

"I'm weak in my strength," he answered. "I served God easily when everything was going my way. But He took my father, and I fell away from Him. It seems that I lack resolve during the storm, and my emotions are so strong that I can't control them."

Zach had been so vulnerable with her that Ruth felt like she could do something that she had never done. She reached over and put her hand on his. "I've lost everything, but when I found God, the emptiness in my life went away. My strength is strong and so is my mind, but my heart and soul are both remote ideas that scare me. Maybe we could help each other."

"But I'm scared of opening the pain of my father's death. I know it will break me," Zach said.

"I know," Ruth said. "But isn't the breaking supposed to be necessary? I'm admitting to you that I have the emotional aptitude of a five-year-old. Won't you at least be open to seeing what God will do? It has to be better than running Sleepers to Efficientists," Ruth said.

"Wow, I'm impressed, Ruth. You said a joke—well, kind of. You're dabbling with humor now," Zach said and leaned back into his chair, giving Ruth's hand a gentle squeeze before letting go. "Okay, I will walk down this road with you. But I'm not ready to talk about fathers right now. I won't mention yours and you don't mention mine."

"Sounds good to me," Ruth said. She didn't mention that she already felt peace about her dad after discussing him in detail with Pastor Tom. Her mom, though, was an entirely different emotional package to claim.

Naomi wiped away her tears and gently closed the door to her bedroom. She had heard soft whispering coming from the kitchen. When she peeked out of her door, she could see her son and daughter in a deep discussion. She knew that Zach had come in late that night, and she feared that her children would be discussing her fall four days ago. Instead, though, they were having the most amazing spiritual breakthrough.

Before climbing back into bed, she replayed the deal her children had made. They were going to help each other overcome their heartaches. Naomi knew she had little time left. The one thing she wanted before she went to be with Jesus in heaven was for her kids to get along. God not only answered her prayers, but He surpassed them. Ruth had challenged Zach's complacency. And Zach had challenged Ruth's heart. Hopefully, together they would encourage and strengthen each other.

As Naomi closed her eyes, she couldn't help but thank God. "*Your way is perfect, Lord. And Your timing is right. Forgive me for questioning Your will all those years. I didn't understand, and I couldn't see past my own hurt. Help Zach to find peace in You. Help my Ruth to experience the warmth of Your love. Direct their paths, Dear God. I know soon we'll all be together in heaven, but help them to fulfill the purposes for which You have created. I pray this in Your Son's name, amen."*

CHAPTER EIGHT

"You didn't have to change jobs for me, Zacchaeus Mark Daniels," Naomi said in a false firmness. "I'm able to care for myself, and I have Ruth here to help me whenever I find myself in a bind."

"Mom, you fell again and sprained both wrists," Zach said, stirring the soup mix into boiling water. "Ruth is not a doctor, and since you won't go see a real doctor, I need to take extra precautions. Besides, they've been wanting to put me in a management job since I started working at the plant."

"Well, at least I caught myself this time when I fell," Naomi said with a smile. "Could have been worse."

"How do you like your new position?" Ruth asked. "How do you like being in charge?"

Zach looked at his sister, pulling puffs of raw cotton into tiny strands using the thread wheel that he assembled. Over a month in his care, and his sister had faded to bone white, and her high cheekbones were accentuated by sullen cheeks. "I hate it," he finally admitted. "I'm close to home and I get off early, but I have to work in close contact with a few Efficientists."

"You don't like them?" Ruth asked. "I have never met any of the Efficientists who worked on location."

"The honest truth, and I'm not trying to be arrogant, but I'm smarter than all of them," Zach said, setting the spoon down to let the soup cool. "They don't even stay on their LPSs very long. They walk around the plant, throwing their weight around, and I really don't know why they are there. They seem more like watchdogs to me."

"I'm curious," Ruth said, wrapping the last of the thread around the spool. "Are you able to maintain your casual mannerisms in your new position or are you having to adjust?"

"There," Naomi inserted. "Ruth hit the nail on the head. You can't act all laidback when you're expected to be the boss, now can you? You've been a Runner for almost five years now, and it has offered you a carefree lifestyle. No attachments. No heartache."

"Let's change the subject," Zach said, getting out the bowls. "Two against one isn't fair odds." He ladled soup into each bowl and set them at the table.

"Speaking of which," Naomi said. "Guess who was running errands for her father and happened to stop by this afternoon?"

"Someone came by?" Ruth asked.

"I'm sorry, Sweetie. You were writing, and I didn't want to disturb you," Naomi said. "But Pilar left of a dozen corn tortillas—they're in the refrigerator—and some apple marmalade that her mom had bartered for."

"What did she want?" Zach asked, eyeing Ruth from the corner of his eye.

"Oh, she wanted to chat," Naomi said. "I know how you like to keep everyone in your life compartmentalized, but we can't all help knowing each other. She said that Bear hasn't been doing well since he stopped recording his sermons now that they're illegal. You better go visit him soon. You know how he gets when people tell him he can't do something. She also said that her younger sister was proposed to last week. They'll be getting married at the Levington's winter bazaar."

"I went to see Bear several weeks ago and had a good talk with him. He's doing okay, Mom. He's trying to figure out what to do with his life," Zach said.

Naomi stopped. "I guess both of you have some serious choices in life to make," Naomi added. "Bear said that he would do the honor of marrying them, but I know Pilar really wants you to conduct the ceremony. The whole town will be invited. Everyone is looking forward to it."

"Reyna's only like twenty-two years old," Zach said. "Levi isn't worried she's too young?"

"Twenty years old is plenty old enough to get married. Plus, Javier and Reyna are perfectly suited for each other. Levi is already teaching Javier the family business," Naomi said, scooting her bowl toward her. "Anyway," she continued. "Pilar is already twenty-five. She should be getting married first."

"Mom, if I would have known that you would be discussing my personal life with me being home more often, I would have kept being a Runner," Zach said.

"It's hard to run away from stuff when you're home, isn't it?" Naomi said, looking into her son's eyes for a moment. "Anyway, the topic is making me weary. Ruth, why don't you come over here and have some soup with us. Come on, Zach, sit down."

Ruth looked at her brother. His cheeks were flushed, and he looked like he was about to leave the room. Finally, his shoulders relaxed and he pulled out his chair to sit down. Ruth put her spool of thread in the basket by her feet and walked over to the table. "This looks like a new soup," she said.

"I was getting tired of minestrone and chicken noodle. I wanted something with beef in it. This one is a little more expensive, but there was a surplus," Zach said, giving a mischievous grin. "And since I am now management, I grabbed everything that was available."

"What is it?" Ruth asked, sitting down.

"It's beef stew," Zach said, triumphantly. "And I hope you like it because I got about five cases of it."

"How many are in each case?" Naomi asked before taking a bite. "It's delicious."

"There are about thirty freeze-dried bags that each contain three to five servings in the case."

"That will feed us for months," Ruth said, tentatively taking a bite. "I like it."

"Well, I'm glad you both like it since absolutely no one in this house is capable of cooking," Zach said. "With the soups and the milk and bread deliveries, I think we'll do okay. I can always stop by the farmers market too, and pick up nuts and jams."

"Speaking of jams, Zach, go into the fridge and grab the tortillas and apple marmalade that Pilar brought. That dear girl—I just love her. They will be a nice addition to our soup," Naomi said.

"Is there any more water left in the jug?" Ruth asked.

"Not in this jug," Zach said, getting up. "But I loaded my truck with five jugs full of water. I put them in the fridge. Now you don't have to worry about going to the pump. Whenever you're on your last jug, let me know, and I'll refill all five of them."

"I would like to go to the farmers market with you when you're off from work. I've made a few shirts and slacks on the sewing machine, and I want to barter them," Ruth said. She hadn't left this house since she came over a month ago. She sensed that Zach was trying to keep her hidden.

Zach sat down with the tortillas and jam and set them on the table. "I—I would, but Mom can't go with us. She's too weak. I don't want anything to happen to her while we're out."

"Nonsense, Zach. You can go out for a few hours this Saturday while I take my afternoon nap. I'll be fine." Naomi said. "Besides, Ruth needs to meet people. You know everyone in town. You can introduce her. Take her to Levington, and let her meet Levi and Maria. She'll love them. They are the town's founders. "

"We'll see how it goes, Mom. Mom? What's wrong?" Zach said, shooting out of his seat.

Ruth ran to her mother who was sliding off of her seat. She was clutching her chest. "Zach, what's wrong with her? She's hurting!" Ruth exclaimed.

Zach grabbed his mother's small frame and gently pulled her back on the chair. "We must get her to the hospital."

Naomi stirred and her eyes focused onto Zach's face. "No, no—I'm fine. I felt a twinge is all," Naomi said. "Just get me to my room, so I can lie down."

"Ruth, go into the cabinet next to the oven and get mom those pain pills," Zach said.

Instantly, Ruth got up and headed into the small kitchen.

"I don't want them," Naomi insisted. "They make me feel funny."

"Well, then I'm taking you to the hospital," he said, firmly.

"I will not step one foot in the hospital! I already let them poke me and cut me up. I'm done," Naomi said, trying in vain to get up.

"Fine. Then you will take the medicine," Zach said, taking the bottle from Ruth. "Can I have your water on the table?"

"Yes, here it is," Ruth said, trying to calm her shaking hands.

"Here, Mom. Swallow these," Zack said, putting two pills into his mother's mouth and tipping the glass of water on her lips.

"Okay, now help me to my room. I want to pray before this medicine takes effect.

Zach helped Naomi to her room, and Ruth covered her with a blanket and closed the curtains. Zach didn't want to admit it, but he had never seen his mother look so sickly. His father died instantly, and now he was forced to watch his mother die slowly. Zach wanted to be angry, but he was too tired and hurt to feel anything other than his brokenness.

"Are you feeling better, Mom?" Ruth asked. "Is it hard for you to breathe?"

"I'm fine, baby girl. Would you mind if I talked to your brother alone for a moment?"

"Not at all, Mom. I'll be working at the HMS," Ruth answered before giving her mom's hand a squeeze and quietly closing the door on her way out.

As Ruth walked to the HMS, her mind was far from writing. She wanted to help her mother, and there was only one person she knew who was qualified. She didn't know if she could trust him and the consequences of contacting him could be devastating, but after seeing her mother suffer, she didn't care.

Dr. Michael Linton examined the last of Randall's newly hired workforce—thirteen very intimidating men, ranging from all backgrounds. "Are you excited about your new employment?" he asked, looking down at the printouts in front of him. "Matthew Coughlin is your name, correct?"

The dark man looked into his eyes. "Yes, but you can call me Matt. I'm honored to be used for a good purpose."

Dr. Linton smiled and said nothing. The man was massive, but his naivety was apparent. Dr. Linton didn't want to spoil his childish view of his service to the World Government. He had felt the same way before he realized the truth. "I can see why Randall has chosen you for his team. You are as healthy as they get. What's your area of expertise?"

"I protect," Matt answered.

Dr. Linton flipped through a few more pages of the man's history. "I think you're the only applicant who hasn't worked for the World Police. You went straight into service as a bodyguard at a young age. You've protected several Elite Efficientists through the years. What made you decide to apply for the World Government?"

The man thought for a moment. "I felt I was ready for a higher purpose."

"To be frank, I'm surprised Randall hired you. Your training is limited," Dr. Linton said honestly.

"I believe he hired me based on my test scores and my interview," Matt answered plainly.

"Hmm, let me look," Dr. Linton opened his portable. "Ah, I see. You scored very high in analytical thinking." He set the Portable down back on his lap. "But all the men have IQs that are off the charts. They are each brilliant in different areas. A few are experts in weapons and warfare. Several are technological geniuses. One even hacked into the World Government site in less than five minutes. One man has a near photographic memory. Another can build an engine with scrap metal. So what's your specialty?"

"It wasn't the aptitude test I was talking about. Look at my personality test," Matt answered.

Dr. Linton looked back down at his Portable. Finally, he saw the difference between Matt and the other hirelings. "I see. You are a team player. You scored high in loyalty and integrity." He leaned back into his chair. "Randall may be one of the most planned men that I've ever met. Of course, he would need a team player—the glue to keep all these mavericks together. So are you an honest man?"

Matt gave a broad smile. "I'm honest to a degree."

"So where's the degree end?" Dr. Linton asked intrigued.

"Loyalty overrides integrity," Matt answered.

Dr. Linton chuckled. "Loyalty is definitely a rare commodity around here. And you're right. If you can't lie to protect the truth, then you're no good to us. Make sure all this loyalty and integrity doesn't get you into trouble."

"Okay," he said, placing the printouts on the desk behind him. "You and your comrades each have your own apartment in the building. Obviously, you've been to Randall's. Neil Elder's apartment is right above us, and we are using this place as kind of a home base."

"This is not your home?" Matt asked.

"No, I live outside the city. I have no desire to stay in this building and definitely not this apartment," Dr. Linton said, looking around at the sparse furnishings. "Randall will be sending your schedule for the week to your Portable. He's letting you have today and tomorrow to get situated in your home."

Dr. Linton looked down at his Portable and froze. "I'm sorry. Can you hold on for a second?" Dr. Linton grabbed his Portable and got up from his seat, walking quickly towards the kitchen. He couldn't believe what he was reading. He wrote a reply to the message.

"*How do I know this is Eve Pallue?*" he quickly typed.

"*You helped me at the Colonial Hospital. I spoke Long English for the first time since I was a girl. You gave me numbers to Life Therapist. Randall was my bodyguard. He shortened your Emergency Medicine Internship,*" came the reply.

Dr. Linton stared at the Portable screen. "*I'm in a compromising position,*" he wrote.

"*So am I, but I need your help,*" appeared on his screen.

Dr. Linton looked at Matt sitting quietly on the couch. "*Contact me again in 5 minutes.*"

He clicked off the strand of messages and erased them. His hands were shaking, and he could feel cool beads of sweat forming along the hairline of his forehead. He needed to leave immediately. If Randall saw his condition, he would know something was wrong. He quickly walked to the sink and splashed water on his face and hands. He tried to collect himself. He dried his face with the back of his sleeve and walked back toward the living room. "Matt, I have to cut the interview a little short. I got word that one of my patients has an emergency. You are in perfect health, and I know you will be an asset to the team. I'm not a Life Therapist, but if you do need to talk, please feel free to contact me."

Matt got up from the couch. "Thank you, sir. I look forward to working with you and the team."

The two men shook hands. "Let me see you out, so I can lock the door," Dr. Linton said, hoping not to sound too rushed.

"Of course," Matt said, grabbing the key and ID badge that Dr. Linton had given him. "I hope everything is okay with your patient."

Dr. Linton opened the door. "It's a critical situation, but I'm sure I can take care of it," he said as he locked the door behind him.

CHAPTER NINE

"**C**an I help you?" Zach asked, after opening the front door of his small house and shooing away one of his mother's cats. A man in his late twenties or early thirties stood on his porch. His medium build body had a tidy appearance, and Zach instantly knew he was an Efficientist. He smelled sterile and his facial features seemed soft, though, there were dark circles under his eyes.

The man fumbled a little bit. "I—I was contacted to come here. I was told that you needed my help," the man finally sputtered.

Zach straightened his tall, lean body and automatically shielded the door with his stance. He saw the solar car parked on the side of the street. "Who sent for you?"

The man intimidated by Zach's aggressive composure looked like he was about to run away. "My name is Dr. Michael Linton. I was contacted by a previous patient of mine who lives here. She said that her mother needed my help."

Zach looked at the man for a long moment before he turned his head over his shoulder and called out. "Ruth, come here please."

A few seconds later, Ruth came to the door. When she saw the visitor, her expression filled with relief. "Dr. Linton, thank you so much for coming. I know it had to be difficult for you."

Dr. Linton stared at Ruth in stunned speechlessness. "I can't believe it," he whispered. "You're alive. I thought I was losing my mind."

Zach suddenly turned to his sister. "Ruth, what are you doing? Who is this man?"

Ruth's cheeks reddened, but she firmly looked up at her brother. "This is Dr. Linton. He helped me after my

68

Awakening. I contacted him after mom fell from her chair at dinner two nights ago."

"Are you kidding me?" Zach said, trying not to raise his voice. He knew his mother was sleeping on the other side of the window next to the porch. "Do you know who this man is? Have you read the World News lately?"

Ruth's jaw went rigid. "Yes, I read the World News. Yes, I know who this man is. What do you want me to do, Zach? Watch mom die and do nothing. I just got her back. I can't lose her again."

"This man works for the men who tried to have you killed!" Zach hollered louder than he would have liked. He looked around to make sure none of their neighbors could see them. "What were you thinking, Ruth? He is the personal doctor to Neil Elder and to your old bodyguard who beat me to a pulp and left me for dead! Now they have an elite team of mercenaries. If they find out you're alive and living here, they will come after you!"

"Look," Dr. Linton finally interjected. "I'm not here to call you out. My life is just as much at stake as yours. I'm supposed to still be at a factory, checking up on pharmaceutical production. I drove almost three hours further to get here, which I only did because Eve was my patient and she asked me to come...and I have questions about her supposed death."

Zach looked at the doctor intently. "How do I know you won't go back and tell everyone that Ruth is alive?"

Dr. Michael squared his stance with Zach's. "Because I have no doubt that if I did, they would question me and kill me. The moment that Eve contacted my Portable, my life became endangered. I mean nothing to them. I've learned not to take sides."

Zach thought for a moment and his tense countenance was replaced with worry. "My mom is sick."

Dr. Linton looked surprised. "I thought she was Eve's mom."

Ruth waved the doctor into the house. "It is our mom, and my name is no longer Eve. It is Ruth."

"I will tell you honestly. I can do a blood test and run her numbers, but I can assure you that she will not make it much longer. Her blood pressure is very faint, and from what you've told me, there is nothing to be done. Even if you took her to the colonial hospital, they could not help her," Dr. Linton said, putting his stethoscope around his neck. "Look, we don't save cases like this, but even if we did everything possible, there is no saving her. I've seen death written on faces before, and I doubt that your mother will last another week. The most you can do is make her comfortable."

Dr. Linton watched the response of the siblings hovering over their mother. The entire surreal situation with Eve Pallue would take him many days to consider, but what made him most curious at this moment was their reaction to the knowledge that their mother was dying. He was always intrigued by the raw emotions unveiled at death's door.

He watched as the mother opened her eyes, and each of her children grabbed one of her hands.

"Oh, my children. I longed for so many years to have you both next to me—side by side. You don't know how much seeing you together fills me with so much joy. What I feel right now was worth every moment of waiting. I feel like heaven has descended on me."

Dr. Linton was taken back by the mother's reaction. He hadn't sensed any fear in her like he had with others. He almost detected a feeling of expectancy in the dying woman's voice.

"Zach, you remember what I told you—protect my baby girl. I know she's in God's hands, but I'm counting on you to be here for her."

"Yes, Mom," Zach said quietly.

"And Ruth, don't forget how much I love you. Even when I couldn't physically be with you, my thoughts and prayers were always directed towards you. I loved you with an ache that never ceased until the day you showed up on my front porch."

"I know, Mom," Ruth whispered.

The mother tried to cough and winced in pain.

"Mom, we have some new pain killers for you. They will take all the pain away. Do you want them?" Zach asked, looking at the bottle of pills on the nightstand that Dr. Linton had given them.

"No need," the mother said with a faint smile. "I feel nothing but the glory of God wrapping around me like a blanket. I'm going home to finally rest. My years of struggle have ended. I know you will both miss me, but I long to go home to be with the Father."

The mother's eyes closed slowly. Dr. Linton immediately walked over to check her pulse. "She's still breathing, but barely."

"I've never seen her so peaceful," Zack said, watching as his mother fell back asleep.

Dr. Linton examined the mother's face, noticing her serene expression. "To be honest," he replied. "I've never seen a patient of mine look like this."

Dr. Linton looked at the woman who now called herself *Ruth*. When he first met her, he thought she was a Colonial prostitute. Next he found out she was Eve Pallue. Then she died in a fire at the same building where he treated her sunburns. And now she was a Colonial going by a different name. Everything about Eve Pallue, Neil Elder and the World Government was distorted and chaotic. He needed some answers.

"Eve—I mean, Ruth, may I talk with you for a moment? I must leave soon, so I can get home before dark. I need to ask you something."

Ruth nodded and followed the doctor out of the room. They both walked quietly to the front door.

"I'm sorry to bother you during this time, but I have a feeling I won't be seeing you again. I need to know something," Dr. Linton started.

"About my death?" Ruth asked.

"Yes, the World Government labeled it an accident, but obviously it wasn't since you are here alive. Either you planned it to fake your own death or someone tried to have you killed. All I know is that it didn't take long for Neil Elder to clean up the mess and move into your penthouse."

"Why are you so concerned?" Ruth asked.

Dr. Linton set his doctor's bag on the ground. "Look, I'm going to be honest with you. Ever since I started working for the World Government, I have found that I don't know who to trust. I thought Randall was a good guy, but now I don't know who's on my side. I'm living under an element of stress that I wasn't expecting."

"You can't trust anyone," Ruth finally answered. "Especially, Neil and Randall."

"Was the fire planned to kill you?" Dr. Linton asked.

"Yes," Ruth said, flatly.

"Who did it?" Dr. Linton asked. He still couldn't believe that she was alive and that she survived being attacked.

"I know that Neil made the decision, but Randall is who carried out the orders," she answered.

"How do you know Neil ordered it?"

"He stole something from me," Ruth said.

"Did you write *Life Plethoricity*?" Dr. Linton asked stunned. "Is that what he took?"

"Yes," Ruth answered.

"That makes sense," Dr. Linton said, rubbing his chin. "And how do you know for sure that Randall is the one who carried out the orders?"

Ruth looked up at Dr. Linton. "As I was driving away, I saw Randall behind the wheel of his truck, watching the building burn," she said. "You can never trust him."

CHAPTER TEN

"I'm very pleased with the incline of your health," Dr. Linton said, looking at the numbers of the blood pressure cuff.

Neil grinned. "I took my doctor's advice. I found the cure to *Life Plethoricity*."

Dr. Linton noticed Neil Elder's relaxed expression. "Well, that's a first. Care to share your discovery?"

"Actually, this time I'm keeping it a secret. However, you will be invited to the release party in a few weeks. It's perfect, and I have you to thank for it."

Dr. Linton nodded and smiled slightly. He was uneasy with getting too much credit for any new development. "I'm only your soundboard, sir. Any precedent you create is solely to your credit."

"I was hoping you'd say that," Neil said, giving Dr. Linton a sharp pat on the shoulder. "Well, now. How was the pharmaceutical plant that you inspected last week? Was everything in working order?" Neil asked, eyeing Dr. Linton closely.

Dr. Linton took the blood pressure cuff off of Neil's arm and brought it back to his bag on the couch. "I found a few issues of concern, especially in the area of cleanliness. I'm concerned not only about the pharmaceutical plant, but all the plants making consumable products for Efficientists," Dr. Linton said, believing his own concern.

"What do you mean?" Neil asked, rolling his sleeves back down.

"It is my opinion that the Efficientists in charge of the plants may have too much free reign. I saw little consistency in their performance and, honestly, the Colonial manager who showed me around appeared to have more sense about what was going on. The Efficientists seemed more concerned about the extra-curricular activities they would be engaging in after work than the work itself."

Neil thought for a second and sat down at his LPS. "This is not good. We can't have the Colonials outperforming the Efficientists. The Colonials must not feel like they have the upper hand or we could have a revolt on our hands."

Dr. Linton tried to hide the tension that was building within him. "Did you want the names of all the Colonial management?"

Neil turned to his LPS. "No, no. The Colonials are only doing what they are paid to do. They're simple-minded enough, and we need the ones who are good at running the floors. They need to remember the pecking order of things. The Efficientists are there to remind them of how things are run in the World Government. How was the security?"

"I'm not an authority on security, but the officers conducted themselves with professionalism, and I didn't see one person in uniform without a weapon of some sort," Dr. Linton answered honesty.

"That's good to know. Randall is doing his job well. I think he has sent out his thirteen men to inspect all the plants. They'll put the fear of the World Government into anybody. So it looks like the person who has dropped the ball is me. I think I know exactly what I'll do. I'll put one of my Elite Efficientists in charge of it. I'll buffer his rank and get him out of the LPS. You see all of the Elites regularly, don't you?"

Dr. Linton nodded his head.

"Out of all of them, which one do you think may want to go?"

Dr. Linton thought for a moment. "All of them but two have marital status—Charlie Liu and Julian Drighton. Julian is older, and he's very focused on his research."

"Yes, he has taken over Eve Pallue's work on Dormant Layered Thought Process. I need him to stay at his LPS, so he can continue supervising the research team. What about Charlie?"

"Charlie is unattached. I think both of his parents were moderate ranking Efficientists, but they are both deceased now. They were aged when they decided to have a child. He works hard, but he still hasn't established any new precedents. I know he was working on a few things, but none of them have proven relevant."

"Yes, Charlie has been very good at doing research for me and a few other little odds and ends that I assign to him, but I can easily have him replaced by another top Efficientist. He's good at communicating without causing alarm. I think he'll be exactly what those factory Efficientists need. He'll intimidate them a little with his elite title, but he'll easily talk some sense into them. Well, that's decided," Neil said, turning off his LPS. "I've sent a message over to Charlie, letting him know that you will be there shortly. I'm glad I enacted those new laws that allow me to buffer rank of those I choose. Please explain the situation to him. Make sure he finds adequate housing that's locally situated. But make sure he doesn't stay in a factory village. I don't want him getting too close to the locals if you know what I mean. I'll make sure his rank stays intact, and he will communicate directly to me."

"Very good," Dr. Linton said, feeling very relieved by the outcome. Again, he was passing the baton onto someone else and taking his seat back on the sidelines. "Is there anything else you need me to do?"

"Yes, in fact there is. I know I usually involve Randall in most of my decisions, but I think I will leave him out on this one. We don't want him knowing too much, do we? I think it is better that I have a man doing my dirty work for me that's not on Randall's radar. Let's keep Charlie Liu out of the picture. We'll detail on his records that he's simply relocating for a time."

"Understood," Dr. Linton said.

"I'll document the necessary changes and send them over to Charlie. I want you to personally assist him in making the necessary arrangements. I want him gone by the end of the week."

Pilar parked her father's truck in the barren cornfield behind their house. She had finished her father's deliveries for the morning, and she didn't think she could speak to one more person. Everywhere she went, people asked her about her sister's engagement to Javier. Inevitably, the conversations would always lead up to her relationship with Zach and the absence of any kind of proposal.

"How is Zach doing?"

"I heard Zach took a management position at the plant."

"Is Zach finally settling down?"

"Is he thinking about proposing to you finally?"

Pilar couldn't handle any more questions. Zach had told her briefly about his promotion at her last delivery to his house, but he had been distant—or maybe preoccupied—since his sister came into his life and his mother was not doing well. Pilar took the keys out of the ignition.

"His mother is dying," she whispered to herself. "You saw her a few days ago. You could see how weak she's become. Give him some more time." In her heart, she tried to forget that she had already given him many years of her youth. She loved him, and she had to wait until he worked through his heartache.

She bowed her head on the steering wheel and prayed. *"God, You know how sensitive Zach is. He covers it up so well, but he's hurting all the time. He's pushed me out because he's scared to feel, and I think scared to love again. His father died in the fire and now his mother is dying. You have taken much from him, but I know he is strong. I remember how he preached, Father, so powerfully, yet with so much compassion. I feel like there is nothing I can do to help him. I feel like all You want me to do is wait. But You know waiting is so difficult for me. I'd rather run across the world and back for him, but waiting is killing me. Help me to put him into Your hands. I don't know why his sister has suddenly shown up, but help her to help him. I want to trust You, Father. Please, I need Your peace in my life again.*"

"Pilar, can you come here, please?" the low voice of her father called out.

Pilar grabbed her things and opened the door. She saw her father's face and hands dusted with ground cornmeal. He had taken off his apron, and she wondered why he had cut his day's work so short.

"How did the deliveries go?" he asked.

Pilar could tell there was more to his question than he was revealing. He was searching her eyes, trying to discover if there was something wrong. She didn't want to go into a debate about Zach again, so she lightened her expression. "Everything went well, Dad. I sold the surplus you gave me this morning, and everyone was happy with their deliveries."

"You didn't hear the news then?" he asked still searching.

"No, nothing new. Everyone still asks about Reyna's engagement, but other than that, I haven't heard anything." She wondered if her father had found out about Zach's sister. She knew Zach wouldn't tell anyone, and he made her promise to say nothing. No matter what Zach was putting her through, she was not a gossip. She had plenty of secrets buried in her heart, and she'd carry them to her grave before telling them.

"Zach's mother passed away early this morning. Bear came by to let us know. Zach contacted him late last night, so he went to Zach's house to say his goodbyes. It seems that he got there just in time. She passed away before the sun came up. He was pretty shaken up about it. He wanted to stay and talk with you, but he needed to get home to build a casket for Naomi."

"Where is the grief gathering going to be held?" Pilar asked.

"She told Bear to bury her body under the ashes of the church where Pastor Austin died in Cedar Wood. Seems fitting for her body to lay with her husband's ashes. Though, from what I gather from Bear, Zach is not too happy about going back to the church. It's probably why Naomi asked Bear and not Zach," Levi said, exposing his white teeth with a broad smile. "Naomi was always a clever one. She knew people's reaction before they knew it themselves."

"Did Bear say anything else?" Pilar asked. She wanted to know if he had met Zach's sister yet.

"He asked if we would prepare some food for the grief gathering tomorrow. They'll be driving her body to Cedar Wood before sun up. Bear and Zach will carry Naomi in the casket to the old church grounds. I've already talked to the other town leaders, and they have declared tomorrow a day of mourning."

"Did Bear mention any other visitors with Naomi?" Pilar asked, trying to sound vague. Pilar knew that she and Bear were two of the few people Zach told about his half-sister, but she didn't know if Bear had met her yet.

"No, he didn't mention any visitors. Did you see anyone there when you visited?"

"No, I—I just wondered if Zach had contacted anyone else," Pilar stated. She knew her father would presume that she wanted to make sure Zach didn't put her further down on his list of his confidences, but she'd rather him think she was acting insecure than to let the secret about Zach's sister out.

"Look, Pilar. Zach would have told you himself, but he knew Bear was coming by here. You would have known right away, but you were out running deliveries. You got to let that man be. He's hurting and running away from God. His mother's death is not going to help this situation," Levi said, firmly.

"I know, Dad. I shouldn't have asked. Do you mind if I help you get the food ready for tomorrow?" she asked. She was done talking for the day. She wanted to disappear in the mundane task of combining and baking ingredients.

"Your mother already got the black maize ready for the masa. It's in the outdoor kitchen. I'm about to get the dried pinto beans from the storeroom. Why don't you go help her, and I'll meet you in there?" Levi asked, placing his heavy hand gently on Pilar's shoulder. "Don't you ever forget, Pilar, that you are a beautiful, smart woman with the honesty of a saint and the passion of a prophet."

"I know, Dad," Pilar whispered and made her way to the kitchen. *I wished Zach would see that*, she thought to herself.

CHAPTER ELEVEN

"**W**hy didn't you wake me?" Ruth asked her brother when he came into the room. She could tell by his facial expression that their mother had died. "Why am I not with her now? How did I get in here?"

"You fell asleep, Ruth. I carried you into my room. You were so worn out. You needed the rest," Zach said, sitting on the corner of the bed next to his sister. His sister looked skinnier than she had when he first met her in the city. Her cheeks were sunken and her skin pale white. If he didn't do something, he would lose her too.

"But I wanted to see her before she died," Ruth said as tears began to make their way down her angular cheekbones.

"You did, I promise," Zach said, reaching for his sister. He brought her into a soft embrace and gently patted her back. "She only lived a few hours after you fell asleep. Bear came over earlier to say goodbye, and he prayed over her passing spirit. He held her hand as she went to heaven. She wasn't alone."

"Where were you?" Ruth asked, wondering why Bear got to have the final goodbye.

"Bear was angry with me because I hadn't contacted him sooner. He loved Mom like his own mother. She seemed pleased to see him, so I let them have their moment. She whispered to him, and I could see a faint smile on her face. I don't know why Mom chose to die with Bear holding her hand, but she did."

"I need to contact Deborah and Esther and let them know," Ruth said, leaving Zach's embrace. "I don't know what I'm going to do without Mom. I knew she was dying. I thought I was ready, but I'm not. I don't want her to leave so soon. I only found her," Ruth cried as fresh tears continued to drench her already wet cheeks.

Zach took Ruth back into his embrace. "I've already contacted Pastor Tom. He and Cindy are going to try to make it to the grief gathering in Cedar Wood tomorrow. He's going to let Deborah and Esther know, but they probably won't be able to make it. They have several Efficientists staying at the farm with them and neither of them should be driving long distances."

"I'm alone again," Ruth whispered through her tears.

"No, you are not alone. I'm here. I will take care of you. You will stay with me, and we'll figure everything out as we go. Let's not worry about the future right now. Come with me. You can tell her goodbye, and you can see how peaceful she looks," Zach said and stood up, reaching out his hands to Ruth.

Ruth looked up at her brother. "Why are you so strong in grief?" she asked.

Zach stared at his sister. He didn't want her to know about the words his mother had whispered to him after she fell from the dinner table so many nights ago. She pleaded with him to take care of Ruth. She could die in peace, knowing that her little girl was in Zach's protection. He had promised his mother that he would do everything to keep Ruth safe, and right now, he needed his sister to say goodbye to death, so she could focus on living.

"I may be strong at carrying grief, but I haven't found the strength yet to let it go. Maybe I can learn how from you," he finally answered as he lifted Ruth from the bed.

Ruth felt weak. Her pajama bottoms that she had only recently made were now drooping toward her hips, and she had to keep pulling up the waistline as she walked. She feared seeing her mother dead. She had seen Christina Straight, the Life Therapist who had led her to Christ, only hours after her death, and the image kept making its way into the forefront of her thoughts.

"I don't think I can do it, Zach. What if she looks sick? I don't want that image to be the last thing I remember about her," Ruth said, pausing in front of her mother's room.

"I wouldn't let you see her if I thought she would scare you. I can't explain, but she honestly looks very peaceful—more peaceful and beautiful than I could ever imagine. I think seeing her will actually be a comfort to you," Zach said. "Trust me?"

Ruth nodded her head.

Zach opened the door and let Ruth enter first.

Ruth's eyes had to adjust because the curtains were open wide, and the early morning light flowed like water over her mother's bed. A white sheet was draped over her mother's body, and her hair was brushed to the side of her face.

"Did you prepare her like this?" Ruth asked, keeping her eyes focused on her mother.

"No, Bear did. He has a lot of sentimental tendencies," Zach said.

"Isn't he a fighter?" Ruth asked, looking toward her brother.

"Well, yes, but he—" Zach stopped, searching for the correct words. "He's also very passionate."

"Like King David," Ruth added.

"Yes, he's a lot like King David. He's very intense with his emotions, yet very literal with the things of this world. It's hard to explain because many times he's an enigma."

Ruth returned her gaze to her mother. "Yes, we are all enigmas. Some of us are better at hiding it."

Ruth walked toward her mother. She could feel the heat from the sun engulfing her mother's body. She peered down at her face and stared for several seconds.

"Yes, she does look beautiful. She seems younger now. The burden of her children is finally lifted. She almost looks like I remembered her in my dreams."

Zach smiled. "Mom is home now. She is resting in the arms of Jesus."

Ruth said nothing for a moment. "I wish I could go with her."

Zach walked to his sister and grabbed her hand. "If God wanted you, Ruth, He would take you. Obviously, you are still needed down here, so don't you dare entertain thoughts of leaving before your time."

Ruth no longer noticed the tears. "Sounds like you've had the same thoughts before."

Zach held Ruth's hand tighter. "I have, and I'm telling you like I tell myself. We will be with her soon enough, and I'll see my dad again." Zach's voice cracked. "And we won't have to suffer anymore and lose people we love. But we can't give up on this life. There is more we have to learn—more we have to offer."

Ruth held to her brother's hand and matched his firm grip. "Then promise me that I won't be trying alone. I will do what God wants me to do. I will struggle to stay faithful in this life, but you need to do it with me. You can't run into your world of indifference any longer."

Zach reached for his sister's other hand. "Yes, I promise. I will try. I will let go."

"Then I will too," Ruth whispered.

Zach bowed his head and closed his eyes. "*Lord, please forgive me for running away from You when my father died. Help me to let go of my pain. I'm so worn out from carrying all of it. I'm tired of always hiding from hurt. Heal me, God. Heal Ruth. We are broken, Lord, but we are receptive to You. And bless our mother. She has been so faithful to You. Let us live to honor her. I pray this in Jesus' name, amen.*"

CHAPTER TWELVE

"**P**astor Tom!" Esther exclaimed, opening the back screen door. "Come on in. It's raining sheets of water. What brings you all the way to our farm today?"

Tomas Isaacs pulled off his hat and stepped into the kitchen. "I hope you don't mind. I'm all wet. I came to the back door, so I wouldn't get your living area dirty," he said. He wanted to remind Esther that she wasn't supposed to call him pastor anymore, but she and Deborah had found it difficult to simply call him Tom, so he gave up mentioning it.

"Well, you shouldn't have. Now you got yourself even more soaked. We don't mind pulling a towel out for you. Wait here, and I'll run and get one."

"Would you mind getting Deborah while you're at it? I need to talk to both of you," Tom said in a serious tone.

For the first time, Esther seemed to notice his countenance. "Is everything okay, Pastor Tom? Anyone hurt?" she asked, stopping at the entrance to the hallway.

"Why don't you get Deborah, so I don't have to explain it twice. Is there anyone else in the house?" Tom asked, looking around.

"No, our three guests have actually headed your way to the Trinity Trading Center. They're going to try their hand at bartering today. I pray that they don't get taken advantage of," Esther said, obviously worried about the three Efficientists living in her home.

"Don't worry about your guests. Cindy is there, and she'll make sure everything turns out fair. She knows their faces, so she'll take care of them," Tom said, taking a seat at the table.

"Well, let me get Deborah. I think she's reading her *Bible* in the front room."

Tom waited for only a moment before he could hear Esther's and Deborah's voices conversing. He heard what sounded like the closing of a book and then brisk footsteps back to the kitchen.

"Is it Ruth, Pastor Tom? Has something happened to her? How's her mother? I know she wasn't doing well when Ruth wrote several days ago," Deborah said, winded from her fast paced walk to the kitchen.

"Why don't you both have a seat, and I'll go over everything," Tom said, motioning to the chairs across from him.

"Here's your towel, Pastor Tom," Esther said, reaching over the table to hand Tom the towel before taking her seat.

"Obviously, you both know that Ruth's mother, Naomi, was very ill," he began. "She passed away early this morning, and Cindy and I will be driving to Cedar Wood for the grief gathering."

"Well, we'll go with you," Deborah said. "We can pack up today and be ready by morning."

"I know you both love Ruth more than anyone," he continued, looking from Deborah to Esther. "But I believe right now you need to stay with your guests. They need consistency only you can provide. I've already spoken to Zach, and he said that he would be taking care of Ruth."

"But she belongs here with us," Deborah demanded.

"Deborah, hold your voice down," Esther chided. "Sorry, Pastor Tom, Deborah and I want to be open to what you have to say before we do anything hasty."

"I know you want to rescue her and have things as they were before, but believe me I've prayed about this. Ruth should to stay with her brother. They need each other. They have both lost their last living parent. This is the time that they can really bond and get to know each other."

"Pastor Tom, I don't mean to criticize, but isn't Zach a Runner? How can he take care of Ruth when he's gone all the time?" Esther asked.

"Actually, he has taken a management position at the plant, so he won't be traveling anymore. And from what I've gathered from our conversations on the HMS, I don't believe he'll be at that position for long. I can tell that he has future plans of getting Ruth as far away from the World Government as possible."

"Yes, but is Zach really what Ruth needs right now? Can he provide the safety and security that we provide?" Deborah asked still unconvinced.

"I know you both know about Zach and his situation. This young man is gifted, but he's been running away from God ever since his father died. He and Ruth are certain to grow and push each other. In fact, Ruth has started reading much Christian literature while she's been living with Zach, and she's written some amazing articles about faith."

"Really?" Deborah asked. "So soon?"

"She's had a lot of time on her hands with Zach being gone and her mother ill," Tom said.

"How is her writing?" Esther asked.

Tom thought for a moment. "She's very learned, which is obvious in her writing, and though I've studied the Efficientist world for many years, I'm struggling to fully understand. She assumes too quickly that the reader understands her points, so she doesn't do well at explaining. I think the biggest hurdle for her, however, is that her writing is very dry. It lacks the emotional appeal that people need to be moved by words."

"You think she'll get better with time?" Deborah asked.

"I've been giving her pointers, but I don't have as much time at my HMS as I used to. God's moved me out of the pulpit and into the world, so to speak. But I know someone who I believe will bring the best out of her writing," Tom said, pausing briefly. "Zach Daniels. That boy had more emotional appeal when he preached than anyone I've ever seen. I was able to save a few of his video sermons before the World Government erased them all."

"I remember hearing about him," Esther confessed, "but that was many years ago. Do you think God can restore his ministry?"

Tom leaned back into his chair. "I don't think Zach ever really let go of his anointing—he idled a bit. Zach has a special calling on his life, so his time wandering the wilderness has been brutal to him, but God is preparing that young man for something great. I feel it," Tom said, reverting to his preaching voice.

"Okay," Deborah said, nodding her head. "Maybe Zach can take care of Ruth, but what about Levington? What kind of town is it? I know it's close to one of them government plants. It's a fairly young village. We knew the town's founder, Levi Jones, briefly when he was a young man. We haven't been able to contact him though. They don't have connections for the HMS where they live."

"Levington is a good town full of good people. They have a rule against using HMSs. Yes, Levi is the founder, and he and the other leaders do a good job at leading by example. I have heard, though, that he doesn't like being in the public eye. He does not own an HMS. He prefers to stay close to his family and stick to the bakery that his family operates. He is a hard man to get a hold of unless you interact with him on a daily basis. There is a core of elected leaders at Levington, and they have a firm handle on all the dealings. They often communicate with Levi if they have a difficult situation on their hands. The town is close to the government factory, but they don't rely on it for survival," Tom said, noticing that the rain had stopped pounding on the windowpane.

"Yes, but does the town have a pastor?" Esther asked. "I know that they were somehow connected to Zach's dad."

"Well, Austin Daniels was the pastor before he died," Tom replied.

"But his church was in Cedar Wood," Esther said confused.

"Austin used to drive out to Levington on Saturdays to preach. Zach preached during his summer breaks, and there were plans for him to take over after he finished graduate school. That was until the fire occurred." Tom hesitated. "Zach's longtime family friend is a pastor of sorts. He used to record video sermons until they were recently outlawed. I think he's struggling like I did when the World Government made my life's work illegal."

"Pastor Tom," Deborah began, "Are you certain that you believe Ruth should not come back here?"

"Yes, I believe that is the next step of her journey. You don't want her near the other Efficientists living here, and I know that she and Zach are bound together for something great," Tom said firmly but showing his fatigue.

"And do you know for certain that is what she wants?" Esther asked.

"Ruth gets the final say. No one is pushing her to make any decisions. Even Zach said that he would help her come back if that's what she wanted. But he does want her to stay. Ruth is all the family he has, and he's willing to change his life to be a part of her life."

"Well, that settles it," Deborah said. "Will you let her know when you see her that Esther and I will be praying for her? And tell here we are waiting and believing that her Elite Efficientist friend will arrive soon. We've already gotten three guests, but we are keeping a room ready for her Charlie Liu."

Tom smiled. The sisters had already told him about Ruth's prophetic image of an Elite Efficientist named Charlie Liu sitting at their table. "I'll let her know. And I doubt he'll use his real name when he gets here, but I'm sure you'll be able to figure out who he is when he does arrive."

"Also, Pastor Tom, what is the name of the pastor in Levington? I would like to send him a letter through the HMS about our Ruth," Deborah asked.

Tom set his towel on the table. "I don't know how to say his name in the language it is derived from, but in English his name is Fighting Bear. But people call him Bear. And from what I've heard, he threw his HMS in the Trinity River when the government banned all religious materials, so I doubt you'll get a hold of him either."

"What kind of name is that?" Deborah asked.

"His mother was Ka'to Indian and his father was in the fighting circuit," Tom said, hoping to avoid the following question he knew would be coming.

"He was a fighter?" Esther asked shocked. "How long has this Bear been preaching?"

"Ever since Austin Daniels died, I believe," Pastor Tom said.

"What did he do before he started preaching?" Deborah asked.

"Well—well, he was a fighter like his dad," Tom said, trying not to fumble his words.

"You're kidding," Esther said.

"Not at all," Tom said, collecting himself. "God uses all types of people to serve His purposes on earth."

CHAPTER THIRTEEN

Bear slammed shut the rusted door of his truck and looked toward the sun. It was almost midday. He swept back a few strands of his polished black hair that had strayed from the leather tie, which secured the rest of his mid-back length hair. Lately, he had been noticing grey, wiry strands of hair intermingling with the rest. His face had a weathered look, yet he knew the years had only added substance to his already distinctive appearance. His 5'11" stature was stronger than ever, and he liked the tighter and leaner shape of his muscles that formed after he quit using steroids over five years ago.

At thirty-five years old, Bear was entering his prime years. He had worked hard all of his life to prove himself, and now he walked in the respect that he had created for himself over the years. He was almost the same age his dad was when he took him into the circuit and started training him to fight. His mind flashed back to the last image he had of his dad, and he felt chills race up his arms. His dad who was once able to intimidate the world now looked broken and decayed. His drug use and wild living had finally caught up with him. Bear silently thanked God for rescuing him from following in his father's footsteps. He had Naomi to thank for that.

Bear looked back at the sun. He had precious little light to make the casket for Naomi. It would take him well into early morning if he constructed it alone. He could skip the adornment, but he wouldn't do that for his surrogate mother. She had prayed the blood of Jesus over him when the demons had filled him and controlled him. The façade of her delicate, motherly nature had lifted before his eyes, and she stared those demons down with an intensity that scared even him, the fighter.

"*Father,*" he prayed. "*Send me help for Naomi's casket.*"

He walked briskly toward his house. Even in his rush, he still eyed his home and storage shed. The locks on the doors were still in place and nothing looked disturbed. The last man who dared to break into his storage shed would regret it for the rest of his life. Bear had followed his trail for almost two days and broken the fingers on his right hand. Most people with any sense stayed far away from the piece of land that he claimed when Austin Daniels, the man who took him in at a young age, had died. Five years ago he had built his house on the crescent-shaped parcel of land that hugged a small section of the Trinity River and there he remained.

His demons stayed with him, tormenting as he built his new home, until Naomi brought the power of the cross to his door. After he was freed, he stopped his drug use, cut his hair and said goodbye to the fighting circuit. He would no longer fight for the praise of man. Yet his hair had grown back and Naomi had died. No matter how hard he tried to protect himself, life always sent him heartache. His thoughts focused on Zach. He met Zach as a zealous little boy, so charged up for God and dedicated to His word. Zach could quote Scripture before Bear could barely read, and Bear was seven years his senior. Life had thrown Zach some blows in recent years, and he still stood dazed from the hits.

Bear scanned the river's edge and saw his grandfather, sitting on a stump, holding a corroded shotgun. "*Aha-enah*," he called out.

His aged grandfather looked at him. His long grey hair, blended with the running river behind him. He put his finger over his lips in a signal for quiet.

"I see two men on the other side of the river," he said, pointing upstream. "By the looks of them, I'd say they were fighters. Maybe they're here to challenge you."

Bear shaded his eyes and saw the men. They looked to be in their late teens or early twenties and in fighting shape. "Too young for a challenge. Maybe a lesson." Bear thought for a moment. "Put your gun down and wave them over. I'll get my gear."

It took several minutes for the two men to wade across the shallowest part of the river. One man carried a tattered bag over his head. They walked first to the old man, but he waved them toward the house. Bear watched the two young men walk up the hill toward his house. The white man reminded him of his father. He towered at about six feet and six inches tall, and he had layers of lean muscle. The darker man was under six feet but much stockier. They both were young with a resolute presence, but Bear could see the insecurity and intimidation beneath their strong veneer. When they arrived, Bear had already prepared the fighting ring. The floor was made of flattened rubber tires, and the parameter was lined with sharpened branches that held different kinds of cordage.

"Are you the Shaman?" the dark man asked.

"That is no longer my name. You will call me Bear. Are you wanting a lesson?" Bear asked, knowing that his time was limited.

"Yes, we are both in preparation for the circuit, but we need more training. We have brought you some items for your services," the man said, motioning for his partner to open the tattered bag. "We know you are the best and that your training is highly valued, so we have brought you something worthy of your time."

"I am honored, but I don't need what you have in that bag. What I need is your strength and time. I will train you each for three rounds, and then you will assist me with a project that I need to finish tonight."

The tall, white man with the bag stopped. "Would you like to see what it is first before you refuse it?"

Bear walked toward the man. "I cannot be bought with trinkets. Already you have wasted my daylight with talk. The sun is heading west now, and I must complete my project. I will train you each, and then you will work for me until I am satisfied."

The man set the bag down. "I'm honored that you will teach us. I will gladly do work until the job is finished."

Bear looked at the dark man.

"Train us three rounds and we will complete your task," the young man said.

"Good," Bear said. "You first."

The man got into the ring with Bear.

Bear turned to the man waiting outside the ring. "You see the metal disk? Strike it with the hammer after five minutes."

"Do you have some kind of timer?" the man said.

Bear gritted his teeth. "Count to 60. When you are done, make a strike in the dirt. Are you capable of doing that 5 times?"

The man's pale face reddened. "Yes."

"Good. Begin counting now," Bear said and faced the other man who had entered the ring.

"Now let me ask you a question. Do you simply want to win or do you want to be the best?"

The man stood confused. "I don't understand what you mean. Aren't they the same thing?"

"No," Bear said. "To simply win means to submit your opponent without getting hit. To be the best means that you must win only after you put on a show for the crowd. I can train you how to avoid getting hit, but you will not be the best in the eyes of your audience. They want to see a performance, and many of them will walk for days to experience whatever it is that you will give to them. They don't want you to simply win. They want you to give them something to talk about for years to come. Now, before we begin. Do you want to win or do you want to be the best?"

The man thought for a moment. "I want to be the best."

"Good," Bear nodded. "Otherwise, you should skip the circuit altogether."

"You can read the men who only want to win. Their performance is almost always the same. They don't last very long in the circuit. They're too predictable, too boring. Are you better on the ground or standing?"

"I'm better at grappling," the man said.

"Okay, don't show it. Work only on your striking. Work on your ground technique when training. Save your grappling until after you've had a few fights. Wait until your name gets known. When the crowds come out and they all want to see what's being rumored about, then you take your opponent down to the floor. Make sure it's someone worth beating. He will only know about your striking, and you will take him off guard. That is the only time you can win without being hit."

The pounding of the disk sounded.

"Good, round two."

"But we didn't train," the man said.

"Believe me, you'll get plenty of combat training as you fight, but what I'm telling you will make your name famous. Now let me see your striking."

The man threw a punch.

"You are about an inch shorter than me, but I can already see you are used to fighting to the height of your opponents. Do you train with your friend a lot?" Bear asked, motioning to the man quietly counting to sixty.

"Yes, I spar with Jason and his brothers, and they are all tall," the man said.

"What is your name?" Bear asked.

"Sentinel," the man said.

"Is that your stage name?" Bear asked.

"No, it is the name given to me by my father," he answered.

Bear stopped. "Who is your father?" he asked.

The young man straightened his shoulders. "Watchman," he answered.

Bear looked into the young man's eyes. "I knew your father. He was a good fighter and a good man. He would tell me about Jesus, and I greatly disrespected him. I apologize. I was hiding from God, and your father exposed me."

Bear wanted to say more. He wanted to apologize for tearing Watchman's labrum and taking out his shoulder. He knew what he was doing at the time. He was tired of the old man's words about God, and he didn't want to hear them anymore. So when he got his chance, he took the man out of the circuit for good.

"My father holds no grudges towards you. Some time ago, a man traded him several disks of your video sermons, and he plays them for the fighters who come to him—he is a chaplain of sorts. He is the one who sent me to you. He said that I needed to have your perspective before he will let me enter the circuit. He is the one who gave us the gift for you," Sentinel said, motioning to the tattered bag at the feet of his friend.

The pounding of the disk sounded a second time.

Bear quickly brushed the new information aside and focused on his student. "Round three. You punch like you are ashamed of your height. You are not a tall man, but being shorter also has its strengths. You need to find those strengths. You are faster. You have better balance. You will not strike up. Face punches are overrated. You will punch to the ribs. You will kick to the legs. Knock your man off balance and get him to the ground. You will respect your movements and not waste energy fighting to your opponent's strengths. Let me see your stance."

The young man positioned his body.

"Keep your chin down. You will disappear behind the power of your fist. Move quickly and waste away the energy of your opponent. You must train your heart to not tire out. Run as fast as you can every day until your heart feels like it will explode and walk to catch your breath. Then run again. Do this over and over again until sweat has drenched your entire body. Then you will need to balance. Walk across fallen trees, balance on fences and hop from rocks in a stream. You must get the core of your body stable and strong. Do you have weights?"

"Yes, I use my father's old set," Sentinel said.

"Stay away from steroids. They may make you look bulkier, but they play with your emotions. Your mind must be clear and precise, not ruled by passions. Alternate days of lifting heavy and lifting light and burning out on reps. Don't lift for looks. You don't want to injure yourself. When you feel a tug on a muscle, put the weight down and do something else. Leave the injuries for the ring. You'll get plenty of them," Bear finished and hesitated.

He continued. "I entered the circuit as a young Christian, but my strength of faith grew weaker as my strength in fighting grew stronger. Your father was the only example of a fighter I've seen who was strong both spiritually and physically. The Spirit in you will let you know when you are compromising. Don't give in even a little. I saw your father praying a lot. And I see now why it was important. He was in a place without light and surrounded by people without light. You will have to pray harder than the rest of us. Why is it that you want to win?"

The young man's eyes matched Bear's staunch gaze. "God has called me to win, so I've accepted His challenge."

The metal disk sounded a third time.

Bear looked across his small living room to the two young fighters sleeping on his floor. They all three worked several hours into the night and early the next morning. They were both receptive to his instruction and showed an obvious desire to please him. Bear could tell that Watchman had raised his son with the same integrity and a good work ethic that he lived by.

He looked to the corner of the living room where his HMS once stood. He had rigged a satellite to steal web access from the nearby government factory. When the World Government banned religious documents of all kinds, he had thrown the machine into the Trinity River. Bear sighed. Why did he let his emotions always get the best of him? He had recorded small sermons for whoever wanted a copy. He'd only make a few dozen a week, and many times people seemed to take a copy out of obligation. He never heard very much feedback, except from a few of his close friends—Zach and Pilar. Once in a while, a stranger would contact him through the HMS and thank him, but those occasions happened rarely during the five years he struggled to learn the *Bible*—a feat he was still struggling with.

Bear's eyes traveled to the window, and he could see the freshly painted casket on the bed of his truck. Naomi had watched every one of his sermons and had given them to the women she mentored. She praised him even when he knew his explanations were rudimentary. "*Someone is going to be blessed by your words, Bear. Wait and see. Your obedience will bear fruit even if you can't see it now*," she had said.

Bear looked back at the young men sleeping. Watchman—a man known for his love for Jesus—had watched his sermons and had shared them with others. That was fruit he had never anticipated.

"*Ne'aw-ze.*"

"Yes, *Aha-enah*," Bear said, turning towards his grandfather's bedroom.

"Will you be leaving soon?" his grandfather asked, looking toward the living room where the fighters were still sleeping.

"Yes, *Aha-enah*. They should be waking soon. Will you take them to the river when they are ready?" Bear asked.

"Did you finish the casket for Naomi?" he asked.

"Yes, we finished early in the morning. They did a good job. I'm heading to Cedar Wood now. Will you give them this gift from me?" Bear said, handing his father two small burlap bags.

"*Bahey?*" the grandfather asked, taking the two sacks from Bear.

"Yes, beans and some cornflour for their journey back," Bear said, grabbing a larger bag. "And this is for the gathering."

"They must have greatly honored you for you to be this generous? *Cabena Sa Ne'aw-ze* does not give up his food stores lightly," the grandfather said, raising his silver eyebrow.

Bear knew that his grandfather only mentioned his full Ka'to name when he was trying to make a point. "Yes, *Aha-enah*. They brought me good news that my heart needed to hear," he said, placing the large bag over his shoulder. "I will be back in a few days. Protect my home."

"Ah—my *ba-kinchi*, you know I always do," the grandfather said.

Bear nodded and silently opened the door to his home, closely it gently behind him.

CHAPTER FOURTEEN

Zach had almost hoped that Bear would be delayed. He needed to bury his mother, but the memories of his father's death were rising up. He had been back to Cedar Wood as a Runner many times, yet he had always made sure to avoid the church grounds where his father died. He was emotionless at his father's funeral. He allowed his mother to cry on his shoulder, and he shed no tears for several weeks after. His heart felt like someone had poured cement over it. He finally cried a few times over the past five years, but the full force of what he carried never came out. He only wept enough to alleviate the pain that seemed to always simmer just beneath.

"I see lights," Ruth whispered, looking into the early black morning.

"That's Bear's truck. We will carry Mom out. Do you mind getting the rest of our things?" Zach asked, looking at his sister. She looked pretty in her tailored black dress. Her eyes seemed larger now that her face had thinned out even more. She had dark circles around her eyes that gave her a weary look. She wore no makeup, but her eyes were outlined with her long, black lashes. Her face looked flushed, and he wondered if she was getting ill. Her brown, straight hair hit below her shoulders, and he noticed for the first time how uneven the ends looked. He realized that she probably hadn't trimmed it since the night he tried to warn her at the PR event. He didn't like thinking about that night.

"How do you feel, Ruth?" he asked, instinctively placing his hand to her forehead. "I think you have a fever. Have you eaten anything?"

"I think I had something yesterday, but I do feel thirsty. I went to get some water last night, but the jugs were empty," she said, looking back out the window as a shadow across the yard slammed a squeaky truck door shut.

"Ruth, you have to let me know when it runs out," Zach said, frustrated with himself.

"It was late after I finished altering Mom's dress to fit her. She had grown so thin since she originally wore it."

"You're no better, Ruth. You are disappearing before my eyes. You need to take better care of yourself. Go sit at the table." Zach led his sister to the table and pulled out a chair. He grabbed one of the water bottles and met Bear at the door.

"Are you ready?" Bear asked when Zach opened the screen.

"No, not quite. Can you pump some water into this jug really quick? I need to get some food into my sister. I think she's getting sick," Zach said, handing Bear the jug.

"I was waiting for you to take her by the house, so my grandfather and I could meet her. She's been here for almost two months," Bear said, trying to look around Zach's body.

"You know I would have brought her by. We've been busy taking care of mom, and I started that management position," Zach said.

"I know. Naomi told me to lay off a little. She said you were working through your issues again. Has Pilar met her?" Bear asked. Pilar was the only other person that Zach had trusted with the secret of having a sister.

"She found out about her the day Ruth arrived, but she hasn't formally met her yet either," Zach said.

"You've done a pretty good job at keeping your sister under wraps, but you're going to have to let go of the secret today," Bear said, taking the jug without looking away from Zach.

"I know," Zach exhaled. "I need to let go of a lot of things today."

"I'll be right back, but we should go quickly. I want to get there before the sun rises."

Zach closed the door and headed back to the kitchen. Ruth had her elbows on the table and she was crying into her hands. Zach felt an instant urgency to take care of her.

"Ruth, how about some beef stew?" he asked, trying to sound positive.

Ruth lifted her face to look at her brother. "Honestly, Zach, I can't take one more bite of stew. I'm done. That's all I've eaten for the last week, and I can't stomach it any longer."

Zach thought for a moment. He opened the refrigerator door, but there was nothing there. "Do you want another soup? We have a few cans of chicken noodle soup."

"No, Zach," Ruth said, trying to wipe away the fresh tears. "I don't want anything right now."

Zach shut the refrigerator door harder than he intended and thought for several moments. "Well, we can't leave here until you eat something, Ruth. You are sick and you have lost too much weight. I'm afraid your body will not have the energy it needs to make it through the day if you don't eat something."

"You know how sensitive I am about food. I've eaten enough soup to last me for the rest of my life. There's nothing in the refrigerator or the pantry."

Zach walked over to one of the cabinets. "Yes, there is a bag of flour right here, Ruth. All you need to do is add some water and bake it in the oven."

"I don't know how to use the fire in the oven," Ruth said, looking at the cast iron cook stove.

"What did you use at Deborah and Esther's farm?"

"I told you that they had electric appliances, but even then I didn't cook much. Deborah did the cooking," Ruth said.

Zach straightened and looked towards the soup. "How have you been heating up the soup?" he asked.

Ruth looked away from Zach's stare. "I've been eating it cold."

Zach kept his eyes on Ruth. "The oven hasn't been burning coal for several days. Are you cold at night?"

Ruth looked back at her brother. "Yes," she whispered.

101

Zach let his hands fall to his side. "Ruth, I'm so sorry. I didn't realize."

"No, it's not your fault. Mom was so good at keeping the house warm and cooking our food. I didn't think to learn. I didn't realize that she would be leaving so soon. I feel so helpless, and I'm embarrassed. It's my own pride," Ruth said, trying to wipe the tears dripping down her cheeks and chin.

Zach walked to the table where Ruth was sitting, and he knelt beside her. "Mom told me to take care of you, but I'm obviously failing. Give me a second chance, and I promise that this will never happen again."

The front door swung opened, and Bear hauled the water jug into the living room on his shoulder. He walked into the kitchen and set the water on the counter. He turned toward Zach, and watched as he got up from the floor. He then stared at Ruth for a long moment.

"She's sick, Zach," Bear said.

"I know. I've got to get her to eat before we go," Zach said. He was feeling ashamed at the state of his sister. He saw her through Bear's eyes and knew what he was thinking. She was too thin and too tired to go to the grief gathering.

"Are you determined to go with us?" Bear asked Ruth, keeping his eyes fixed on her.

"Yes," she answered.

Bear walked over to Ruth and gently took her wrist in between his thumb and first two fingers. His calloused hand enveloped Ruth's small hand.

"Her heart rate is very slow," he said, drawing his hand away lightly. Bear said nothing more for a moment and finally spoke as if he made a decision. "You will go, but you will need to eat and drink something on the way. Once you are done, you must lie down, so bring a pillow and a blanket. You're likely to get cold. I will stay in the back of the truck with the casket to make sure nothing happens." He turned to Zach, handing him the keys from his pocket. "You will drive my truck."

"But no one drives your truck," Zach said stunned.

"Today is different. Do you have a thermos to pour some water in?" Bear asked.

"Yes, I'll get it."

"Good, let's load up the truck and then we'll come back for Naomi's body."

Ruth got up from the table, relieved to get away from Bear's stare. She entered her mother's room and grabbed a small pillow and blanket from the closet. She looked at the bed where her mother's body rested and walked to the edge of the bed. She leaned over her mother's body and adjusted the single pearl strung on a strand of nylon at the base of her neck. Ruth made her mother the same necklace that Cindy had made her. It was only two short months ago that she left the farm, but it already felt like an eternity. She unconsciously fingered her small pearl, dangling slightly below the neckline of her black shirt. She had only one pearl left. She would have to keep it for something important.

"I don't want to say goodbye, Mom," she whispered. But her mother said nothing, so Ruth turned away and left the room.

When Ruth met Zach back in the kitchen, he had a thermos of water ready for her. They both grabbed several bags for the grief gathering before heading out to the truck. A thin layer of clouds covered the moon and stars, so the path leading through the yard to the curb was hard to see. Zach noticed that the air was chilly, but the wind had kept still, like it was holding its breath. He felt much the same way—he was trying to hold everything in one more time, but he knew it wouldn't last. He would break.

Bear came to the passenger side, carrying a large burlap bag.

"Ruth, here is a corn muffin for you and some dried nuts and berries," he said, pulling items out of the bag. "Once you are done eating, I want you to drink all the water in that thermos. Then you must wrap up in the blanket and lay down. I'll be in the bed of the truck, so there will be plenty of room for you to stretch out. You have a fever that needs to break. We will be driving slowly because of the casket, so you'll have almost two hours to sleep. You must use all of that time to rest. Do you understand?"

"Yes," Ruth said, taking the food from Bear's hand.

"Zach, let's go get Naomi."

Zach and Bear quickly walked into the house to where Naomi's body rested. They each grabbed two corners of the blanket and lifted her body off the bed. They slowly maneuvered through the small house and out the screen door, carefully walking down the front steps. They moved slowly because the early morning still slumbered in darkness. Then they lifted her on the bed of the truck. Bear opened the casket and they arranged Naomi's body inside.

"Thanks for making her casket," Zach said when they finished. "I can't really see it, but I know it will honor her."

Bear nodded. "Yes, I was able to make something worthy of Naomi with the Father's help."

"Did you need anything before we leave?" Zach asked. Zach sensed that Bear had something to say.

"Your sister, she looks nothing like you or Naomi."

"I know. She favors her father's side of the family," Zach said.

"Do you know her father?" Bear asked.

Zach paused. "I never met him personally. He died several years ago."

Bear stared off into the darkness. "I'm glad Naomi confirmed her identity to me before she passed or else I wouldn't have believed it."

Bear stayed quiet for a moment longer. He moved closer to Zach, so he could see his face. "Zach, I've known you since you were an irritating kid, telling me how I needed Jesus. You brought me to your house, and I envied your perfect life with your perfect parents. But we all take our turns walking through hell—no one gets the easy road all the way through."

"I know," Zach said.

"God knows that I'm no one to judge. I've made enough mistakes to last a lifetime, and I'm doing what I need to do to make up for it," Bear said, pausing long enough to see that Zach was listening.

Bear nodded and continued. "But that girl in the front seat was Naomi's dying wish, and you can't hide in your heartache any longer. I watched my own mom slowly die, and your sister has the same look about her—like she's giving up. You need to get her out of the dark place she's in or she might not make it."

Zach felt his face heat up against the cool morning air. "I know I've messed things up, but I will make it right," he said. "She is my sister, and I will take care of her."

"The worst thing you can do is isolate her, Zach. I know this from experience. She needs to connect with others. She needs to get out of that house."

Zach stared at his friend. He knew Bear would not let up until he was satisfied that he was being understood. "Let me get through this day, and I will fix everything."

Bear leaned back against the truck's cab, sitting next to the casket. "So long as you do. Now let's go bury your mom in the ashes of your father."

CHAPTER FIFTEEN

Bear kept a firm grip on the casket as the truck drove down the darkened streets. He loved the black abyss surrounding him; it allowed him a feeling of safety as his thoughts consumed him. The image of Ruth filled his mind. Her body frame was small and slender like his mom's, but that was the only thing about Ruth that was like his mother. There was something different about Ruth that he couldn't quite grasp. He knew it was the same feeling that he got when he talked to Zach, like there was a depth to her thoughts that he was unable to reach.

Her lack of makeup and adornment would have made her look simple and young if it weren't for the mature presence of her eyes. Her black suit fit her petite, youthful figure perfectly, and he noticed she didn't have her ears pierced or a ring on her finger. She wore only what looked to be a small, white pearl attached to some kind of clear thread around her neck. He had stared at her for several seconds, trying to read her reaction to him. But she showed no emotion. Death of a loved one could knock the wind out of you for a time, but soon enough, it would cause you to buckle over in pain. He wondered how long it would take Ruth to feel the full loss of her mother.

Bear felt his truck dip into a pothole on the street, so he instinctively grabbed hold of the wooden casket. The truck slowed, and he was grateful that Zach was driving carefully. The bottom of the casket jumped half an inch, but it landed quietly back on the bed of the truck. Though it was still dark, Bear could see faint light rising in the horizon. The sun would be up soon. Bear looked behind him through the window of the truck. He couldn't see Ruth's face, but he could tell that her head was lying on the pillow against the passenger door. Her small frame was curled across half of the bench seat. He could see the profile of Zach's face, concentrating on the road ahead of him. Bear knew his friend was working through his thoughts.

Zach had the same look on his face when Bear saw him drive up to the training grounds the summer before his father died. Bear hadn't come home that summer to visit. He was too caught up in his drugs and women and winning his fights on the circuit. He didn't want to admit what he was doing to Zach's dad. He didn't want to see the disappointment in Naomi's eyes. He wanted to stay blind to the path that he allowed the circuit to take him on. He was famous and people loved him. He was the Shaman—or at least, that is what the crowds called him and he had fully embraced his new title.

Bear leaned his back against the side of the truck and let the memory unfold.

"How did you find me?" Bear asked, as Zach made his way through the crowd of fighters and fans. He was sitting on the bed of his truck with a young woman who was massaging his hands.

"The whole area knows that you were fighting today," Zach said, his face held tight to keep in the emotions. "Why haven't you come home to visit? Mom is worried about you and Dad was about to come and get you, but I told him that I would go. He can't just stop preaching to go chase you around. You only stayed a few days for Christmas and you forgot to come home this summer. I start school next week, and we were supposed to do some fishing together. What's going on, Bear?"

"What do you care, Zach? You're not my keeper," Bear said. The other fighters were noticing the confrontation between him and Zach. He wanted to avoid making a scene, but he knew Zach. He wouldn't let up until he spoke his mind...or heart.

"What is that supposed to mean? We care about you. Your dad isn't even fighting anymore. Why do you continue to do it? You told us you were mainly trying to get to know him," Zach said, forcing his voice to stay calm.

"I'm good at fighting. I make a living at it. I don't expect the preacher's kid to understand, but you have no right to judge me," Bear said, taking his hands away from the young woman next to him.

Zach looked at Bear. He looked like the old images he saw in history class. His long black hair was spiked in a Mohawk. He was shirtless with nothing but a thick, leather necklace of large bear teeth around his neck and chest. He wore a leather sarong around his waist and little else.

"I don't stand in judgment of you but God's Word does," Zach said, firmly. "Why are you dressed up like this? I've been hearing things about your fighting performance."

"What do you know about it?" Bear scoffed, feeling uncomfortable with Zach's posture of attack. Zach wasn't a fighter, but he was good at using words. And the way Zach was standing now reminded him of a story Zach's dad used to tell of the prophet Elijah, raining down fire from the heavens. "Are you going to start preaching to me?"

"I will if that's what God calls me to do and there is nothing you can do to stop the will of God," Zach said, noticing the crowd of people circling around them.

"Go ahead, preacher boy! Preach us a sermon!" one man shouted out.

The young woman that was sitting next to Bear slipped out of the bed of the truck and put her hand across Zach's shoulder. "I might need some saving, preacher boy. Let's hear what you've got to say."

Bear jumped off the truck bed. "Don't you touch him!" he shouted at the girl.

"Why are you getting so upset all of a sudden?" she said, obviously offended.

"He doesn't mess around with your kind," Bear said, throwing her hand off of Zach's shoulder.

"Look, I don't want to involve all these fighters," Zach said, looking around to the young men around him. "Can I talk to you for a moment alone? I promise. I won't bother you again. I have something that I want to give you," Zach said.

"Fine, go sit in my truck," Bear said and then directed his attention back to the small crowd. "What are you all staring at? Does someone want to fight me? I'll take you on right now if you don't walk away now!"

Instantly, the crowd began to disperse. The young woman who had been massaging Bear's hands tried to make her way back to him, but he pointing her away. "Get out of here. I don't want to see your face again."

Bear made sure there were no more stragglers and walked back to his truck and slid into the front seat. "Okay, what do you want to tell me?"

Zach took a deep breath. "Look, I'm not trying to judge you. The only reason I'm here is because I care about you. If I didn't care, I would turn a blind eye to the road of destruction that you're on, but I can't. I'm accountable to call into light the darkness that I see engulfing you."

"You know I hate it when you talk like that. Now talk to me plainly," Bear said, frustrated. He didn't learn to read well until Naomi had started teaching him when he was younger. Even still, it became clear that Zach, though many years younger, caught onto language quicker and better than he ever would.

"I told you outside that God's Word stands in judgment of you, so I wrote down a list of verses and stories you need to read. Read them and compare them to your life and to your choices. God says that he sets before us blessings or curses. You may feel like your choices are getting you rich and famous, but I promise you it will not last. Disobedience to God's commands always comes with a price, but I know that God is gentle and He gives us many chances to obey," Zach said. "He's not mad at you and you're not in trouble, but you need to take the way out before you wind up like your dad."

"What have you heard?" Bear asked.

"I know your dad is dying. He's an addict and he's going to die like your mom did. It's a selfish lifestyle. You know more than anyone."

"The only reason I'm not smashing your face in right now is because I know you're not trying to dishonor me. But you have no right to bring up my mother," Bear said, squeezing the steering wheel of his truck so hard that it started to screech.

"Why? You want me to ignore the choices she made? You want me to pretend that she didn't choose drugs over you? Do you want me to deny the fact that you are headed for the same fate?"

"I don't have any kids," Bear said in his defense.

"You're having sex with many women," Zach said without flinching. "You could conceive a baby any time now. You might already have a baby out there somewhere."

"Sex? Is that the worst you can come up with, Zach? Don't tell me you're jealous." Bear said, laughing.

Zach stared at Bear for a long moment. "Those are God's daughters you are exploiting. He loves them. He died for them. He will hold you accountable for what you are doing to them."

Bear stopped laughing. "They pursue me," he said.

"If their boundaries are that loose, someone in their past has hurt them. They've been touched by a dad, a brother or someone close to them and you are simply taking advantage of their pain," Zach said. "You hold no value for those women and they are crying out for love. They need real love. They need the love of the Father, not the counterfeit substitute that you're offering them."

Bear looked away and stared out the window.

"I also heard that you are experimenting with peyote," Zach said. "You are using it as part of your Shaman routine. You're singing old Ka'to songs, invoking the spiritual world. There are only two spiritual forces out there—good and evil. When you use that stuff you are opening doors to a darkness that you won't be able to run away from in your own strength. People do not stand alone. We were created as vessels, and we will be filled with God or Satan. If you are not careful, you will be ensnared by demonic forces."

Bear looked back at Zach. "I haven't done it for several months now."

Zach could sense something that Bear was not telling him.

"What's going on? Have you been spiritually attacked?" Zach asked.

"I remember your dad saying that once you are a Christian that Satan can't touch you," Bear said, uncertainly.

"Satan has lost the final battle, yes, but He can still feed on the darkness that you let into your life. Your salvation is a covenant signed in the blood of Jesus. No one can snatch you from the Father's hands. But if you are not letting Jesus have all control, the Enemy can create misery in your life," Zach paused. "Bear, look at me. Do you understand how much the Enemy hates you? As much as the Father loves you, Satan has a hatred for you that is supernatural and evil. He knows that God has a purpose for your life. He knows that you are a masterpiece made in the image of God. Satan wants to wipe you across the ground with his foot so the rest of the world can walk over your decayed body and laugh at the destruction of God's beautiful creation. Don't let him do it. Don't fall into the same trap that your mom and dad fell into. The women, the drugs, the fame, the wealth—none of it is worth losing the real fight. God has so much He wants to do through you."

"But I'm not like you, Zach. I'm not a preacher boy. I can't talk like you do. You sit with God for hours, and I could barely sit fifteen minutes with Him," Bear said.

"Bear, the worst thing you could ever do is compare your relationship with God to mine or to anyone else. You are designed differently. God has special plans that are unique to you. You interact with God in a personal way—a way that I never could."

"That's easy for you to say, Zach. When I'm with you, I'm always second. I'm the one who has to hear how great you are and how your words are changing lives. But here I'm first. I'm the one people talk about. I'm the one people want to see."

"So instead of making decisions based on God's glory, you are going to make decisions based on your own?" Zach asked.

"I'm done talking with you," Bear said. "I know what I'm doing and I don't need Zacchaeus Mark Daniels to share his words of wisdom with me. Go home. Go back to school and go be the good boy everyone knows you are."

"Fine. I will leave you alone, but don't forget that I came out here because I care about you. Mom, Dad and I are not looking the other way. We are praying for you and we love you. Here is the paper with the verses on it. Just look over it."

Bear grabbed the paper out of Zach's hands and crumpled it in his fist. Zach took hold of the door handle and pushed the car door open. He turned to leave, but stopped and looked back at Bear. "If I lost everything? If I were to become destitute and lose my will to preach? If the only words people said about me were words of pity and of shame? Would you consider coming back? Would you walk away from this path of destruction if you saw my perfect life fall apart? Would that satisfy you?"

Bear looked in Zach's eyes. "That's not going to happen to you," Bear said.

"You don't know the plans that God has," Zach answered. "Don't let my life dictate your decisions. You must always stay obedient to the Lord's call on your own life."

"I don't know what that call is," Bear said.

"Well, you won't find it unless you fight for it," Zach replied and stepped out of the truck door, slamming it behind him.

Bear watched Zach walk away. He felt like it would be the last time he would see him, but he would never have believed that very soon Zach's father would be burned alive in the church.

Bear felt the truck jerk, and he instantly grabbed hold of the casket again. Zach took a turn off the road, and the truck began to bounce around on the grassy path that led to the remains of church. Bear looked at the horizon—hues of gold and pink spread across the skyline. He gripped the casket, steadying it while the truck drove slowly on the overgrown dirt road.

Bear tried to relax his face. He knew he wore the emotions from the memory of his talk with Zach over five years ago. Today they would honor Naomi's life, and he wouldn't bring the mistakes of the past into the grief gathering. As Zach parked the truck in front of the charred remains of the church, Bear couldn't help confronting the truth: Zach had lost everything.

CHAPTER SIXTEEN

Cindy Isaacs looked diligently at the map of the Trinity Trading Center grounds that she held in her hand. She stood at the front station of the trading center, and only a few people could be seen walking through the aisles looking at the different commodities available for barter. It was early in the morning and the center was still waking up to the buzz of commerce.

"Tom," Cindy said, placing the map on the counter and walking toward her husband who was labeling a load of winter grapefruits that a Trinity resident dropped off the night before. "Would you mind watching the front for a few minutes? Jim isn't here yet, but he said he would get here as early as possible. I need to do some work at home on the HMS. Almost everything is ready for the trading expo tomorrow, but I need to check if we got any more vendors wanting a section for their goods before we leave for the grief gathering."

"I'll watch the front. I'm sure he'll be here any minute. Everything is packed up in the truck, so we're ready to go. What do you think of the Henson family's crop this year? I think they're finally worth something," he said with a broad smile. "This batch of winter grapefruits should provide them with a few goods they've been needing."

Cindy paused and looked at the grapefruits. "Yes, I think you're right. They look much bigger and pinker than last year."

"Did you hear anything from those people coming from the north, bringing several dozen head of cattle? That will be a nice draw for the people coming out. Cows have been running low in Trinity and the surrounding areas, and I know of several families saving to barter for a pair of them," Tom Isaacs said, as he walked to the front station of the trading center.

"They should have contacted me on the HMS before they left this morning. I'll let you know if they decided to come down. Was there anything else you need while I'm on the HMS?" she asked.

Tom looked around quickly. "Yes," he said in a hushed voice. "I'll be leading the *Bible* meetings all day tomorrow. Can you go over the list and contact the people still missing?"

"Yep, that was on my list of to-dos," she smiled. "And don't worry. This time I'll make sure to send one of the kids down to bring your lunch and dinner. We won't let you starve like last time."

"I didn't notice," Tom said, putting his arms around his wife's neck and giving her a quick hug.

"When you're giving the Word, you don't notice anything," she whispered in his ear.

"But I do love to talk about God," he whispered back and gave her a knowing wink.

"The generator is fueled up, right?" she asked, reaching to the front counter and grabbing the map of the trading grounds.

"It should be unless the kids were using it without permission," Tom said.

"They better be doing their homeschool. We should check on them before we leave. They know I'll be checking all of it when we get home tonight," Cindy said behind her as she opened the front door.

"If they're not, I'm sure you'll get them in line," Tom yelled before the door shut. He smiled to himself. His wife was definitely not one to cross.

Cindy closed the door of the main storeroom behind her and walked through the halls of what was once Trinity Church. It had changed a lot since they began renovations to make the church into a trading center. She shook her head in thought. The church had doubled in size since they began doing secret meetings in the basement. Never would she have comprehended what a little persecution would have done to their church. Instead of going straight to the office where the

HMS was located, she veered to the side door of the building. She opened it and peered across the lawn towards her home. She could see her kids sitting at the kitchen table doing their schoolwork. It was one of those rare mornings when all of her kids were in cheerful moods. She even overheard her eldest helping the smaller ones with their assignments before she left early that morning. She loved when her children worked together—it made the entire day so peaceful. She knew they would be okay while she and Tom were gone. Several women from the church would be stopping by to check on them.

She closed the side door and headed toward the office. "Thank You, Lord, for surrounding us with caring people," she whispered. When she entered the office, she reached down to the generator and turned it on. After a few moments, she switched on the HMS. She noticed a stack of printouts next to the machine. Her husband still stayed up-to-date with what was going on with the World Government and the Efficientists. Tom felt that Neil Elder was up to something. He wasn't scrambling to make peace like he had been, and he was beefing up his bodyguard personnel. Tom would read into the night all the printouts from each day until she demanded that he come to bed. Cindy knew her husband was good at putting the puzzle pieces together. He had figured out that Eve Pallue was still alive.

As the HMS warmed up, Cindy thought about the petite girl she knew as Ruth—the adopted daughter of Esther and Deborah. She still couldn't see her as Eve, but she wasn't the one who kept up with the Efficientists' happenings. That was her husband's passion. They had talked with Deborah and Esther the week before. The elderly women were bringing some of their guests to the trading center. They were a diverse group of people—all appearing like fish out of water. None of them knew how to take care of themselves in the colonies. They were like children in a new world, having to be trained all over again. Unlike the other Efficientists she had seen come through the trading center, the people living with Deborah and Esther had no family or friends in the colonies. They were completely isolated and alone—much like Ruth was when she first came to Trinity. Deborah and Esther were the perfect surrogates for them.

Cindy looked at the sun coming up strong over the horizon from her window. She knew she needed to get done fast. She checked her list of people who hadn't responded to the secret church meeting invites, and she sent coded messages to each one. Since the World Government outlawed all religious activity, they had to do church secretly. However, instead of disbanding the church members, Cindy knew that they had formed an even stronger bond together. Her husband's greatest fears turned into his biggest experience of faith. His congregation may appear to be nonexistent, but it was growing larger every day.

When the HMS was finally ready, she sat down in front of the screen. Then she went through her vendor contacts and wrote down the ones who verified they would be attending tomorrow's trading expo. She was happy when she saw that the people from the north with the cattle were already on the road. They should get here late tonight. She scribbled some notes on the trading grounds map, and marked a large section for the cattle. She was thankful that they put the fence in a few months ago. When God led them to start the Trinity Trading Center, they had no idea what they were doing, but after a couple of months of trial and error, she believed they were finally providing a much needed service to the local area—not to mention they were able to continue to preach the Good News of Jesus Christ.

Cindy completed her work and erased any trails, like her husband taught her. She was about to sign off, but a message suddenly appeared on her screen.

TO: Thomas Isaacs
FROM: Inside the World Government
RE: World Religion

Neil Elder and his team have developed a World Religion Holy Text called "The Unum Vernum," which means "The Only All." He and his researchers have knitted together pieces of all religious documents, including the Tripitaka, the Koran, Course of Miracles, Vedas, The Book of Mormon, the Old and New Testaments and other religious documents of different societies and religions throughout history. Be warned this document has been designed to further the World Government's agenda of control, and nothing of the text carries any value of the existing religions from which they were taken. Prepare your people for this lie, so they will not be fooled. The deity of Jesus Christ has been completely erased. Print and erase this message immediately. I will contact you further. Attached is the encryption code.

Cindy fumbled a moment before the training her husband had gone over with her kicked in. She knew she only had seconds to erase the message before a trail would be left. She pressed print. The blank page being sucked into the printer felt like it took an eternity to get into position. Once the ink started zipping across the page, she pressed delete. She waited without breathing until the page finally printed out. She reread the message several times not believing what she saw. Her husband's prayers had finally come true—there was a mole in the World Government, and he had contacted Thomas Isaacs.

Esther sat on the porch, petting one of the farm cats that jumped onto her lap. She watched as Deborah was overseeing the division of the goats. It was time to wean the babies from their moms. They had to start their lives as adults now, and from their cries, they were not happy about it.

"They sound like children crying," a man's voice rang out from behind the backdoor screen.

"Li, you startled me," Esther jumped and the lazy cat jumped from her lap. "Did you find your breakfast on the table?"

Li opened the screen door and stepped on the porch. "I did. Thank you. I washed the dishes and put them away." He looked back out on the farm. "I'm glad I got house cleaning duty this week," he said, staring at two of his housemates who were running after a young goat.

Esther pointed to one of the rocking chairs. "Why don't you join me and we will watch them together," she said. She noticed he was carrying one of the *Bibles* they had given each of their new houseguests.

Li turned the chair slightly and sat down, placing the *Bible* on the porch railing.

"How is your reading going?" Esther asked, motioning to the *Bible*.

Li stared toward the goats. Though, his eyes were no longer focused on the action in the pen. "It seems strange. I read the Tripitaka, knowing that my family's history is Buddhist, but the words were not logical to me. Then I read the *Bible* and these words also do not seem logical, but they are touching me somehow," he said, placing his hand on his chest. "I feel them in here, even though I fight them in my mind."

"Are you reading the Gospels like we suggested?" Esther asked.

"I am. The words of Jesus are difficult for me to comprehend. This spiritual kingdom He talks about is backward. It is about serving. It is about giving. It is about being last. I do not understand. How can one be last and yet first? How can one serve and yet be the master?"

"Those are good questions, Li! You are starting to see the difference between God's way and our way," Esther said. She looked back towards the goats. "You see those baby goats?"

Li focused his attention back on his housemates' work of fathering the goats. "Yes," he said.

"There are mom goats and baby goats. Which goat serves the other?" she asked.

Li thought for a minute. "The mom goat serves the baby her milk," he answered.

"Yes, she does," Esther nodded. "But which goat is the master?"

Li thought again. "The mom goat is the master because she directs her young."

"Precisely!" Esther exclaimed. "The mom goat serves out of her abundance. It is the baby that takes out of his lack. She is the servant because she is the master."

Li looked toward Esther. "If Jesus is God, and God created all things, then Jesus is the ultimate Servant because He gives from an endless supply of abundance."

Esther nodded excitedly.

Li stood up and placed his hand back onto his chest. "And if Jesus is the ultimate Servant, then He is the ultimate Master."

"Yes!" Esther said, getting up from her chair and grabbing both of Li's shoulders. "Just like the mama goat! But instead of milk, God gives us life. He has an endless supply of life, so He serves it to His creation. But we must be like the baby goat and drink from Him."

Li stared into Esther's aged eyes. "And when we learn to take from God, we can be the endless supply to others," he said tentatively. Esther felt a tear run down her cheek. "Like what Deborah and I are doing on the farm. We are serving, teaching and preparing you because God has blessed us with plenty."

"Thank you, Esther. I am starting to understand now. Would you mind if I go back into the house? I would like to read and think on these things." Li said.

"Of course, Li. If you have any more questions, Deborah and I are here for you," Esther said.

Li smiled and made his way back into the house.

Esther leaned back in her chair. The cool wind blew over her, so she picked up the knitted blanket on the back of the chair and laid it over her. She knew exactly who Li was. He was Charlie Liu—the very man Ruth had predicted would be here. Esther knew that he played an important role in what was happening in Trinity. She and Deborah were already making plans to introduce him to Pastor Tom. They informed him that their long-awaited visitor had finally arrived.

Esther shook her head and smiled. Li had asked many questions about God and faith. In fact, all of their guests had asked many questions and continued to ask questions. Ruth's time at the farm had prepared her and Deborah with the ability to bring God's truth to them. The Efficientists were highly intelligent, yet their questions were very basic. Making a bridge from their intelligence to their faith took patience and clarity of thought. Esther couldn't wait to introduce Li to Pastor Tom. Pastor Tom could explain the mysteries of faith to a doorpost and win it to Christ if it were possible.

CHAPTER SEVENTEEN

Bear jumped out of the bed of the truck before Zach put the truck in park and walked to the passenger side. He looked in the vehicle and saw that Zach's sister was awake and alert. He opened the door and put his hand toward her face. She instantly jerked back.

"I'm only going to feel if the fever broke," he said and placed his wrist against her forehead. "Did you break into a sweat?"

Ruth looked embarrassed. "Yes, my clothes were damp when I woke up, but they are dry now."

Zach came around the front of the truck. "She's been awake for about fifteen minutes. She ate a little more and drank some water."

"We will begin digging Naomi's gravesite on the church grounds, so we will make you a seat near us. Or would you rather stay in the truck?" Bear asked.

"No, I would prefer to be next to my mom's body," Ruth answered.

"That's what I thought," Bear said.

"Zach, let us move your mom's casket next to the gravesite, and then you can move Ruth while I begin to dig," Bear said. "The tree over there will be a good place for her. We will be out here all day, so you don't want her to burn." Bear examined Ruth's skin. She had taken off her jacket, so her arms were exposed. They were pale and he could see a few bruises.

"You are not eating enough meat," He said, picking up one of her thin arms. "You are bruising too easily. And you need to watch where you are walking. I bet your legs are bruised from bumping into bed frames and running into the kitchen counters."

Ruth took her arm back. She had worn pants to cover up the bruises on her shins and thighs from walking into things. She had been absentminded ever since her mom became severely ill.

Bear looked at Ruth a moment longer. "Put your jacket back on and stay in the shade of the tree. You are too sick. If you burn, you may not recover. I will borrow a hat from someone when people begin to arrive. The day should be cool, but there are no clouds to cover the sun."

Bear shut the door, and he and Zach went to the bed of the truck. Zach jumped in while Bear opened the bed of the truck. Zach pushed the casket over the edge of the truck as Bear gently brought it directly back. When the casket was almost completely off the bed, Zach jumped back out and grabbed the other end. Together they slowly walked the casket to the church grounds.

Ruth watched them walk, seeing for the first time the image she saw in the newspaper when Zach first arrived at her flat in the city. It looked almost the same except that the steeple had rotted out even more, decomposing into the earth. The two men gently brought the casket to the ground. Bear got up quickly and looked away from the truck. Ruth leaned forward, looking through the windshield. She could see several cars coming from the distance. Bear began to walk toward the cars, and Zach looked back toward the truck where Ruth sat. He began to walk in her direction.

"Are you ready to come out or do you want to stay a little longer?" "Zach asked her.

"I'm ready to get out. I want to be near Mom," Ruth said, putting on her jacket.

"There is a tree right next to where the gravesite will be. I'll put you there." Zach opened the door and helped Ruth to the ground and closed the door. "Give me a minute to grab everything."

Zach reached into the truck, gathering a blanket, food, water and other items. He closed the door and gave Ruth his arm. "Take my arm. I know you can walk on your own, but there are a lot of holes in the ground and rocks scattered about. I don't want you to trip."

Ruth took Zach's arm and they began to slowly walk toward the tree. "Zach, I don't want you to think my condition is your fault. We both lost Mom. You are grieving as much as I am—in fact, probably more. You loved Mom, and I know that we are both mourning her loss."

Zach stopped walking for a brief second before continuing their slow steps. "No, Bear is right. I should have taken better care of you. I haven't taken care of anyone besides Mom, and my actions have been self-absorbed. God has been exposing a lot of unrepentance in my life, and I need to deal with it. But I promise you that I will be a much better brother."

Ruth still felt awkward with the word *brother*, but somehow it made her feel more secure. As they continued to walk, she noticed Bear talking with a group of people, standing near the parked cars. He was dispersing shovels and pointing toward the casket. "I notice that when you are around Bear, you let him lead. It is obvious to me that you have more knowledge than he does—spiritually and intellectually. Yet, he is the one who takes command. Why is that?"

Zach chuckled under his breath. He leaned down to Ruth but kept his eyes on Bear's location. "Bear is not very concerned with abstract ideas and concepts, but he can read people like a book. His strengths come out when he is around groups of people. He is a natural leader. People follow him and do their best to keep to his high standard of performance. It's hard to explain, but you'll see," Zach whispered. "He struggles with basic Biblical revelation and understanding theoretical information, but he can expose deception or ulterior motives in people when they themselves don't see it. He's also very good at the day-to-day details of life. Nothing gets past him."

"Is that why you both get along so well?" Ruth asked.

Zach stopped when they reached the tree and placed the items on the ground. "What do you mean?" he asked.

Ruth looked at her brother. His face too had thinned out, and he appeared to have aged several years since she met him less than a year ago. "You don't know how to deceive. Your feelings are clear to anyone close to you," she said.

Zach looked away and leaned down to grab the blanket. He unfurled it and laid it on the ground. "You are mistaken. I've deceived myself for many years."

Ruth gently sat down on the blanket and looked up at her brother. "You hide your feelings. There is a big difference," she answered.

Zach stared into the distance. "I got pretty good at hiding. Mom always said that I was an open book. I guess when the book got too difficult for me to read, I slammed it shut."

Ruth thought for a moment. "The best books have the greatest heartache."

"I don't know," he answered. "My book felt pretty good when everything was going my way. My dad was alive. We were doing ministry together. Mom was always sick and heartbroken over having lost you, but I figured that was a hardship I had to live with. But when Dad was murdered, I couldn't bear it."

Ruth was about to speak, but she heard footsteps crunching through the stiff grass. "Zach, we need to begin. People are arriving, and we need to have the grave dug before the sun rises too high."

"Okay, I'm coming," Zach answered.

Bear looked at Ruth. "Here is a hat from one of Naomi's friends. She wants you to have it. You don't need it now, but when the sun feels hot on your face, put it on."

Ruth took the hat from Bear's hand. "Thank you."

"We will be digging for about an hour. Do you need anything before then?"

Ruth looked up at Bear, surprised that he had remembered the hat he had promised her. Zach was right. He thrived in leadership because he was good at the details—the details found in the external world and in people. "No, I'm fine. I feel a lot stronger now. I'm sure I can make my way if I need anything."

"Do you want to join us later after the dig? I will warn you that people will not only share their words, they will share their touch—a hug, a pat on the back or even a kiss on the cheek," Bear said. "You'll come in contact with many people, and I don't know if you are up to it."

Ruth tried to cover her look of distress, but she knew that Bear had seen it. "Yes, you're right. I'm not up to it. I would prefer to stay here—away from the crowd," she said.

Ruth directed her attention back to her brother. "When Pastor Tom and Cindy arrive, will you direct them to me? They said they would be leaving Trinity early this morning, so they will be a few hours behind us."

"I'll let them know," Zach said. "I'm looking forward to catching up with Pastor Tom. I'm also anxious to hear about the trade center and any other news he might have for me. Stay here and try to rest. I'll look your way every now and then. If you need me, give me a wave."

Ruth watched as Bear and Zach walked back toward the casket. Bear was several inches shorter than Zach, but much broader in the shoulders and stockier in the limbs. She still was surprised by how well they worked together, even though they were so different. She thought for a moment, and her mind finally found the running theme—the same theme found in Deborah and Esther's relationship. There was no ego to protect.

More and more cars and trucks filled the church grounds. Men had gathered around the gravesite where Zach and Bear were digging. The two men were now shirtless, and Ruth could see Bear's tan shoulders and Zach's white torso moving in sync with the shovels. Ruth noticed that although Zach's frame was lean, the muscles in his back and arms were prominent. The manual labor involved with delivering Sleepers had strengthened his form. Bear, on the other hand, had mature muscle mass developed over years of fighting. Ruth observed that even when Bear rested for a moment, his muscles stayed taut.

Although a few men gestured to help Zach and Bear with the dig, neither man relented his shovel. A ceremonial custom unfolded before Ruth's eyes, and she began to look around her with great interest. The men around the gravesite were taking turns speaking, and the entire group listened to his words. Ruth realized that the men were telling stories to keep Bear and Zach's attention while they dug. Gestures of help were only offered when Zach or Bear took a slight break, but each hand of help was denied. Ruth realized the offerings of help were only a form of custom. Bear and Zach would dig the entire grave themselves, and everyone knew and respected it.

She scanned her eyes to her mother's casket, which was several feet away from the gravesite. The casket was opened now, and people were taking turns kneeling by Naomi's body. Some people reached in and touched the body. Other's simply looked at the body with tears glistening in the sunlight. A few people never looked into the casket. Instead, they touched the carved wood encasing her mother and bowed their heads. For the first time, Ruth looked at the design of the casket. It wasn't a simple box that she had expected. It was beautifully constructed, and Ruth felt the urge to examine it.

She placed the large brimmed hat on her head and got up from the blanket, astonished by the strength she felt in her legs. She walked toward the casket, passing groups of families that had blankets and chairs dotted around the churchyard. She briefly peered at the gravesite and saw that they were almost done. Bear stopped shoveling and looked toward her direction. She quickened her steps, so he wouldn't reprimand her for leaving her spot under the tree. She saw that the sun was directly above her. She was glad that the hat shielded her face from its blaze, but it also shielded her from the curious eyes of others.

Ruth knelt by the casket and ran her hand over the bottom corner of the wood. The design was simple but graceful, and every corner complimented the other. Ruth felt like the casket gave an accurate view of her mother—purposeful, beautiful and unassuming. She felt someone near her.

"I'm sorry about your mother," said a woman with an elegant tenor's voice.

Ruth looked toward the open mouth of the casket and saw the face of the woman she had seen when she first arrived home. "Thank you," Ruth replied. "I'm glad that I got to be with her before she died—even if for only a brief time."

"I am friends with your brother," the woman said. "I also loved Naomi."

"My mother told me about you," Ruth said. "You are Pilar Jones. Your father is the founder of Levington. Your family owns and operates a bakery. Somehow, I have missed your arrival whenever you delivered goods to our home. I appreciated everything you brought us. It was my main sustenance over the past few weeks."

"Is that all Naomi told you about me?" Pilar asked.

Ruth looked at the exotic face in front of her. Pilar's dark skin, black hair and bright green eyes made her look intriguing. "Mom said that you and Zach were almost engaged before his father died."

Pilar exhaled and glanced toward the gravesite where Zach and Bear were finishing the dig. "Yes, that about sums me up. Oldest daughter of a baker who is in love with a man who won't love her anymore."

"I'm sorry," Ruth said.

"Does he talk about me at all?" Pilar asked.

Ruth rubbed the wood of her mother's casket one more time. "You are one of two people Zach won't talk about."

"Who's the other person?" Pilar asked.

"Austin Daniels, his father," Ruth answered.

The two women knelt side by side at the casket a moment longer, letting their heartache linger. Pilar was the first to speak again. "My family brought food for the grief gathering, but I saved you and Zach a special bag, so you won't have to wait in the lines," she said, handing Ruth a burlap bag. "Your mom said that you're not much for crowds—kind of like my dad. He didn't make it here today, but he's praying for your family."

"Tell him thank you for the food. I am grateful. He and I have mutual friends. We both stayed with Deborah and Esther, the two elderly sisters in Trinity." Ruth said.

Pilar brought a cloth to her face and dabbed the tears away from her perfectly applied makeup. "Yes, he has told us about them. He stayed with them before moving here. His short time with the two sisters changed his life. My entire family owes them a debt of gratitude. They showed my father the love of Jesus, and he in turn has shown all of us. Will you tell them the next time that you contact them that we are blessed by the help they gave my dad?"

Ruth smiled, thinking of how much Deborah and Esther complained that God wasn't using them. "I think they will appreciate your words." Ruth looked back to the casket but avoided looking at her mother's body. She already had an image of her mother from early that morning that she wanted to remember her by.

"You better get back to your tree," Pilar said, motioning to Ruth's blanket lying in the shade. "Grief gatherings can be intense, so you may want to hang back and mourn in your own way."

Ruth walked back to her spot in the grass and left Pilar kneeling at the casket. Pilar closed her eyes and whispered a short prayer. She looked toward the gravesite and watched Zach jump out of the grave that he and Bear finished digging. He put on his shirt and looked toward the casket where his mother's body waited to be buried. His eyes locked with Pilar's, but he gave no expression of how he felt. Pilar looked away. She got up with resolve and stood a few feet away from the casket. Ruth could tell that Pilar would grieve the death of Naomi despite the conflict in her relationship with Zach. Ruth felt a closeness to Pilar. She realized that Pilar must have really loved her mother.

CHAPTER EIGHTEEN

The churchyard was packed with people, and Ruth was glad the tree was outside the crowd. She got comfortable on her blanket and placed the bag that Pilar gave her protectively next to her. She had a high regard for Pilar's food, and she did not want the bag of hand-baked breads and pastries to leave her sight. She looked toward the grave site. The digging had stopped. Zach and Bear walked toward the place where Naomi's body rested. Ruth could see Pilar standing with a group nearby. Zach kneeled by the open casket, and Bear stood erect, opening his arms out and facing his palms up.

Ruth couldn't make out what he was saying, but she sensed the quiet that moved across the churchyard like the cool breeze. She knew he was praying with his eyes opened and looking into the heavens. Suddenly, Bear's voice grew louder and morphed into a melodic bass. He was singing. She couldn't decipher the words, but the tune sounded like a worship song she had heard sung at Trinity Church before it closed. The pleasantness of his voice surprised her. All around her, she heard quiet whispers, but the stifled cries soon started to ring out. Bear continued to sing, and the voices of the crowd began to join him.

She moved her focus back to Zach. He remained motionless by his mother's side. She could tell his prayers had become more passionate because his lips began to fervently move, and she saw tears dripping from his chin onto the carved wood of the casket. Bear began another melody—one that sounded even more mournful than the previous one. The crowd's cries transformed into wails, and people began to grab hold of each other in sorrow.

She saw Zach's eyes shoot open. His flat hands on the casket turned into fists. His cheeks were red, and Ruth wondered if he had worn himself out during the dig. She quickly changed her mind when he began methodically beating his fists against the edge of the casket. Bear cut the chorus he was singing short and let his hands drop to his side. He looked down at Zach who had now grabbed hold of the casket's edge and was leaning the weight of his exhausted body on it. Bear tenderly moved Zach's hands away, so he could close the casket door. Zach straightened his torso as his knees dug into the dirt. His hands grasped the hardened, cool dirt and he leaned his head back and lifted his face to the sky, "My mom is dead! My mom is dead! Why God? Why have You taken them both away from me?"

The crowd was silent, and Ruth could hear the words of her bother. She couldn't stop the tears that spilled down her face. Pilar, who was standing behind Zach, fell on her knees next to him. She didn't disturb him, but she rocked back and forth, mixing her cries with his. Bear began to shout out, "Naomi is gone. She touched the earth. She touched our hearts. Her body was weak, but her love was strong. Lord, take up Your daughter, Naomi. She was obedient even to despair. Claim Your child, Lord! She was a wife, a mother, a friend, but she lived a life for You, Lord!"

Bear walked behind Zach and Pilar and placed one of his hands on each of their shoulders. "Protect those who mourn, Lord. Help us not to be offended by what You have chosen. Yes, let us be angry. Let us be hurt. Let us grieve. But let us not turn from You. Naomi is with You now and joined with her husband. Let her finally rest in peace." Bear went to his knees and wrapped his bronze arms around Pilar and Zach. The beauty of the image awed Ruth: three shades of skin blended into one sorrowful embrace. The cry of the crowd came forth again. Ruth felt her own rigid composure break, and she began to allow the sorrow that she had unknowingly been harboring to join the others at the grief gathering.

She felt a hand squeeze her shoulder, and she saw Cindy's familiar face hovering above her. Cindy knowingly smiled and sat down next to Ruth, pulling her tight into her arms. Ruth let go of her guard and began to cry out for her mother. She felt another hand petting her head and knew that Pastor Tom had joined them. She allowed the two people she had come to trust to share in her grief. She hadn't realized how hard the last couple of weeks had been on her. She knew that God had protected her in Trinity, giving her rest before meeting her mom. She almost wished that she could be back with Deborah and Esther away from all the pain, but she knew that they had a house full of guests. The sweet time that Ruth had with them was over. She didn't know what the future would bring, but there was no turning back for her. She would cling to the only family she had left.

By the time Ruth opened her eyes again, she saw her mother's casket slowly being lowered into the grave. Ruth watched as Bear commanded the men with the ropes while they inched Naomi's body to her final resting place. She scanned the church grounds for Zach, but she found him exactly where she had last seen him. Instead, this time he and Pilar were hand-in-hand, facing each other and exchanging whispers. Pilar's dark thumbs were gently stroking Zach's light wrists, and their light-colored eyes stay deeply fixed on each other.

"Ruth, how are you feeling," Cindy said as Ruth lifted her head from Cindy's shoulder.

"I'm tired, but I do feel lighter somehow," Ruth acknowledged.

"That's what grief gatherings are for. They allow for a powerful release of emotion, so people are freed from the bondage of despair. Many people grieve their own sort of loss at grief gatherings and most walk away with their pain and heartache buried along with the dead."

Ruth rubbed her eyes and tried to straighten her rumpled jacket. "I'm glad you both came. I don't know anyone here very well except my brother, and he has taken Mom's death the hardest."

"Actually," Tom chimed in, "I think your brother is mourning the death of your mother and his father. I wasn't at Austin's grief gathering, but I did hear that Zach did not shed a single tear. I think it was too great at the time. But what we saw today is definitely a start to his letting go."

Ruth looked toward her brother again. He and Pilar were getting up. Pilar gave his hand one last squeeze, and she began walking back toward her truck.

"Is that the daughter of Levi Jones? I've heard a little about her."

"Yes, that is Pilar," Ruth said. "Levi couldn't make it, but he did send food for the grief gathering."

"Did you hear the news about Charlie Liu?" Tom asked.

"Yes, Deborah sent me a note a few days ago about his arrival," Ruth said.

"Well, I'll be meeting him tomorrow at my *Bible* study. I'll let you know how it goes," Tom said. "I hope you ladies don't mind. I need to have a quick word with Zach while he has a free moment."

Ruth watched as Tom got up and walked toward Zach who was chatting with a couple who were offering their condolences.

"That's my husband," Cindy said with a sigh. "He can only relax for so long before he's planning something."

Ruth saw Tom whisper in Zach's ear and they both wandered away from the crowds. "Your husband has a great gift of linking ideas and concepts together," Ruth said, thinking of how he guessed her true identity. "What has he discovered today?"

"I best let your brother explain the details to you. Tom has sworn me to secrecy. But if you know Tom, you'll probably guess what the information is related to."

Ruth knew Tom was discussing something important that happened in the World Government that had an effect on the Efficientists and Colonials. She had to suppress an urge to join the two men and listen to what they were saying. Yesterday, Ruth didn't want to know anything about what was going on in her old life, but suddenly today she felt a strong desire to get involved. She wanted to know what Neil Elder and Randall were up to. Maybe Cindy was right. Maybe a grief gathering allowed for people to let go of more than the deceased. Maybe they were able to let go of the past, as well.

CHAPTER NINETEEN

"**W**hat do you mean we didn't get the response we were anticipating," Neil said as he turned away from his LPS screen. The light from the high-rise streamed through the double-stacked windows.

"The Efficientists reactions are right on par with what the researchers suggested. In fact, they seem to have an even more favorable initial reaction to *The Unum Vernum* than we were expecting. We will let the book permeate a little longer before we establish it as the World Government's new sacred text and preferred religion," Randall said as he shielded his eyes from the sun's rays filling the room. "I thought you were going to get blinds put over the windows."

Neil looked up to where the rays of light were flooding the room. "They are already measured and they are coming to install them next week. I really don't know how Eve worked with all the light coming into this room. It's blinding."

Randall said nothing at the mention of Eve's name. The image of her lifeless body lying on the floor filled his mind. He knocked her out the night of the fire, hoping she would somehow wake up and tell him that she changed her mind. He wanted to hear her say that she needed him and that she wanted to be with him. But she never woke up as he opened the base of her Sleeper and caused a spark with the exposed wires. He had to pour gasoline in lines throughout her flat because she owned very little that was flammable. It was as though he was burning a blank slate—the plastic of the Sleeper and LPS wouldn't burn without assistance.

"Randall!" Neil said impatiently. "You can't daydream every time I mention that woman's name. You won't work effectively if you are too emotionally attached."

Randall's eyes refocused on Neil and spoke in an even, forceful tone. "If I was too attached to her I wouldn't have been able to permanently dispose of her. I have a long list of deaths under my name and none of them have caused me to compromise my position with the World Government."

"Good," Neil said, sitting down on the couch. "Now, if the response from the Efficientists is favorable, what has been the response from the Colonials?"

"There hasn't been much of response at all," Randall said.

"Well, isn't that a good thing? Weren't we expecting a backlash or riots or some kind of boycott? Am I wrong to want the Colonies to stay busy in their own pathetic lives and out of my way?" Neil said.

"But they are showing absolutely no signs of curiosity at all. The HMS clicks on the book have been very low. It's like they are ignoring it," Randall said.

"That's what I want. I want them not to care about it. I want them to look the other way, so they can stop being a thorn in my side," Neil said.

"But that's the problem. Are they ignoring it because they don't care or because they already know about it?" Randall asked, handing Neil his Portable.

"Do you see those two graphs?" Randall asked, pointing to the screen. "One graph represents the HMS hits on the World Government links only two weeks ago. The other graph shows the HMS hits on the World Government links today."

"The graph from today is more static," Neil said, looking from one graph to the other.

"Either the Colonials have suddenly lost interest in us or someone is tipping them off," Randall said, taking back his Portable.

"What do you mean *tipping them off?*" Neil asked.

"You may be right and the Colonials don't care about *The Unum Vernum,* which has chopped up their precious *Bible* and mixed it with other pieces of religious material from across the globe.... or," Randall paused, ensuring that Neil was listening. "They already knew about it."

"That's ridiculous. How could they already know about it? The world media didn't even know about it until it came out," Neil said incredulously.

Randall waited a beat before talking. "There may be a mole."

Neil quickly got up from the couch. "Who do you think would possibly be leaking information?"

"I don't know. I've already checked the men on my team, and they are clean. I didn't find anything unusual on their Portables. I need your permission to check the researchers and the writers who worked on the project."

"Yes, do what needs to be done," Neil said. "But don't alert them to anything. The problem with the Colonials may be a fluke. They could start boycotting next week for all we know. I don't want us to entangle ourselves with delusions of deception."

"I understand," Randall said. "This brings me to my other concern."

Neil stopped and turned to Randall. "Which is?"

"I need more funds. It costs a lot of money points to complete my work and the allotment you have me on is barely enough to pay my staff."

"Maybe if you took your girlfriend off the payroll, you would have more money," Neil quipped.

"Ada makes sure that the public loves us. She is the one that keeps the other Efficientists busy with the latest trends and newest products. She is doing what needs to be done to keep people's appetites for entertainment and distraction satisfied. The media loves her, and she keeps us looking good. Public support is the foundation of all we do here. Without it, we might as well give up."

"One day we may not need public support," Neil said flatly.

"Until then, we need to do what needs to be done to appease them," Randall finished.

"I can't ask for any more money from the World Government. I've used up too much for the *Unum Vernum* project." Neil said, stroking his hands through his thinning grey hair. "Believe me, I'd figure out a way to get more if I could."

"What about Eve's estate?" Randall asked. "She has jewels in the World Bank right now that would fund everything we need and more."

"I know. I know. But we can't touch it for three more months. A full year needs to transpire before we can liquidate her accounts. I've already spoken with the manager of the World Bank, and he won't let me in before the one year is up without her keycard," Neil said, sitting in front of his LPS and turning on the screen. "You should have gotten it from her. You were the last to see her alive."

"I didn't know I needed it or else I would have gladly retrieved it," Randall answered.

"It doesn't matter. What's done is done. In three months, we will secure her accounts. Until then we will have to find another way to secure money points to see if your mole theory is correct."

"Also, there is an Efficientist missing. He hasn't logged onto his LPS for several weeks," Randall said.

"Why would I care?" Neil snapped.

"Because he's an Elite Efficientist—Charlie Liu," Randall said and waited.

Neil froze for a moment. "I sent him on an errand."

"You sent him to the Colonies," Randall said flatly.

"How would you know that?" Neil asked. "Did he bring his Portable?"

"No, but I checked his Portable when I entered his house. He had maps printed and logged interactions with several of our factory sites outside the city. If you send an Elite Efficientist into the wild, you may want to let me know. I shared a lot of classified information with him."

"Has he tried to contact you?" Neil asked.

"No, the bodyguard we assigned him notified me that he stopped communicating with him," Randall said keeping his voice even. Charlie's disappearance had been a sore spot for him.

"I'm glad he knew nothing about the *Unum Vernum* project. I sent him away before we started it. What do you think happened?" Neil asked.

"I don't know. I've already started a search for his vehicle. Sending him out into the Colonies may have sounded good to you in theory, but Charlie has no family or experience there. I think he's like a fish out of water. If he didn't make it to the factories by now, he probably didn't make it," Randall said.

"Do you think he deserted *Life Efficiency*?" Neil asked.

Randall looked at his hands for a moment. "No, I don't. I've interviewed him before assigning his bodyguard, and I've never found any desire in him to leave. Why didn't you let me send a man with him?" Randal pressed.

"I didn't want to bother you with the details of something so small. I needed a man I could trust overseeing the factories in our area."

"Your lack of judgment probably cost him his life," Randall added. "I don't need to be aware of everything that goes on in the World Government, but when it comes to the Colonies, I'm the best man you got."

"Well, there is no use getting upset about it now. What's done is done," Neil said. His irritation was obvious.

Randall looked at Neil sitting at his LPS and thought over his words. "What if I declare him dead? Are we able to liquidate his accounts and retrieve his money points? He's only been an Elite Efficientist for less than a year when Trent had his Awakening. He doesn't do well at PR events and his work hasn't made any noticeable contributions yet. His death would barely be noticed."

Neil's eyes widened and he quickly turned his chair to face the LPS screen. He gave a few commands and moved his fingers across the keyboard. "It looks like Charlie Liu not only has his own money, but he inherited money from his deceased parents—and a lot of it. Sending Charlie to the Colonies has turned out to be an excellent gamble."

"Hopefully, that gamble will pay off," Randall said.

Neil turned back to Randall. "You know what to do. Report him missing and then report him dead. I don't care about the details. Just make it happen, and I will get you your money points."

Randall turned to leave. "What if he turns up alive?"

Neil turned away from Randall and stared at his LPS screen. "Then make sure he doesn't stay alive for very long."

Randall slowly examined his men. They lined up in his high-rise flat. He loved the feeling of being in charge, and savored the respect that his men gave him. They were now an elite force group, distinguished from the rest, and they held that title tightly. For so many years he took orders, but now he was the second most powerful man in his district of the World Government. He was not even forty yet, and he still had the rest of his life to enjoy his new position. He liked being second in command. He got the power but wouldn't take the fall for anything. That was Neil's role.

His men looked sharp. They were all dressed in suits, they were fit and they were intelligent. If there were a mole in the World Government, he wouldn't be found on his team. He had checked all his men's accounts. They were clean. Just being around these men gave him a sense of purpose that he had been longing for. He had a girlfriend who was beautiful and cunning—albeit she wasn't nearly as intelligent as Eve. And had a team of highly trained men at his disposal. He was exactly where he wanted to be. His life was finally perfect, and he would let nothing destroy the world that he had built for himself.

"Everyone is to be watched very closely. I gave each of you added surveillance duties. I don't care how much you like the people on your list, you will view them as a threat until you find proof otherwise. We are not certain, but we believe there may be a mole in the World Government somewhere, feeding information to the Colonies."

Randall walked up to Matt Coughlin. "I have entrusted you with Dr. Linton on your list. I want you to check him out—and I mean everything. His house, his LPS, his Portable, his car—make sure that he has no suspicious activities. He went to the Colonies to survey a pharmaceutical plant. Check to make sure that he made no other stops. He trusts you. You're a nice guy. Don't let him think he's been targeted or else he'll get suspicious. Let him know that you are doing a mandatory checkup on all World Government employees."

Matt nodded his head. "Yes, sir. I'll get right on it."

Randall walked down the line looking at each of his men. "Charlie Liu, one of the Elite Efficientists, was sent on assignment to the Colonies. Regrettably, I was not told about his assignment, so we had no way of ensuring his safety. He was an Efficientist all his life who spent his time doing research. He knew nothing of the Colonies, and I doubt he survived out there. We need to find clues about what happened to him. I've already assigned the team leader and crew for his recovery. If you do happen to find him, tell no one. Bring him straight to me, and I will deal with him. Do you understand?"

"Yes sir!" voices rang out.

"Before I dismiss you, I want you to remember that you are here for a reason. You have been chosen because you add value to our team. I know you all work hard, but I want you to remember that when you are at PR events, you still represent me and this team. Believe me, I want you to enjoy yourselves, but the World Media is always watching. Make sure to conduct yourself as professionals both during work and play. Do you get me?"

"Yes sir!" voices shouted out again.

"Good. You are dismissed. I want reports sent to my Portable by the end of this week," Randall finished.

CHAPTER TWENTY

"**D**id Tom receive another letter?" Ruth asked, turning on the lamp next to the HMS and tying her robe tight around her waist.

Zach blinked his eyes, as they adjusted to the light. "Yes, I printed it out, and I'm about to decode it," he said, pulling out the drawer of the desk where a stock card was taped.

"You don't need it," Ruth said, taking the encrypted letter in her hands. "I have memorized the code."

"Is that what you do while I work all day? Memorize the code to decipher the letters from Tom?" Zach asked and replaced the drawer into the desk.

"It didn't take me long, Zach. You know what I do all day. I read the books in the closet and write. It's important that we have the code memorized if something were to happen to the house. I know you don't like your job, but you shouldn't take your frustration out on me."

Ruth read the paper quickly and placed it back down on the desk. She thought for a moment while Zach waited. He was used to Ruth's need to think before she talked.

"I'm sorry about complaining. What does it say?" he finally asked when she looked him.

"My writings are making an impact on the Efficientists. The World Government has labeled them propaganda and has banned them," she said.

"We knew that it wouldn't take long, especially since you write so many a day. Maybe you should back off a little bit. Tom and I are struggling to keep up."

"I only write three a day. If I could choose so, I would write more," Ruth said.

"Yes, but only a few people could produce as much work as you do. The World Government will become suspicious.

They need to think several people are writing your letters. I can only alter your writings to a point. And Tom is maxing out his capacity to post your writings and cover his trail. We have to find a new system," Zach said. He looked at the clock. He had to be at work in less than three hours.

"How many letters have there been since the mole?" he continued.

"This is the fourth one," Ruth said.

"And it's been almost three weeks since Mom's funeral. So that's more than one a week. Do you think Dr. Linton is the mole?" he asked.

Ruth looked at her brother. He had regained his strength since the funeral. Pilar stopped by twice a week to bring them both a variety of baked goods. Pilar and Zach had come to a decision that they would put their relationship on hold for a while. Pilar said she needed to keep her focus on her sister who was getting married, but Ruth believed that Pilar was protecting herself from heartache again. Ruth knew how she felt. Ruth had exposed her heart to her father for many years, seeking his approval. She watched him die, and he never gave her the love she needed. She had merely been a strategy piece in his agenda.

"Dr. Linton is not the mole," she said with finality.

"How do you know that?" Zach questioned.

"He lives strictly to serve himself. He would never put his life on the line for someone else."

"How do you know he won't turn on you?" Zach asked.

"He's already kept the secret too long. If he tells now, Randall will kill him," she answered.

"What if Randall finds out he visited you?" Zach asked.

"Randall will kill him and come after me," Ruth answered.

"That is why I need to stop working at the factory," Zach said, stringing his fingers through his blonde hair. "We need to get out of this house. I feel it in my spirit. I have to get you out of here soon. Tom said we can stay with him at the trading center."

"We can't endanger them," Ruth reminded Zach. "I can't go back to Trinity. There are too many people I care about there."

"I know. You're right. I need to trust that God will provide us with what we need when it's time."

Ruth smiled. "I enjoy listening to your faith. It gives me comfort."

Zach leaned back in his char. "I had forgotten how much of my identity was wrapped up in my faith. I feel like my old self again. I have this freedom that I lost when my dad died. I know that I will see them both in heaven. Everyone I love will be with me one day. It makes it easier to love others knowing that."

Ruth thought of her father and knew he was lost to her forever. Her mind wandered to Christina Straight. "In a small way, Dr. Linton is responsible for me being here."

"What do you mean?" Zach asked.

"He is the one who gave me Christina Straight's name and suggested that I see her for counseling. He did it for self-serving reasons. He wanted to get his internship shortened at the hospital and a recommendation as a house doctor for Efficientists. But even so, God was able to use Dr. Linton to bring me one step closer to a relationship with Jesus."

"I still have trouble believing that this woman who led you to the Lord was the Apostle. My dad collected all her writings."

"I know," Ruth said. "They are in the book closet. Mom must have kept up printing her writings after your dad died because I was able to read her most recent ones."

Zach looked at his sister. "Have you read everything in that closet already?" he asked. Somehow he knew what the answer would be.

"Yes, I finished a few days ago," she answered. "Do you think Pastor Tom has more material I can read?"

Zach got up from his chair. "No, Ruth that is enough for now. I need to get you out of this house. Mom was right. You need to meet people and get into society. She warned me not to let you stay at home all day."

"But the letter claims that my writings are making a difference," Ruth said. "What I'm doing is helping. Isn't that what Pastor Tom wants?"

"Your writing is important, but I'm talking about balance. You are too involved inside of yourself, Ruth. You need to get out. I'm protecting you far too much," Zach said with conviction. "I need to let you lead your life."

"I don't have anywhere to go," she said.

"Look, I didn't want to mention it, but Bear says that he has several bolts of fabric that he won at his last fight. He's willing to give you some if you make him and his grandfather some new clothes. Bear will be conducting Reyna and Javier's wedding, so he needs a new outfit for the occasion."

"What would I do with the rest of the fabric?" she asked. "Is there a way to sell the clothes I can make from it?"

Zach nodded his head. "Yes, Levington holds a bazar a few times a year where everyone sells their merchandise. The winter bazaar is coming up soon. It's the busiest one since the harvest is over and people have more time to work on their goods. Pilar's sister will be getting married the evening of the final day. You can sell your clothing there."

Ruth felt an excitement rush through her body. "I could still write one article a day while I begin to sew again. It will be nice to provide for myself—even in a small way. I wish I had more time, but I can create many pieces before the bazaar."

"Okay, Ruth. I can see that you're enthusiastic. I can take you by Bear's house after breakfast. If he's there, I'm sure he'll let you take his measurements and pick up the fabric. I—" Zach hesitated. "I don't want you to get too close to him."

"What do you mean," Ruth asked, noticing that Zach was clearly thinking about his words before he spoke them.

"Bear has been clean for many years. And he's made a lot of changes. He hasn't dated anyone since he's moved here after my dad died. With that being said, he once was a womanizer—he used women for pleasure only."

145

"If he has been celibate for five years like you say, why would I need to be cautious of him?" Ruth asked, wondering if her brother was hiding something. She could tell that he was uncomfortable with their discussion.

"Yes, he has shown great self-control, but I think the main reason he has avoided temptation is because he has isolated himself in his house, and Levington really doesn't have many women his age to choose from. Most unmarried women are too young for him. He kept himself busy recording his sermons and training his fighters. But now that the World Government has banned his religious work, I think he is floundering a bit. Plus—" Zach fumbled.

"Plus what?" Ruth asked. She couldn't understand why Zach was making a big issue of something so minuscule.

"Look, Ruth. I know you don't wear makeup anymore and you don't dress yourself up like you did as Eve Pallue, but you are a beautiful person and Bear will notice."

"Why are you bringing up how I used to look as Eve?" Ruth asked. Now she definitely knew that Zach was hiding something.

"Because," Zach said, "Bear used to have—well, let's call it a thing for Eve Pallue when he was younger. Whenever I would return from the city and he was visiting after one of his fights, he would ask if I had seen you. He followed your PR events, and he had a few images of you printed out. But that's not who you are anymore, so I think it's best that he doesn't find out."

Ruth said nothing for a long moment. "He has made no attempts to pursue me."

"I wouldn't be too sure. Mom died, and you were sick. You might not have noticed."

"I have been pursued by many men through the years, and I know when a man is interested in me. Bear has given absolutely no indication that he is attracted to me," Ruth said, trying not to sound offended.

Zach shook his head. "That's probably because he thinks you are younger than you really are."

"I'm not a girl, Zach. I'm thirty-two years old. Doesn't he know that I'm your older sister?"

"Yes, growing up I told him that my sister was from my mom's first marriage, but I don't think that fact has dawned on him yet. He looks at you and sees an innocent, young girl, and he goes by what he sees. But he will eventually figure it out," Zach said.

Ruth looked at her brother. "How old do I look to you?" she asked.

Zach squirmed in his chair. "I'm sorry I brought up this topic."

"I know that Deborah and Esther said I looked young, and Cindy treats me like I'm a daughter, though, I'm probably only a few years younger than she is. How old do I look?" she asked again.

"I'm not good with ages, but you don't wear makeup and your face looks young. Remember when I met you in the city? I thought you were a servant or maybe one of the daughters. I would have never expected that you were Eve Pallue. In the media, you are always shown wearing so much makeup and form-fitting dresses. How you look now actually works to your advantage because no one seems to recognize you in the Colonies.

"How old would you say Bear thinks I am?" she finally asked.

"He probably thinks you're a teenager or at most your early twenties," Zach admitted.

Ruth said nothing, and Zach could tell she was lost in her thoughts. "Look, I'm sorry. I'm anticipating things that may never happen. I should have never brought it up," Zach said. "Let's forget that I even mentioned it."

Ruth nodded. "I'm going to take a quick bath before we leave. Is there water still available in the basin?" she asked.

"Yes, I filled it up last night."

"Thank you," she said and headed toward the bathroom. Once Ruth closed the door, she examined her face in the mirror. She never worried about how she looked when she was an Efficientist because she always paid someone to do it for her. The media had always loved her and given her more attention than she desired, but now she couldn't even capture the attention of a single man. She lifted her chestnut brown hair, which was now several inches below her shoulders. She turned her head, remembering Ada saying that her golden-brown eyes and high cheekbones were her best features. She let her hair down once more, and sat on the edge of the tub. She allowed the image that she had tucked into her memory to fill her mind. She saw Bear standing alone in the middle of a field. His arms were outstretched and he sang a sad melody.

Ruth tried to wipe the memory of Bear away as she rinsed her body with cups of cool water from the basin. She knew she was attracted to him, but she did not know if her feelings were reliable. She had only exchanged brief words with him, so the allure must be merely physical. She looked down at her hands. The burns from the fire were mostly faded. Only minor scar tissue remained, which wouldn't be noticed unless examined closely. She quickly toweled herself off and stood up to look at her reflection once more. She smiled. She could see the missing tooth she lost in the fire. She suddenly saw what everyone else in the Colonies was seeing: a plain-looking girl who didn't know how to make herself beautiful. She may no longer be as glamorous as Eve, but Ruth could be appealing too.

Ruth jumped when she heard a knock at the door.

"Ruth, it's Pilar. I stopped by to bring you food, and Zach says that you're heading to Bear's house. If you want, I can give you a ride. I have a delivery for him too."

Ruth opened the door. "What does Zach say?"

Pilar exhaled and looked over her shoulder. "He's being a typical brother. He's acting overprotective and overly concerned, but I told him that he needs to stop worrying."

Ruth tightened the towel around her and looked down the hall to where her brother stood.

Zach shook his head. "Fine, go with Pilar. You have my contact code at the plant. I'll have the Portable thing they gave me with me all day. You can reach me anytime."

He looked at Pilar. "Will you take her right home?"

Pilar waved a hand of dismissal at him. "I'll get her home safely. She'll be fine, Zach. It's a beautiful winter's day. The air is crisp, the fresh bread is warm, and there is beauty all around us. You both need to get out of this dark, dreary house," Pilar said, looking around. "You got books lying all around. Papers scattered on your desk and table. You two are too intense. You need some downtime away from whatever it is you two are up too."

"We aren't up to anything," Zach said awkwardly.

"Zach, you know that you are a horrible liar. I know you and Thomas Isaacs are up to something, and I've already connected the dots with that *Unum Vernum* letter that was sent out to the Colonials with an HMS."

"Please, Pilar, if anyone were to find out," Zach said.

"Zacchaeus Mark Daniels, do you take me as a fool? I've known you since I was sixteen when you were preaching next to my daddy's bakery. I don't take what you and Pastor Tom are doing lightly. I know it's important work. But God made us to work the fields, enjoy our rest and eat from our harvest. You both have had a hard couple of weeks. I know that Naomi would want Ruth to get out and meet people, so you're going to have to give her some space."

Zach crossed his arms. "I already told Ruth that she needed to get out of the house. Is your monologue finished?"

Pilar crossed her arms in return. "No, I also have my *little* sister's wedding to help plan. I have the privilege of being the *oldest* bridesmaid in the group, so I wanted to see if Ruth wouldn't mind adding something to my sister's dress."

Pilar turned her attention back to Ruth. "My mom made Reyna's wedding dress, and it is simple and beautiful, but I wanted to surprise her with something special for her wedding. I was able to get a spool of lace as a trade from a woman from another town. As a gift, I wanted to add the lace to her dress. I have some ideas about where it should go, and I wanted to see if you could help me. Naomi said that you are an amazing seamstress, especially with delicate stitching."

"I've never sewn on lace, but I'm sure it will be easy for me to learn. I would love to help," Ruth said.

"Perfect, now you let me know what I can do for you in return. And don't forget that you and Zach are going to the wedding. Don't let your brother talk you out of it. Hurry up and get dressed. I brought over breakfast and then we will head out."

Ruth smiled. "Okay." As she walked into her room, she knew exactly what she would ask Pilar for in exchange for sewing the lace.

CHAPTER TWENTY-ONE

"We are almost there," Pilar said, turning the wheel of her truck down a car-width path in the brush. "Bear lives next to the Trinity."

"The Trinity River goes through this area?" Ruth asked, looking around to the naked trees and dried brush around them.

"Yes, it's a long river. It continues all the way up to the top of Old Texas."

Ruth felt foolish for not knowing. Her father never encouraged her to study geography. He said that she would never use the information. She decided that when she got home that evening, she would download some maps from the HMS and get acquainted with her whereabouts.

"Is Levington on the river?" Ruth asked.

"No, being too close to the river in these parts isn't safe. There are a lot of gangs that stay near the water for survival. My dad and a few of his friends built the water well in Levington before I was born. The town only started with a few families, but once the well was built, more families came. There are now about thirty families that live in our village."

"There were a lot more families in Trinity where I lived, but the people were more spread out," Ruth said.

"Trinity is more of a farming community that provides food to a larger population in the surrounding area. They have been established a long time. Levington is newer and unconnected to the World Government. None of our people own an HMS, and we never use money points. My dad does owns several fields of beans, corn and wheat, but we mainly provide food for the village. We only sell what's leftover to outsiders. My younger brothers are able to work the fields now, so my father stays with my mom working the bakery. He'd much rather dig his hands in dough than dirt. A few of the other families own chickens for meat and eggs and some other small animals, like goats and pigs. We all trade for different things that we need. "

"And you deliver the food?" Ruth asked.

"I mainly deliver to the government housing where you live and to a few houses on the outskirts of town a couple of times a week. Gasoline is very valuable, so they have to pay me with items worth my drive."

"What do they pay you with if they can't use money points?" Ruth asked.

"They pay me with different items that they buy. The government workers will usually give me items from the factories where they work. People like Bear always have something on hand that they can trade. One woman pays me in milk once a month. I take the milk home and Dad makes some sort of cake or dessert. That's what he'll be using for Reyna and Javier's wedding cake."

"Will a lot of people be at the wedding?" Ruth asked.

"We won't know how many people will be there for sure, but we will get a good idea on the first day of the bazaar. I have a feeling that it will be a lot more than we think. Dad and Mom will be cooking into the night to get ready. But the other families have all offered to help bring food, drinks and other things."

Ruth looked away from the window and turned to Pilar's face. "I notice that you wear makeup," she began.

Pilar laughed and looked back at Ruth. "I notice that you don't. Is that normal for Efficientists? Whenever I see photos of the PR events they're always dressed up, but I guess you don't need makeup if you're working at your LPS."

Ruth squirmed a little in her seat.

"I didn't mean to embarrass you," Pilar added. "Only Bear and I know that Zach had a half-sister who was an Efficientist. We haven't told anyone. He only mentioned you a few times, but we never thought we would actually meet you. I've heard that a lot of Efficientists have left rank and are coming into the Colonies. You're the only one I met so far, though. Will they all be like you?"

"I once believed that all the Colonials were the same, but you are all different. That is the same with Efficientists—we are all different, but most of us are lost, especially if we don't have family in the Colonies."

"That makes sense," Pilar said. "I asked Zach what rank you were, but he wouldn't tell me."

Ruth looked out the window again and said nothing.

"It's okay," Pilar said. "I'm being nosy."

"When can I look at your sister's dress?" Ruth asked, changing the subject.

"I don't think I should bring you to the house to look at it because my sister will get suspicious. I may sneak it out when I get home and bring it here before I take you back home. That way you can work on it without her knowing."

"I wanted to ask you—in return for adding the lace—if you could help me," Ruth said, searching for the right words.

"Sure, what do you need?" Pilar asked.

Ruth pointed to Pilar's cheek. "I would like some makeup. Can you help me purchase some?"

Pilar laughed and tapped her stirring wheel. "I make my own makeup. In fact, I'll be selling my collection at the bazaar."

"Can I have some like yours?" Ruth asked, relieved that Pilar could help her.

"Ruth, your skin is way too pale to have makeup like mine, but I will create a few colors that will match *your* complexion."

"Can you do that for me?" Ruth asked, trying to muffle her excitement.

Pilar slowed the truck and put it into park. "Look at my face. Do you see how much artistic talent it takes to create this image?"

"You look gorgeous," Ruth said.

"Well, I can make you look just as good," Pilar said. "You make my sister's wedding dress stand out, and I will give you an individualized makeup kit."

"Will you teach me how to put it on?" Ruth asked.

Pilar stared at Ruth for a moment and smiled. "Girl, you are too much—an Efficientist who doesn't know how to put on her own makeup."

Ruth looked at her hands on her lap.

"I'm only playing with you, Ruth," Pilar said in a serious tone. "I would be delighted to show you."

"If you don't mind, can we keep the makeup between me and you? I don't want Zach asking me a bunch of questions."

"Lord knows that man has kept secrets from me. I would be glad to actually have one of my own," Pilar said. "Why the sudden interest in makeup?"

Ruth looked out of the windshield and saw Bear walking toward the truck. "No particular reason," she replied.

"Tom, can I speak with you in private?" Li asked.

The secret *Bible* study in the basement of the Trinity Trading Center had finished.

"Sure thing, Li. Let me say goodbye to few more people. Do you want to meet me upstairs in my office?"

"Yes, that would be good," Li said.

Tom watched Li make his way up the stairs. He looked different from when he first met him—almost like the transformation he saw in Ruth when she first came. Li had filled out some, and his skin darkened more. He also wore western clothing. He even had a cowboy hat on this morning, which he took off when the *Bible* study began. This had been Li's third time at the *Bible* study, and Tom was impressed at how quickly Li grasped the more difficult aspects of faith. Exactly like Ruth, Li had been thirsty to learn. Tom knew Li's true identity. He was Charlie Liu. He did his own research to make sure that Ruth's prophecy was accurate, and it was. He wondered why he wanted to speak with him.

Tom was finally able to break away from the few people that lingered. He reached his office, and he found Li quietly sitting in one of the chairs.

"I like your outfit today, Li. I didn't know you embraced the western look," Tom began.

Li looked down slightly embarrassed. "I wanted clothes that helped me fit into the Colonies better. Deborah and Esther had several outfits my size, but they were all from a particular young man who enjoyed this western look," Li said.

"I think it suits you," Tom said.

Li smiled. "I have to admit, I do like how I look. I've always been intrigued with the Old West. Deborah and Esther said they would try to trade some of their goats for a few horses, so I can learn to ride. They had a lot of newborns this season."

"I'm sure we can find a pair of fine horses for you at the trading center. We get lots of people wanting to trade livestock. I used to ride horses in my younger days. I'll be happy to teach you to ride. It might be nice to start it back up again. There are lots of folks around here who use horses as their main transportation," Tom said.

"I would like that," Charlie said not hiding his excitement.

"I look forward to it. So, how can I help you, Li?" Tom began, taking a seat at his desk.

"I've been reading those articles that you told me about. Only one came out today, but they are helping me to understand much about faith. At first, they were hard to find, but I have gotten better at locating them," Li began.

"That's good. I'm impressed how quickly you have been able to find them," Tom said. He realized he had to be careful with his words. Although he knew Li's real identity, he did not know why he was there.

Li sat in his chair for a moment, thinking. "I grew up in *Life Efficiency*. My parents had me at an old age. They hired a Mother to raise me, and when I was thirteen, they sent her away. I soon discovered she killed herself. I was always angry with her. I had planned to go to the Colonies myself when I was older and take her home, but it was too late. It didn't take her long to take her life."

"I'm sorry to hear about that," Tom said and waited.

Li continued. "Something happened to me when I was driving to the Colonies. I was supposed to make it to a factory east of here, but as I was driving, the map I had been given blurred on me."

"What do you mean?" Tom asked suppressing the dozens of questions he suddenly wanted to ask.

Li hesitated. "I don't understand myself. I had studied that map over and over again, but halfway to my destination, the map went blurry. I could see the trees through the car window. I could see my hands on the steering wheel. But the map was a haze of red and black lines. I had to stop my car on the side of the road."

"What happened when you stopped the car?" Tom asked, fidgeting in his chair.

"I felt like I needed to gather my things and walk into the woods."

"And let me guess," Tom added. "You found Deborah and Esther's farm?"

"That's the thing that really confuses me," Li said. "When I was told that I would be driving into the Colonies. I looked up all the places on the way that would be safe for me to stay in case something happened. Deborah and Esther's farm was one of the places that I marked. I found it on a Colonial website. But when the map went blurry, I couldn't tell if I was close to it or not. Something inside of me told me exactly where to go. When I finally made it onto their property and saw the sisters, I knew precisely where I was at."

"Li, when you say that you were supposed to drive to one of the factories, are you saying that you are here as a representative of the World Government?" Tom couldn't cover up the fear in his voice. If Li had been sent to the Colonies to gather information, the Trinity Trading Center would be destroyed and he and his family's lives would be at stake.

"I was sent to watch over the government factories in the area. I believe God sent me here," Li finished.

"Look Li, I'm going to come clean. I realize that my family's lives are in danger. I know that you are Charlie Liu. However, I didn't know that you were sent to the Colonies on government business. I believed you were deserting your life as an Efficientist. Have you spoken to anyone? Have you talked with Neil Elder? Is he the one that sent you?" If Neil Elder knew about the Trinity Trading Center, a trail of clues could eventually lead to Ruth and Zach.

"That is why I wanted to speak with you," Li said. "I have chosen—or rather it was chosen for me—I want to stay here in Trinity. I want to embrace this life of Christianity. I've studied your Jesus, and I'm ready to trust Him by faith. I feel something supernatural moving in me, like God's spirit—the Holy Spirit as you call it—pressing into me. I feel like I belong, like I have purpose. No matter what I did in *Life Efficiency*, I have never felt that."

"Have you prayed the salvation prayer? Have you received salvation through Jesus?" Tom asked.

"Yes, last night Esther led me in what you call the salvation prayer," Li said. "Now all I want is to be used by Him."

"When you say *it was chosen for you*, what do you mean?" Tom asked.

Li leaned back into his seat. "Well, it seems that Charlie Liu has been declared dead and all of my points have been absorbed by the World Government. I was able to see who claimed them."

"Let me guess, Neil Elder," Tom said.

"Yes," Li answered. "So it looks like my name is now Li for good."

Tom felt the anxiety in his body begin to relax. "So you will not turn me and my family into the World Government then."

Li smiled. "No, I want to be a part of what you are doing."

"How so?" Tom asked. He knew that having Li on his side with his set of skills would be extremely beneficial.

"The first thing I want to do," Li continued, "is to help you hide your trail better when you post the articles."

"What do you mean?" Tom asked unable to hide his surprise.

Li straightened up in his seat. "I've traced three of the articles that you asked me to read to this HMS," he said pointing to the HMS behind Tom. "I know you are the one who has been posting them."

"You found my trail?" Tom asked.

"Yes, I also know that the articles are written by the same person. Though, I can tell someone is trying to cover it up."

Tom said nothing and waited.

Li continued. "And I know that you are not writing them."

"How do you know that?" Tom asked.

"I've studied your writing," Li said. "You write well enough, but this person has a breadth of knowledge that makes many connections in very few words. Only a high ranking Efficientist can write the quality of these articles in such a short amount of time."

Tom felt uneasy.

"I also know that a young woman named Ruth left here almost two months ago. She had been in a fire and Deborah and Esther cared for her."

"Deborah and Esther would never divulge information that would harm Ruth!"

"They did it unknowingly—as you are doing now," Li finished.

Tom got up from his chair. "Li, these conclusions that you are making can be devastating to all of us!"

Li stood up and matched Tom's stance, facing him eye to eye. "I want to be a part of what you are doing. I can't stay on that farm all day—tending goats and washing dishes. I was born for something greater. I have watched you, Tom. You have an energy that comes from doing something that is making a difference. I need that or I won't make it very long on the farm!"

Tom stared into Li's eyes. He finally placed his hands on Li's shoulders. "You remind me of me, Li. You know that? I think I would waste away too on the sisters' farm. They mean well, but they can only offer so much."

Tom patted Li's shoulders and chuckled. "It's ironic."

"What is?" Li asked.

"I asked Ruth to do what you are so eager to do—to get involved with my work—and she wouldn't. I used to think she simply didn't want to, but now I understand that she simply wasn't called to. You are."

Tom let go of Li's shoulders and sat back down into his chair.

Li sat down and faced Tom.

"Do you know what's even more ironic?" Tom asked.

Li raised his eyebrows.

"Ruth knew you were coming," he answered.

It was Li's turn to look surprised. "Eve Pallue knows that I'm here?"

Tom nodded his head. "She is the one who told us you would come."

CHAPTER TWENTY-TWO

"**W**here is Zach?" Bear asked when he reached Pilar at the driver's side of the truck. He looked in and saw only Ruth with Pilar.

"He said that I could bring Ruth over. She and I had a few things to discuss," Pilar said.

"I had a question that I needed to ask him," Bear said not trying to cover up his displeasure.

"Well," Pilar said, "you could ask him while he was at work if you hadn't thrown your HMS into the river."

"It doesn't matter," Bear snapped. "I'm done with that machine anyway. I'll find the answer that I need."

"Why are you sweating?" Pilar asked, pointing to the sweat discoloration on his shirt. "It's sixty-five degrees out here."

"I finished a session with some kids who needed to get training in before their morning chores," he answered.

"Was my brother here?" Pilar asked.

"No, he said that he would be busy until after Reyna's wedding."

"Mom and Dad have all of us working to get ready. She's the first of us to get married, so my parents feel a pressure to make everything perfect."

Bear noticed the aggravation in Pilar's voice. "You know Zach loves you," he said plainly.

"It doesn't matter anymore," Pilar snapped. "I've thrown that relationship in the river next to your HMS."

Bear laughed. "Whatever you say, Pilar. You don't fool me."

Bear looked past Pilar toward Ruth. "Are you ready? You can measure me and then my grandfather."

Ruth nodded her head and said nothing.

160

Bear took this opportunity to evaluate Ruth's face. He had only met her once at Naomi's funeral and she looked close to death then. She had gained a little weight and lost the dark circles under her eyes, but she still looked nothing like Naomi or Zach. It had dawned on him a few nights ago that Ruth was Zach's older sister, so that made her in her earlier thirties. But he didn't see it. If Naomi hadn't told him herself that Ruth was her daughter, he would never have believed it. He still didn't trust her.

"Do you mind if I finish my deliveries and run home to get something? It won't take me more than a couple of hours and I'll come back to bring Ruth home," Pilar said.

Bear looked at Ruth. "Is that okay with you?"

"Yes," she answered.

Bear looked back at Pilar. "Where's my delivery?"

"Hold on, and I'll get it." Pilar reached back behind her and grabbed one of the bags on the floor of the truck. "Here's yours. Tell your grandfather that I brought the sweet bread for him."

Bear opened the bag and peered in. "You know he's an old man. You should save your sweets for someone who can actually trade you something for them."

"Now why do you have to be so mean to your own granddaddy? I know he looks forward to what I bring him, and I'm not going to disappoint him on account of you. Not everything in life needs a fair bargain. Sometimes it's good to give without expecting anything in return."

"That kind of thinking will get you in trouble," Bear said.

"Actually," Pilar smiled, "it's that kind of thinking that will get me blessed."

Bear ignored her last comment. "Ruth, let's go."

Bear started back towards his house. He could see his grandfather sitting on his favorite tree stump close to the river's edge next to a fire that he had started. His grandfather never liked sitting inside the house—even when it was cold outside. He noticed that he didn't hear any footsteps behind him. He looked back at the truck and watched as Pilar got out of the truck. "What are you doing?" he yelled.

Pilar dismissed him with a wave. When she reached the passenger door, she opened it for Ruth. Ruth climbed out and said a few words to Pilar before walking in his direction. Bear took this time to look at this woman who was supposed to be Zach's long lost sister. She wore pants and a thick sweater. She looked a lot healthier than the last time he had seen her. He noticed for the first time how much red she had in her brown hair. She was very petite—five feet and maybe a few inches. Zach was over six feet tall, which was another reason why their kinship seemed so unlikely. She looked his way, and for a moment he saw a flash of Naomi. Maybe it was in the cheekbones. Naomi's face was rounder, but her cheekbones were high like Ruth's.

"What is taking you so long?" he asked when Ruth finally caught up.

"I couldn't get the door opened," she said.

"You have to push harder," he said and continued to walk toward his house.

"I did," Ruth said, trying to keep up with Bear's pace.

"Did you bring something to measure us with?" he asked.

"Yes," she answered. "What's your grandfather doing by the river?"

Bear looked toward the water's edge. "He's sitting there," he said matter-of-factly.

"He looks more Native American than you," she said.

"That's because he's full-blooded Ka'to Indian," he answered.

Ruth stopped walking. "That's not possible. No full-blooded Native Americans of any kind have been reported since before the Second Civil War."

Bear stopped, irritated by her statement.

"You may be confused about your family and where you come from, but I'm not. He is my grandfather," Bear said pointing. "Our family up north lives with many other Ka'to families where Old Oklahoma used to be. The reason why no full-blooded Native Americans have been reported to the World Government is that they don't want to be found."

Ruth said nothing.

"Now," he continued his walk to a wooden table next to the front door, setting down the bag of baked goods that Pilar gave him. "You can measure me here." He tugged off his shirt and pulled down his drawstring pants and set them on the table next to the bag. He wore only a handmade, cotton sarong that was wrapped between his legs and around this groin. Bear waited for Ruth to get her measuring tape. When she didn't move, he snapped his fingers at her.

"Are you going to measure me?" he asked impatiently.

"You don't have to take off your clothes," she struggled to say.

"What do you mean? This is how I've been measured in the past," he said.

"I know how to compensate for the fabric on your skin," she mumbled.

Bear looked at her closely now. She stared at the ground, and he could see her cheeks brighten to match the highlights in her hair.

"You cannot be who you say you are," he said crossing his arms and not bothering to get dressed. "Zach says that you're the daughter of his mother's first relationship. That would make you several years older than him. But look at you. You look like a girl. You act like a girl. You blush at the sight of a man like a girl. You can't be Naomi's daughter."

Ruth lifted her head and her almond eyes formed like daggers piercing past her reddened cheeks. She dropped the measuring tape to the ground. "How dare you accuse me of lying about my mom? I lost her when I was a young girl only to get her back to watch her die. I gave up everything to find her—my money, my home, my work—and my life. Someone tries to burn me alive, and I barely escape with my life. And now I humble myself as a seamstress and come out here to work to earn fabric, so I can actually do something to support myself. And you treat me as if I'm a lesser person than you.

What happened to the man who gave me a hat to keep me from getting sunburned?"

Bear was amused. He trusted her more now that she was yelling at him, sharing her emotions—even if they were emotions of anger. "At the funeral you were on the verge of death. You are better now, so you don't need people babying you anymore."

"People don't baby me," she said indignantly.

"You can't even open a truck door without Pilar helping you," he said, growing more impressed with himself that he got a reaction from her.

Ruth looked at Bear for a long moment.

Bear could see her guard going back up.

She leaned down and picked up the measuring tape from the ground. She unraveled the tape, got on her tiptoes and reached around his chest, pinching both ends at his sternum. She loosened her grip and brought the loop of tape around his waist, pinching the ends at his navel. She let go of one end and brought the tape across his shoulders and then down both arms. Then she bent down and brought one end of the tape to his waist, bringing it down past his groin and around one thigh. Finally, she let go of the end around his thigh and knelt, bringing the measuring tape down toward his foot.

She got up. "You can get dressed now."

"Don't you need to write down my measurements," he asked.

"I've memorized them. Now can I see your grandfather?"

Bear grabbed his shirt from the table and pulled it over his head. Then he got his pants and slipped them on. "I have some things I need to do. I will show you the fabric and then you can measure my grandfather. Follow me," he said, tying the drawstring of his pants.

He walked to the storeroom next to his house. Several large locks hung off the door and Bear squared his body over the door to unlock them, shielding Ruth's view from his movements.

"I'm not going to memorize the code to your locks," Ruth said.

"I know you're not," he replied. "Because you can't see them."

He opened the door, revealing a room filled with various items. He went straight to several of the barrels and made sure the lids were on tightly. Grains and legumes filled each large cylinder container, and he wanted to ensure that no critters had gotten in.

"How do you have so much stuff collected?" Ruth asked, looking around the room.

"I won them in my fights," he answered.

"Are you not too old to fight?" she asked.

"I'm only a few years older than you," he answered, looking directly at Ruth's face. "Besides," he said, turning his back on her once more. "I'm retired now. I train young fighters, and they pay me."

Ruth walked to a tarp on the ground that had several rolled bolts of fabric on it. "Is all of this for me?" she asked.

"Of course not," Bear said. "You are only making me and my grandfather a few new shirts and pants. I'll let you keep the leftover from the two bolts of fabric that you use."

"But you have seven bolts of fabric here," Ruth said.

"Each of the bolts has about 50 yards of fabric. You can make 20 shirts with that much fabric. With two bolts you can make about 20 shirts and 20 pairs of pants. Minus the ten or so items for me and my grandfather, you will still have almost 30 items you can sell. I think that it more than fair."

"But I would like to make some dresses also. I will have to use the masculine fabric for you and your grandfather, which won't do well for dresses," Ruth said and pointed to a bolt of lavender fabric. "I would like some of that fabric with the floral design. Can I take half bolts? That way I can make a few feminine pieces, as well."

165

Bear shook his head. "The value of the fabric goes down if it's not in a complete bolt."

"What can I do to earn the bolt of lavender fabric?" she asked.

"Nothing," Bear answered. "I don't need anything and you have nothing to give me."

Bear could see Ruth's disappointment, but he was pleased that she covered it well. "Measure my grandfather and let me know how many yards you need. I'll cut it for you and Pilar can take it to Zach's house for you. When I approve of the finished product, I will give you the rest of the fabric."

Ruth nodded her head.

When they made their way out of the storeroom, Ruth waited while Bear secured all the locks. Then he walked over to the table and grabbed the bag of baked goods. "Come with me," he said to Ruth.

They walked toward the river's edge where Bear's grandfather sat on a stump. A rusty shotgun rested on the ground only a few feet away from him.

"*Aha-enah*," Bear called out. "Pilar has brought you another sweet," he said, reaching into the bag.

Bear handed the sugar-covered bread to his grandfather. The grandfather quickly took it and turned his eyes to Ruth. "Who is this?"

"This is Ruth. She's a family friend of Zach," he said.

The grandfather's face was aged and leathered. His hair was long and white. He gave Ruth a toothless grin. "You are a sweet *baynit*. Like a little white dove," he said.

Bear looked toward Ruth one last time. "That description fits her perfectly—white and helpless," he answered. "My grandfather likes to talk too much. Just ignore him. When you're done, you can head back into the house, and I'll cut the fabric for you."

166

Pilar looked toward the sun and grimaced. She pulled into Bear's land and parked her truck. She saw Bear exiting his house with an armful of fabric. He began walking up the hill toward her, but she didn't see Ruth. She got out of the truck to meet him halfway. "Sorry, I'm late. My dad had a list of wedding errands for me when I got home. I can't wait until my sister finally marries Javier, so I can be done with all this extra work. Where is Ruth?"

Bear nodded toward the river. "She's been talking with my grandfather for several hours now."

"Your grandfather definitely has a lot of stories to share. I always feel bad rushing passed him when you're not home. Maybe we should go rescue Ruth."

"I tried a couple of times, but she ignored me," Bear said, staring intently at the river's edge where Ruth sat on the grass, listening to his grandfather who was sitting on the stump. "The first time I walked down and offered them food, but neither of them took it. The second time all she did was tell me how much fabric she needed."

"What was he talking about?" Pilar asked, joining Bear's stare down toward the river's edge.

"He was telling her about his life—from beginning to end. When I got there the first time he was talking about my mother—when she was a little girl."

Pilar said nothing for a long moment. She took the fabric from Bear's hands, and when they reached her truck, she opened the back door and placed the fabric across the seats. After she closed the door, she looked at the ground and asked softly, "What did he say?"

Bear crossed his arms and looked off into the distance. "He said that she loved animals. She would steal newly weaned animals from their moms and raise them as her own. She would care for them during the day and sleep with them at night. Until—" Bear stopped.

"Until what?" Pilar asked still staring at the ground.

Bear re-crossed his arms and changed his stance. "One time she befriended a small, brown bunny. She loved him and

167

cared for him, and he grew strong and fat. But a severe storm came through their village and no one could leave their homes. My grandmother took the bunny while my mother was sleeping and cooked it against my grandfather's wishes. She tried to serve it the next morning, but my mother knew what had happened. She wouldn't eat or drink for three days. Finally, the storm broke and my grandfather traded one of the neighbors a knife for a piece of bread and a glass of milk. My mother ate it, but after that day, she never cared for another animal."

"I'm sorry," Pilar said quietly.

Bear loosened his arms and placed them on his hips. "All my life my mother never took care of anything—not even herself. To me she was like that small, brown bunny that needed to always be cared for. I did everything for my mom, but the drugs slowly devoured her. I promised myself the day she died that I would never baby anyone ever again. People need to learn to be strong," he said. Then he looked at the river's edge to where Ruth sat on the grass. "People need to learn to take care of themselves."

Pilar followed his gaze and frowned. "That's interesting," she said.

"What is?" he asked, looking back at Pilar.

"Your mother probably said the same thing when her bunny died," she finished.

"Are you saying that expecting people to be strong is wrong?" he asked.

"No, but what I'm saying is that life is not built on extremes. It's built on filling the needs of those around us. Sometimes they need to learn on their own and sometimes they need to be helped. It's up to us to let God show us what to do."

Bear said nothing.

Pilar quickly changed the subject. "What was he talking about the second time you went down there?"

"He was listening the second time," Bear replied. "Ruth was telling him about Jesus."

"But your grandfather doesn't want to know about Jesus," Pilar said surprised.

"So he has told me hundreds of times. But today was different. Today, I could sense a presence with them—like God was there."

"You think the Holy Spirit was working in your grandfather's heart?" Pilar asked, helping Bear find his words.

"Yes, like that. I can't explain it. It was like the air around them was warmer and lighter somehow. I almost turned back around because I didn't want to step into their talk. But I needed to cut the fabric, so I walked up to her."

"What did she do?" Pilar asked.

"She gave me the length of fabric I needed to cut before I even asked and continued talking to my grandfather," he answered.

"I wonder what happened," Pilar said.

Pilar and Bear both looked at the river's edge. Finally, they saw Ruth kneel next to the aged man and place both her hands on each of his knees. They bowed their heads for several moments until Ruth grabbed both of his aged hands and stared into his face.

"They are smiling," Bear said.

"Yes, they are," Pilar agreed.

CHAPTER TWENTY-THREE

"Did you just make it home? I've been trying to contact you on the HMS all day," Zach said as he entered the house.

"Pilar dropped me off a few minutes ago. She wanted to stay, but she needed to get home."

"I really need to get out of this job," Zach said. "I can't keep expecting people to watch you all day," Zach said, shutting the front door and walking over to the couch.

"I don't need to be watched," Ruth said.

"I don't mean that. I only mean people shouldn't be burdened with taking you places. I should be taking you," Zach said, sitting down. "But it's more than that. I just really hate this job. I hate working at the plant. I hate overseeing the production of Sleepers. I'd rather be working in the soup department. And I hate interacting with the Efficientists—no offense to you, Ruth. I feel like I need to be home. I need to be with you and available to Pastor Tom."

"Why can't you leave?" Ruth asked.

"Because I have nothing. I used up all my money points on getting Mom her surgery. I sold my family's house when I became a Runner and we moved here. I'm not qualified to do anything else. I'm of no value to anyone."

"But you have a degree from a colonial college," Ruth said.

"I can preach," Zach said, getting up. "That's all I'm qualified to do, but I haven't preached in over five years. I don't know if I can even do it anymore. Who wants to hear me talk?"

"Why can you not preach?" Ruth asked. "Doesn't God speak through you? Can you not make yourself available to Him? Everyone I've talked to about your preaching said you have a gift of speaking God's Word. What has changed?"

"Ruth, it's not as simple as that," Zach said, pulling his fingers through his blonde hair. "Since my dad died, I lost something."

"Then you need to find it," Ruth said. "You make it too hard for yourself. I talked with Bear's grandfather today, and I told him about Jesus. I didn't have to do anything. I study the *Bible* and the Holy Spirit takes out what is needed for him. I make myself available."

Zach stood up. "You talked to Bear's grandfather about Jesus. What did he say?"

"I listened to him at first. I learned about his family and his life. I could see that he did not know Jesus, so I shared with him what I knew."

"And he listened to you?" Zach said.

"Why is that so hard for you to believe," Ruth asked.

"I've witnessed to that man for many years, and so has Bear. He has been so resistant to everything about faith. We all gave up."

"He was worried," Ruth said.

"What was he worried about?" Zach asked.

"He didn't want to accept salvation because he is worried that his wife and daughter did not. They have already passed, so he didn't want to leave them alone."

Zach sat back down. "What did you say?"

"I told him that when I almost died, I reached out for God. If I had known more about Him, I think I would have received salvation at that moment. But if Mom had talked to me about Jesus, I couldn't remember. It was buried too deep. Thankfully, God allowed me to live, and I received salvation with Christina."

"How did that help him?" Zach asked confused.

"I asked him if there was a chance that someone had talked about God to his wife and his daughter, and he said that your father had talked with both of them before they died."

"Yes, he and I visited them several times through the years," Zach said. "But they never would accept salvation. It was like they thought they were too unworthy of it."

171

"That seed you and your father planted in them may have been dormant for many years. But if they had asked God to come to them before they died, that seed would have sprung to life. It is possible that they are in heaven."

Zach leaned back. "But it is still possible that they are not," he said.

"He said that too," Ruth said.

"What did you say?" Zach asked.

"I said it was better for him to continue living with his wife and daughter's memory in him than to allow that memory to die forever," Ruth finished.

"That point resonated with him?" Zach said, reclining in his seat to think.

Ruth smiled a bit. "I think what may have motivated him most was Bear."

"How so?" Zach asked.

"He doesn't trust Bear to be a good carrier of his wife and daughter's memory. He says that Bear harbors too many bad feelings toward them. He feels like he needs to be the one to keep their memories safe."

"And so he is," Zach said, matching Ruth's smile. "So he accepted Jesus as his savior?"

Ruth nodded. "He was ready."

"Did you tell Bear?" Zach asked.

"I don't like talking to him. He's abrupt, rude and condescending," Ruth said.

"Bear doesn't forgive easily, and he expects too much of people. I think maybe because he's had to fend for himself for so long."

"He didn't have a good relationship with his mother?" Ruth asked.

"You definitely couldn't call it good, but he cared deeply for her. His grandfather and grandmother came down a few years before she died, but it was always Bear who took care of his mother. He would have done anything for her, and all he wanted from her was to get well. But she never did. Bear's dad would come into town, stay a couple of days and leave. He would give Bear money, but his mom would always find it and buy more drugs."

Ruth walked over to where the wedding dress was hung from the wooden frame that outlined the entrance to the kitchen.

Zach noticed the dress for the first time. "Is that Reyna's dress?"

"Yes," Ruth said. "I will be adding lace to it. Pilar is going to leave it here until the wedding, so it can be a surprise. She is telling her sister that with all the food being stored for the wedding, she didn't trust it at their house anymore."

"It's probably safer here anyway," Zach said. "No one cooks in this house."

Ruth smiled. "No, we don't."

"Will you be starting on Bear's clothes when you're done?"

Ruth ran her fingers along the silky edge of the wedding dress. "Yes," she whispered in thought.

"What's wrong?" Zach asked, getting out of his seat and walking towards his sister.

"I can see how Bear's past interactions with people are dictating how he interacts with people today, and it makes me grateful that God took everything from me."

"Why is that?" Zach asked.

"I have no idea how to interact with people now. It feels like I'm learning everything as a child again, but at least I don't have to always distinguish between actions that are caused by my past and actions that are rooted in truth. But there is only one problem I struggle with."

"What is that?" Zach asked.

"I'm supposed to interact with people out of love, like I see you doing. But I don't have the love you have for people— the type of love that hurts."

Zach leaned against the counter. "Maybe God designed you that way?"

"Why would God wire me not to love?" she asked.

"I think you do love, Ruth. You don't get emotionally involved. You led Bear's grandfather to Jesus today. That is love by choice, not by emotion. I envy you. I think I could do so much more for God if I didn't feel everything so deeply."

Ruth looked up into her brother's eyes, noticing for the first time the deep, solid blue they contained. "Maybe God designed you to feel deeply. Maybe instead of hindering you, those feeling will lead you further than you can imagine."

Suddenly, they heard a rustling at the front door and saw a silhouette through the curtains.

"Don't move," Zach whispered.

They both stood there motionless. A car door slammed shut, and they could hear an engine come to life.

"Someone was here," Ruth said quietly. "Are you expecting any deliveries?"

"No, and if it was someone I knew, they would have knocked," he said.

They heard the car drive off, but neither of them moved for several seconds.

"They are gone," Zach said. "Stay here."

Zach went to the front window and pulled the curtain back a few inches and peered out.

"What do you see?" Ruth asked.

"Nothing," he said, looking toward the street. "Wait a minute. I see something on the porch. It looks like a blanket or something."

Ruth watched as Zach cautiously opened the door. He leaned to the ground and grabbed something heavy, pulling it into the living room. "What is this?" he asked when he finally shut the door.

"It is a bolt of fabric," Ruth said.

"What is it for?" Zach asked. "Did you order it?"

Ruth stared at the lavender fabric with the floral pattern. "This is the fabric I wanted from Bear, but he wouldn't give it to me because I had nothing of value to offer him in exchange."

Zach shook his head and smiled. "Well, I guess you had something of value after all."

174

"What is that?" Ruth asked.

Zach hoisted the fabric off of the floor and started making his way to Ruth's room. "Your willingness to listen and obey."

CHAPTER TWENTY-FOUR

"**W**here did you go, *Ne'aw-ze*?" Bear's grandfather asked, walking up the slope from the river's edge. He stopped and placed the shotgun on the ground.

"I had a delivery to make," Bear said, continuing his walk to the house.

"You don't make deliveries."

Bear stopped and looked at his grandfather. "My heart is happy this day for you, *Aha-enah*."

"You sound so surprised," the aged man said with a gummy grin. The wrinkles around his eyes thickened as his smile broadened.

"*Aha-enah*, I have prayed for this day for so long. I have talked with you many times, but my words were not heard," Bear said.

"Ah, I knew you were not the one who could give me the right words, so I waited. When you brought that little *baynit* to me, I knew she was the one."

Bear looked at his aged grandfather, crossing his arms. "Why Ruth, *Aha-enah*? She is a helpless little girl. She knows nothing of the world around her."

"She may not know a lot about this world," the grandfather said, spreading his arms wide. "But," he continued, placing his index finger on his gray hair right of his temple. "She knows more about what's in here."

The grandfather then placed his hand on his chest over the location of his heart. "She knows more about what's in here too. She is very smart in a world you know nothing of because you do not value it."

"Being smart about things that do not exist does not feed or clothe you," Bear said.

"You have all your heart in a faith that cannot be seen, yet you don't understand it," the grandfather said. "You can't be all heart and action, *Ne'aw-ze*. You must also have understanding."

Bear uncrossed his hands. "I try, *Aha-enah*. You see me read the *Bible*. I don't understand it. "

"Does this mean you give up?"

"I want to ask Zach questions, but he's a manager at the factory now. I saw him more when he was a Runner. Who else can I ask? I don't have the HMS anymore. I have no one to guide my understanding."

"That little *baynit* told me about the fabric she wanted. You said she had nothing of value to give you," the grandfather began.

"I gave her what she wanted," Bear said. "That was my delivery."

"I know what you were doing, *Ne'aw-ze*. Do you think I am blind? I'm speaking of your ignorance. You see no value in what you don't understand, but she can teach you. Ask her your questions. She answered all of mine, and she helped me to understand."

Bear shifted his feet on the dried grass. The cool winter breeze felt good against his heated cheeks. "You want me to ask her for help?"

"Yes, you need her help and she needs yours."

"Do you think she needs more fabric?" Bear asked.

"No, she needs to learn to protect herself. She does not stay aware of her surroundings. She is too inside of herself," the grandfather said, placing both of his fists gently on his chest. "She is like a pearl outside of the oyster. She will not last long without help."

"She needs to learn to take care of herself," Bear said firmly. "I tried to tell her."

"Yes, but not by your words, *Ne'aw-ze*, and your arrogance. She needs guidance, like you do when you read. You are strong, and it makes you unwilling to show your weakness, but you will not take hold of what you are looking for unless you get help."

"She has Zach to help her."

"You said it yourself, Zach is working. Besides you are a better teacher for this. Give her a foundation for how she can protect herself. She is smart. She will learn fast."

"I'll ask Zach, but I don't know if he will agree. He shields his sister."

Bear and his grandfather started to make their way back to the house together. The grandfather placed the old shotgun over his right shoulder. "Will you tell me what she teaches you?"

"About what I'm reading in the *Bible*?" Bear asked.

"Yes, I want to know more about this Holy Book, but I'm too old to learn to read."

"Don't you think you've had enough to drink?" Randall asked. He watched Neil's behavior become more and more affected by the alcohol as the evening progressed. The PR event was coming to a close. The dinner and desserts had been presented and eaten, and the attendees were enjoying a few drinks before they were taken back to their high-rise homes. Back to their work and their LPSs.

"Why don't you enjoy your little princess over there and let me worry about my own PR event? Don't forget that you work for me. I pay you," Neil said.

"Actually, Charlie Liu is paying me," Randall said evenly.

"You know what I mean," Neil said, trying to mask his anger.

"We found what was left of Charlie's vehicle," Randall said.

"Did you find a body?" Neil asked.

"No, but that doesn't mean he's alive. He was probably killed and thrown into the woods. The vultures and coyotes have eaten him to the bones by now. There was almost nothing left of his car. It was completely stripped."

"Will you continue to look?" Neil asked, sounding more sober than he had previously.

Randall stopped talking when one of the PR photographers came near to snap a few photographs. Neil and Randall smiled for the camera, and the man moved on.

"There is no need to look. Charlie Liu is dead," Randall said. "He wouldn't survive in the Colonies by himself."

"What about those essays that have been discovered on the web? You are sure that Charlie Liu hasn't written any of them?" Neil asked

"Not possible. Those posts are written by people who are learned in the *Bible*. I've checked Charlie's reading history, and he has never downloaded it. Although his parents had no religious tendencies, if they did, they would lean toward being Buddhists, not Christians."

"And it does appear that many people are writing these posts," Neil said. "The team I assigned to analyze the posts believes it is a group of people writing them. They've compared much of the writing, and they say there is a subtle difference in writing styles."

"Do they believe Efficientists are writing them? Could it be the Apostle or someone from the Efficientists Christian Sect?" Randall asked.

"No," Neil said, shaking his head. "This seems to be something entirely new. They believe it is a group of highly intelligent Colonials who are writing the posts because they are not writing in a variety. I never thought that would be possible. I've underestimated Colonials."

"That doesn't mean anything," Randall said. "You hate writing in variety and you are now considered the top Efficientist."

"That's because I am old. The current generation of Efficientists don't mind talking in Long English, but they only write in a variety. They don't have the patience for Long English. That's how they've been trained," Neil said.

179

"I've read a few of those articles, and there is no way Colonials could be writing them," Randall said.

"You underestimate them," Neil said. "Some of them are smart enough to put these so-called top Efficientists to the test."

"You forget that I grew up in the Colonies. There is no way that they could be writing these articles. They don't have enough spare time to be so analytical. They must all work to provide a living," Randall added. "The person or persons writing them has time to think."

"Am I interrupting something?" Ada Armel came in between the two men. "Your conversation seems a little too tense for this occasion, I think"

"There now," Neil said. "A woman with common sense. You have a very sophisticated look this evening, Ada. No crystals or dye to entertain us today?"

"Sadly, the days of extreme went away with Eve Pallue." Ada stood at eye level with Neil because of her three-inch heels. Her face was round, and her blonde cropped hair framed her jawline. She had round hazel eyes and a petite nose. Her flawless complexion was highlighted with hues of gold to match her gold suit dress.

"Has Eve's death caused such a decline in the public opinion polls?" Neil asked.

"I hate to admit it, but, yes, it has. What can I say? An artist is only as good as her material. Eve Pallue was the perfect backdrop for my work."

"Can you find another Eve?" Neil asked, intrigued.

"I've tried. There are no female Elite Efficientists, and the other top Efficientists don't have what Eve had."

"And what is that?" Randall asked.

Ada waited for a second and leaned in to whisper. "Her absolute indifference. She couldn't care less about popularity, which made her even more alluring. Honestly, I used to be so infuriated by her lack of concern about the image I was giving her. All she wanted to do was keep her face in that Portable of hers, but I never realized that what I had was nothing short of supernatural. Now that she's gone, a gaping void has been left, and I'm incapable of filling it."

"Don't be so theatrical, Ada," Neil said.

Ada wiped a tear that had slipped down her cheek.

"Are you crying over Eve's death or your loss of material?" Randall asked, tersely.

"Don't be a brute, Randall. We both worked with her. Anyways, unless we can figure out how to fill in the hole that Eve left, I guess sophisticated is all the world is going to get," she said draping her hands down the sides of her skirt.

"Can't you be that girl?" Neil asked.

Ada threw her head back and gave a well-rehearsed laughed. "I am not willing to waste my entire life on an LPS. Eve was bred to work, which is why her outings were so spectated. No one can replace her. She was a one-of-a-kind gem that people clamored to see. At least, I know that her final PR event will be an image ingrained in the minds of the entire world. My crystal-encrusted queen will be remembered for eternity, and I will share in that glory."

CHAPTER TWENTY-FIVE

"I don't know how you can do all that," Tom said to his new friend. "I thought Efficientists only knew how to use an LPS. I didn't think they knew how to build one."

Charlie Liu leaned behind Tom's HMS. "I can't believe you had all the equipment that I needed in the trading center."

"People wanted food, so I traded them for whatever they brought me. I saved all the LPS boxes and wires in the basement, hoping one day they would be used," Tom said. "There is a factory near Levington that produces LPSs and Sleepers among other things."

"Isn't that where Zach Daniels works?" Charlie asked.

"Yes, but from what I hear, he won't be there for long," Tom answered. "He wants to go into full-time ministry again."

"It will be interesting to finally meet him, since I have heard so much about him," Charlie said and plugged in a few more wires before standing up and staring at his creation. "If this works, I can gain access to almost anywhere on the web, but we'll have to be careful. Every move I make must be subtle, so I don't expose my presence."

Tom stared at the young man who had given himself freely to God's work. "You think this will help us disguise our writings?"

"I received a few more writings of—Eve," Charlie fumbled. "I'm sorry. I keep forgetting to call her Ruth."

"That's quite alright. You met her first as Eve, so I can see why it's difficult. I think if you saw her again, though, you would find it easier to see her as Ruth. She is not the same woman she used to be."

"And I'm not the same man," Charlie said. "I of all people should understand that."

Tom patted Charlie on the shoulder. "You have been a God-sent to me."

Charlie's crescent eyes disappeared as his round face opened up with a wide grin. His unkempt black hair had grown shaggy over the few weeks, and his tan skin had darkened in the sun from helping Esther with the goats in the fields. His thin frame had thickened from the manual labor and Deborah's cooking.

Charlie began again. "Zach sent me more of Ruth's writings, so I'm hoping these will last longer on the web. There is so much being published every day by Efficientists that these won't be noticed until several Colonials download them. By then it will be too late. They will be printed out by the leaders that you have set up."

"God has opened doors beyond my capabilities. He has sent men and women my way who have influence in their local towns. I could have never set up what He has done," Tom said emphatically. "I only hope that our presence on the LPS won't be discovered."

"You are good at connecting and leading people, and you believe in your work, which helps motivate the rest of us," Charlie said.

"I was so worried when the World Government made me shut down my church, but their limitations only enhanced my talents," Tom said. "Now let's see if this machine you built will work."

Charlie sat down in front of the LPS that he had created. "I can't use my thumbprint because the World Government has declared me dead, so we will continue using yours. Would you mind?"

Tom reached his hand out and placed his thumb on the print identifier. The screen of the LPS breathed to life.

"The first thing I want to do is to see what the World Government has done to my accounts." Charlie deftly works his fingers across the keyboard and gave short commands.

"That's it!" Tom exclaimed.

Startled, Charlie stopped his work and looked at Tom. "I have not found anything yet."

"I'm sorry for my outburst," Tom said. "I was watching you work, and I realized that when Ruth came into my office the first time, she worked like you. I think that is what started me thinking about why she seemed so different. It was how she was working on my HMS that had me first start analyzing her."

Charlie looked up at Tom. "What was the clincher for you?" he asked.

"She is missing a tooth, and I remember reading an article that all that was found of her body in the fire was a tooth."

Charlie looked back at the screen. "This makes me wonder why the World Government declared me deceased so quickly. Obviously, none of my body has been found." He began typing quickly on the keyboard, giving short commands. After a few moments, his typing stopped and he leaned back in his chair.

"What is it?" Tom asked.

Charlie looked up at Tom. "They have taken all of my money points. Everything I own has been confiscated."

"But they're not supposed to do that for a year, I thought," Tom said, staring at the screen.

"They aren't," Charlie agreed. "But no one has noticed, and I think that's what they were wanting."

"Can you see who did it?" Tom asked.

Charlie faced the screen again and began typing. "There's a lot of movement, but I think it's all leading to Eve's old bodyguard, Randall."

"But bodyguards don't have that kind of authority!" Tom said, incredulously.

"This one does. He is now Neil Elder's number one man."

"He's also the man who tried to kill Ruth. What do you know about him?"

"I don't have to look that up to tell you," Charlie said. "He's a mercenary. He kills for money."

"Neil Elder had Ruth killed, so he can claim *Life Plethoricity*, and he hired Randall to do the dirty work for him. Randall was Ruth's bodyguard for years, so he had access to almost everything."

"Let me check something," Charlie said, giving a few short commands to the LPS. "That's interesting."

"What?" Tom asked, looking at the screen.

"All of Eve Pallue's accounts are still frozen. None of her assets have been touched."

"She must be too high profile even for Neil Elder," Tom said.

Charlie continued typing on the keyboard. "There are only about two months left and it will be a year since she was declared dead."

Tom thought for a moment. "Is she able to access her accounts?"

Charlie looked up at Tom. "I could easily unfreeze her accounts, but when she accesses them, the World Government will start tracking the culprit, which may eventually expose her. And even if she got the money points, she wouldn't be able to use them for very long without leaving a trail."

"I know Zach has been wanting to quit his job at the factory. He feels God leading him into full-time ministry, but he won't do it unless he is able to provide for Ruth. We could help him here, but he doesn't want to do anything that would endanger me and my family. Any connection between us would not be good for the trading center and our work here. It's too bad they can't touch those money points."

"There is an alternative to money points," Charlie said.

"What?" Tom asked.

Charlie made a few strokes on the keyboard. "Do you see that?"

"Is that a jeweler?" Tom asked.

"No," Charlie said, shaking his head." That is merely a portion of what Eve Pallue has allowed the public to see from her vaults at the World Bank. She collects jewelry."

"I remember reading about that in some of the PR articles, and my wife mentioned something about Ruth's pearls coming from the World Bank before the fire."

"If she went to the World Bank in person, they may possibly allow her into her vault. But we would have to get someone on the inside to help us. The only problem, besides getting caught, is that everyone will know that Eve Pallue is alive."

"Zach would never allow that. She will be on the run for the rest of her life," Tom said, shaking his head. "And everyone who knows her will be endangered, as well."

"Did Charlie meet up with Pastor Tom again?" Deborah asked. The elderly sister was kneading dough in the kitchen. The windows were open and the cool breeze slid over the table where she worked. She could hear the goats calling out in the distance. She glanced through the screen door. Some of their houseguests were sitting around the rock fire pit that they finished building. The fire brightened their faces in the twilight of the evening.

Esther set down the glass jars she was carrying on the table next to where her sister was working. "Yes, he said something about doing some mechanical work at the trading center. I can tell he doesn't want to tell me much."

Deborah powdered the table with flour. "He doesn't want to endanger us," she said. "You know how Pastor Tom is always telling us to not discuss too many details with others. He said we were the reason Charlie figured out Ruth was still alive. Thank the Lord Charlie is on our side now." Deborah paused, deciding to change the subject. "How is the fire pit working out? It looks mighty fine from here."

Esther looked out the window. "They constructed it well. I'm impressed with how many large stones they found near the river. Jordan is leading the *Bible* study tonight."

"Are they still going through Isaiah?" Deborah asked, taking her rolling pin over the flattened dough.

"Yes," Esther answered, opening two of the jars. "Some of them love Isaiah's prose and a few of them feel like he needs to get to the point."

Deborah laughed and wiped her hands on her apron. "It seems that Efficientists always want to get to the point. Ruth wasn't like that when she came here. She never rushed."

"It's probably because she was like a newborn babe. Everything was new to her, and she was learning how to live life over again. How I do miss that girl," Esther said.

"Me too," Deborah admitted. "She seems content enough in her letters. She is getting ready for the bazaar near Levington. She is making clothes to sell there. I hope she's careful. A lot of people from the surrounding area attend it."

"Isn't it something that our Ruth befriended Levi and his family? Who would have thought that the young man we took care of for a while would start a respectable, God-fearing town?" Esther asked, getting out a pie pan from the cupboard.

"And to think that God sent Ruth to his village and she is good friends with his daughter. God never ceases to amaze me. I wish Levi had an HMS, so we could contact him, but the village is totally disconnected from the World Government, which—seeing the current state of things—is probably best." Deborah placed the dough on the pie pan and took one of the jars that Esther opened.

"I felt blueberry would be good for tonight," Esther said.

"Sounds good to me," Deborah answered and poured the crushed blueberries from the jar into the piecrust. "I only wish that Zach didn't live in government housing. He needs to take Ruth to stay with Levi's family."

"The only reason she is there is for her brother," Esther said. "We have to trust that he knows what he is doing."

Esther sat down at the table and stared as her sister poured the blueberries from the second jar into the piecrust. "I talked to him," she finally admitted.

Deborah stopped. "What do you mean?"

187

"I wrote him and he responded. I told him that I was worried for Ruth, and that I hoped he had a plan to get her out of government housing."

"What did he say?" Deborah asked.

Esther looked out the window. "He said that he was working on it."

"Did he say anything else?" Deborah asked, wanting to know every detail.

"He said that he knew you and I are prayer warriors, so he asked us to pray for him," Esther said, meeting her sister's gaze.

"What does he want us to pray for?"

"He feels God's call on his life to preach again," Esther said.

Deborah pushed the pie to the center of the table and sat down next to her sister. "Well, that will mean two things. First, it means that Zacchaeus Daniels has stopped running away from God. Second, it means that our Ruth will no longer be able to hide if he starts drawing a crowd like he used to."

CHAPTER TWENTY-SIX

"**R**uth, wake up. We have to go," Zach said, knocking on Ruth's door, trying not to allow the emotions of his dream to affect his demeanor. "Ruth, open the door," he continued, impatiently.

The door finally opened and Ruth peered her brown eyes up toward her brother's flushed face. "What's going on, Zach? It's still dark outside. You don't have work today, do you?" she asked. She had gone to bed late finishing a writing project that had been weighing on her.

"No, the factory is closed, which is why we must go now. Bear will be training all the young men from the factory, and we need to get there first."

Ruth's eyes opened wider as the feelings of sleep instantly vanished. "Why would we go to his house right now? I can give him the clothes that I made for him and his grandfather later today," she said, looking back at the clothes neatly piled on her dresser top. She had also completed the wedding dress for Pilar, which was hanging securely in her closet. Pilar was true to her word and had made her a makeup kit with all the essentials she remembered that her image consultant, Adel Armel, once used on her. She hadn't been able to research how to apply the makeup, though. And Pilar promised that she would apply her makeup before her sister's wedding.

"We need to get to his house before the sun gets too high and he starts his training. He'll be busy all day, and I need him to train you," Zach said with tension building in his face.

Ruth opened the door all the way. "He's a fighter," she said. "Why would he train me?"

"Remember when I first met you at the gas station, and that man was attacking you?"

"Yes," she said flatly.

189

"You had no idea how to protect yourself and that man was a drunk and way beyond his youthful years. He could sense your ignorance. Otherwise, he would have never attacked you in broad daylight," Zach said.

"I dislike that word, *ignorance*," Ruth said, crossing her arms. "Besides I have to start sewing the pieces for the bazaar in two weeks. I want to have a full collection of clothes before it begins."

"Look, Ruth, you are my sister, and I don't want to offend you, but you are too vulnerable. You're not aware of the world around you. You don't do the normal things to protect yourself," Zach said.

"Like what?" she asked.

"You never lock the front door. I always have to check it. You don't lock your car door either, and you leave the window rolled down when it is parked. We don't live in the safest of neighborhoods," Zach said, trying to calm his voice.

"We haven't gone many places, Zach," Ruth said. "I'm in this house every day either working at the HMS or at my sewing machine."

"I know! That's why I don't want to take you places because you are not aware of your surroundings. You are extremely intelligent and you make connections in your writings that have profoundly changed the way that I view my faith. I've read every article that you've written so far, and they are brilliant. I'm learning a lot, and I value all the insight I have gained. So please believe me when I say that you too need to learn something new. We live in the Colonies now, and there is always an element of risk everywhere we go, and you are not ready."

Ruth looked at her brother. His eyes were filled with concern. "You are highly agitated. Did something happen? Why are you all of a sudden concerned about me getting hurt?"

Zach looked down. "I dreamed of that man attacking you again, but this time I was unable to protect you. I tried to move and yell out, but I was frozen. I couldn't stop him," he said. He looked back at his sister. "I felt the Holy Spirit's urgency to help you when I woke up. I know how to fight a little. I've wrestled with Bear through the years and he's taught me here and there, but he is an incredible teacher. He is the only one who can help you learn to protect yourself. He will evaluate you and give you your best fighting chance to stop an attacker if I'm not there."

"How do you know he will help me?" she asked.

Zach straightened his shoulders. "I never ask anything of him unless it is important to me and he knows that."

Ruth leaned on the doorframe. "But I wouldn't feel right taking his services without giving him something in return."

"You don't have to worry about that. I got something in my truck that I know is worth more than his training, and he will want it."

Bear set up his training equipment. He knew that he would have a lot of would-be fighters there today. He'd have to divide them in groups, and have some of the men do strength training exercises while he trained the other group. Maybe he could get a few spars going on early in the day. The men were eager to learn.

Bear paused and looked at his set-up. He strung rope across the designated fighting area. He would be doing some movement drills with the men too. He played the image of the different fighting moves in his mind.

He heard movement and looked down toward the river. His grandfather was up and heading to his stump by the river's edge. Bear shook his head. After all the years of persistent badgering, his grandfather finally received Jesus in his heart. And the person who finally got to him was Ruth—the helpless girl who had somehow won his grandfather's favor. She actually wasn't a girl. She was only a few years younger than he, but nothing about her face was aged. Maybe there was more to her than he could see. She was hard to read. The only time he had sensed any emotion from her was when he accused her of not being Naomi's daughter. At least she showed some feeling about that.

Bear saw the first rays of light creep along the river's edge. He thought of his HMS deep in the mud of the river. Five years of work, sacrifice and obedience gone in one move. The World Government banned his work, so he threw it all away. He had tried to do everything God had told him to do. He stayed home, read his *Bible* and created sermon videos. He even hired a small band of Runners that he had been training to take the videos to the nearby people. He had become a pastor of sorts. Now he didn't know what he was. Zach was back, and he was the rightful pastor of the town. Bear could feel his sense of purpose slipping away.

Maybe, my time of service to God is over, he thought. Even as he thought the words, he knew that they contradicted what he felt was building inside of him. Something new was about to happen. There was more to his life than simply training fighters.

Bear heard the noise of a car's engine in the distance, and he quickly spotted a small yellow car, slowly making its way through the brush that led to his house. He had never seen the car before, so his guard was up. He heard the sound of his grandfather's footsteps behind him and the cocking of his shotgun.

"No, *Aha-enah*," Bear said, raising his right hand. "I see Zach in the car."

"Are you sure, *Ne'aw-ze?*" the grandfather said, stopping a few yards behind Bear.

"Yes, his hair is yellow like the car. It is him."

"Is he alone?" the grandfather asked.

"No, his sister is with him. In the sun her hair looks like the leaves of a red oak tree in the change of season."

"Tell her to visit with me before she leaves. And remember what I told you. She needs your help and you need hers," the grandfather said and headed back to the stoop.

The car pulled up next to Bear, and he leaned near the driver's window. "Why have you come so early?"

"I need you to train Ruth. She is unable to protect herself from attackers," Zach said.

Bear could sense fear in Zach's voice, which was unusual for him.

"Has something happened?" Bear asked.

Zach got out of the car and walked a few paces from the car, keeping his voice low. "She was attacked when I first met her by an attendant at the gas station."

"What happened?" Bear asked. He felt the protective instinct in him automatically surge.

"He was trying to make an exchange with her that she was unwilling to make. He was drunk and old, and she couldn't stop him. Only by the grace of God was I there at the right time."

Bear leaned back on his heels and crossed his arms. "Zach, she is very weak and small. There is only so much I can teach her. I cannot make her into what she is not."

"Look, all she needs to know is how to get away from an attacker. She is very smart and learns quickly. She has absolutely no body awareness. She grew up never playing sports or even playing around with other kids. And as an adult, she doesn't have any physical contact with people unless they are giving her a hug or a pat on the back. She is completely ignorant, and I can't let her go to the bazaar without any clue of how to handle herself."

"Why don't you teach her?" Bear asked.

Zach looked toward his sister who was still sitting in the car and looked back at Bear. "She needs to experience what an attacker will feel like, so she can overcome him. I would let up too easily. With me she would only learn how to defend herself against a brother who loves her. She needs to learn how to defend herself from an attacker who wants to destroy her."

"And you trust me?" Bear asked. He knew that Zach was fully aware of his past with women, and he wouldn't train Ruth unless Zach would allow him full rights to train her his way.

Zach was a few inches taller than Bear, so he tilted his head slightly to look straight into his friend's eyes. "I am choosing to trust you because you have submitted your life to the Lord. But—" Zach said, trying to keep his voice even. "If anything happens to her, I will fight you until my last breath."

"Good," Bear said. "I will train her."

They both heard the car door open and watched as Ruth came out. "I'm going to talk with *Aha-enah*," she said, slamming the car door behind her.

Bear watched Ruth walk toward the river. "She has a good Ka'to accent already," he said impressed. "And she showed good strength slamming the car door. What is that she is carrying in her arms?"

Zach watched his sister walk carefully through the brush. "I don't know," he said. "She was working on something late last night at the HMS, and she printed it out this morning. It must be something for your grandfather. Oh, and she finished your clothes already."

"All of them?" Bear asked surprised. "It's only been a few days."

Zach leaned into the opened driver's side door and reached into the back seat. "She's really fast at the sewing machine," he said, grabbing a stack of clothing. "Here you go."

Bear looked at the clothing. He grabbed one hem and studied the stitching. "Her lines are perfect," he finally admitted. "I will get the rest of her fabric."

"Before you leave, I have something to exchange for you helping Ruth," Zach said, walking to the back of the car.

Bear already knew what he wanted to trade for his services, but he was intrigued to see what Zach had brought. "Why have you driven this small car to my home? Where is your truck?" Bear asked.

Zach popped the trunk of Ruth's small car. "My truck has a tracking device from the World Government. I'm trying to use it less in case something happens. The fewer places the truck leads the better."

"What is this?" Bear asked.

"This, my friend, is one of the older models of the LPS. A few of the managers got upgrades, so I decided to take this one home."

"How were you able to get it out of the factory with no one seeing you?" Bear asked, amazed that Zach would steal something.

Zach smiled. "I took it apart piece by piece and placed the parts in soup boxes."

"I can't accept it," Bear said.

"Why not?" Zack asked.

Bear put his hands on his hips. "Because I need to ask your sister to help me understand a few things in the *Bible*. I have many questions that need to be answered," he said.

"Why don't you ask me?" Zach asked.

"You have to be at the factory during the week, Zach. You have the weekends off, but those are my busiest training days. I need someone who has the time to show me what I need to know."

Zach leaned on the bumper with the palm of his hands and shook his head. "That is why I need to get out of this job. It takes all of my time. I'm barely able to read Ruth's writings."

"I've heard people talk about these writings. I have read a few of them," Bear said. "People say Pastor Tom is writing them. They have too many difficult words."

"I've been trying to make Ruth's writings easier for Colonials to understand. She assumes too much of the reader, but what she conveys is very relevant for us today. She writes mainly to Efficientists, which is why you are having difficulty. Tom has actually been writing some too. He is writing mainly to Colonials. I'll get you a few copies of his writings."

Bear looked at his friend, trying to quench his own frustration. "These writings are changing things, and I feel that I am missing out on something important."

"Ruth can go over them with you. We have them all printed out. She can be difficult to understand at times, but if you ask her to explain, she will make it clearer."

Bear looked toward the river where Ruth sat on the cross near his grandfather's stump. "She is reading those pages to him."

"We can let her stay with him while I set up your LPS," Zach said. "I still want you to have it. I need to be able to contact you while Ruth is here and I'm at work, and I don't want to keep it at my house. You didn't throw your satellite dish into the river, did you?"

Bear looked at the LPS. "No, it's still on the side of the house. I wouldn't mind having an HMS, but I don't know how to use this one."

"After I set it up, I can go over it with you. Ruth will be here too, and she knows more about how to use it than I do. She can help you."

Bear thought for a moment. "I will not take it without a trade," Bear said.

"We can worry about that Monday," Zach said.

"No, we must exchange something now," Bear said, thinking. "Wait, I know."

Bear turned around carrying the folded clothes that Ruth had made him and his grandfather and began walking in the direction to his home. He got to his front door and opened it, placing his clothes inside. Then he headed toward the padlocked door of his storehouse. He disappeared inside for a short moment and reappeared with two bolts of fabric under each arm. He walked up to the opened driver's side door and placed all four bolts of fabric across the back seat. Then he walked back to Zach who was watching him.

"I put the two bolts of fabric leftover from our clothes in her car, and I added two more for the LPS. I will give you two more on Monday once I learn how to use the machine. So that is the two I owe her for the clothes and four more for the LPS. Is that fair?" Bear asked, only slightly winded from carrying the heavy loads.

"Yes, I think Ruth will like that," Zach said.

"My men will arrive any minute now. Let me help you carry this LPS to my house, and you can set it up while I train."

Zach looked at the river again. "I guess Ruth will be keeping herself busy with your grandfather this morning," he said.

CHAPTER TWENTY-SEVEN

Bear sat staring at the final page of Ruth's manuscript. His chair was tucked under the large, wooden table that ran across one wall of his small living room. His legs were crossed on the chair, allowing his bare feet warmth under the backs of his legs. The LPS sat on the other end of the table. He hadn't touched it for fear he would somehow break it. He knew Ruth would be coming today, so he would wait until she showed him everything he would need to know to use it.

"So what do you think?" his grandfather asked. He had been sitting at one of the chairs near the wood-burning stove. He nursed the fire while he listened to his grandson read the book to him.

"This is what she read to you the other morning?" Bear asked. He was biding time, searching through the mass of feelings flooding him.

"Yes," the grandfather stoked the fire some more. "I had to tell her that I never learned to read. She hid her surprise well, *Ne'aw-ze*. She covered my shame. She read the pages to me, and the story lived before my eyes."

Bear looked at the manuscript again. It was only around forty pages, but it detailed his family's history from the time of the Second Civil War until now. He shook his head. "But how could she know all of this?"

"The first day I met her—when you gave me the sweet bread from Pilar—she sat with me. She listened while I talked. She would ask me a question, and I would talk some more."

"Did she write anything down?" Bear asked. He couldn't understand how someone could have one conversation with a person and then know that person's entire family history.

"Ah, *Ne'aw-ze*, I think if we truly listened, we wouldn't have to write anything down. She listened, and I was able to paint our history into her mind. And look," he said, pointing to the book on the table, "our family lives on in these pages."

"But why would she write it?" Bear asked. "We did not ask her."

"We did not know to ask," the grandfather said.

"But we have exchanged nothing for it," Bear said. "Why should I pay for something I did not ask for?"

"You anger me, *Ne'aw-ze*," the grandfather said, turning his full attention to Bear. "Something like this is a gift. To pay her would devalue what she had done."

"I'm sorry, *Aha-enah*. It is difficult for me to receive a gift," Bear said.

"So you decide not to embrace this gift because you are ashamed to accept it?"

Bear said nothing.

"For years you tell me to receive the gift of salvation for free. You say that I can do nothing to earn what Jesus had done for me, and I should not be ashamed to take such a gift. But now you will not accept a gift from Ruth because you don't like people helping you."

Bear stood up in frustration, and the grandfather patiently sat back in his chair.

"You are becoming upset, *Ne'aw-ze*, but you don't say why you are angry," the grandfather said. "Stop and think for a moment before you speak. Why are you upset?"

Bear looked at his grandfather for a long moment. He finally sat back down in the chair. "I know why I'm upset," he said.

"What is it?" the grandfather asked.

"The end of her book, she writes about the video sermons I used to make," he said, struggling to hide his emotions. "But that's the end of it. *Aha-enah*, what am I to do now? Zach is back, and he and Ruth are writing these articles that everyone is talking about. I hear Pastor Tom has leaders in every village, working on spreading these writings. The five years I spent reading the *Bible* over and over again—making those video sermons—none of it seems to matter now. I stayed in this house, trained my men and studied, and for what?"

The grandfather leaned in his chair. "Maybe your videos were like the gentle showers before the storms. You softened the earth, so it would be ready to receive the hard rains."

Bear thought for a moment. "So my work is done?"

The grandfather chuckled. " *Ne'aw-ze*, you are too much like a hawk. He circles big and proud over his prey for all to see. Yes, he is strong and quick, but too predictable. You need to fly like a bat."

"A bat? They are clumsy flyers with no pattern to their path," Bear said, shaking his head.

"You do not see because you are too busy trying to be the important hawk. The bat is the better flyer. His skin is flexible and his muscles can bend in many different directions. The shape of his wings changes to match the wind that blows him. His flexibility is his strength."

"Am I not flexible?" Bear asked, leaning forward in his chair.

"You want to circle high in the sky over the villages, but maybe it's time to fly into the farms, the churches and the homes, like that bat. He is found everywhere."

Bear stood. "God has been showing me something, but I don't understand what it means. But what you say makes me think of it." Bear quickly got up, making his way toward one of the bedrooms. When he got back to the table, he sat down holding a large stack of papers.

"It is in here in the *Bible* that I printed," Bear said, showing his grandfather one of the pages. "But I don't understand it."

The grandfather stared at the page and then looked back at his grandson. "That is why you must ask Ruth for help. The *Bible* is living in her mind. Like you see the forest and the river with your eyes and hands, she sees the *Bible* with the eyes and hands of her mind."

"But why won't God show me?" Bear asked.

The grandfather got up and put his aged hand on Bear's shoulder. "Because he wants the hawk to become the bat."

Zach walked into the factory, skipping the lines of people working the machines. He was supposed to be the mediator between Colonials and the Efficientists, ensuring that both groups were doing their part to serve the World Government. The Colonials were the backbones of production and the Efficientists were the brains, but Zach knew that all of it was one big ploy to keep everyone busy and out of the way. The Efficientists and Colonials were on two separate streets, going in the same direction.

He was nearing the office of the Efficientist in charge. He, of course, was not there. Zach had been doing much of his work on the LPS lately. The director was a middle-aged man who would never be more than a lower Efficientist. He was a drunk and partied with the young women of the factory who were half his age. Zach looked over his shoulder before entering the man's office. The director put too much stock into Zach's ignorance, but Zach knew more than he let on. He had worked this man's LPS for weeks until he knew exactly what he needed to do.

Zach sat at the LPS and touched the screen. The Efficientist always left it on, so Zach could check in for him every morning. Zach quickly typed on the keyboard and gave quick commands. He had to laugh at the irony of events. Less than a year ago, he would have never been seen behind an LPS screen. Now he could build and work one. He typed a quick note and pressed send. Then he began his other normal duties of checking in all the divisions of the plant. They were all accounted for. He finished the morning reports and let the LPS stay idle. The director would be coming soon, and Zach needed to get on the factory floor.

As Zach made his way down the steps, he thought of his sister. He had dropped her off at Bear's house. Zach exhaled a breath of surrender. He might not be able to control everything, but he at least wanted to be a part of what was going on. Pilar was ignoring him. Bear was training his sister. His mother had died. All of the freedom he thought he had was gone. The responsibilities at the factory were weighing on him. He was lying to these people, giving them hope in the World Government to keep them quiet and out of the way.

And he had been feeling God's call to preach pressing on him harder every day. He could imagine himself preaching to the trees if no one else would listen. He dreamed of preaching to crowds, and he would give sermons in the cold showers. Ruth had even caught him a few times, pacing the backyard and preaching to the wind. He finally understood what the Prophet Jeremiah meant when he said that God's Word was like a fire in his bones that he couldn't contain.

After he dropped off Ruth this morning, he knew what he had to do. Come this afternoon, he would no longer be an employee at the factory. His boss would receive a notice of Zach's discharge from employment. The director would grab one of the other floor managers and give him Zach's old job, knowing that the World Government would take too long to fill the void. Then Zach would move everything out of government housing. Now Zach only hoped that Bear would let them move in with him until they figured out what to do next. He didn't care where he lived as long as he was no longer a World Government employee.

CHAPTER TWENTY-EIGHT

"**I** don't need your help, *Aha-enah*," Bear said, making his way to the makeshift ring in his yard. Bear's grandfather had pulled a chair from the house and set it next to the training ground.

"I asked him to watch," Ruth said, fidgeting in the cool winter breeze.

The mornings had gotten cooler, and Ruth wasn't used to being outside away from the warm oven at the house that Zach made sure to light every morning for her. She wished that she could be back at the HMS writing her articles or at the sewing machine, creating new clothes. She didn't want to learn how to defend herself. What could she really do when faced with people like Randall? He had knocked her out without her even knowing he was there. She was too weak and too small, and she never trained for anything physical while growing up. She was always at her LPS or studying with her tutors. Ruth put her focus back on Bear. He was not happy about his grandfather overseeing the training. He never tried to hide his emotions.

"How can I train you to protect yourself if you don't trust me?" Bear asked, folding his arms when he reached her.

"I trust you because Zach trusts you. He wouldn't have dropped me off here if he didn't believe you could help me. But you and I see things differently, and I believe we need a third party observer."

Bear stared at Ruth for a brief moment. "I see you brought him something sweet."

The grandfather smiled and held up a pastry that Ruth brought to him right when she arrived.

"Pilar was helping me with something yesterday evening, and she brought a few sweets over. I wanted to bring one to your grandfather in exchange for his help overseeing our training."

"Pilar was at Zach's house yesterday? What was she helping you with?" Bear asked.

"I would rather not say," Ruth answered.

"Is she still ignoring Zach?" he asked, not detoured by Ruth's unwillingness to answer his first question.

"She is not ignoring him," Ruth said. "But she is not actively interacting with him either."

"I'm glad," Bear said, unfolding his arms. "She has waited for Zach to make up his mind for far too long. She needs to move on. Maybe she'll meet someone at the bazaar."

Ruth said nothing. She glanced up at him, wondering why he seemed to be procrastinating. Suddenly, she realized that he looked nervous. "Is there something that you want to tell me?"

Bear looked away from her direct eye contact. "How did the fabric turn out that I gave you?" Bear asked.

"I like it," Ruth said, thinking. "Zach said that I will be showing you how to use the LPS today. And he said that you were giving us two more bolts of fabric."

"Yes," Bear said. "That was the deal for the LPS."

"Would you mind if I picked out the fabric?" Ruth asked.

"That would be fine," Bear said.

"Zach also said that I would be explaining some things in the *Bible* for you. And I brought some of my writings and some of Pastor Tom's to go over with you," Ruth said. She was trying to figure out what Bear was not saying. He was anxious about something, but he obviously hadn't discussed it yet.

"Are you ready to train me?" she finally asked.

"I have a question," he said quickly.

Ruth waited.

"Why did you write that history of my family?" he finally asked.

"The Ka'to history stops at the Second Civil War, so I finished it," she said. Ruth had hoped that Bear wouldn't even have read the book. She wrote it so quickly without analyzing her motives and gave it to Bear's grandfather on impulse.

"But I looked for it at the Ka'to archives, and it is not there," he said.

"I did not publish it," Ruth said.

"What could you possibly gain from writing it then?" he asked.

"I did not write for any purpose other than to finish the story of the Ka'to Indians."

"But you didn't finish anything," Bear said, allowing his frustrations to show. "It feels like you placed the entire Ka'to Nation on my shoulders."

Ruth stood quietly for a moment, trying to discern the root of Bear's frustration. "I did not intend to make you feel responsible for the Ka'to family that you have left and the Ka'to People as a whole. I apologize. I wrote from a limited perspective."

"I don't want an apology from you," Bear said. "It is difficult to see your life written out on paper, but I can handle it. But what I don't understand is why you wrote it."

"I told you that I wrote it to complete the history of the Ka'to Indians," Ruth said, feeling her own heart start to quicken its pace.

"If that was your only reason, you would have published it," Bear said. "Since you kept the book personal, you need a personal reason to write it. Did you write it for my grandfather?"

Ruth stared into Bear's eyes. His structured face kept the age lines around his eyes from being too linear. Their ebony color made distinguishing his pupils impossible. "I simply wrote it. I didn't analyze why," she finally admitted.

"You wrote it differently," he said.

"What do you mean?" Ruth asked. Now she felt like her life was on the spotlight. She should have deleted it the instant she wrote it.

"I've tried to read your other writings, and they are difficult for me to understand. But I read the book about my family, and I can understand it. Why did you write it like that? Is that why you won't publish it?" he asked.

Ruth said nothing, so he continued. "I know my reading level is not like Zach's. I know that books are not my strength. I don't know how you did it, but you wrote this book on my level, and I want to know why."

Ruth felt her cheeks heat up in the crisp, cool day. She looked away from Bear's stare. "I don't know why I did it."

"Ruth, I know you wrote that book for me, but I don't understand why," he finally said. "I may not be book smart like Zach, but I can read people, and I can see their motives always before me. You are harder to read than anyone I've ever met, but I can still sense things in you. Do you want something from me? Is there something you want in return?"

"Does that mean you liked it?" Ruth asked.

Bear looked at his grandfather. "It helped me see better," he admitted. "I've been stuck in this house for a long time, and I've lost direction. When I read your book, I had better eyes to see what God is doing. I'm grateful for that."

"Can I say that I wrote it because God told me?" Ruth asked.

"Is that the truth?" Bear asked.

Ruth looked at the ground. "No, I didn't ask God specifically. But I felt His pleasure when I wrote it. I always feel His pleasure when I write."

"Then tell me why you wrote it, Ruth. I want to train you, but we need to lay everything out on the table. I will be too distracted with second-guessing myself, and I won't do it."

"You fascinate me," she finally blurted, looking back at him.

Bear nodded his head. "Why? Because of my Ka'to heritage?"

"Yes," she admitted. "Your Native American heritage fascinates me. But it is more than that."

"What?" he asked, folding his arms again, waiting for her reply. "You had to do a lot of research about me in order to write what you did. You knew my fights. You knew my Shaman routine. You knew about my father and the many women in my life and how I treated them. Why did you add all of that to the book?"

"Because I wanted you to know that I understand," Ruth said, unable to communicate feelings that she barely understood herself.

"Understand what?" Bear asked. "That I lived like a heathen?"

"No," Ruth said. "I understand what it feels like to walk away from everything." She didn't know how else to describe what she was thinking.

"How can you possibly understand how that feels?" Bear asked.

"Because I walked away from more," she answered.

Bear looked at her. "Who are you?"

"I am a seamstress and Zach's sister," Ruth said, looking down at the ground. She wouldn't say anymore.

Bear put his hands on his hips. He waited for Ruth to continue talking, but she didn't. "Do you think it is fair for you to know more about my life than I know about yours?" he asked.

Ruth looked back at him. "You know as much as you wanted to know," she answered.

Bear was about to say something, but his words were cut off. "That is enough, *Ne'aw-ze*," his grandfather said.

Bear looked at his grandfather. "I will let you interrupt our talk, *Aha-enah*, but don't interrupt my training."

"Then get on with it," the grandfather retorted.

Bear held out his right hand. "Make a fist and punch my hand."

"What?" Ruth asked.

Bear grabbed her hand and formed it into a ball. "Now, hit my hand with all your strength."

Ruth looked at Bear's hand and then at her fist. She brought it back and lunged it toward his open palm.

Bear's hand barely moved by her force.

"Your lack of strength will be your biggest weakness," he said. "I'm going to grab you, and I want you to try to get out of my arms."

Bear walked behind Ruth and put his arms tightly around her shoulders and across her chest. "Now try to get free."

Ruth froze in his embrace. Her mind stopped, and she couldn't force her body to react.

"Ruth, you need to fight me. The battle is lost if you can't respond to danger. Now move!" Bear said, firmly.

Ruth tried to wiggle free, but his grip was too tight. She could feel the pulse of his wrist on her arms, and the beat of his heart on her back. His face was next to hers, and his deep voice vibrated in her ears.

"Ruth, use your hands. Use your feet. Use your body. Try to get free. You are freezing up. You need to fight."

"I can't!" Ruth yelled. "You are holding me too tight. Let me go!"

"An attacker will not let you go, Ruth. He will hold on tighter. You must react. Fight me!"

Ruth started pushing her feet into the dirt, pressing against Bear's embrace, but he barely moved.

"You are too weak. You must do something else. Think! What can you do?" Bear asked.

Ruth started to cry out.

Bear instantly covered her mouth with his palm. "An attacker can easily silence you. Your voice will not save you. You are small and light. He will carry you away. You need to react before he does."

The tree line in Ruth's view began to spin out. She became lightheaded and she had a flashback to her Sleeper. She was stuck in the plastic chamber again about to have her Awakening. She couldn't do it again. She had to wake up. She began to kick and flail, but Bear only picked up her from the ground. She wiggled her face free from Bear's hand and took the meaty side of his thumb into her mouth. She bit as hard as she could and felt a spray of warmth across her face.

In an instant, her feet were back on the ground.

"Good! Good!" Bear said. "That is the only thing you can do. But instead of standing there, you must run. You will only have a few seconds before the attacker recovers, so run into the trees. Stay quiet. Don't yell out. Run as fast as you can and then hide. Stay hidden until morning. He will not pursue you for long."

Ruth stared at Bear. She was unable to talk for several seconds. She watched him untuck his shirt and cover his bleeding hand with the soft edge. When she felt her heart rate calm a bit, she slowly walked toward him.

"Did I bite you hard?" she asked.

His smile was broad, and Ruth was taken back by its sincerity. "You almost bit an entire chunk off," he said. "It's still hanging on by a quarter inch. Are you missing a tooth?"

"Yes, I'm missing one," she answered.

"Good thing," Bear said. "I think my skin can be sewn back on."

Ruth stood stunned. "You are happy?" she asked confused.

"What is a bite if you learn to save yourself?" he asked. "You don't have strength, Ruth. Even if I trained you every day for a year, you will never have the strength to push off an attacker. The only weapon you have is your teeth. But next time bite harder."

Bear's grandfather walked up to Ruth and handed her a small cloth. "You have blood on your face. You can use this to wipe it off. Here is some water too," he said, handing her a small jug. "You were like a mouse, but you rose up like a snake. Well done."

"Do you train your men to bite?" Ruth asked confused.

"Never," Bear said firmly. "But you are not a fighter. And a man who tries to attack you is a coward. He doesn't deserve proper fighting rules."

The aged man walked up to Bear and inspected his hand. "You will need a few stitches," he said.

Bear opened the cloth and looked at the bite. "You think you can do it?" he asked.

The grandfather shrugged. "I'm too old to work a needle and thread, but you have Ruth here. She can make it look new again." He patted Bear on the back and chuckled.

"Am I done with training?" Ruth asked.

Bear laughed. "Not even close. I still want to practice some basic self-defense moves with you and create a getaway plan, but at least I know that if someone attacked you today, you won't freeze up."

"I've been attacked three times in less than a year, and every time I was scared," she admitted.

"Do you know the area?" Bear asked. "Do you know how to get from here to Zach's house and to Levington Village?"

Ruth nodded. "I printed and studied a few maps."

"The maps may be of some good, but we should hike to both places. You need to get acquainted with the real terrain and not merely trust maps on paper. Tomorrow wear shoes that you can hike in. I'll take you to Pilar's house."

"I've never met Pilar's family," Ruth said. "And I would like to introduce myself to her dad, Levi. We have mutual friends."

"Training is done for today. Come into the house and sew me up, and I will ask you those questions from the *Bible*."

"*Aha-enah*, let me know if anyone comes," Bear said, as he continued to the house holding his bloodied hand.

"Yes, *Ne'aw-ze*," the grandfather said, grabbing his rusty shotgun. "I will let you know if I see anything."

Ruth followed Bear back to the house. She had never sewn skin before, but she was up for the challenge.

"That's ten stitches," Dr. Linton said after he put the last strip of medical tape over the gauze. "It's a wonder that that knife didn't sever your axillary artery."

"Thanks, Doc," Matt said, trying to button up his shirt.

"Just leave it alone. You can't go anywhere for a while anyway. You'll be on bed rest for a couple of days. You are lucky you are such a large man. It would take a knife 12 inches long to penetrate through your thick muscle," Dr. Linton said, patting Matt's uninjured pectoral muscle.

Matt chuckled but quickly stopped when he felt the pain radiate down his chest and arm.

"Best not to laugh too hard," Dr. Linton said. "Are you sure you don't want some pain pills?" Dr. Linton sewed Matt's knife wound without any anesthesia. Matt felt the pain, but he never yelled out.

"No, it really doesn't hurt much. I don't want to take anything that may compromise me. I want to stay aware of my surroundings," Matt said.

"Always on duty," Dr. Linton said. "That's why I like to live on the outskirts of the city. I want to know that when I leave the city limits, I am no longer anyone's doctor. I'm Michael—a man who likes to enjoy his peace and quiet."

"No one is ever off duty when part of Randall's team," Matt said, looking at Dr. Linton.

Dr. Linton brushed off his words. "Well, I'm glad I was still in the city. Otherwise, I would have missed sewing you up. I haven't done stitches since I left the Colonial hospital. So tell me what happened. Randall was too brief with his description. He is never good with the details."

"A man tried to attack Neil and I stopped him. Not much to tell," Matt said, reaching his good arm for the cup of water on the nightstand near his bed.

"Was he a Colonial?" Dr. Linton asked.

Matt shook his head slightly. "No, he was an Efficientist. He was young. Probably mid-twenties. He said nothing as he approached us. I wouldn't have seen it coming, but the light from the sun reflected off of his knife blade. Right when I saw it, I pushed Neil out of the way, and the man stabbed me. Randall intervened before he could take the knife back out."

"It's a good thing that the knife was left in. It kept you from bleeding too much until I could get to you," Dr. Linton said.

Matt smiled. "You seemed to enjoy pulling it out."

"Like I said, I haven't seen anything interesting since I started working for Neil Elder. It's nice to work on a trauma case again. Even if for one afternoon."

Matt said nothing for a while and watched as Dr. Linton packed up his bag.

"Are you sure you don't want me to leave you anything for the pain for sleep perhaps?" Dr. Linton asked.

"No, but thank you," Matt said.

"Well, if that is all, I'll be leaving now," Dr. Linton said, turning to go.

"Wait," Matt said. "I wanted to ask you something."

"Sure thing," Dr. Linton said, walking up to the side of the bed.

"Randall has me in charge of monitoring all the cars being driven by Neil Elder's team. About every few weeks, I check their tracking device."

"Just making sure no one decides to up and leave, I guess," Dr. Linton said, smiling.

"I check yours, as well," Matt added, quietly.

Dr. Linton's expression went cold. "I didn't know that I was being watched."

Matt nodded. "Everyone is being watched."

"Where is this conversation going?" Dr. Linton asked, setting down his bag.

Matt thought for a moment. "I know that you have been to the Colonies."

"Neil had me check up on a pharmaceutical plant a little while ago," Dr. Linton said, getting anxious. "Why?"

"The tracking device indicated that you drove several hundred miles past the pharmaceutical factory that you visited," Matt said and paused, watching Dr. Linton's expression.

When Dr. Linton said nothing, he continued. "I assume you were seeing an old patient or friend of yours from the Colonies. I know you mean well. And I trust that you're not up to anything. I want you to be more careful in the future. I like you. I think you're a good doctor. If you decide to make an additional stop, notify Randall, so there won't be any mistake of your intentions."

Dr. Linton kept eye contact with Matt. "It was an old friend from med-school. I didn't realize that all of my actions outside of my job for the World Government would have to be approved."

"I understand," Matt said. "I want you to be more careful in the future. We wouldn't want anyone getting hurt. But you have no need to worry now."

"Why is that?" Dr. Linton asked.

"There was a malfunction with the old tracking device in your car. As of a few days ago, I had to get rid of it and install a new one. So there's no harm done. I wanted to give you a heads-up for future reference. Thank you again for sewing me up. I think I'll rest my eyes now."

Dr. Linton watched Matt fold his dark arms across the creamed-colored sheets and close his eyes. He picked up his bag. He was about to turn to leave when he asked. "If there is anything I can do for you, just let me know."

Matt kept his eyes closed. "Stay off the radar."

Dr. Linton turned toward the door. "I can certainly do that."

CHAPTER TWENTY-NINE

R uth watched Bear as he washed his hands with a thick bar of soap and water from a nearby bucket. He then grabbed a bottle from one of the shelves in his kitchen. The kitchen was even less sophisticated than the kitchen at Zach's house. Bear had no refrigerator, a bucket for a sink, shelves lining the walls and a large multi-fuel oven. She had read about houses like these in the 1800s, and she felt like she jumped into one of the old photographs she had seen. She knew the Second Civil War had created a culture similar to long ago, but it was difficult to perceive from her LPS in her high-rise flat. Again, she was thankful that the first house she came to when she got to the Colonies was Esther and Deborah's farm. She prayed silently that the World Government would not discover them.

"Here," Bear said, sitting down next to Ruth at the table. "Pour this over the wound and then you can sew it up."

Ruth looked at the bottle on the table. "What is it?" she asked.

"It's whiskey. I won it at my last fight. Pour it on my thumb, but don't waste it. This is very valuable."

Ruth grabbed the glass bottle. "How do I open it?" she asked.

"Just pull the cork off," he said, not hiding his frustration.

"Look, you may be well versed in alcohol retrieval, but I'm not. You need to be more patient. I plan on being patient with you when I discuss the *Bible* and issues of faith," she said.

Bear looked at the table and exhaled a deep breath. "I know. You're right. My adrenaline is wearing out, and my hand is starting to throb."

Ruth uncorked the bottle and placed the cloth that Bear's grandfather had given her on the table. "Put your hand over the cloth," she instructed. She looked at the fold of skin. She could see his dermis. She lifted the skin and quickly let go. "I can see your subcutaneous tissue," she said.

"I know, Ruth. You bit hard. I'm glad you did, but now you need to fix it," Bear said, holding his right wrist with his left hand. "I won't be using my right hand for a while."

Ruth slowly poured out the amber liquid over his wound. Bear didn't say anything, but she could see the muscles in his arm tense. She opened the flap again with the tip of her finger and gently poured a little more. "I want to make sure that the inside is clean before I stitch it together," she said. "Do you have a needle and thread?"

"Don't you have one?" Bear asked, surprised.

"I wasn't anticipating sewing anything at your house. I didn't bring any of my supplies," Ruth said.

Bear quickly got up, holding his injured hand. "I know I have something in the storehouse. Wait one second," Bear said, walking out of the front door and leaving it open.

Ruth waited at the table. She realized that she didn't know if she still had blood on her cheeks, so she got up to look for the bathroom. She walked toward the only two doors she could see. She opened the first one and saw a mattress on the floor with a blanket. Shelves on the wall, which were used as some sort of dresser. There were printouts also hanging on the wall. From a distance, Ruth could tell they were of different fights that Bear had been in. She had seen several of the same ones when she researched him. There was a large chest by the mattress with a few fighting items on top, which she didn't recognize. Ruth saw no other doors. She left the room and opened the other door. This one also had a mattress and some shelves, but there was nothing on the walls. Again, there was no other door.

"What are you looking for?" Bear asked from the living room.

"I wanted to use your bathroom," she asked.

Bear smiled. "The bathroom is behind the house," he said, setting a large tin canister on the table.

"Why have you separated it?" she asked confused.

"Because it is an outhouse," he said back.

"You mean that you have no septic tank?" she asked.

"Unlike government housing, our water does not go down some drain and into a holding tank with all the other waste water. We have to get rid of our water the normal way—by dumping it. We have an outhouse when you have to go and we have the river when you need to wash."

Ruth could not hide her look of horror, and Bear couldn't hold back his laughter.

"Zach's Efficientist sister having to rough it out in the Colonies. I've been to some of those places in the city where you lived. A few Efficientists would ask me to come to their PR events—the Shaman performing his peyote song for the brains. They would provide me a place with running water, a refrigerator, an oven and all the prepackaged food and drinks that I could want. I only lasted a day in those shiny, cold apartments. I want the trees, the dirt and the hills. I would rather wash in the Trinity River than bathe in the hottest showers in all the world."

Ruth recovered from the shock and sat down at the table. "That's the difference between you and me," she said. "You could only last a day in a new environment, and I'm choosing to last a lifetime." She began searching through the metal canister for a needle.

Bear sat down next to her and put his hand back over the cloth. "You're still pampered in government housing. Let's see you last more than a day at my house."

Ruth ignored his words. "Is this all you have? This needle is larger than what I need."

"That's all there is. I don't sew much," Bear said. "Now, can you sew this hand up, so I can be done with it?"

Ruth held up the needle to thread it. And the size of the needle looked even bigger in Ruth's small hand.

"Wait a minute," Bear said. He uncorked the whiskey and took a large drink and wiped his mouth with his good hand. "If you are going to be sticking me with that thing, I better be relaxed."

"Aren't you used to pain?" she asked. "You've had so many broken bones that it was painful to write of them in your book. I listed ribs at least a dozen times."

Bear recorked the bottle. "It doesn't matter how many times you get hit, the pain is always the same—it hurts like hell."

It was Ruth's turn to laugh. "Zach never talks like that," she said.

"I don't judge him for talking like a preacher. And he doesn't judge me for talking like a fighter," Bear said.

Ruth thought for a moment. "You each have your own audience to reach," she said.

"What does that mean?" he asked.

"When you made your video sermons, who gave you the most feedback?" she asked.

"I trained two young men before Naomi's funeral. He and his friend are the ones that helped me finish her casket. The young man said that his father, Watchman, watches my videos and shares them with people. They are fighters."

"You also gave them to the people in Levington. What did they think?" she asked.

Bear looked at his hand. "Naomi always encouraged me. The people from town would say they liked them, but I could feel their pity. They would watch them only because I asked them to. They knew I had changed my life, so they wanted to be nice. The Shaman making sermons—what a joke."

"Doing God's will is never a joke," Ruth said. "Jeremiah had to carry a loincloth, which would be like underwear today, many miles to the Euphrates River. I'm sure people would make fun of him and pity the assignment that God had given him. But he did it anyway, and God used his obedience to teach something to the people who were rebelling against God."

"What was God teaching them?" Bear asked, intrigued by the story she told.

"The people were too sheltered in their blessings, and because they would not be used by the Lord, they were good for nothing."

Bear looked at Ruth and waited with unveiled anticipation.

"It is better to be a fool for the Lord than good for nothing, don't you agree?" Ruth asked.

"Yes, I do agree, and I see what you mean. I know I have read that story before, but I've never seen it like that."

"I'll tell you more stories, as I sew your hand. I think you will like King David. He reminds me a lot of you. He was a warrior, but he also sang."

"King David sang?" Bear asked.

"Yes, many of the Psalms are written by him. The Psalms were like songs to the Lord. He would play the harp and sing them. He had to manage an army made up of rebels and misfits. He needed to train these men, but most importantly lead by example. When I read his songs, I imagine that he is frustrated with being in charge, and he might have wanted to give up. Many of his Psalms were about wanting to quit, but in the last brief moment of his song, he would tell the Lord that he would trust in Him. Every day while he was hiding from King Saul, waiting in the caves for God's promises on his life to come true, he would have to encourage himself in the Lord. He couldn't expect anyone else to do it."

"How can I encourage myself in the Lord?" Bear asked.

"You read the *Bible* every day?" Ruth asked.

"Yes, I do, but so many times I don't understand what I read or how it can help me," he said.

"This may hurt a bit," Ruth said, pricking the meaty part of his thumb with the needle above the left corner of his wound.

Bear tightened his grip on his wrist. "It's okay. It's not so bad. Just talk as you sew."

"The *Bible* is alive and active, and the Holy Spirit wants to speak to you. He wants you to be encouraged. There are promises found in the *Bible,* and they are all yours, but you have to find them and claim them. So as you read, make a list of any promises that the Holy Spirit shows you. When you feel doubt come over you, say those promises over and over again."

"I think there is a promise that the Holy Spirit is trying to give to me. I've been reading it ever since I threw my HMS into the river. The passage comes to me. It's like it is chasing me wherever I go. I look through the Scriptures and there it is. But I don't understand what God is telling me," Bear said, watching as Ruth nimbly made each little stitch.

"What is the passage?" she asked.

"It's about King David. It says that h*e went out and came in*. I don't understand what that means."

Ruth broke the string with her teeth. "I am done. It should heal, but you will have a scar."

"I don't mind scars," Bear said, taking back his hand. "I have plenty of them. But this is my first one from a woman," he said, analyzing the small bite marks from Ruth's teeth.

Ruth felt heat flood her cheeks. "Where is your *Bible*?" she asked, getting out of her seat.

"It is in my room on the bed," Bear answered.

"You need to keep that wound clean or it will get infected. If you have to train in the dirt, cover it with a clean cloth. Wash your hands every chance you get." Ruth went to the bucket where the large bar of soap and jug of water stood. She washed her hands thoroughly and dried them on her pants. "May I go into your room?" she asked when she had finished.

"Go ahead," he said. "You already know everything about me."

Ruth went back into Bear's room and walked to the mattress on the floor. She noticed that he didn't use pillows and he only had a light sheet to keep him warm at night. At first she couldn't see a *Bible*, but then she saw a thick pile of tattered printouts. She picked them up and read the top page. It was the *Bible*. She flipped through some of the pages. There was no page numbers, and she noticed that some of the verses were out of order. She held the stack of paper and walked back to the living room.

"Is this your *Bible*?" she asked.

"Some of it," he answered. "I have the New Testament in another pile. I used to listen to the *Bible* on my HMS. I am better at hearing it than reading it. But one day I went to my HMS and it was gone. I had this printed out several years ago, but I didn't start reading it until I lost my HMS."

"Zach has an extra *Bible*. Why didn't you ask to use his?" Ruth asked.

"Isn't that the same thing? I don't need another *Bible* when I already have one," he answered.

"Tomorrow, I will bring you another *Bible*," Ruth said and sat back down at the table, setting the stack of papers in front of Bear.

"The passage you are thinking of is in 1 Samuel," she said, flipping through the pages. "Here it is. Read it to me."

"I would rather not read out loud," Bear said. His discomfort was obvious.

"I will read it since you are still in pain, but I expect you to read tomorrow," she said, turning the pages toward her. "*But all Israel and Judah loved David, for he went out and came in before them,*" she read. "This is chapter 18 verse 16."

"So what does that mean," Bear asked.

Ruth thought for a moment. She wanted to explain the principle without getting bogged down by too much detail. "It simply means that he was no longer a shepherd boy. The shepherds in that day spent days by themselves away from all the crowds. This was good for David. He learned to use a sling. He learned to play the harp or lyre, as it was called. He learned to care for his sheep. He probably even read the Scriptures that were available to him at the time. But now his time of isolation was over. He needed to spend time with people, gaining their trust and favor."

"So he needed to walk around with the people?" Bear asked. "But what does that mean for me?"

Ruth looked at Bear. His learning ability surprised her. In so many ways Bear seemed almost arrogant, but she sensed a humble spirit in him, wanting to learn. She no longer felt afraid of him. "It means that it is time for you to go and come before the people," she answered.

Zach drove through the bumpy land that led to Bear's house. He felt nervous, but he never felt so free. A noose had been constricting around him for many years, and the tension grew stronger as he worked in the factory. But not anymore. He was now on his own. He had no idea what he would do, and he had his sister depending on him, but he knew that he needed to depend on the Lord. He shook his head and laughed under his breath. All these years he thought he would have a *come-to-Jesus-moment* that would get him back on the right path. He never realized that his moment would come in gradual steps of letting go of the pain and embracing the calling God had for him. He was meant to preach. He felt it. He didn't care who listened or if he had an audience. He needed to talk about what the Holy Spirit was showing him.

He thought of his sister. Never would he have guessed that she would show up in his life and light a fire in him. Her writings are what helped him to see beyond his hurt and disappointment. She had a way of explaining faith that exposed any deception in his heart. Ruth had walked away from a life of fortune and fame and had fully embraced the idea of faith, which helped her to explain her faith in such a brilliant way. He knew many of the Colonials wouldn't understand her writing. She made allusions to literature, ideas and historical events that the unstudied would miss. Even he had to look up many of the parallels she packed into each paragraph of her writing. Each one would open up a world of ideas and meanings that brought the point she was making to life.

He enjoyed editing her work. She frequently left out articles and prepositions that he would insert back into her writing. She had written so often in T-variety that she almost always lapsed back into it. He had taken a course in the

Varieties at college, so much of the information he had learned was coming back to him. But, of course, he had to refresh his memory time and time again. He only hoped that he could change the voice of her writing without the relevancy of her words being altered. He needed the World Government to think that many people were writing these papers. They could handle one person—he knew too well what could happen when one person was singled out. His father had been burned up in flames at his church. However, the World Government could not so easily get rid of many people, and Zach needed everyone to believe that many voices were shouting out.

Zach knew that Pastor Tom was writing more. His writings were gaining more exposure with the Colonials. Zach patted the steering wheel unable to stop his smile from growing. The World Government was getting hits from two people—Tom and Ruth. Another Elite Efficientist, Li, was working with Pastor Tom, and now he was about to enter the scene. Zach knew that a move of God was about to unleash—all the pieces were falling into place.

Zach spotted Bear's house in the distance. He couldn't see anyone outside. As he slowed to a park, he finally saw Bear's grandfather on his tree stump near the river's edge. The old man loved to sit outside and watch the day rise and fall. Zach thought that he was probably spending his time reliving old memories. His mother had done that before she had passed away. Zach looked around his truck for something to give the old man. Pilar had started the trend of giving him something whenever she visited. Zach's mind centered on Pilar. She had been ignoring him. He understood why. He had mishandled their relationship for so long that she no longer trusted him. In fact, he no longer trusted himself. He had let fear seep deep into his heart—a fear of losing those he loved. He knew he loved her deeply, which is why he was so good at shutting her out. He had shut her out so long that he no longer knew if he could let her back in. He hoped that since he would no longer be at the factory, they could spend some time together, getting re-acquainted without fear constantly interfering.

He remembered two boxes of crackers that he had placed in the backseat of his truck before he left today. There were extras at the factory, and he was always on the lookout for food he could give Ruth. She wouldn't cook anything, so packaged food was all she ate. Zach knew that she needed to eat more meat. She was thin and her muscles had weakened since she had arrived almost two months ago. When she lived with Deborah and Esther, she worked in the garden and in the vineyard. Now, Ruth either sewed or wrote all day. She rarely got out of the house. And Deborah's cooking was notorious in the area, so he knew that Ruth had eaten very well when living on the farm. Now all she ate was packaged foods. That would all change, though. Zach would be home now, and he would make sure that she ate better and got out more.

Zach grabbed one of the boxes of crackers and got out of his truck. He headed to Bear's grandfather. As he got closer, he noticed the old man's eyes were closed. But when the grass crunching under his feet got within earshot of the old man, his eyes flew open and he grabbed his rusted shotgun. Zach threw up his arms.

"It's Zach," he said.

The old man stared at Zach for several seconds and then noticed the box in his hands. "It took you so long to get out of your truck that I forgot you were there. Is that for me?" he asked.

Zach smiled. "Yes sir," he said and handed him the box. "They are only crackers, but they'll fill the belly up nicely."

"Thank you for these," the old man said and ripped open the top. He placed one of the crackers in his mouth. "These are good. If you come across more, I will take them."

Zach laughed. "Okay, if I find more, I will make sure to give them to you."

Bear's grandfather placed another cracker in his mouth. "They are inside," he said.

"Did they train?" Zach asked.

"Yes," the old man said.

"How did she do?" Zach asked. He wanted to gain the grandfather's perspective. Ruth had said that she would be asking him to stay while they trained. Zach wondered why he hadn't of thought of that first. It made him feel much better knowing that a third party would be there.

"At first fear stopped Ruth from fighting, but then something happened in her and rose up like a snake," the grandfather said, smiling.

"Did Ruth bite Bear?" Zach asked, struggling to capture the image in his mind.

"She almost bit a chunk right out of him. She did well. We were both proud of her," the old man said.

"Was Bear upset?" Zach asked.

"Of course not!" the old man snapped. "She protected herself. Isn't that why he is training her?"

Zach understood that fighters got hurt a lot, but to be happy about it seemed strange. The old man must have seen Zach's look of confusion, so he explained further.

"If you are teaching your son to get honey from a hive, does it matter if you get stung if he succeeds? The sweetness of the honey for your son is worth the sting of the bee."

Zach nodded. "I'm glad I asked Bear to train her. How long have they been inside?"

Bear's grandfather looked up at the sun. "I would say several hours now."

Zach felt a twinge in his stomach. "What are they doing?"

The old man looked at Zach. "Ruth is speaking to Bear, and he is listening to her."

"Well, I best go check on them. I'm sure she's hungry," Zach said.

"You will feel it when you enter the house," the old man said and put another cracker in his mouth.

"What will I feel?" Zach asked.

"You will see," the old man said in between bites.

CHAPTER THIRTY

Zach walked toward Bear's house back up the hill. He was glad he visited Bear's grandfather first. Maybe Pilar knew what she was doing when she brought him treats whenever she came by. Bear was ruled by his emotions, and talking to the aged man helped Zach prepare the correct mindset when approaching him. This was especially important since Zach was about to ask Bear if he and Ruth could move in with him until he was able to figure out what he was going to do next.

Zach passed the storehouse. He noticed that the locks were not secure and the door was slightly opened. Zach knew Bear was protective of his commodities. Zach stopped and quickly shut the door and secured all the locks. He couldn't believe that Bear had left his storehouse unlocked and opened. Bear trusted no one—not even his own grandfather.

When Zach made it to the front door, he knocked lightly and waited. After a few seconds, he cracked the door open. He could hear Ruth's voice talking quietly. She was discussing the time the Apostle Paul preached to the Athenians. Zach recognized the energy in Ruth's voice. Whenever she spoke about things in the *Bible*, her pitch elevated slightly, and she spoke faster than usual. Zach pushed the door even further open. Bear's eyes were wide, staring into the direction of Ruth's face. But Zach knew that Bear had images in his mind, painted by the words Ruth spoke.

Zach felt something turn in his gut. He knew instantly it was jealousy. He reprimanded himself. He couldn't hide Ruth forever. He wished that the factory hadn't taken so much of his time. There was nothing he could do about it now. Their life in government housing was over. Zach noticed the opened bottle of whiskey on the table.

"Isn't it a little early for a drink?" he finally asked, interrupting Ruth's narrative.

Bear blinked. "Are you off work already?"

"The sun is headed west," Zach said. He looked at Ruth. "Are you hungry? I brought you some crackers. They can tide you over until we get home."

Bear got up. "Why don't you both stay for dinner? I have some beans and rice and some dried deer meat."

Zach was surprised by Bear's hospitality. "Are you sure, Bear? I didn't bring anything besides the crackers. I don't have anything to offer."

Bear crossed his arms. "Does everyone think I'm unable to accept and give a gift?"

"No, it's only that you like a fair deal," Zach said uncomfortably. Zach knew instantly that something was different about Bear. His entire house felt changed somehow.

"Look, Naomi and your father always fed me when I needed a meal. They were always there for me when my mom would get really sick. It's time I repay their kindness."

Zach stared at Bear unable to decipher if he was being genuine or if alcohol had affected his judgment. "How much have you been drinking?"

Bear looked at the bottle of whiskey on the table and began to laugh. "I had one drink a few hours ago to ease the pain of the stitches, Zach. Believe me, I'm in my right mind. It would take a lot more than a drink to make me so generous."

Zach smiled pleased at his friend's mood. He realized that he had forgotten the free-spirited man Bear once was. "It seems a cloud has lifted from you, my friend."

"Yes, it has! Ruth has explained some things to me about the *Bible*, and I see now how they fit in my life. I no longer want to be a hawk, soaring alone above the village. I will be as the bat, coming and going before the people!"

Zach waited for an explanation, but Bear stood staring at him with a boyish smile on his face. "I have no idea what you're talking about, Bear, but if that bat has made you like this, then I'm happy for you."

"Bear is pulling together something I have discussed with him and something his grandfather told him," Ruth said, getting up. "The Holy Spirit is showing Bear a few things, and we were discussing it. Bear has learned a lot today. We also discovered that he's very good with oral learning and oration."

"Oration?" Zach asked.

"You remember my Shaman routine when I would tell stories of my old fights to the crowds?" Bear asked.

Zach nodded his head. Bear would sing in his deep voice and a hush would pass over the crowd. Then he would go into the details of his previous fights and every ear would listen to each word. Bear was excellent at drawing the crowd into stories.

"All this time I've been trying to preach like your father did. I made video sermons like a teacher, and I was never good at it. But I'm not a teacher. I am a storyteller. And I don't like talking on videos because I can't see the reaction of who I'm talking to. I need to see each person's face and hear their whispers. I don't like large crowds that I can't interact with. I like just a handful of people—a dozen at most that I can sit down with. That is why I am a bat. I need to be pliable like Paul, letting the wind shape me into what I need to be!"

Zach couldn't help smiling. "You look young, my friend. If it weren't for the silver strands, running through your black hair, I would think you were a kid again."

"I feel free again!" Bear added. "Your sister has helped me!"

"Well, I heard that she bit you like a snake," Zach added, nodding his head towards the bandage around Bear's hand. "Is it okay?"

"It's fine. She froze up at first, but she found the strength to fight back," Bear said, looking at the bandage. "It throbs a bit, but at least she was able to sew up the hole she made."

Zach nodded his head and smiled, but he sensed that Bear was withholding something. He would have to ask him later. "Did you know that you left your storehouse wide open?"

Bear's shoulders became rigid. "I did?"

"I went ahead and locked it for you. It didn't look like anyone got in. Your grandfather would have fired his shotgun if he saw anyone."

"I was getting a needle and thread. I was rushing and forgot to relock the door. Thank you for securing the locks for me. Would you mind helping me get the food for our dinner?" Bear asked Zach.

Zach could read Bear's intentions. He knew that he wanted to talk privately with him. This was good for Zach because he needed to discuss the issue of living with him for a while. Zach normally would be worried about what Bear would say, but somehow he knew that God was going to take care of everything.

"Ruth, would you ask my grandfather to boil some water from the river? I'm sure he's already started the fire for the evening."

"Yes, that would be good. I want to ask him about starting fires," Ruth said, turning and walking toward the door.

"Ruth," Zach said. "You have blood on your shirt."

Zach could see Ruth blush.

Ruth looked down. "I didn't know," she said. "I will clean it when we get home."

Zach watched his sister walk through the door. Unlike Bear, Ruth was almost impossible to read. She showed sadness when their mom died and happiness when she finished a sewing project. Other times, though, he hardly knew what she was thinking or feeling. He never took it personally, though. He had a lot of experience with Efficientists, and the higher the rank, the harder to read.

Zach turned his attention back to Bear. "Man, it's good to have the old Bear back. I didn't realize how much you had changed these past few years until now."

Bear nodded. "Ruth is very wise. She is like a young girl with an old mind," Bear said.

"She's not a girl, Bear. She's almost your age," Zach said.

Bear started making his way to the door. "I saw it today," he said.

228

Zach started to follow Bear and stopped. "What did you see?"

Bear turned around. "Ruth pulled her hair behind her ears, and I saw some gray in between the red."

Zach nodded. "I saw that too. Don't say anything. Although she doesn't show it, I think she is particular about her looks."

"I noticed that she had makeup on today. Not much, but enough to make her appear...different," Bear said and continued outside.

"I think Pilar has been helping her," Zach said, following Bear into the open air. The day was turning to evening and the temperature was getting cooler. He remembered seeing Ruth making coats with some of the fabric she had received from Bear. He hoped that one of them was for her.

"When I first met her she looked plain, but now there is something about her that feels familiar somehow."

Zach said nothing. Up till now, Bear had asked very few questions about Ruth. He hadn't told anyone that she was Eve Pallue. Pilar and Bear had been content with knowing she was an Efficientist and nothing more. He knew they were unclear about the ranking systems of the World Government, so he never mentioned it. He hoped the subject would never come up, but he realized that someday they would start asking more questions. He wondered if that was another reason why he had been shielding Ruth from others.

When Bear got to the doors, he began unlocking the locks. He didn't bother blocking the view. Bear opened the door and walked in and turned around. "I wanted to ask you something about Ruth."

Zach masked the tension he felt. "What's your question?" he asked as casually as he could.

"I've been to the city, and I've talked with Efficientists whenever they've invited me to their PR events. They all seem the same at first, but once you get to know them, there were certain differences," he began. "I remember a few of them telling me about the differences, and it was about how much

229

they produced or how much they knew or something like that. There was this system to rank them that you told me about," Bear said, trying to recall the conversation in his mind.

Zach jumped in, hoping to turn the conversation. "Yes, the higher ranks produce more and they are less social, is that it?"

"Yes, that's it!" Bear said.

"And you're thinking that my sister had a higher rank?" Zach asked.

"Yes, that is my question. When I touched her, she froze up. It's almost like she doesn't know how to act. I've trained women before, and all of them will kick at me or try to wiggle free. But she did nothing for a long while—like she didn't know how to react. Finally, she fought back and bit me," he said.

Zach shook his head. "When the man attacked her at the gas station she kicked and pushed at him. She even bit his hand, like she did you. Although, I don't remember any blood. She did not bite him hard enough," Zach said, trying to remember.

"Then why does she freeze up with me?" Bear said, looking confused. "Do I scare her?"

Zach thought for a moment. "What did she put in that book she wrote about the Ka'to Indians?" he asked.

Bear thought. "She wrote about my family during the Second Civil War and everything that happened up to now."

"Did she write about you?" Zach asked.

Bear nodded. "She knew everything about me. Things that I've forgotten, she knew. It was like reading my entire life in a book. There was stuff in there she could have only heard from you or Naomi and stuff that she had to get on the HMS. It was like she sewed all this information together," he said.

"She's good at doing that. Did you ask her why she wrote it?" Zach asked.

"She said that I fascinate her," Bear said.

Zach looked at Bear. He didn't want to go further into this conversation until he talked to Ruth. "I think maybe since she researched so much about you that it's making her react differently. It's easy to fight a stranger, but harder to fight someone you know."

Bear nodded. "You're probably right. I'm glad to know. I was going to say something else."

"What were you going to say?" Zach asked.

Bear wavered on answering. "I was going to say that her reactions are much like a girl—not a woman in her early thirties."

Zach looked at the floor for a minute, gathering his thoughts. "I'm going to be honest with you. Ruth was a very high-ranking Efficientist, so she will be different than what your common sense tells you. She looks young because she never went outside. She is very smart because she studied all of her life. She doesn't interact well with people because she wasn't around a lot of people growing up. Many of the Efficientists were a little like her. You may never understand her because you don't know much about Efficiency."

"It would be easy to get on the LPS you gave me and do some research. It won't be hard to find the information that I need, so I can understand her." Bear said, defensively. "I never researched *Life Efficiency* before because I never found it necessary."

"I don't mean to offend you," Zach said, feeling tense. "There's no need to do a bunch of useless research about Efficiency. The system is changing anyway, since *Life Plethoricity* was created."

Bear only looked at Zach.

"It doesn't matter now. She's not an Efficientist anymore. She lives here with us," Zach finished.

"Why do I feel that you are keeping something from me, Zach?" Bear said, crossing his arms. "There's something about your sister that you are not telling me."

Zach looked at his friend. He didn't want Bear to find out that Ruth was Eve Pallue until he got to know her as Ruth first. He didn't understand Ruth's reaction toward Bear, but he hoped it was fleeting. He couldn't think of two people more different than Ruth and Bear. Even he and Pilar were more matched together with their vast array of differences. "You know that I've prayed for my sister all my life and to have her home is a miracle. I'm not trying to deceive you, Bear. But I will protect her until I feel that she is safe," Zach said.

Bear put his hands on his hips and nodded. "You are doing the right thing. I apologize. She has left her place at the World Government, and we need to be cautious. I will respect your wishes."

Zach put his hand on Bear's shoulder. "Thank you, my friend."

They paused for a brief moment, and Zach took back his hand.

"Speaking of the World Government, I have a favor to ask you," Zach said.

Bear looked at his friend. "What is it that you need?"

"As of today, I will no longer be working for the factory. Ruth and I will need a place to stay for a while. Can we stay here until we make other arrangements?"

"Why did you quit? Are you going to start preaching again?" Bear asked.

"Yes," Zach said.

Bear thought for a moment. "Naomi would be pleased. You both can stay with me for a few weeks until you figure things out," Bear said.

"Will you help me to move tomorrow morning? We will stay home one more night and get everything packed up," Zach said. "If we use both of our trucks, we can take everything in a few trips."

"What will you do with your extra furniture?" Bear asked.

Zach crossed his arms. Bear's practical side had returned. "I was thinking about giving some of it to Javier and Reyna as a wedding present, but I want to refinish the wood on the table and one of the beds first. I was hoping I could use some of your tools."

"I will help you with the project. I'm better at working wood than you," Bear said.

232

"Good," Zach said. "The furniture can be from both of us."

"And Naomi too, since the furniture was hers," Bear said.

Zach smiled. "I'm looking forward to focusing on preaching again. It's funny. The very thing I've been running from is now the very thing I'm running to."

"Now it's your turn to be the hawk," Bear said. "I am no good at it."

"I still have no clue what you're talking about, but a hawk sounds good to me," Zach said. "Now let's get this dinner going. I'm starving."

CHAPTER THIRTY-ONE

Ruth looked at the piles of clothing that she had been working on. She hadn't realized how much she had accomplished until seeing her items stacked up together. Thanks to Bear's gift of fabric, she had plenty to sell at the bazaar coming up shortly. She scanned the room. Everything she owned was placed on her mother's old bed. It didn't seem like much. She eyed the small bag that she had constructed out of fabric pieces. In it was the makeup Pilar had given her, her last pearl, the keycard from the World Bank and her *Bible* from Deborah. She had her blanket from Esther folded next to it.

She had her sewing machine and thread wheel against the wall. She would definitely be taking those. She also had a few items from her mother, including a few boxes of photos. Ruth liked looking through them. Although she never met Austin Daniels, he seemed like a nice man. He took her mother in when she was destitute and for that Ruth would always be grateful to him.

Ruth fingered the single pearl necklace around her neck that Cindy had made her. It gave her comfort that her mother was wearing the same necklace even as she rested under the earth. Ruth's mind went to Bear, singing at her mother's funeral. She knew moving in with him would be difficult. Zach and Bear were both strong personalities, even though they were vastly different. Ruth was glad Bear's grandfather would be there. Many times she went to him for peace and quiet. He had no worries to deal with. He simply lived in the moment. Ruth liked that about him.

But Ruth knew that moving in with Bear would be difficult for other reasons. She realized that she needed to let go of whatever feelings she had for him. She could sense his ambiguity towards her. She felt foolish for writing that book about his family's life. She had confessed that she was intrigued by him, but she knew there was no attraction on his part. At least now, he saw her as a teacher and not merely a liability. She had to admit her pride had taken a blow. Never in her life had someone treated her with so much disinterest. She hadn't realized how accustomed she had become with people's biases towards her as an Elite Efficientist and daughter of Arthur Pallue. And when she moved to the Colonies, Deborah and Esther had treated her like a special daughter.

"Knock, knock," a voice came from the door.

Ruth turned around and saw Pilar standing in the doorway. "Come in, Pilar. I'm glad you are here."

"I came from Bear's house. He told me what was going on. Zach was there too. They were moving some of your stuff into Bear's house," Pilar said. "I wanted to pick up my sister's dress, so you wouldn't have to move it. I don't want to burden you with keeping it safe. I have another home for it until the wedding."

"Good, I was worried about it. I can keep it clean at this house, but Bear's house is unkempt," Ruth said, trying to find the right words without sounding condescending.

"He definitely has a bachelor's pad out there by the river. I don't know how you're going to do it," Pilar said, honestly. "He lives much the way we do, except more rural. Our bathroom is attached to the house. Bear doesn't even have proper flooring in his house."

"I've spent the last year adjusting. With every move God never gave me more than I could handle," Ruth said.

"You know, you are welcome to stay with us," Pilar said. "You would have to sleep with me in my room, but I promise it is clean."

Ruth shook her head. "Thank you for offering. Deborah and Esther have also offered for me to move back with them. In fact, I think they may have begged me. I miss them a lot. And their home is so tempting for me. It has most of the comforts that I grew up with. But I feel like I need to stay with Zach for now."

"My father told me about the sisters. He lived with them for several weeks when he was a young man. He said that their relationship with the Lord was so real and he wanted that same thing, so he prayed to know God. That's when his life changed," Pilar said. "We invited them to Reyna's wedding. We sent word with a friend who was heading to Pastor Tom's trading center. We invited Tom and his family, as well. That Trinity Trading Center is becoming well known in these parts."

"I speak with Deborah and Esther frequently on the HMS. I'll message them an invite, as well," Ruth said. "It will be nice to see them again. They don't live so far away."

"Are you going to miss government housing?" Pilar asked. "You have to leave the HMS here. How will you write?"

"Zach gave Bear an old LPS that he found at the factory. We will be using that one. Although, we won't be able to use it often. If people from the World Government find its signature being used in a Colony, they will become suspicious," Ruth said.

Pilar scanned the room, trying to buy time to gather her thoughts. "I've read a few of the articles that you have written. I learned a lot, but I must be honest. Much of what you wrote I couldn't understand."

"My main audience is Efficientists. I'm writing about faith in a way most of them would understand," Ruth said. "Pastor Tom has been writing also, and most of what he shares can be understood by Colonials."

Pilar leaned against the large, solid dresser. Her long height allowed her to rest her elbows on the flat surface. "I read a few of his too. Yes, his are easier to understand. I was just wondering," Pilar said. "I remember there being a ranking system of Efficientists. I used to follow their fashion trends a lot when I was younger. I had a friend who lived in government housing, so we would get on her HMS and look at all the PR events. Did you go to some of the PR events?"

Ruth sat on the edge of the bed. "Yes, I went to some of them."

"Were they as glamorous as they seemed?" Pilar asked.

Ruth stared at her friend. "Do you remember what you told me about the packaged food the World Government produces?"

Pilar thought back. "You mean about how horrible it tastes?"

"Yes, you said that the packaging looks amazing, but when you open it, the food tastes horrible, like it is fake food."

Pilar nodded. "I don't know how you and Zach can eat it."

"I'm used to it, but you are right. When I lived on the farm in Trinity, Deborah cooked my meals. There was no comparison. Her food tasted more alive than the packaged food I grew up on."

Pilar nodded her head.

"That is the PR event. They look nice on the outside, but the entire thing is fake. We are all merely playing a role to keep public interest high."

Pilar thought for a moment. "That's what I was wondering. Still it would be nice to have all those cameras taking your picture and all those people writing about you."

Pilar left the dresser and began looking at the piles of clothes on the bed. "Do you think I saw you in some of the PR events?" she asked.

Ruth said nothing for a moment. "You might have."

"Oh well. I have my sister's wedding to look forward to. I might not be getting married, but I can still shine."

"Are you sad about Zach?" Ruth asked.

Pilar sat on the bed next to Ruth. "I feel like I wasted my life waiting for him. I've waited and prayed, but he seems more distant than ever."

"Love and grief have hurt him greatly," Ruth said.

"I know," Pilar said.

"He feels deeply. He's different from you and me. You have to give him time," Ruth said.

"I've given him five years," Pilar said.

"Can I suggest something to you?" Ruth asked.

Pilar tensed. "I've been given a lot of advice on how to deal with Zach. Now I see him making all these changes that I asked him to make a long time ago, but I'm not a part of them. He's leaving the World Government, and Bear told me he would start preaching again. I'm furious that he's pushed me off to the sidelines."

Ruth held her breath for a moment, considering her words. "You think you are letting him go by ignoring him, but you are not. You are still trying to be in control."

"What do you mean?" Pilar asked.

"You really need to let go of him," Ruth said. "That is my suggestion to you."

Tears began to stream down Pilar's cheeks. "But God has promised me happiness in marriage," she whispered.

"I believe you. That's why you need to let him go. We all must watch our dreams die in order to see them resurrected again."

Pilar covered her face with her hands and wept. Ruth was still uncomfortable with offering touch, but she knew from experience how necessary it was. Her mother had held her when she cried with sorrow. And Deborah and Esther had always petted and held her. Ruth put her arm around Pilar's shoulders and drew her close.

"I'm okay," Pilar said after a while. "Thank you for helping me. I'm ready to let go."

Ruth got up from the bed. "Here is a handkerchief. I made many of them with scraps from my sewing. You can have it. Your makeup is starting to smear."

"I love wearing makeup, but I hate crying in it," Pilar said with a smile. "I don't want to keep you. I know you are trying to get everything packed up before Bear and Zach return."

"Before you leave I wanted to give you something. You have spent hours helping me learn how to apply the makeup you gave me and you trimmed my hair to make it even."

"Girl, I don't know how you let yourself walk around with that haircut. Whoever did it needs to find a new trade."

Ruth smiled. The last haircut she had was when Ada Armel shaved her head. "I appreciate you fixing it for me. I didn't notice until my hair started getting longer. And thank you for pointing out my grey hairs. I didn't notice those either."

Pilar laughed. "I was so surprised to see them. Your face looks so young that the grey shocked me. You have been genetically blessed with a young face, but our age always catches up on us somehow."

Ruth leaned over the bed and grabbed a small pile. "I made this for you," she said, handing Pilar the stack.

"What is it?" Pilar asked, unfolding the first item.

"That is a blouse, skirt and jacket set," Ruth said. She knew the size was right, but she didn't know whether Pilar would like it or not. Pilar liked her clothes form-fitting to show her curvy figure. Ruth only hoped that this would appeal to her.

Pilar said nothing as she examined the material. "I love it!" she finally said. "I will wear this at Reyna's wedding. It is gorgeous!"

"I hoped you would like it. There's green in this fabric that matches the color of your eyes, so I knew that I wanted it for your blouse."

"It's perfect, Ruth. Thank you so much. And thank you for your words. You are right. It is time to let go and give God control."

Pilar leaned down and gave Ruth a hug. "I thank God for you," she said. "Now, I better leave before Bear and your brother get back. I don't want them to see me with my makeup smeared and my eyes all red."

"I put your sister's wedding dress over there," Ruth said pointing to the closet. "I asked Zach to leave the box he brought home from the factory in the living room. You can put the dress in there and hang it up right away, so it doesn't wrinkle."

"Thank you, Ruth. I'll do that," Pilar said.

Ruth hesitated. "Before you leave, Pilar. I have a question for you."

"Ask me anything, Ruth," Pilar said, turning to her friend.

"When you first met Zach, how did you know you loved him?" Ruth asked, feeling her cheeks redden.

Pilar stared at Ruth. "Why do you ask?"

Ruth looked down at the floor. "It's only that I've never been in love before, and I'm curious how it feels."

Pilar put a hand under Ruth's chin and drew her head up. "If I didn't know any better, I would say that you are smitten with someone. But I do know better and you've only been around a handful of people since you've been here. You like Bear, don't you?"

Ruth shrugged her shoulders. "I don't know what I'm feeling," she said, honestly. "All I know is that what I'm feeling is different and new, and I don't know how to handle myself."

Pilar dropped her hand and placed it on her hip and shook her head. "Girl, you are in deep trouble. You think you don't know how to handle yourself now, but wait until you move in with that man."

"Zach will be there and Bear's grandfather. I should be fine. I'll sew and write a lot," Ruth said.

"Does he suspect anything?" Pilar asked.

Ruth shook her head. "He sees me as Zach's sister and a teacher and nothing more."

"That's because you give him nothing to look at," Pilar said, waving her arms toward Ruth.

"You are a beautiful woman. And I know you have a figure under all those clothes you wear," Pilar said, looking at Ruth's wardrobe.

"It's wintertime. I'm cold. Although I would love to wear one of my summer dresses, I can't. I would freeze to death," Ruth said.

"I'll be honest with you. Bear is used to women throwing themselves on him. And he's been out of the dating game for a long time, locked up in that house of his and training all those young guys. Unless you wave some sort of flag and scream to him that you are interested, he will not notice."

Ruth crossed her arms. "I am not one of those women. I will not be throwing myself on any man."

240

"Do I detect a little pride in Miss Perfect?" Pilar laughed. "It's good to know that you have your flaws."

"It was easy to feel perfect when I was an Efficientist because I was always alone. But the more I am around people, the more my flaws show," Ruth said, seriously.

"Leave it to people to bring out the worst in us," Pilar said. "But at least seeing the worst will help us to be better in the end. Maybe that's what Zach and I are doing. We are bringing out the worst in each other now, so we can be better later on."

Ruth watched Pilar's face. She could tell she was thinking.

"Anyway, you don't have to throw yourself at Bear, but you do need to leave him a trail to follow. He is good at tracking, but he needs a few hints to get him going."

"I'm not good at doing any of that," Ruth said.

"Now, come on, Ruth. Don't play like you don't know how to work a man," Pilar said. "You look young, but those grey hairs tell the truth. You were an Efficientist. They are notorious for loose relationships."

Ruth shook her head. "All my life I always worked. I never had time for relationships—not even loose ones."

Pilar put her hands on Ruth's shoulders. "Are you telling me that you've never been with a man?"

Ruth shook her head. "A man kissed me once, but he turned out to be a liar." She thought of Randall. She wanted to say more to her friend—to share some of her burden—but the events seemed strange and distant now, and she didn't want to scare Pilar.

Pilar laughed. "And all this time I pitied myself for being the oldest virgin in the village."

"I would appreciate it if you did not laugh at me," Ruth said.

"I'm sorry, Ruth. I'm not laughing at you. I'm laughing at myself for throwing such a pity party for so many years. No matter how bad we have it, there is always someone who has it worse."

"That doesn't make me feel any better," Ruth said.

"I'll be honest with you. I have no idea how you and Bear will figure things out, but if it is meant to be, it will happen," Pilar said.

"Now you sound like me giving you advice about Zach," Ruth said.

"I guess you're right. It's easier to see the answers when looking at someone else's life. It's harder when your own emotions are involved. Does your brother know?" Pilar asked.

"He suspects something. I wrote a book about the Ka'to Indians after the Second Civil War. I saw him reading it the other night. He must have copied it from our HMS and printed it out," Ruth said.

"Why would that make him think you like Bear?" Pilar asked.

"Because the entire book was about Bear's lineage and life," Ruth said.

Pilar looked at Ruth for a moment, and Ruth fidgeted under her stare.

"What made you attracted to him?" Pilar finally asked.

"I saw him singing at my mother's funeral," Ruth said.

"He's a beautiful singer," Pilar said. "But that's not enough to cause the heart to stir, is it?"

Ruth looked at Pilar. "He was open with his emotions. His body language was so expressive. I could feel his energy. It was alive and vibrant, and he awoke something dormant in me."

"Poor thing, that sounds like love to me. Same thing happened to me when I saw Zach preach for the first time. I couldn't get his image out of my head," Pilar paused. "Now whenever I think of Zach all I feel is heartache. I wonder if that can change?"

"God can change anything," Ruth said. "I'm proof of that."

Pilar walked over to Ruth's closet and opened the door. Inside hung Reyna's wedding dress. "I'm glad my sister is getting married and not me. These past years have taught me a lot about myself. I've become stronger. No wedding dress could ever make me give up the person I am today—with or without Zacchaeus Daniels."

Cindy quietly closed the door to her home. The kids would be asleep for another hour, so she had time to get the trading center ready before it opened. She walked across the crisp grass of the old churchyard. She loved winter days. Although it never got too cold in this southern region, the weather still slowed life down a bit. People usually visited more often. The trading center provided a place for people to keep in touch, but it wasn't the same as it was last year when they could openly talk about the *Bible* and God. Cindy slowed her pace.

She wondered if all the changes the World Government implemented would stay for good. Tom kept her up to speed on most of the happenings, and things were not looking good for Christians. Tom was already at the trading center. He enjoyed doing his personal *Bible* study in the basement of the building early in the morning. He was preparing for a secret meeting that was happening in a few days. Many pastors in the surrounding areas were coming by their trading center to discuss the changes the World Government was implementing. A few of them were curious about starting a trading center as a cover for their church as Tom had done. People needed church. They needed to meet together in order to stay strong.

Cindy entered the building and headed down the hallway. She noticed that light flooded under the door that led to the main store area of the trading center. She wondered why her husband would be up there. She opened the door only to find Charlie Liu behind the counter.

"Cindy, glad you are here," he said without looking up.

"What are you up to so early?" she asked. Charlie had been working more and more at the trading center and less and less at Deborah and Esther's farm. Tom had mentioned making a room for him at the trading center, but they didn't want to offend the aged sisters. It was obvious that Charlie did not like the slow pace of rural life, and he definitely didn't like caring for the goats.

"Tom showed me the books that you keep on paper, and I wanted to make it easier for you," he said, looking up and smiling.

"Yes, it's been hard since I had stop using the HMS. Tom doesn't want the World Government to trace any of our steps and everything on the HMS has the potential of being hacked," she said, reciting her husband's words.

"I have solved your problem," he said, as his smile lengthened.

Cindy walked up to the counter. "What is that?" she asked, eyeing the strange machine.

"This is a computer!" he said.

"Like the computers used before the Second Civil War?" she asked.

"Yes. Someone dumped several of them here a few days ago. Tom didn't want them, but I said that I had a plan for them. I've put all of the trading center's books and other records on this one. I've even installed cameras in the store that feed directly into the computer," he said, pointing to two cameras on either side of the large room.

"Does it connect to the World Government?" she asked, staring at the simplistic design.

Charlie thought. "I haven't connected it to the Internet, but it could if you wanted it to," he said. "I added a strong enough satellite to the side of the building for the HMS, but we could use that for the computer too. We get a good signal here. I've rigged up some solar panels on the roof of the trading center, so you don't even need gasoline to power it. It is completely solar-powered, and I have hooked it up to a secondary battery power if the solar panels don't gather enough energy. That way your computer should never shut down on you."

Cindy walked around the counter amazed at what she saw. "Is it easy to use?" she asked.

"You don't talk to it and there is no print identifier. You simply turn it on and off," he said.

Cindy brushed her fingers across the simple machine. "So can Tom use this to publish his writings?" she asked.

Charlie stood for a moment, thinking. Suddenly, his smile disappeared and his eyes widened. "I made it mainly for you to keep the trading center's books, but Tom could definitely publish his articles from it. We may not be able to have complete access to all the sites, and the computer may not run most of the systems, but we could definitely get limited mobility online."

"And we won't be detected by the World Government?" Cindy said, wanting to be sure of what she was hearing.

Charlie thought for a moment. "I don't think so. It is hard to explain. We would be like an insect in a large building. The World Government won't see us because they won't be looking for an insect."

"How many more do you have?" Cindy asked.

Charlie looked at the computer. "I think there is three more. I might be able to put a fourth together if I have the right pieces. We also have several old satellites. Why do you ask?"

Cindy tried to calm her breath. She didn't want to get her hopes up, but if what she was thinking could be possible, everything would change. "If we set up these computers in different towns with satellites, could they communicate with each other through the Internet unnoticed?"

Charlie stared at Cindy for a long moment. "If we were careful and stayed clear of the World Government sites, I believe that we would not be noticed. None of the World Government's systems are compatible with us."

Cindy smiled. "We would be like a family of quiet crickets, chirping to each other in the center of the ruckus."

Charlie nodded his head. "The World Government wouldn't hear because they wouldn't know what to listen for."

CHAPTER THIRTY-TWO

"**I** will not wash in the river. I've already learned to use the restroom outside in that hole in the ground, but you can't expect me to bathe in freezing water outside for all to see!" Ruth said. Zach, Bear and she were sitting at the breakfast table.

"Bear, don't you have some kind of tub in your storage room that she can use for a bath?" Zach said. He never realized how difficult this move would be on all of them. It was the morning of the third day and already tension was high. He had to admit that sleeping on the couch in the living room for the past two nights had been uncomfortable. He wasn't looking forward to several more weeks of staying there. He needed to find an alternative home quickly. Bear had trained Ruth the past two days, and she in return was teaching him from the *Bible*, but the warm feelings they had from their first day of training had all but diminished.

"She already has a room to herself and now she wants a warm bubble bath? Ridiculous! Take some water to your room and wash off like the rest of us," Bear said.

"I'm sorry that you have to share a room with your grandfather, but I am the only woman in this house. I need my own space. And I've already tried to wash off in my room, but it's not enough," Ruth said. "You are training me to fight in the dirt. You are making me hike these hills. I have so much dirt in my hair and on my skin that it won't come off. I need to immerse myself in water!" Ruth said, getting up from the table.

"Maybe we should take a break from training," Zach said, getting up next to her. "The bazaar is coming up next week, and I know that you had a few things you wanted to finish. I saw you fighting with Bear and you are doing much better. And you walked to Pilar's house yesterday, so you have a better understanding of the layout of the land."

"I'm thankful Pilar was there to take us home. Otherwise, we wouldn't have made it back until dark," Ruth said.

"Don't whine. It was only a six-mile hike," Bear interjected.

"Six miles may sound easy to you with your muscles and your strength, but it was difficult for me, Bear. You would not slow down for me," Ruth said, glaring up at him.

"If you are being attacked, you won't be able to stroll through the forest. You will have to move quickly, "Bear said matching her glare. "I'm trying to train you, not spoil you, like your brother."

"Wait a minute! Let us calm down for a minute. Ruth, didn't you finally get to meet Pilar's family? Wasn't that worth the effort?" Zach asked.

"Yes," Ruth looked down and nodded. "And I got to experience Levi's baking first hand. He's a very nice man. I know Deborah and Esther would love to visit with him again. I hope they can come to Reyna's wedding." Ruth looked at her brother and smiled slightly. "Though, he's not happy with you."

"I know," Zach said. "I have some apologizing to do, which brings me to something I've been meaning to ask you both."

"I don't like the sound of your voice," Bear said as he sat at the table. "Are you both going to stay standing or will you sit back down, so we can talk like adults?"

Ruth and Zach both sat down. Bear and Ruth both put their attention on Zach.

"Tom messaged me yesterday through a coded message, which means something is going on and it's important. He is having a meeting at the trading center tomorrow, and he really wants me to be there."

"Will I get to see Deborah and Esther then? I can take a bath. I'm sure their house is heated in the winter," Ruth said, excitedly.

247

"I'm sorry, Ruth. Tom doesn't want you to come yet, and I have to agree," Zach said, waiting for his sister's protest. He knew she would want to come back, but this meeting was definitely not the right time for her to show up.

"Why would he not want me there?" Ruth asked. Her voice trembled. "Deborah and Esther have been wanting me to visit ever since I moved here."

"Look, he's not trying to keep you from seeing them, but he is conducting a very important meeting. Many of the Christian leaders are risking their lives and the lives of their families to meet with him. There is something very important he needs to discuss with us."

"You told me about this meeting already. I thought you said that you weren't going," Ruth said.

"No, this is different. Something happened or something has changed. I really can't tell from his letter. I know it is urgent. Tom couldn't give me any specifics, but he did tell me that for everyone's safety that you need to stay here at this time."

"Why is Ruth such a risk?" Bear asked.

Zach leaned back in his chair. "Ruth is a high profile Efficientist that left rank with valuable information. The World Government cannot know where she is. It would make everyone a target."

Bear looked at Ruth. "Is that why I've been training her?"

"That's part of it," Zach answered. "I've already told your grandfather that I would be leaving for a few days. I told him a little about Ruth, as well. I need you both to know what's going on, so you can help me keep her hidden."

"I'm understanding a little more," Bear said. "But you are very limited with the information that you give."

"Will you go alone then?" Ruth asked.

"No," Zach said. "I'm taking Pilar with me."

"And her father said that would be okay?" Bear asked incredulously.

"Tom's wife offered to let Pilar stay at their house. I will be staying at the trading center. Your friend, Charlie Liu—or Li as he is called now—is living there," Zach said motioning to

Ruth. "Tom has made a sleeping quarter for him, and I'll be rooming with him. I asked Pilar last night when she dropped you off. She said she would ask her dad, but she was pretty sure that she could convince him. She excited to go to Trinity."

"I gather no one has told Deborah or Esther about the meeting," Ruth said.

"They know there is a meeting, but they don't know how important it is. Tom thinks it's best to shield Deborah and Esther from some of what's going on. They housed you for so long that they would be a target if you visited them again. Besides, you will see them soon. They both will be driving up with Tom and Cindy for Reyna's wedding."

"Why is it okay for Ruth to see everyone at the bazaar if she is so high profile?" Bear asked.

"Because it is a public meeting place. There will be many people there," Zach said.

"I will be one in the crowd," Ruth added.

"Don't be upset, Ruth. I will be home in a few days. I need to have time with Pilar. I've been selfish these past several years, and I need to make amends."

Ruth heaved a breath. "Yes, you do. Pilar is a wonderful young woman and my only friend. Will you do me a favor?" Ruth asked.

"Anything!" Zach answered. He was relieved to see that his sister took the news better than he was anticipating.

"If you happen to see Deborah, will you ask her for a piece of pecan pie for me?"

Zach smiled. "I will ask. I know that Pilar wants to meet them, since they've had such a profound influence on her father."

Zach turned his attention to Bear. "Let Ruth rest until I get back. I'm grateful for everything you have shown her so far. I know it will help her."

"That's fine," Bear said. "I wanted to work on that table that you want to give Reyna and Javier. I'm going to sand it down and use that dark varnish that I have in the storehouse."

"Thank you for doing that for them. Pilar said that the table will be most welcomed," Zach finished and got up from the table. "Well, I'm supposed to pick up Pilar this morning to head out. I've already got my bag packed in the car. Is there anything you two need from me before I leave?"

Bear and Ruth glanced at each other and quickly looked away.

"No," Ruth said. "I'll probably write several articles, but I'll save them for you to edit when you come back home."

"Be careful on that LPS, Ruth. Don't stay on for more than ten minutes at a time," Zach said.

"I know," Ruth said. "I plan what I'm going to write before I get on."

"Okay," Zach said, then looked at Bear. "Can I speak with you?"

Bear got up from the table. And the two men walked outside.

"If you are going to lecture me on being too hard on your sister, I don't want to hear it. You asked me to train her and that is what I did," Bear started out.

"No, it's not that, though, I do want you to stop training her for now, I can tell she needs a break," Zach said.

"Then what else is it? I will make sure she has food. I will make sure that no one bothers her. But I will not give her a tub," Bear said, tersely. "She knew that things would change when she moved here."

"Fine, Bear, she doesn't need a tub...for now. But I want you to know that I trust you. Otherwise, I would take her with me regardless of Tom's warning," Zach said.

"Then what is it?" Bear asked.

"When I talked to Pilar last night, she kept asking me these weird questions about you and Ruth. And she didn't say it directly, but I'm starting to see all the hints piling up," Zach said.

"What? That Ruth hates my guts?" Bear said.

"No, not quite," Zach said. Never in a million years did he think he would be having this conversation with his friend.

"No, I think Ruth likes you, so I just want you to tread carefully around her."

"If she likes me, she covers it up well because I have seen nothing but dislike in her," Bear said, unamused.

"You don't like her, do you?" Zach asked, uncomfortably.

"Not in the least," Bear said. "She is not my type."

"I'm glad to hear that. I was worried because the other day when I interrupted your conversation with her in the kitchen, I thought you may have shown some interest in her," Zach said.

"That's because she helped me understand something about my life, but that doesn't mean that I find her attractive."

Zach looked at Bear. He always wore his emotions for all to see. The only problem was that his emotions turned as suddenly as the weather. "Good, let's keep it that way. Let her do her own thing for the next few days. She's good at staying busy."

Zach knew that when Bear looked at Ruth, he only saw a woman who seemed helpless and who covered herself from head to foot with clothes because of the cold. Zach only hoped he could get Ruth out of Bear's house before the spring and the warm weather came. He wanted to keep Bear ignorant for as long as possible.

"Was there anything else that you needed?" Bear asked.

"Yes, I wasn't exaggerating when I said that Ruth is a high profile target. The World Government has tried to have her killed and she survived. I know you've seen the light burns on her hands. This is no joke. She needs to stay hidden."

Bear became serious. "She mentioned something about that, I think. They tried to burn her alive?" Bear asked.

"Yes," Zach nodded.

"What is it with the World Government and fires?" Bear asked.

Zach felt his heart begin to pound. "What do you mean?"

"They burned your father in the church. They tried to burn your sister? I wonder if the same man is doing it or if the World Government prefers fire as their silencing tool?"

251

Zach felt his fists tighten. "I don't know," he said. "But I will assuredly find out."

"Daddy, you know Zach. He would never do anything to offend you. I will be staying with Pastor Tom and his family," Pilar said, as she leaned over the counter in her father's kitchen. "Let me have a few more of those for the road." She reached and grabbed several of the pastries that her father was making.

"You'll be back in two days?" Levi asked. He was a balding, tall man with dark brown skin and green eyes. He wore a burlap apron that was covered in flour. "Your sister's wedding is next week, so we need all the help we can get."

"I know, Dad, but I need a break. I've already made all the deliveries for the week, so everything is caught up. I will be back in time to help make the final arrangements for the wedding before the bazaar begins. Zach finally wants to talk to me. He wants us to work things out."

"You know that I worry about you, Pilar. You may be twenty-five years old, but you are still my baby girl," Levi said, kneading the dough on the counter a little too briskly.

"Yes, honey, she will be fine," a woman's voice could be heard coming in the doorway. "Ah, Mijita, you look beautiful this morning!"

"Thanks, Mama," Pilar said, looking at her mother. She was a small lady with tan skin and black hair that was turning grey.

"I'm trying to protect our girl, Maria," Levi interjected.

Maria ignored her husband's words and turned toward her daughter. "Do you have everything you need?"

"I'm all packed up and ready to go. Zach should be here any minute," she said.

"Will you be going to the farm that your father went to when he was a young man?" she asked.

"Zach said we may stop over there. What were the names of the sisters?" Pilar asked, turning to her father.

"Deborah and Esther," he answered. "Give them my blessing when you see them. God used those two ladies to change my attitude and turn me back to Him," he said.

"I hope I get to visit with them," Pilar said, sincerely.

"I can't believe they are still living after all this time. They were old when I was young," Levi said, laughing. "Bring some of those pastries to Deborah. If I remember correctly, she was the one who used to cook."

"I will, Daddy. Thank you for being so supportive of me," Pilar said.

Levi wiped his hands on his apron and walked around the counter toward his daughter. He drew her into an embrace. "Out of all my kids, you are the strongest. You have been faithful to God even when you didn't understand. I am proud of the person you are today, Pilar," he said.

"Levi, you're getting our daughter dirty," Maria said, pushing him away. "She has flour all over her clothes. Here let me wipe it off."

Maria used a towel to get the white powder off of her daughter's clothes. "There now. All better," she said.

A truck could be heard coming up their rocky driveway.

"That's him," Pilar said, grabbing her bag. "I'll see you guys in a few days."

"Not yet you don't," Levi said. "I need to have some words with that young man first."

Pilar rolled her eyes and exhaled. "Please be soft with him."

"Don't you worry," he said. "I want to make sure that Zach knows that this papa cares about his little girl."

CHAPTER THIRTY-THREE

Ruth woke up and turned in the bed. She didn't want to start the day. Everything was dirty. The ground was dirty. Her body was dirty. The sheets she slept in were all dirty. She needed to do laundry, but she didn't know how to do it. Zach had a washing machine at his old house that had to be filled with water from the pump, but at least it would wash the clothes. The water would drain by itself into the holding tank that the government housing shared. She would hang the clothes in the room and a large window opened at the top of the laundry room, drawing the wind in and drying the clothes. But everything here was different and difficult. Bear was different and difficult. She wished she could stay on the bed forever, imagining it was a pillowy white cloud in the sky—clean and light.

She looked at the makeshift shelves on the wall. She had over a hundred pieces of clothing she had made. Her hands hurt. Her foot ached from pressing on the pedal-powered sewing machine. She couldn't think about clothes anymore. She only hoped that some of her handmade items would sell at the bazaar. What if the Colonials didn't like her designs? Most of her pieces were functional, but many of them were fashion conscience—or so she hoped. Ruth thought of the jacket she made herself. She was tired of the cold. She wanted to wear her summer dresses again, like she did on the farm. She remembered how much she hated the heat when she was outside with Deborah and Esther, but now she would take being hot over being cold any day. She wondered how cold it would be today.

She decided to look out the window. Bear's grandfather always dressed for the weather. She knew it would be a particularly cold day if he had his deerskin jacket on. She got up to peer out the window. She saw the aged man sitting on the tree stump, but he wasn't wearing his coat. In fact, he wasn't even wearing his light jacket. She got up further. The sun was shining. She got out of bed with the blanket that Esther made wrapped around her body and placed her hand on the glass of the window. It was warm. She tried to open the window, but it wouldn't budge.

She let the blanket fall from her shoulders and felt the air. It wasn't cold. She had on a small, sleeveless nightgown that went mid-thigh. She had been meaning to make warmer pajamas, but she didn't want to waste material on something that wasn't absolutely necessary. She put the blanket on the bed and stood in the room, letting her body adjust to the temperature. It felt like the temperature she kept in her high-rise apartment—about seventy-five degrees. She grabbed her blanket and made her way to the door. She peered out, but Bear was not in the living room. She knew he was probably in his storeroom working on the table for Pilar's sister. She passed the kitchen table and noticed a bowl of dried nuts and berries left for her. She scooped up the bowl and walked outside. It was a warm day. She felt the sun all around her. She wanted to lie still under its rays and let them penetrate her body.

She saw the small table that Bear had on the outside of the house. It was placed against the sidewall, so the roof put the entire width of it in the shade. Ruth set her berries on a large rock and walked toward the table. She grabbed one corner of it and pulled it away from the house. She was impressed that she was able to move the table a few inches. She went to the other side and moved it. Then she went back to the first side and moved it some more. She went back and forth until the table was completely in the sunshine. Then she retrieved her breakfast bowl, popped a few nuts and berries into her mouth and walked back to the table. She set the bowl down on the corner of the table, and spread the small blanket out.

She carefully got on top of the blanket and placed the bowl on her lap. She ate her nuts and berries and quietly enjoyed the sunshine. When her breakfast was finished, she set the bowl on the ground and lay down. The warmth of the day enveloped her. The burden of everything lifted from her. The articles she'd been writing. The clothes she'd been making. The changes that she had endured all lifted up. Even all the dirt seemed to be lifted. She couldn't help thanking God for this moment. She quietly prayed herself to sleep.

Bear finally finished stripping the table and the chairs last night, so he began the tedious task of painting them. He was glad to have an excuse to work on something. It had been one full day since Zach had left with Pilar, and he had spoken only a few words to Ruth. If she liked him, she sure didn't leave any hints. She stayed in her room all day, working on the sewing machine. The only time she came out was at mealtime or when she worked the LPS. Then she would go right back into her room.

He was glad he had canceled his training for a few days. He didn't need a bunch of the young guys at his home, asking questions about Ruth. He made them all go home this morning. They respected his wishes. He was glad a warm front had blown in. He didn't feel as bad sending the men home when the weather was nice. A little exercise in the sun would do them all some good. He told them they needed to rest up for the bazaar. He was conducting several spars and training camps during the festivities, so they needed to be ready. Several other trainers and their fighters would be attending. They would enjoy a few bouts and exchange valuable training methods and insights with each group.

He hoped the warm front would last until Javier and Reyna's wedding. It would be a nice change from the cold fronts they've been having lately. Plus, warm weather was always better for weddings. He was supposed to conduct the ceremony, but he would ask Zach to marry the couple instead. Zach was preaching again, so he could do the honors. Pilar did ask him to play the drum and sing a song, so he would still do that. He enjoyed singing. It was an outlet for what he was feeling. He thought about Zach and Pilar. He was glad they were getting some time away. For so many years Zach was a Runner in the cities, always traveling alone. It was good for him to travel a little bit with Pilar. And whatever Pastor Tom was doing, Bear was glad that Zach was there. He wanted to make sure that they were a part of any resistance to the World Government. He had heard that Pastor Tom was a simple country preacher, but now Bear knew better. Tom was a thorn in the World Government's side.

Bear looked at his hand. The bandage was off and the bite mark was healing. He would have a permanent scar, though. He thought of his mother. He didn't know why his thoughts went to her, but when they did, his heart ached. He realized that she had scarred him too—not a scar that could be seen—but one that damaged his heart. She had neglected him all of his life, and he had gotten back at her by using women all his life. He remembered Zach's words to him a long time ago. He hurt women who were already hurting. He had asked forgiveness for his behavior. He knew that he had never been in a functional relationship with a woman. Zach's mom and dad gave him his first idea of what a good relationship looked like, and he had never experienced it. Maybe that is why God had kept him away from women for so long. Maybe he was like his father. He didn't know how to take care of a woman, and he never would have the chance to learn.

Suddenly, Bear needed to get out of the workroom. He had to get away from his thoughts and do something active. He pulled off his stained shirt and threw it on the ground. Maybe a nice dip in the river would do him some good. He had sponged bathed often enough, but there was nothing like full immersion. He would run into the house and get his soap. He could also grab his clothes and wash them, as well. That was the perfect idea. Doing laundry while it was warm was always best.

He opened the storeroom door and walked into the sunshine. He closed the door and locked all the padlocks. As he began walking to his house, he noticed something white on the table. Had the table moved? What was his grandfather doing? He neared the table and saw something that froze his steps. Ruth was lying on the table asleep in the sunshine. She was wearing a small white dress, lying on a colorful blanket that he had never seen before. Bear stared at her form. Her body was small, but he could tell she was definitely a woman. He hadn't noticed her figure under all the clothes she had been wearing. Her skin was white and smooth. Her hands were outstretched above her head. He could see the faded pink scars on her hands from the burns that Zach was talking about. He wondered what had really happened to her.

He quietly walked closer to the table. He could see the red tints in her hair that ran along strands of brown. Her hair looked different. The ends were more even than they were a few days ago. Her legs were bent at the knee and her hips were turned to the right, but her shoulders and head were flat on the table. She looked longer without all the layers of clothing covering her. Her body was petite, but very proportionate. He heard steps behind him. He looked back to see his grandfather.

"Why are you staring at her, Na-aw'-tsi?" he asked quietly.

Bear straightened and looked away. "I didn't know how beautiful she was," he whispered.

"I saw her beauty from the first time I met her. You are too ruled by your eyes," his grandfather quietly reprimanded. "She has beauty in her, but you did not see it."

Bear looked as his grandfather. "I see her beauty now, *Aha-enah*. She is the most beautiful woman that I have ever seen."

"Yet, you almost missed it," the aged man said. "You missed it because you have no imagination within you."

"Life has been hard. It has taken my imagination," Bear said.

"I think it is time that you claim it again," the aged man said.

Bear looked back at Ruth sleeping. "I think you are right."

Bear bent down and grabbed the corner of the blanket that hung over the table, and he slowly spread it over Ruth's waist and legs.

"Zach says that she likes me," Bear said.

"I already knew that," the aged man chuckled. "You don't see the way she looks at you because you do not look."

"Maybe I don't look because I don't deserve to," Bear said. "I have mistreated women all of my life. Even now I am too harsh."

Bear's grandfather nodded. "You carry too much of your mother with you."

Bear looked at his grandfather. "What do you mean?"

"Ruth has told me about forgiveness. If we don't forgive the evil done to us, we continue to carry the evil with us. It continues to affect our words and actions."

Bear looked back at the table. "If I forgive my mother, I can be free of her?"

"No, Na-aw'-tsi, not free of her memory, but free of the pain and hate," he answered.

"I believe I'm ready to forgive her. Now that I see what I can have in exchange, the choice has become easier," Bear said.

CHAPTER THIRTY-FOUR

Ruth heard footsteps approaching her. She didn't want to open her eyes. The sun enveloped her like a hammock, and she couldn't remember feeling this peaceful since she left Deborah and Esther's farm.

"Ruth," she heard. It was Bear's voice, but it sounded different. It was the voice she remembered when she first met him at her mother's funeral. His usual terse tone had turned to tenderness. Maybe something happened to Zach. She quickly shot up from the blanket.

"Is my brother okay?" she asked, staring into Bear's dark brown eyes.

Bear was holding a wide piece of thick fabric around his waist with his right hand, and his left hand held a net filled with damp clothing. His wet, black hair draped down his back and across his shoulders and water droplets covered his tan skin.

"I assume he's fine. The last I heard was what you told me that he and Pilar arrived at Trinity safely," Bear said, looking confused. "Did you have a dream?"

Ruth stared at Bear unable to think. "No—no, I don't think so," she stammered. "I'm sorry. The way you sounded made me feel like something was wrong. Why are you all wet?"

"You've been asleep for about an hour. The sun is getting higher, so I thought you might want to take a swim in the river. I finished bathing and washing my clothes, so I was going to hang them up. If you wanted to do your wash, I will hang yours with mine."

Ruth was confused. "You will help me wash my laundry in the river?"

Bear's eyes widened. "Yes, I can help you with that. Let me put some clothes on, and I will go to the river with you and show you what to do."

"What did you wear to bathe?" Ruth asked. She had never bathed in a river before. The only other time she had been in the river was for her baptism. She had worn a summer dress for the occasion.

It was Bear's turn to look uncomfortable. "I have built a stone wall in a small inlet of the water. I use that when I bathe as a covering. You can use it also. I will help you wash your clothes, and then I'll leave you to wash yourself."

Ruth quickly looked at her arms. "I've been out here an hour. Do you think I am burned?" she asked, showing Bear her arm.

"No, it is too late in the season and too early in the day to burn. The sun is getting high, but another fifteen minutes outside won't hurt you."

"Do you have another net for my clothes? I would also like to wash my bedding," Ruth said, getting up from the table.

"I'll empty this one out and let you use it," he replied.

"This day is so sunny and warm. Do you think this weather will last?" Ruth asked, as she neatly folded the blanket Esther had made for her.

Bear watched as Ruth gathered the colorful blanket and secured it in her arms. The V-neck nightgown she wore exposed the smooth line of her décolletage and the sweep of her shoulders. He followed several feet behind her as she made her way to the house. He was surprised by the youthful curve of her legs and the feminine way that she moved. "I hope it does," he replied.

"I don't normally use this scrubbing board myself, but most people do. Here, sit on this rock," Bear said. He took Ruth's hand and led her to the large, flat rock where he normally did his wash.

"Oh, the water is so cold!" Ruth exclaimed, pulling her foot back out from the water.

Bear tried to stifle his laughter. Ruth stood in the center of the rock, gripping the net that held her dirty clothes.

"You'll get used to it after a while," he said.

"I don't think so. That water is much colder than the showers at Zach's government house," she said, staring at the cool, bubbly stream of water around her.

"Well, it comes down to this. Do you want to be clean? Or do you want to be warm?" Bear said, smiling. He hadn't laughed in a while. He was in the mood to watch the scene with Ruth unfold. Apparently, his grandfather wanted the entertainment too. He sat on his stump turned toward their direction.

"*Aha-enah*, we don't need an audience. Why don't you go get lunch?" Bear called out to his grandfather.

"I will stay and protect her from invaders!" the grandfather called out.

"I am here. I will make sure she stays safe," Bear called back.

"You are the invader that I'm most worried about!" the grandfather called back.

Bear eyed Ruth and ignored his grandfather's words. He turned back to Ruth. "Now, take a deep breath and sit down with both feet in the water."

Ruth looked down at the churning water around her. "I do want to be clean. Is there not a tub that you can get? We can warm up the water, and I can take a nice bath inside my room," she said.

"Ruth, you're not even taking a bath yet! I'm trying to get you to wash your clothes. Look, I promise I will look for a tub at the bazaar next week. Let's just wash clothes until then. Okay?" Bear said. He almost enjoyed the tug-of-war of words with Ruth. Her helplessness now amused him. He wondered why it had irritated him before.

"Okay, as long as this is the first and last time I wash clothes in the river," she said. Ruth bent her knee and placed it gently on the rock. Then she bent the other knee and put it down softly. "Can I do laundry like this?" she asked.

Bear shook his head. "You'll need leverage when you wash the clothes. You'll have to sit, so you can place the scrubbing board in the water. You can place your feet against the smaller rock in front of you."

Ruth finally sat down and slowly put her feet in the water. She pressed them down to the ground until the water hit almost to her knees. She kept her eyes closed, waiting for the shock from the cold to subside. "It's better now. I think my legs have gone numb," she said.

"Good, now place the scrubbing board between your legs. They will have to hold it in place while you wash your clothes against it. Open your bag and take out something to wash. Here is the soap," Bear said, handing Ruth a large, thick bar.

Ruth took out her first item and placed it on the board. Then she took the soap from Bear's hand.

"Dunk the shirt in the water first. Good, now rub the bar of soap against it. Okay, now put the soap down next to you and rub the shirt against the metal ridges of the board with both hands."

Ruth began to scrub the shirt on the wrong side of the board.

"No, you have to flip the board. The ridges need to be away from you, so you can reach around and scrub the shirt. You will be able to use more of your back and shoulder muscles," Bear said, reaching down and flipping the board.

Ruth reached around the board and gently moved the shirt up and down the ridges.

"That's pretty good, but you will have to use a little more force than that to get it clean," Bear said, putting his hand on his hips and smiling.

"This is a delicate shirt," Ruth replied. "I want to move it softly, so I won't compromise the fabric."

"I forgot," Bear said. "Women have things that need a soft touch. Everything I own already has holes in it, so I scrub as hard as I can to finish the job quickly."

Ruth placed the shirt in the water again and twisted it. "I know how to do this part. At Zach's house, we didn't have a dryer, so I had to wring the clothes and hang them."

"Here if you put the dirty clothes next to you, we can fill the net back up with your washed clothes," Bear said.

Ruth dumped her dirty clothes next to her on the rock and placed the clean shirt in the net. She was running out of space on her rock.

"I'll take the net. I can hold it for you while you wash the rest," he said, grabbing the bag.

Ruth stared at Bear for a brief moment. "Thank you for helping me," she said.

Bear nodded. "You're welcome. I'm sorry I hadn't been more helpful before," he answered.

"If you would like, I can fix the holes in your clothes," Ruth said, motioning to the rip in his drawstring pants.

"You don't have to do that," Bear said, looking down. "I've gotten so used to them. I haven't left the house much in the past few years, so I stopped worrying about them."

"I would like to sew them if you allow me. I've finished with all my clothes that I will be selling at the bazaar, so I have some free time. It will be nice to have another project to do," Ruth said, as she continued with her wash.

"Okay," Bear agreed. "And I never formally thanked you for the clothes you made for my grandfather and me. They were nicer than I had expected."

"I noticed that you haven't worn any of them yet," Ruth said.

Bear thought for a moment. "I haven't had an occasion to wear them," he answered.

"Only the outfit I made for the wedding is for a special occasion. The rest are for everyday use," Ruth replied.

Bear shook his head. "No, they are all very nice. I don't want to wear them unless I'm going somewhere important," he replied.

Ruth looked up at Bear. "Every day is important."

Bear looked down at Ruth. At one moment she seemed innocent as a girl, but the next moment she transformed into a woman who was wise with age. "Lately, I've been feeling like every day has been the same, like nothing is important anymore. When you talked to me about going before the people, I had hope again—hope that God was going to use me. But it seems that God is choosing Zach for his special purpose."

"I disagree," she said. "I think this moment with you is special."

"There's nothing special about this moment. I'm only teaching you how to wash your clothes," he whispered.

"I wouldn't trade this moment for a thousand other special moments," she whispered back.

Bear looked at Ruth. She had become soapy from the suds of the wash. She held the scrubbing board in one hand and the bar of soap in the other. Her hair moved slightly in the wind, and her feet flowed gently in the current of the river.

"Your legs are turning red from the cold water. Let me finish your wash for you. You can go beside the stonewall over there and bathe. I won't look, but if you're uncomfortable, you can leave your nightgown on and wash it on your skin."

Bear helped Ruth to her feet and brought her to the shore. He handed her a large piece of thick fabric for a towel. "Here take this to dry off with." He grabbed the soap from her hands and broke it in half. "And take this soap. I'll use this piece to finish your clothes."

Ruth took the soap and towel into her hands. "You won't leave me, will you? I'll try to wash quickly."

"Take your time. I'm not going anywhere," he said. "If you need anything, call out. I'll hear you."

Ruth smiled with relief. "Thank you, Bear," she said and turned to the path that led to the small inlet of the river.

Bear watched as Ruth carefully walked down the short path to the rock wall of the bathing inlet. She placed the towel across the ledge of the wall and disappeared behind it. He saw her slender arm reach out and set her white nightgown on the rocks next to the wall he built. He stared for a moment before

265

stepping back onto the flat rock that was still warm from Ruth's body. He sat down and put the scrubbing board between his knees and rested it against his chest. Then he grabbed another piece of her clothing and immersed it into the water. He ran the soap across the garment and began to rub it gently along the ridges of the board. Ruth was right—this day was special. His mind was filled with questions about Ruth and her past. But more than anything else, Bear knew that after all these years of waiting, God had placed a treasure in his hand, and he didn't care who she was as long as he didn't have to share her.

CHAPTER THIRTY-FIVE

"**H**ow is Ruth?" Zach asked, entering into the house that was now his home—even if it was only temporary. It was late and he had dropped off Pilar. They had a good trip, but their relationship was overshadowed by the news from Tom. Things were about to get worse for the Colonials. Bear sat at the table, reading Ruth's *Bible*. She must have loaned it to him until he could get a new one. "You know, I have an extra *Bible* that you can have. I'll search through my stuff and find it for you."

Zach sat and placed a pan on the table.

"I would appreciate that," Bear said. "Ruth is fine. She is sleeping. What's that you brought?"

"It's the pecan pie that Ruth requested," Zach said.

"You better keep it away from my grandfather or he'll eat it all," he answered and went back to his reading.

"I'm sure Ruth will share," Zach said.

Zach was surprised that Bear easily accepted his gift of the *Bible*. He said nothing about trading anything for it. Zach knew he was indebted to Bear for letting them live with him for a time, but even then Bear would mention that it would be a part of the payment for housing. Zach waited for Bear to look up from his reading. He had so much to talk about. He watched Bear read for a short moment. His fighting friend looked strange lost in thought. Bear almost always walked around shirtless when the weather was warm. A warm front had blown in, so Zach wasn't surprised to see him shirtless at the table. He always wore loose, cotton drawstring pants, which he wore now. Zach noticed that a patch had been sewn onto the knee of the pants.

"Did she sew that patch on your clothes?" Zach asked.

Bear looked down at his pants. "Yes, she went through my clothes and patched and sewed up everything needing it. She also took out some clothes that weren't any good. I think she has plans for the old material," Bear said, closing the *Bible*.

Zach was surprised at his friend's words. He couldn't envision Ruth sorting through Bear's clothes. "Why did she do that?" he asked.

Bear shrugged. "I guess she didn't like the holes," he said simply.

Something had changed in Bear's reaction towards Ruth. She was no longer simply a teacher—she was much more. Zach tried to calm his breathing, which tempted to expose his anxiety. "Did you research my sister on the LPS?" Zach asked. "Do you know who Ruth is?"

Bear looked at Zach. "I don't need to know her past to know who she is today. Just like me she made a clean break from everything."

Zach sat down next to his friend thankful that he did not research Ruth's previous identity. "You are the same person you were then. You aren't tangled up in sin anymore. Ruth too is the same person, but she's free to be who God created her to be. She no longer has to live by the expectations of this world."

Bear nodded. "Yes, I am the same me. I was like a spider, trapped in my own web. But I'm free from it. Over the past five years, God has brought me out of that life."

Zach paused. "I know that I'm not one to talk because I ran from God for many years, but I want you to know that God has a specific purpose for you, and He designed you for that purpose. You don't have to be a different person. You don't have to be like my father or like me. I feel like you've been trying to be someone you are not. You can be Fighting Bear who is free from sin. You are one of the most interesting, complex people I know. You don't have to hide that."

Bear said nothing, but Zach could tell he was soaking up his words. "You know when I did that last fight—the one on Enchanted Rock?"

Zach nodded.

"I didn't understand why God called me to fight one last time, but now I know," Bear said.

"Why?" Zach asked, leaning closer to his friend. He wanted to keep their voices low, so they didn't wake Ruth.

"I was surrounded by the women and the cameras and the crowds—all the things that I used to love. And I realized that they no longer had a hold over me. I don't need those things anymore, but I still feel an emptiness—like a hole has been left. Ruth told me that I need to imagine something beyond what I'm used to. She said God would do a new thing. I can't imagine anything else than what I've known, so I've decided to keep my mind clear for God. Maybe he will put the images in me."

"I think that is wise," Zach said. His friend was talking in abstract truths, and Zach couldn't help but be impressed. Ruth's words were having an influence. Zach wondered why he could never affect Bear the way Ruth had, but he knew Ruth had a special gift of seeing a person's difficulty and speaking truth into it. Hadn't she done that for Bear's grandfather? Hadn't she done that for him, as well? Didn't his change begin when she moved in with him and began speaking and writing words that helped him overcome his hurt?

"I wanted to ask you two questions. I know that you don't want me to research Ruth's past. It's a funny feeling that she knows so much about me and I know very little about her, but somehow I trust her. I remember her mentioning something about burns, and when we talked about it, you got upset."

Zach felt his fist tighten. He had done a little research on his own and the results left him with an intensified feeling of revenge. He had been trying to bury it, but he knew that he would have to deal with it eventually.

"You see, already I see anger in you," Bear said, looking into Zach's eyes. "If I am to protect Ruth, I need to know what you know."

Zach knew where Bear was leading the conversation, but he wanted to wait until he heard the actual questions. "What is it that you want to know?"

"The first one is who saved Ruth from the fire?" Bear asked. "Was it you?"

Zach felt the tension in his hands release. A flood of guilt came to him. What if he had never tampered with Ruth's Sleeper? What if she never had the Awakening? He knew she wouldn't be here today. And he had tried to warn her. He didn't know that the Awakenings were killing people. And his warning cost him. He had been beaten by the very man who had changed all of their lives. He told his mother and his friends that he had fallen asleep behind the wheel and crashed into the trees.

Zach thought over his words before answering. Bear didn't need to hear the entire story just yet. "I did not save her. A man named Jonah gave his life to get Ruth out of the fire."

Bear leaned back in his chair. "So the man that saved her is dead?"

"Yes," Zach said. "What is your second question?"

Bear put his elbows on the table and narrowed his eyes. "Who is the man that started that fire, and is he the same man that killed your father?"

Zach stared at his friend. He could feel the heat coming from his friend's face. Bear was never able to hide his emotions, and for the first time, Zach could match his intensity. "Don't tell Ruth."

"She already knows," Bear said.

"How do you know?" Zach asked.

"When I asked her about the correlation between her fire and your father's, she would not answer me," Bear said.

Zach pulled his fingers through his blonde hair. "It totally makes sense now. She has probably known all along," Zach whispered. "She has been shielding it from me. Why did you discuss this with her?"

"I only questioned her about the things I need to know to keep her safe. If someone is trying to kill her, I need to know about it," Bear said.

Zach looked at his friend. He saw something in him that he hadn't seen before. He was showing more protection over his sister, and for that he was thankful. Hopefully, Bear had started to see Ruth more as family and less as a stranger, which would help ease his own burden of protecting her. "His name is Randall, and he is the second in command under Neil Elder."

"Is he still searching for Ruth?" Bear asked.

"No, they think she is dead for now," Zach said.

"What do you mean, for now?" Bear asked.

Zach hesitated. "The World Government is making plans to assimilate all Colonials into their system as a workforce. And Tom has a plan to help us separate before that happens."

"What does Pastor Tom's plan have to do with Ruth?" Bear asked.

"Because the plan involves Ruth exposing her true identity. If we agree, Ruth's past will no longer be dead," Zach finished.

Pilar walked into the large kitchen of her parents' house. She opened the burlap sack that Deborah and Esther had given her filled with jars of grape jelly and bags of pecans. She put all the jars on the counter. Their father would be pleased. He could use the jellies to spread across layers of cake. The aged sisters had given them enough jelly for Reyna's entire wedding cake. Their father would also use the pecans to compliment his sweetbreads, as well. The sisters' wedding present would be greatly appreciated by all.

Pilar sat down and looked at all the shelves stocked full of food. They would be responsible for feeding the entire wedding party, including hundreds of guests. Of course, every person would bring wedding gifts, and many of those gifts would include foods and drinks. Pilar had peace that it would go well. No matter how many people showed up, there would be enough.

"Are those for my wedding?" a familiar voice asked.

Pilar looked up to see her sister. Her sister looked much like their mother. She had their mother's tan skin and brown eyes. She was also small like their mother. Pilar was almost a full foot taller than her younger sister who would be a married woman in a few short days.

"Yes, they are. The sisters that Dad was telling us about gave them to you for a wedding present. And the pecans, as well. And, here, they had one more thing for you," Pilar said. She opened up the near-empty burlap bag and pulled out a small fabric, wrapped box.

"What is it?" Reyna asked.

"They want you to open it right away. It is for your wedding," Pilar said, smiling. "I don't know what it is, but they did say it is part of an old wedding custom."

Reyna opened the box and pulled out a small, laced-lined handkerchief with blue embroidery. "It's beautiful."

"I believe you're supposed to carry it when you walk to Javier during the ceremony," Pilar said.

"This is perfect!" Reyna exclaimed. "Mom wanted me to carry some dried foliage that she had put together, but it was dead and ugly. I would much prefer to carry this in my hand."

"I think the sisters will be pleased," Pilar said, smiling.

"I hope the warm weather stays until my wedding," Reyna said.

"Pastor Tom said it would be close. He's looked at some weather printouts, and he could see a cold front coming the night of your wedding. He thinks there may even be snow. But he's praying that it doesn't come in until after the ceremony," Pilar said.

"I've heard so much about Pastor Tom lately. I'm glad he is praying for my wedding," Reyna said. "Speaking of the wedding, are you sure that my wedding dress is safe? Mom told me not to worry, but I feel like I need to try it on again. What if it doesn't fit anymore? What if the warm weather has expanded it?" Reyna asked.

"Stop worrying. It is fine," Pilar paused. "I wanted to do something for your wedding, so I had a detail added to your dress. I promise you, that you will love it."

Reyna's eyes opened. "What did you add? Who did it?"

"Ruth added it. You know how great her sewing is, but I won't tell you what she did. Just know that you will have the prettiest wedding dress in the history of the village," Pilar said.

"Ruth is so amazing!" Reyna exclaimed. "I received the suit dress she gave me for after the wedding. It is stunning and fits me perfectly. How did she know my size if she didn't measure me?"

"She got the measurements from the wedding dress. She wanted to make you something special as a gift, and I picked out the fabric. I knew you would like it, since you liked the suit she made me so much," Pilar said.

"I think you know me better than I know me," Reyna said, grabbing her sister's hand. "Thank you for working so hard for my wedding. I see everything you have done for me. I know it must have been hard helping me while Zach kept pushing you away," Reyna said. "How was the trip with him? Did you work things out?"

Pilar let go of her sister's hands. "Yes, we worked it out— well, kind of," Pilar said, hesitating.

"What do you mean, *kind of*?" Reyna said.

"We no longer have a wedge between us. He has finally worked out the pain of losing his dad and his mom, but now we have an even bigger problem," Pilar said. "I don't know how much I should tell you. I don't want to scare you before your wedding day."

"What's going on? Is the World Government changing things again?" Reyna said.

Pilar looked at her young sister. She was only twenty-two years old. She wanted to shield her, but the news would soon be out in a few weeks. She only knew what Zach had told her, and she could tell he was withholding some information. Normally, she would have pressed the subject, but the information that he did give her was enough. She didn't want to know more—yet.

273

"Pastor Tom has someone in the World Government feeding him information. We don't know who it is, but everything he has told us so far has checked out. And he gave us the newest update, all Colonials who want an HMS will have to become citizens of the World Government and work for them. And the end plan is to make all bartering illegal, so we will be forced to get an HMS and rely on the World Government's money point system."

"But how can they do that? We don't even have electricity in our village. They can't force us to stop bartering. We would have no way to trade goods," Reyna said.

"Their plan is to eventually move all of us into government housing, but it will take time to build them for all of us. They will need to hire Colonials to build them, so they can make more Colonials into citizens," Pilar said. "It's a horrible cycle they've planned to absorb everyone into the World Government."

"But they can't force us to leave our homes!" Reyna whispered loudly.

"The sad thing is that many Colonials will go willingly. They will punch their time cards, get their money points and sit in front of their HMS all day. That is why Dad prohibited them in our village. He knew that people lacked the ability to control themselves," Pilar said.

"But Pastor Tom's ministry uses the HMS. He keeps us all updated with everything that's going on," Reyna said. "He uses it for good. Bear made those video sermons until he threw his HMS into the Trinity River. I'm not saying I want an HMS, but they can be good. If none of the people who use the HMS for good are able to get on them, how will we communicate? How will we know what is going on in the world? How will Pastor Tom receive the notifications from the spy he has in the World Government?"

"We don't need to use them anymore," Pilar said, as a grin spread across her face.

"What do you mean?" Reyna asked.

"Pastor Tom has passed out the new form of communication, and he has given one to our father," Pilar said.

"Where is it?" Reyna asked, looking around.

"Zach set it on the table next to the couch," Pilar said, pointing.

Pilar followed her sister into the living room. "It looks like a kid's toy. What is it?" she asked.

Pilar looked down to where Zach set down the simple computer. "It's called a computer, and the World Government won't be able to detect it."

CHAPTER THIRTY-SIX

"**R**uth, how much stuff did you make to sell at the bazaar?" Bear asked, holding two bags in each hand filled with clothing.

"I have two more bags. Why? Is it too much?" Ruth asked. "Can you fit them in the back seat of your truck?"

Bear set the four bags down on Zach's makeshift bed in the living room. He wore one of the new outfits that Ruth had made for him. "I have all of my fighting gear in the backseat. I'm going to have to move them to the bed of the truck and tie them down. It will take me about twenty minutes."

"Why do you sound upset?" Ruth asked. Bear easily incorporated his emotions into his facial expressions.

"The sun is already coming up. I told my men to meet me at the bazaar by sunrise. I need to claim our spot before the good ones get taken. We are hosting all the fight teams in the area. Some will even come from miles away to fight and learn. I am the main person in charge. I can't be late."

"Can't you set them in the front seat between us?" Ruth asked. "They will fit."

Bear shook his head. "I would have preferred not to have a bunch of bags sitting up front next to me, but I don't have a choice. Let me put these bags there, and I will see how much room we have left," Bear said, grabbing the bags and leaving the house.

Ruth wished that Zach hadn't left earlier that morning. Trading and bartering would be difficult for her since she had never done it before, and Bear would be busy with his fighting camps at the bazaar. Zach told her that he needed to help Levi set up the computer and show him how to use the generator, but Ruth felt that there was more to him leaving. She couldn't tell if he wanted to be close to Pilar or if he was giving her more time with Bear. He had become distant since he came back from visiting Pastor Tom. Thankfully, though, he did say that he would be available at the bazaar later that day to help her.

Ruth went back into her room to get the other two bags. She saw the makeup that Pilar had customized for her sitting on the table next to her bed. She quickly sat down to put on her makeup, exactly how Pilar had shown her. She hadn't worn makeup since they moved into Bear's house. She had dirt all over her skin from training with Bear, and she hadn't had a good bath until the warm weather came in, allowing her to wash in the river. She finally felt clean enough to wear it. Plus, she knew that she would be in front of people today, selling her clothes. She needed to look her best.

When Ruth was done, she got up and swept her hands over her outfit. She made form-fitting pants out of the dark blue fabric that was almost as thick as denim. She paired it with a light peach, short sleeve blouse that buttoned up in the front. Bear gave her the buttons from the small tin of sewing supplies he had that she used to sew up his hand. She was glad that the warm weather had stayed these past few days. She didn't have to wear a bulky jacket. She hoped it would stay warm until Pilar's sister's wedding tomorrow. She had a dress that she made for the occasion, and it couldn't be worn in cold weather.

She grabbed the last two bags and headed for the door of her bedroom. Bear entered in when she made it to the living room.

"Are those the last of the bags?" he asked, reaching for them. He took the bags and stopped.

"You put on makeup," he said.

Bear held onto the bags and scanned Ruth from head to toe. "Your clothes look tighter too. Have you gained weight?"

Ruth blushed from his bluntness. "I may have gained a few pounds since living here. I have been eating more. But I decided to make a few outfits that were more form-fitting. Most of my old clothes are very loose and formless on me. They worked well on the farm, but I wanted something different for the bazaar," Ruth didn't mention that she wanted to look good for Bear. She recognized that he was looking at her more—not as a teacher or as Zach's sister, but as a woman. And she wanted his interest to continue.

"Is Pilar meeting us there?" he asked, setting the bags on the table. Ruth knew something was wrong. Bear's body had become rigid, and he no longer seemed anxious to leave.

"I haven't spoken to her. She's been busy planning the wedding. Zach is at her house now, and he said that he would meet me there later today."

"I can't leave you alone when we get there. Fighters learn to have self-control in the ring, but they lack it when it comes to women, especially the young boys who think they know everything. If you are noticed, you will become a target," Bear said, matter-of-factly.

"I don't understand. A target for what?" Ruth said, confused by Bear's words. She wondered if she was in some kind of danger. Zach never mentioned the bazaar being a threatening place.

"Ruth, you can't act like a girl and look like a woman," Bear said, pointing toward her. "They will want you."

"Want me?" Ruth asked.

"They will want to have sex with you, Ruth! How are you not understanding me? You grew up an Efficientist, so don't act like you're so innocent!"

"Who cares if they want me? What can I do about what people think or feel?" Ruth asked, wondering why he was getting so angry. Men had tried to pursue her before, but she simply ignored them. "And I'm not trying to act like anything!"

Bear crossed his arms. "Well, you certainly are trying to attract attention like an Efficientist now. Don't play games with me, Ruth. I know how Efficientists view sex. They marry only for alliance, and they'll invite anyone into their beds."

"I'm not wearing anything that I haven't seen Pilar wear herself and you have never criticized her. And how dare you criticize *my* morality," Ruth said forcefully. Ruth could see Bear had become uncomfortable with her words.

"What if they try to force themselves on you? You can't even protect yourself," Bear said, trying to avoid Ruth's stare.

"Now you are starting to act like my brother," Ruth said becoming angry. "What do you care if people look at me and notice me? You certainly haven't shown much interest."

Bear exhaled and began to pace the floor several times before stopping in front of Ruth. "Ruth, look at me. Why are you wearing tight clothes? Why do you have your makeup on? Is it because you're about to be surrounded by young men? Are you trying to get someone to like you?"

Ruth looked up into Bear's eyes. "Yes, I am," she answered.

"How dare you hide your beauty from me and then flaunt it out in front of everyone!" he said, unwilling to quench the anger in his voice.

"Flaunt it in front of everyone?" she said, trying to stifle the cries that choked at her. "I am wearing it for you, Bear. The reason I asked Pilar to get me makeup in the first place was for you to notice me. And you never did!"

"Well, I'm noticing you now!" he said, moving quickly toward her. He grabbed her and lifted her from the floor, pressing her against the wall. He held her up with his body and clutched her jaw with one hand, kissing her hard with his mouth. Ruth tried to respond, but the intensity was more than she could handle.

Suddenly, Bear stopped and stared into her eyes. She knew he was examining her reaction to him. He quickly pulled away and set her back onto the ground. He backed away several feet. "I thought you wanted me?"

"I do want you," she whispered breathless, leaning against the wall.

He looked at her, thinking. Finally, he stepped closer to her. "Have you ever been with a man?"

Ruth looked at the floor. She had never felt so humiliated. "No," she whispered.

"You are an Efficientist, though. How could you have never been with a man?" Bear asked, disbelieving.

"I was always producing, working on my LPS. I never had time for relationships. And the only time I thought of starting one, the man turned on me and tried to kill me."

"Randall," Bear muttered through clenched teeth.

"How do you know about him?" she asked.

"Zach told me his name," he answered.

"What else do you know?" Ruth asked.

"I know nothing, but the time of me being left in the dark needs to end. Tell me who you are. I've met many Efficientists during my time as the Shaman. They would invite me to their little parties and show me off. You aren't like any of them," Bear said.

"Why do you want to know?" Ruth asked. She wanted to hear his intentions first before her true identity was revealed.

Bear took a seat at the table. "Sit down next to me," he said, scooting out the nearest chair. After Ruth sat down, he took one of her hands into his. "I've mistreated women all of my life. I had been so hurt by my own mother that I didn't trust them. But with you, everything is different. I want to learn how to have a real relationship with you—the kind of relationship your mother had with her husband. But before I can do that, I must know who you are."

Ruth looked at the man that she had fallen in love with. She knew life with him would be strange and at times tumultuous, but the alternative seemed stagnant and pale. Something awoke in her when she first met him. She needed to be completely open with him. She got up and walked to the end of the table where the LPS sat. She leaned down and turned it on, typing quickly and giving short commands. After only a few short moments, she straightened back up. "Sit over here. This is who I was," she said, motioning to the chair.

Bear sat down and stared at the LPS. He needed only to look at the image of the woman on the screen and his face transformed with a flood of emotions. Crystals covered the woman's head and went down the side of her face. She wore a small sequin dress, and her bodyguard stood close beside her.

280

Bear flipped the LPS off and stared into the blackness for a long while. Ruth stood quietly, waiting for his reaction. He finally stood and looked at her

"Why have you kept this from me?" he asked, showing no emotion.

"If you wanted to know, you could have found out anytime, Bear. The LPS has been right here the entire time. You have my bodyguard's name. You know I was an Efficientist. You know the World Government tried to kill me in a fire. And you know they thought I was dead. The answer has been here all along, but you never bothered to look. You are to blame for your own ignorance," she said.

"I'm glad that I didn't know. The reputation you have made for yourself is well known, Eve Pallue," he said, coldly. "I might not know a lot about *Life Efficiency*, or whatever the hell they are calling it now, but I know about you. You are very good at playing innocent. You almost had me fooled."

Ruth felt a calm wash over her. She stared into Bear's eyes unable to hide her disappointment. "Then you are like the rest of the Colonials—ensnared by your own love of entertainment and scandal. You believe everything the World Media pumps into your mind. You should have turned your HMS off when you were done recording your video sermons instead of filtering through PR event updates. You let the media image of Eve Pallue seduce you, but I can assure you, I was never the woman they portrayed."

"So you're telling me your whole life was a lie," he said.

Ruth couldn't stop the tears that flooded her eyes. "Yes, that sums up my life until now," she answered.

Bear said nothing for a brief moment. "It's late. We have to go. We will have to talk about this later," he said.

Ruth watched as Bear grabbed the last two bags of her clothing she would be selling at the bazaar. She noticed that he put a stony veneer over his expressions, but his anger and hurt could not be hidden. She followed him to the truck and got in. He placed the two bags in the middle of the front seat, and they were like walls between them. Ruth wondered if those walls

281

would stay there forever. She had revealed the truth about her life and had been honest about her feelings for him. Now the rest was up to him.

CHAPTER THIRTY-SEVEN

Ruth sat in the bed of the truck, watching Bear dictate to the men around him. His anger was obvious. He didn't get the spot that he wanted at the bazaar, and he was forced to locate his team and equipment on the outskirts to get enough room. Bear wanted to be in the center, so his training camp would have higher traffic of people. Now people would have to walk to his camp to watch the fights and training segments. Bear's men could sense his anger, and they were quick to do everything he commanded. No one spoke while he gave the orders.

Ruth liked their location, however. They were far enough from the throng of people building in the center of the bazaar. The weather was still warm, and a nice breeze blew in from the south. Bear had said nothing in the truck on the way over, but like the calm breeze, she felt at peace. She had been honest with Bear, but she would not try to persuade him any further. If he could not see beyond her past, then she wouldn't be with him. She knew his past. She knew about the drugs and the women, but she also knew he had changed. He would have to afford her the same grace that she gave him. Otherwise, she would rather be alone than with a man who judged her.

Ruth looked back over the field. The men had done a lot in the hour they had been there. Even though Bear looked upset, Ruth couldn't help but notice that he looked nice in the outfit she made for him. She used the thick, dark blue material that he had given her, but she was able to integrate a small pattern of bright red fabric that she had owned from when she lived with Deborah and Esther. He liked his clothing loose, so she kept with the same design of the drawstring pants. She wanted to make the shirt reminisce of the Ka'to design, but she had no beading or feathers to add, so she tried to add a subtle thread pattern down the two front panels of the shirt. Bear would never know how long that design took her to create, but she could tell that he liked it when he put it on that morning.

Ruth noticed that Bear looked her way and nodded his head to someone behind her, but he did not make eye contact with her. She turned and saw his grandfather coming up through the clearing. When he made it to the truck, he opened the front door and put his shotgun inside. Then he walked back to the bed of the truck. Ruth patted the tailgate next to her. "Come sit with me?" she said.

The old man smiled and got on the tailgate next to her. "I would have gotten here earlier, but I got sidetracked," he said, opening his hand and presenting several colored stones.

"What are those?" she asked.

"These are the trading stones of the bazaar," he said. "They have different values. The red is the highest price. The blue comes next. Then the green, and finally the yellow."

"What are trading stones?" she asked again.

The old man tilted back his head and laughed. "Are you not bartering the clothes you have made today?" he asked.

"Yes," she said.

"Well, what do you expect in return?" he asked.

Ruth thought. "I don't know. I thought people traded me items for my clothes, and I could agree or disagree," she said.

"On a normal day, yes, that is how it goes. But at a bazaar, there is no time to waste bartering. Levi and the other elders have made a very good system. They have a set amount of colored stones, which they give out to each person for their items," he started.

"Are you saying that they set the price of my clothes?" Ruth asked, intrigued.

"They have certain people inspect your items, and they decide their worth. If you have done a fine job, the price will be high. If the clothes are not so well made, the price will be low. They then give you the stones, and you are free to buy whatever you want until the stones in your hand run out," he said.

"What if all your items don't sell?" she asked.

He shook his head. "They make sure that everything sells out. The stones they give out must all be returned at the end of the bazaar. Everything has to sell, even if you wind up buying your own items. But most people don't want their own items, so they will buy whatever is left on the tables."

"But what about Bear? He offers his services. How does he get paid?" she asked.

"That simple," the grandfather smiled his toothless smile. "People buy things with their stones, and they give them to *Ne'aw-ze* if they want to be trained. He will not trade his services for stones."

"How did you get those stones?" Ruth asked, pointing to the aged man's hand.

"That was why I was late. I saw two fat turkeys on the way here, and I was able to shoot them both. They were heavy and they tired my old bones, but I made it," he smiled.

"I notice you are wearing the outfit I made you," Ruth said. She was pleased to finally see the aged man wear the clothes she had made him.

The man looked at his shirt. "I got a little blood on this one, so I tried to rinse it in the river."

"I barely notice it," Ruth said, smiling. "It means a lot that you are wearing it."

"The lines for the stones will be long soon. Why don't we take your clothes over to the elders, so they can give your set amount," the grandfather said.

"I have six larges bags of clothes. We may have to take a few trips," she said, jumping down from the tailgate.

"I am not so old that I can't help a pretty, young lady," he said, following her.

Ruth opened the door and started getting the bags out of the front seat. She handed him three of them and she carried three.

"The walk isn't long," he said. "We can make several stops along the way when we get tired."

Ruth followed the aged man and said nothing. She looked back to see if Bear saw that she was leaving, but he was busy stringing a rope along the cleared out portion of the field. When they got to the table of elders, she saw Levi. She had only met him one other time when she hiked to his house. It would be nice to talk to him again.

"Here is the talented Ruth!" Levi's baritone voice rang out. "I finally get to meet with you again. My daughters are in love with the clothes you have made them, and now my wife insists on having a new wardrobe made by you!"

Ruth instantly warmed to his jovial presence. He had Pilar's light green eyes and brown skin. He was tall and thin, except for the thickness around his midsection from too many sweets. "I would enjoy making her a new outfit," Ruth said, smiling. She enjoyed the praise.

"*Aha-enah*, how are you? My daughter is still sneaking my treats to you, I presume," Levi said, turning to the old man next to Ruth.

"She has not been around in a while. She has been too busy lately. I have not had a sweet in many days," the aged man said, seriously.

Levi looked around, making sure no one was looking. "She has been thinking about you, and she told me that if I saw you, I was to give you this," Levi said, bringing out a small burlap bag. "There should be plenty in here to last you the day. But don't get too full. We have wedding cake tomorrow night."

The grandfather took the bag. "I shot two turkeys this morning. I traded one for colored stones, but I gave the other to your wife. She was headed home after she dropped you off. She will have it prepared for the wedding tomorrow. It is my present to the bride."

Levi's smile was large and genuine. He moved around the table of elders and walked up to the old man, giving him a large hug. "Thank you, my friend. We have been worried about food. I know your turkey will feed many people," he said.

The grandfather was surprised by the show of affection but no less pleased. He smiled his toothless grin and quickly opened the bag and grabbed the first sweet bread he saw, popping it quickly into his mouth.

"So, Ruth, why don't you show me some of the clothes that I've been hearing all about?" Levi asked, motioning to the bags.

Ruth picked up one bag and laid the contents on the table. Levi inspected them closely. "The stitching looks good, but let me get one of the other elders in charge of textiles. She has more of an eye for this than I do."

Levi walked around the table and waited for a silver-haired lady to finish her conversation with a young mom who was holding her infant on her hip. When she was done, Levi said something to her and pointed to Ruth. She walked around the table and gently unfolded the first piece of clothing, inspecting it for a long time. Then she looked at all the other items on the table carefully.

"Can you place the rest of the items on the table, so I may inspect them?" the woman asked.

Ruth and the old man emptied the bags on the table and placed the items in neat stacks in front of the woman.

"I see that you left extra material on all the hems so they could be easily adjusted," the woman said.

"Yes," Ruth answered. "They should be easy to take in or out, depending on the size of the wearer."

"How long have you been sewing?" the woman asked.

"Only less than a year, but I am a fast learner," she answered honestly.

The woman looked at Ruth in surprise. "I see that some people simply have a knack for things," she said simply. "You obviously have a gift of sewing."

Ruth waited a moment longer while the woman inspected the rest of the clothing. She made two stacks of clothing and put them to the side. Then she arranged smaller stacks in order along the table. She opened the pouch that she had fastened around her waist and placed several colored stones in front of each stack. "You have the best clothing that I've seen in a long time. It is obvious you were patient while making these items. Nothing was rushed and you took care to make them beautiful. They are each a work of art and should thereby reflect a higher price."

Ruth did realize that she had been harboring insecurity about her work until the woman's words relieved her fears. "Thank you. I worked very hard. I'm pleased that you recognize that," she said.

The woman nodded. "I have set two stacks away for myself," she pointed to the clothes she separated. "So I will be purchasing those."

The woman reached into a smaller pouch that she wore around her neck, and grabbed a handful of colored stones. "According to the price I set, here is your payment for those items."

Ruth allowed the woman to put the stones into her hand.

"Thank you," the woman said, smiling for the first time. "I've been wanting some new clothes for some time, but my old hands can't work a thread and needle like they used to."

Ruth nodded her head. "You are welcome."

"Hurry, and scoop those colored stones into a pile. You don't want people to see how much you have. They will be tempted to relieve you of some of them," the grandfather said.

Ruth tried to put each pile of stones into her hands, but they wouldn't fit.

"Why don't you use that small bag that has the sweets in them? They will hide your stones," Levi said. "Never thought you were a rich woman, now did you, Ruth?" Levi said and chuckled. "Hard work pays off."

The old man emptied the rest of the sweets from the bag and handed it to Ruth. She quickly poured the colored stones into them. "Do I take the clothes to one of the tables?" Ruth asked the silver-haired woman.

"Oh, no, you don't want to waste your time standing at the table. You can hire some of the youths to stay by your items and make sure that they are given the right price. In fact, my son needs to earn some money. Wait one minute. Let me get him."

The woman left the table and went to a small group of older kids talking. She pulled a young, tall man aside. Ruth knew the boy must have been about sixteen or seventeen years old. The woman and the boy walked back to the table.

"This is my son. He will stay by your table until the items run out. I don't think it will take long. He will charge two red stones for his services," the woman said.

Ruth reached into the bag and picked out two red stones and handed them to the boy. She was relieved. Not only did she not have to barter, but she didn't have to sell her clothes either. She hadn't been looking forward to being there as people scrutinized over her work, so the two red stones were worth the price.

"Don't worry about a thing. I'll let him know the cost of each item, and he will set them out for you and make sure they get sold," the woman said.

"Thank you," Ruth said.

"Enjoy shopping," the woman said and winked at Ruth before she turned her attention back to her son.

Ruth looked at Levi. "That was easier than I thought," she said.

"That's what makes Levington the best village in the area. We do things that make sense," he said.

Ruth nodded. "Deborah and Esther will be pleased to know that you are doing so well. They have helped so many troubled children, and I know it strengthens their faith when they see their efforts making a difference."

Levi nodded. "Pilar spent some time with them when she went down there with Zach. I will be honest. I didn't want her to go at first, but I think it was the best thing for all of us. It feels like the tension that we've been living with has finally dissipated."

"Do you know where they are?" Ruth asked.

"I know Pilar is at her table. She wants to be able to show people how to put on their products. She is particular about how the women wear her makeup," Levi said.

"I've noticed that," Ruth said. "Where did Zach go?"

"You must have missed him. He went to find you and talk to Bear," he answered.

"I should go see him," Ruth said about to leave.

"Honestly, if I were you, I would spend those stones. The good items go quickly. Pilar has been out there for less than an hour and her items are halfway gone."

"I know I want fabric, but I don't know what else I need," Ruth said.

"Pilar will help you. Take your empty bags with you, and she will show you how to fill them up," Levi said.

"Thank you for your help," Ruth said.

Levi gave Ruth a hug like the one he gave Bear's grandfather. "I feel like you are part of my family. I can see Deborah and Esther in your mannerisms," he said, letting her go.

"I hope so," Ruth replied.

Ruth and the grandfather grabbed the bags and headed to Pilar's table. Ruth wouldn't admit it, but she was looking forward to shopping. She hadn't spent money in a long time. She couldn't be as indulgent as she was when she was an Efficientist. Storing away gold and gems wouldn't help her survive as a Colonial. She needed everyday items that would help her provide for herself. But if she happened to see something beautiful, and she had colored stones to spare, she might be tempted to buy it.

"I see two fighting teams coming in the distance," a young man said, trying to catch his breath. He had run in from the clearing of trees.

"Good," Bear said, tying the last knot in the rope. "We are done here. We are ready to begin. Do you recognize any of the fighters?"

"I think one is Watchman. He has aged, so I barely recognize him from his pictures. But I know his son, Sentinel, is with him, and he is very good. I don't believe he does any ground fighting, but he is climbing the fighting ranks quickly," the young man said. "They will be the first team to show up."

Bear remembered training the young man who helped him carve Naomi's casket. The boy had told him that he was good at grappling, fighting on the ground, so Bear had told him to hide that strength for the right moment and to only win by hits. The boy had listened to his advice. He would like to continue his talk with the boy. He was a good learner and he listened to the advice of his elders—no doubt an attribute formed in him by his father. He was glad that he would also be able to meet Watchman again and officially apologize for the damage that he caused to his shoulder.

"Do you know who the other team is?" Bear asked. He knew there would be at least five or six teams meeting with them at the bazaar. He hoped the leaders would be all men he was on good terms with. It was difficult to control his men when rival teams showed up.

"Yes," the man hesitated. "The leader is easy to recognize. It is the Bald Eagle. He has brought a large team with him. They are keeping their distance from Watchman."

Bear shook his head. The last man he had fought was the red, white and blue painted young fighter. He knocked him out in a little over a minute. The man would have been harboring that loss for months. His presence was not welcomed, but he could not turn any fighting team away unless they disobeyed the rules of the bazaar. Bear hoped they would do something stupid quickly, so he could kick them out before Reyna's wedding.

"Does the Bald Eagle wear a brace around his left knee?" Bear asked.

"Yes," the young man said. "He does."

Bear looked toward his truck, but he noticed it was empty. Ruth and his grandfather had left. "We have about ten minutes before they come. Tell everyone to warm up now."

"Yes, sir," the young fighter said.

Bear walked toward the truck. His heart pounded. Hadn't he told Ruth to stay there? He tried to remember. No, he hadn't. He had been so consumed in his thoughts of being late that he walked away from her when he parked. He was also angry about the truth that she revealed to him, and he didn't trust his words when his temper was high. He couldn't believe that Ruth was Eve Pallue—the same woman he had desired for so many years. He would stare at her images on the HMS, filled with guilt of his want for her. Every time he went to the PR events in the city, he hoped she would be there. He knew that he could get her to want him if they met. But she was never at any of the ones he was invited to. She had the highest rank of all of them. But now she was in his home—innocent, or so it seemed. Was she toying with him?

But hadn't he ignored her and dismissed her as Zach's plain sister. She wasn't acting then. What had changed? She was beautiful, the most beautiful woman he had ever seen. But now she was trying to show it to him, and he shut her out for it. But how could Eve Pallue be the woman who patched all his clothes? He thought of her lying on the table. He could tell when a woman was trying to get him to notice her. Ruth had tried in her own simple way, but he missed it. She had no idea how to entice a man. Maybe she was as innocent as she acted to be. He needed to talk with her. He couldn't concentrate on his fight camp with his thoughts eating away at him like this.

He got to the truck and opened the front door. The bags of clothes were gone. His grandfather must have taken her to the table of elders. Bear was just about to go get her when he saw Zach coming down the path toward him. Bear waited for Zach to reach him. It gave him time to think over how he would word his questions.

"Why are you way out here?" Zach said. "Don't you normally set up inside the bazaar?"

"One of the teams that are coming has a bad reputation. We want to keep them out of the way, so we camped further out," Bear said. He wasn't lying because that was now the truth. It would be better for Bald Eagle and his team to be on the outskirts of the bazaar. Instantly, he knew God had arranged it.

Zach tried to cover his look of surprise. "Thank you, Bear. I know Levi would appreciate you protecting his daughter's wedding like that. I don't think it will affect your traffic, though. Everyone is talking about watching the competitions tonight."

Bear nodded his head. "That is good to know. Zach, I have a few questions for you about Ruth."

Zach's laid-back features tightened. "What have you found out?" he asked.

"She told me who she is," Bear said. "But I'm having difficulty because the Ruth I know does not match what I know about Eve Pallue."

Zach crossed his arms. "I've learned to never believe what the media says. Look, I met Ruth when she was still living in the city. And I can tell you, when I found out who she was, I was as surprised as you. She didn't look or act anything like her media persona, and this was before she became a Christian. The media likes to hype things up, and they did that for Eve Pallue—a lot."

"I kissed her," Bear said and waited for Zach's reaction.

Zach's arms instantly dropped to his side, and Bear could see his hands becoming fists.

"Did you do that before or after you found out she was Eve Pallue?" he asked, as his voice became rigid.

Bear put his palms out in a show of nonaggression. "I can see why you would be angry. But I kissed her before I found out who she really was."

"But you weren't interested in her," Zach said. "I could tell. You appreciated her as a teacher and maybe even as my sister, but you were not attracted to her."

"She wore those baggy clothes and no makeup, and she was always so helpless. I couldn't see her value," Bear said.

"I disagree," Zach countered. "To me she is a beautiful person and the most intelligent one that I know. Her value is obvious—not to mention she is a child of God, which makes her priceless."

"I know. I've treated her poorly, and I am sorry for that. I've realized recently that I have a lot of fear towards women, which is why I mistreat them. Deep inside of me, I don't trust them, and I know it's because of my relationship with my mother. I keep forgiving her, but I'm always having to let go of my anger toward her. I know it affects how I see women, and I'm trying to change it," Bear said.

"I will not let you mistreat my sister like you mistreated all those other women," Zach said. "I know too much of your history."

"But I have done nothing for five years now. Don't I deserve a second chance? Has my past eliminated my value and the value I can bring to a woman?" Bear asked. "Can I not have a relationship like the one I saw in your parents? Before Naomi died, she told me that I was new again. She said that I had a second chance at true love."

Zach hesitated and loosened the tension in his fist. He strung his fingers through his blonde hair and looked at his friend. "My mom said that?" he asked.

Bear nodded his head. "Yes, she did."

"You're right. We all deserve a second chance. And you have shown yourself honorable these past five years—more honorable than me, in fact. When did your thoughts toward my sister begin to change?" Zach asked.

Bear looked embarrassed. "I began noticing her after you and Pilar left. I made a decision to start a relationship with her before I knew who she was."

"Is that the truth?" Zach asked.

"Yes, I saw her laying on my table outside the house, and she was surrounded by the sunlight. I don't know what happened but something in me woke up to how perfect she is," Bear said, trying to hide his discomfort in talking about his feelings towards Ruth to his friend. "It was like my fear was replaced with desire."

"Desire for her body?" Zach asked.

"Yes, I do desire her in that way, but it was more. I felt a desire for her protection, for her happiness, for her companionship....I—I have this desire for all of her," he answered.

"What did you say when you found out that she was Eve?" Zach asked.

Bear looked away. He knew he had messed up again. Ruth had been honest with him, and he lashed out at her. Why did he have so much trouble controlling his emotions? "I became angry with her," he said, honestly.

"Why would her true identity make you angry? I know you had a thing for Eve Pallue," Zach said.

Bear felt awkward talking about this to Zach, but he needed to know. "She has this innocence about her. When I kissed her, she didn't know how to act. I could tell she liked my touch, but she didn't know what to do. She told me she has never been with a man. How can that be? Is she lying to me? I can handle many things, but I can't take lying lips."

Zach put his hands on his hips and tried to stifle his laugh. "Never in a million years would I have ever dreamed that we would be having this conversation about my older sister."

"This is nothing to laugh about, Zach!" Bear said, allowing his voice to carry across the field. He quickly looked around, noticing the stares. He walked closer to Zach, so his words would not be heard. "I need to know if she's being honest with me."

Zach looked at his friend. The stress in Bear's facial expression was apparent. "What do you think? Do you think she is lying to you or being honest?"

Bear thought to himself. "I feel like she is telling me the truth, but I'm struggling to believe her because of everything that I've read about her. And if I can't believe her, I will never trust her."

Zach thought over his words. "Ruth, like yourself, has had a unique kind of life. And she may be innocent in some things, but in other things she knows the wickedness of the world. We each have our own innocence and wickedness at war inside of us," Zach started to say.

295

"I don't need the preacher boy to come out. Just tell me if Ruth is telling me the truth. Is she a virgin or not?" Bear asked, impatiently.

Zach sighed and shrugged his shoulders. "From what I've gathered, I don't believe she's ever been with a man. Her bodyguard wanted to have a relationship with her, but she rejected him and look where it got her. Anyway, I've never known Ruth to lie—she has no reason to."

Suddenly, Bear knew he needed to see Ruth. He had to make everything right and redeem his actions from this morning. "Have you seen her?" Bear asked.

"No, but she might be with Pilar. She is at one of the tables."

"I have to stay here," Bear said, looking back at the fighting grounds. "I see Watchman is here, and the other team will be here shortly. I'm in charge, so I must stay. When you see Ruth, will you bring her to my truck? I need to speak with her," Bear said.

"I'll do that," Zach answered. "I'm expecting Pastor Tom and his wife to be here shortly. They will be bringing Deborah and Esther. I know Ruth would be happy they have come."

"Are those the sisters who took care of Ruth when she came here?" Bear asked, anxiously.

"They are the ones that nursed Ruth back to life. She was badly burned and on the verge of death. They took care of her and helped her heal," Zach said.

"I did not realize how bad it was," Bear said.

"There is a lot about Ruth you don't know," he said.

"Will they be here long?" Bear asked.

"No, they will be leaving the day after the wedding. They are staying with Levi and his family. I better warn you, though. They have come to ask Ruth to live with them again. They don't care if it puts them in danger."

Bear felt his heart thumping in his chest. "Will she go with them?" he asked.

"She knows that I want her to stay, but I am not the one providing for her anymore. You are," Zach said.

296

Bear looked at Zach. "I must go!"

Bear walked quickly back to the fighting grounds. Watchman was there, helping the men get warmed up. Bear walked straight up to him. "Watchman, thank you for coming. I am sorry about your shoulder. I was young and stupid."

Watchman turned to Bear. "You don't have to apologize. What you meant for harm, God meant for good."

"Thank you for your forgiveness," Bear said. "I must ask a favor of you now."

"What do you need?" Watchman asked.

"I must put you in charge of this meeting today. I have greater business to take care of, and I can only trust you to lead the fighting camp. Will you stand in for me?" Bear asked.

Watchman looked at Bear for a long moment. "It is a woman, isn't it?" the man asked.

"Yes," Bear said without hesitation. "I must make her mine before it is too late."

"Then, yes, I will take charge," Watchman said. "Once you find the right woman, you must do everything to keep her."

"I agree. And I must warn you. Another group is coming, and they are not to be trusted," Bear said.

"If you mean the Bald Eagle and his gang, my son has already beaten him," Watchman said. "The training you gave Sentinel did him great good. The Bald Eagle confronted us many miles back, and challenged my son to a fight. My son submitted him in the first round. He took him to the ground and the Bald Eagle was caught off guard. He believed my son was no good at grappling because he had not done it in any of his fights. That is why Bald Eagle and his team have walked so far behind us when we arrived. I don't think they will get into too much trouble now, but I will keep my eye on them."

"Thank you, Watchman. Tell your son that I am proud of his work," Bear said. "His submission will be a story passed along at the bazaar, which will only create more interest in him and encourage more people to see his next fight. He chose his timing wisely."

"Every time my son fights, he tells people of the Lord. He heard that you spoke of God at your last fight, and it gave him strength to speak up. I am honored that you have influenced my son in this way," Watchman said.

Bear nodded and began walking back towards his truck. He heard the whispers from his men as he passed them, but he ignored their reaction. Watchman was a good fighter and leader, and his words gave him the strength to believe that he could do something worthy with his life. He would find Ruth and ask her to be his, and he would learn to have a relationship with her that was honorable and good. He knew she was telling him the truth, and he would not let this gift slip through his hands. Ruth would be his wife.

CHAPTER THIRTY-EIGHT

Z ach saw Bear speaking with an aged fighter that he did not recognize at first. He was a dark skinned man that looked to be in his mid-fifties. His body was strong, but his face showed his age. Zach remembered a man that Bear had fought long ago. His name was Watchman, and he was a Christian. Bear had injured him in some way, but Zach couldn't remember the details. Watchman had a good reputation as a leader, and Zach could tell Bear was putting him in charge. Bear trusted very few people, so Watchman must have shown himself worthy.

Zach watched his friend ignore the whispers of the other fighters. They knew something was going on, but he didn't stop to explain himself to anyone. Bear never did care much of what people thought, especially since he left the fighting circuit. Zach realized that Bear was determined to find Ruth, so he decided that he would follow him. He wanted to see what Bear would do for love. The World Government was pulling the reins tighter on the Colonials, so he needed to be sure that Bear had true intentions towards his sister that were lasting.

Zach followed Bear to the elder's table. Levi pointed in the direction of the tables of merchandise being sold at the bazaar. Zach looked and saw the place that Pilar had set up earlier that morning. Ruth was talking with Pilar, and Bear's grandfather was sitting on a large rock, eating something. Zach assumed it was the sweet bread that Pilar had saved for him. Bear walked toward the table. Zach could see his eyes were set on Ruth. Ruth hadn't noticed him yet. She was looking at something in a small pouch. When she finally looked up, Bear was directly in front of her.

Zach slipped next to the table and stood next to Pilar.
She smiled at him and gave him a knowing look. They would
hear what Bear would say to Ruth.

Ruth looked startled. "Did something happen?"

"I want you to be mine and no one else's," he said, firmly.

Ruth tilted her head to one side. "What does that mean?"
she said.

Bear threw up his hands. "Can you not understand me?
Must I explain everything to you?"

"You will have to because I'm unable to perceive your
intentions—you are too emotional for me to understand," Ruth
said, no longer intimidated by Bear's dramatic responses.

Zach was impressed by Ruth's words. She seemed to have
gotten her footing when dealing with Bear. He realized it must
have been hard for her to adapt to all the changes in her life,
but she seemed stronger now.

"It means I love you, and I won't share you with anyone.
I am older than all those other men, so I have more to offer
you. I will protect you and provide for you. I will make sure no
one hurts you, including that old bodyguard of yours," he said,
eying the crowd that had started to gather around them. He
grabbed her body and pulled her to him. "Promise not to leave
me. I just found you, and I can't lose you now."

"Okay," Ruth whispered, staring into his eyes.

"Does that mean you will be my wife?" Bear asked,
cautiously. "Not according to the laws of the World
Government, but according to the laws of God. I want you all
to myself."

"Yes," she answered. "I don't want to share you either."

Zach looked around the faces that were standing around
them. The people were smiling and whispering into each other's
ears. Others waved friends over to watch the moment unfold.
They all knew who Bear was—his legacy as the Shaman was
notorious. And even though no one as of yet knew who Ruth
was, her legacy was nonetheless profound. Zach would never
say it to anyone, but watching Ruth and Bear linked together in
an embrace felt strangely symbolic to him, like two worlds

coming together. The union of Efficientists and Colonials would be important if the people of God were going to come together, lifted up as one body and one church.

Bear let go of Ruth, but he kept a protective arm around her shoulder. He looked at the faces around him. His showmanship kicked into high gear. "Friends, our fighting camp has begun on the south side of the bazaar. If you would like to train or watch the spars, please head over to our campgrounds. We even have a few surprises for the young kids. Watchman and his son, Sentinel, are there, and they are ready to teach and entertain you. If you have something to offer, you may set it near the ring. If your pockets are empty, join us anyway. We have much to celebrate today!"

The people clapped and cheered. Instantly, the crowd began to disperse. Watchman was well known in the fighting circuit and his son's fight with Bald Eagle had already begun to spread. They also knew when Bear wanted privacy. His words were spoken gently, but they still carried the expectation of obedience.

Zach said goodbye to each person, shaking hands and patting the younger kids on the back. He felt good. He looked at Bear and his sister. Ruth was showing Bear the colored stones that she had gotten for her clothes. Zach could tell from Bear's reaction that he was surprised by the amount she had been given for her work. He scooted back to Pilar's side. The feeling of peace penetrated him. Whatever the World Government was planning, they could not steal this moment from him. He was surrounded by the people he loved, and tomorrow night would be a great celebration.

He looked back at Pilar. She always looked stunning. She was only a few inches shorter than he was. Her body was lean and fit. She intimidated most men, but Zach respected her dominant presence. She was a natural leader, and not having control had broken her. He had asked her to be patient with him, and she agreed. She was content that they no longer had a chasm between them. He could sense her submission to God's authority and the peace it had given her. They would work together to accomplish the next step in their plan to resist the World Government. They were friends again, whether or not their intimacy continued was yet to be seen.

Ruth looked out of the window. She was glad the warm front had stay for one more day. She looked at the empty tree stump in the yard. Bear's grandfather would not be there today. She looked down at her dress. The lavender fabric complimented her pale skin. The deep v-cut of the front allowed her petite form to show itself from under the fabric. She hemmed the knee-length layers of the skirt with lace that she had bought from the bazaar. She wore the single pearl strung around her neck. It complimented her dress well.

"Oh, Ruth, you look beautiful," Deborah said. "I was so worried for you, but look at you. You look radiant with health and vitality."

"Not only health, mind you. I'm sure love has something to do with the glow of her cheeks and the sparkle in her eyes," Esther said, not trying to hide her smile.

Ruth looked at the two beloved sisters who she considered family. They stood in her small room at Bear's house. They were dressed in full-length dresses with their silver hair piled on their heads. "I'm so glad you two were able to make it to the bazaar and the wedding. I have missed you both so much."

"Oh, Ruth dear, don't make us cry. Pilar has done our makeup, and we don't want to ruin her work," Esther said, dabbing at her eyes with the bottom of her sleeve.

"Li sends his regards," Deborah said, changing the subject to prevent her own tears. "He's watching over the trading center for Pastor Tom. He's an amazing young man. He has taken to Pastor Tom. They are always together now, working on something or other."

"Does he go by Li instead of Charlie?" Ruth asked. When Zach came back from visiting Tom at the Trading Center, she noticed that he started calling him by that name also.

"Yes, he asked for us to all call him Li," Deborah said. "That was the name that Pastor Tom used to baptize him."

Ruth thought of her own name change when she was baptized. "His name change is good. I will now think of him as only Li, the Elite Efficientist turned Colonial rebel."

"It might be more appropriate to call him the Colonial cowboy. He only wears western clothing. I think we got him hooked," Deborah said, smiling.

"Isn't it amazing, Ruth, that God gave you the vision of him at our table when you were still living with us? Your words prepared us for him. We knew exactly who he was when he arrived on our porch, so we were patient with him and answered all of his questions the best that we could," Esther said.

Ruth nodded. "And I'm glad you got to meet Levi after all of these years. He has done a wonderful job establishing this village. Your ministry did a great work in him."

Deborah tried to wave the compliment away. "We were staying obedient to God. But I'll tell you that daughter of his, Pilar, is one strong woman. I can see why your brother likes her."

"She has become my close friend," Ruth agreed, but she wasn't sure that Zach's relationship with Pilar would ever be like it used to be.

"They asked us to stay a few more nights, but we have to get back home tonight after the wedding. Our sweet houseguests need us, and Pastor Tom is anxious to get back to the trading center," Esther said.

"Plus, I'm sure everyone will be busy...taking care of family matters," Deborah said, winking.

"That Bear of yours is some kind of man," Esther said. "When he was training those men yesterday, I about fell off my seat. He's quick as a jackrabbit but fierce as a bear. I've never seen anything like him. His name is fitting."

"Ah, but he melts like butter when he's next to Ruth. You know a man is in love when he is unable to keep his guard up when he's around her," Deborah said.

"I'll have to be honest, Ruth. I always judged fighters. They seemed like hooligans to me. But Watchman—why, he loves the Lord! And many of those men were so respectful to us. It was nothing like the stories I heard about the fighting circuit," Esther said.

Ruth knew there was a dark side to the fighting circuit too. She had researched Bear's past and understood that he struggled with many addictions. But she would shield her old friends from the full truth. "Bear speaks to his men about God when he teaches them. Not all of them agree with him, but they do respect him and his words."

They heard a knock on the door. "Ladies, are we ready? Everything is set out here. We better get started if we are going to make it to my sister's wedding on time," Pilar said.

Pilar walked over to Ruth. "You look amazing. I'm glad I saved you that lilac eye shadow. It looks perfect with your dress."

"Thank you for all your help. We are ready," Ruth said. She grabbed a small pouch that she made with the same material as her dress.

The two elderly sisters walked out of Ruth's room into the living room. Pilar clasped Ruth's hands. "Let's do this."

Pilar turned and started her slow walk into the living room and Ruth followed her. Ruth looked at all the faces present in the house. She saw Cindy, standing next to Deborah and Esther. Bear's grandfather stood next to the table. Pilar took her place across from Zach. And Pastor Tom stood next to Bear. Ruth watched Bear's expression when she walked out of the room. She could see it—it was the one thing she wanted all her life from her father. Bear not only accepted her, though. He cherished her.

She walked up to him and he took both of her hands in his.

"God has brought us here together to witness the union between this couple—Bear and Ruth. We all know the strange events that have brought them together, which makes their marriage even more special. I can honestly say that this will be my first time to marry a retired Efficientist and a retired fighter, but I'm all about firsts lately," Pastor Tom said, allowing a smile to spread across his face.

The people in the living room laughed, and Ruth couldn't help notice that Bear only stood, focusing his attention on her. She could feel the intensity of his stare. He loved her, and she knew that. His love frightened her a little, but she knew that he would be patient with her. Her life had been emotionally void for so long. She wouldn't dare shun any of his love away. She would find a way to absorb the heat of his emotions.

"Do you, Bear, take Ruth as your wife before God?" Pastor Tom asked, looking at Bear.

Bear did not look away from Ruth. "I will," he answered.

"Do you, Ruth, take Bear as your husband before God? Pastor Tom asked, looking at Ruth.

Bear felt the blush deepen in her cheeks. "I will," she answered.

"Does anyone have anything to add?" Pastor Tom asked.

"I have something for you," Ruth said, pulling away from Bear's grasp. She opened the small bag that she had carried in her palm and drew something out.

"This is for you," she said, handing him a single pearl strung on nylon wire.

Bear took it. "This is like the necklace Naomi wore in the casket," he said, softly. Tenderness spread across his face. "And it is like the one you always wear," he said, motioning to her neckline.

"It is the last pearl that I have left. God gave me these pearls when I left the city. They helped me find my way in the

Colonies. I don't need them anymore. The last one is for you. I'm here to stay," Ruth whispered.

Bear put the necklace over his head and brought the single pearl to his neck. He fingered it for a moment before bringing his hands back to Ruth's.

"If there is nothing further, it is my pleasure to pronounce Bear and Ruth husband and wife before God and His Children. You may kiss the bride."

Bear bent down and kissed Ruth, trying to hold back the passion that was rising in him. Ruth could taste the salt on his lips and feel the heat from his face.

"I hate to break it to the newlyweds, but we have my sister's wedding to attend to. You'll have to consummate this wedding later," Pilar said with a knowing laugh.

"I think this will be the longest day of my life," Bear said, keeping his eyes locked on Ruth.

CHAPTER THIRTY-NINE

"**I**s this crowd a normal size for a wedding?" Ruth asked. The people were densely gathered, and Ruth was uncomfortable with how close everyone stood together. She sat next to Pilar on a blanket she had laid out.

"My father and mother are well known in these parts. This is the first wedding of one of their children, so everyone came to celebrate." Pilar said. Ruth could see a hint of sadness in her expression.

"Are you upset?" Ruth asked.

"Not at all. I'm happy for my sister. I had to let go of my dream of being married first. Javier and Reyna only met a little over a year ago when his parents moved into the village. I had to swallow my pride when he proposed, and I was still waiting for Zach to get over his father dying. I finally let go of my plans and started trusting God. It still hurts a little. I'm so happy for my sister, but it is difficult to watch someone live out your deepest desire."

"Sometimes the dream that we are waiting for takes longer because its influence is bigger," Ruth said.

"Or sometimes it is not the right dream," Pilar said.

"I see that you and Zach have come to an agreement. I sense peace between you both," Ruth said.

"Yes, we are starting over. What we had before no longer exists—all that I had left for him was resentment and all that he had for me was fear. So we decided we will begin again. We don't know what the end result will be, but at least we're done with the chaos and heartache that had overtaken our relationship."

Ruth heard in Pilar's voice what she had experienced when her mother died. It was a mixture of surrender and heartache.

"Do you still love him?" Ruth asked.

"I do love him, but I don't know if that love has changed somehow," Pilar said.

"He did a wonderful job marrying your sister and brother-in-law. The words he shared beforehand were spoken with power," Ruth said.

"I think he's gaining his authority back," Pilar said. "He used to preach with such anointing that you could feel the Holy Spirit being unleashed on his audience. Maybe that's why I fell in love with him in the first place. I was attracted to God's power in his life. But he's different now. There is a sense of humility and brokenness about him now—and there is an overwhelming sense of love in what he says," Pilar said.

"He loves very deeply," Ruth agreed.

Pilar fidgeted. "That is what I see in him. He loves everyone. But I don't think he'll ever love just one," Pilar said.

Ruth sat in silence.

Pilar changed the subject. "Anyway, what do you think of the bazaar? Was it everything you imagined it would be?"

Ruth looked around at the people in the crowd. "I notice that some people are wearing unique outfits from various time periods in history. I remember reading about different festivals during Old America when I was a girl. Your sister's wedding resembles much of what I read about. I've also seen many people wearing the clothes that I made. Is it normal at weddings for people to be dressed so differently? I would like to know, so I can make a variety of different clothing for the next bazaar."

Pilar smiled. "Themed festivals are still popular today— even fighters, like Bear, dress up to play a part of history. But wearing costumes at weddings and other special events is a new trend. I think it started as a backlash against the World Media. After Eve Pallue died, Colonials no longer wanted to mimic the Efficientists."

Ruth stopped looking at the crowd and faced Pilar. "Did the Colonials also copy Eve's trends?"

"People either loved or hated her. There was something so intriguing about her that even if you didn't have an HMS, you would see a print out of her or hear a story about her. When Zach would come back from the city, people used to always ask if he had seen her. But she was such a recluse. No one had ever seen her outside of the PR events. Maybe that was why she was so alluring."

"Maybe she wasn't alluring at all. Maybe it was all a facade," Ruth said.

"You're probably right. It doesn't matter now. She died. The legacy of Arthur Pallue is gone," Pilar said with finality.

Ruth said no more. She knew that Pilar would find out her true identity soon enough, but she wouldn't reveal the information at her sister's wedding. From what she knew about Bear's response, her true identity was a difficult truth to handle.

The sun was going down, and the breeze had chilled a little bit. Pastor Tom, Cindy, Deborah and Esther left right when the ceremony was over. They wanted to make it home before the snow that was expected to come in that night with a cold front. Ruth didn't think about what was to come. She only wanted to enjoy the moment, sitting next to the woman who had become her best friend. She sipped on her second glass of grape juice. She liked the flavor. She had been nervous all day, so she hadn't eaten much. She always lost her appetite when her thoughts were occupied.

Levi and his wife served food to all that had come to their daughter's wedding. Bear had volunteered to help them since Zach would be conducting the ceremony. Surprisingly, there had been enough food for everyone. Many people had brought food and drinks as a wedding gift. The rest of the presents were stacked next to the bride and groom's table. Ruth saw the table and chairs of Zach's that Bear had refinished. They looked like new. "Do you think Reyna likes the table Zach and Bear brought her?"

"She loved it," Pilar said. "Starting a new home is expensive, but I think her and Javier are off to a good start. I'm happy for them."

People were finishing their food and they were anxious for the wedding festivities to start. Ruth could feel the anticipation of the people around her. She saw that a small band was setting up to play. There were no speakers and no microphones—just a violin, a drum and a couple of guitars. Ruth looked forward to hearing the live music. It had been considered frivolous in *Life Efficiency*.

"It looks about that time for the dance to begin," Pilar said. "Do Efficientists dance?"

"It was frowned upon by *Life Efficiency*, but a few Efficientists did dance. I never did," she said.

"Too busy working, huh?" Pilar asked and laughed. "We need to talk more about your life as an Efficientist."

"I think that will be a good idea," Ruth agreed.

"I'm going to go get your new husband to sing a song for us. I'm sure he's wanting to be rescued from my dad. Will you be okay by yourself for a minute? I'll be right back," Pilar asked.

"I'll be fine," Ruth said.

Pilar walked up to the middle of the makeshift dance floor that had been created. She waited for the crowd surrounding the area to become quiet.

"I wanted to thank everyone who gifted food and drinks to my sister's wedding. We are honored that you would celebrate with us. Also, Javier and Reyna thank you for all the gifts that you have given them, so they will be able to start their new lives together. My parents have opened their hearts to you, and they would like you to stay and celebrate with us. I do want to warn everyone that a cold front with snow is expected later tonight, so we will enjoy this warm weather for as long as we can. We thank the Good Lord for giving this weather to us on this special day."

Pilar paused, allowing the people to nod their heads and say their agreements. "We also wanted to thank Zach Daniels for conducting the ceremony. As many of you know, he has accepted the call to share God's Word with others. He is not allowed to start a church according to the new laws of the World Government, but he will be available at my father and mother's house every weekend to speak with you and your family about faith. Our house will be opened to you. Many of you were expecting Bear to conduct the ceremony, but we have a better treat for you. Bear has agreed to bless my sister's wedding with a song that he wrote. Bear, you may begin," Pilar said, motioning to Bear who was standing next to Levi.

Bear walked to the dance floor next to Pilar and sat down. Ruth felt a sense of accomplishment with how good he looked in the pants and shirt she made for him. He brushed his thick ponytail of hair behind his back and straddled the drum. "Many of you have heard me sing my old Ka'to songs, but today I wanted to sing something that could be understood by everyone. I wrote this song not only for Reyna and Javier, but for everyone who has found someone to love. May your love move like the weather—in seasons of hot and cold, work and rest—I pray that the Most High fills every moment of your love with His presence."

Bear began to beat on the drum, and a hush moved over the crowd. His voice rolled out like a deep barrel of emotion. Ruth could see the small pearl around his neck resting on the dark blue of his shirt. She felt her desire for him move within her. It was the same feeling she had when he sang at her mother's funeral. His spirit saturated in feeling had caused the empty places in her soul to ache. She was bound to this man in the eyes of God, and that thought made her entire body tingle. His words were not profound, but the powerful emotion he conveyed could be felt by all.

Scent of spring moves through
And I've found my love for you
The plants take the sun
And my love for you is young

Summer heats the earth
You were destined mine from birth
The planted seeds grow
And your ways I've come to know

311

Fall's breath cools the land
And my love protects your hand
In the calm of night
I take you into my sight

Frost of winter sleeps
My love for you alone keeps
Your soul does not hide
Lay quietly by my side

She took another sip of the juice and then quickly took the cup away from her lips. She looked back up at Bear. His words began to blur, and her view of the drum began to drift to one side. She brought the cup to her nose. Was this juice she was drinking? She felt weird, and she could feel heat rising from her body. The voices around her began to press against her. She looked up again, but Bear was no longer there. She began to panic.

"What's wrong, Ruth," Pilar said, joining her.

"What am I drinking?" she asked, handing her the cup.

"It's sweet wine, Ruth. Didn't you know?" Pilar said, taking the cup.

"I thought it was juice," she said. "My vision has gotten blurred a little."

"Oh, crap, Ruth! Why didn't you tell me you were such a lightweight? This wine is very weak. How many did you have?" Pilar asked.

"I had one glass and this is my second, but I stopped drinking when I began to feel strange," Ruth said, focusing on every word she said. She would not allow herself to slur.

"Even my sister, who's almost as small as you, can have one cup and not get like this," Pilar said. "What have you eaten today?"

"I don't think I've eaten today. I'm sorry. I've been so preoccupied watching everyone that I haven't taken time to eat. I drank the juice, so I could wait to eat with Bear when he was done helping your father. I wouldn't have had two glasses if I would have known," she said, trying to concentrate on her words.

"How did you not know it was wine, Ruth?" Pilar said.

"Everything tastes different in the Colonies. And this wine was so sweet that I couldn't tell," Ruth said. "Are you laughing at me?"

Pilar tried to stifle another laugh. "No, I'm not laughing at you. I'm laughing at the situation. You are something else, Ruth. I better get you fixed up before I have Bear and Zach breathing down my neck," Pilar said, putting her arm around Ruth's waist. "Good thing you are so tiny. I could carry you if I had to."

"I'm very hungry," Ruth said, struggling to walk straight.

"Let's go talk to my dad. I know he'll have something for you to eat," Pilar said, making her way through the crowd with Ruth.

Pilar and Ruth walked arm and arm to Levi. He was packing up the leftovers.

"Hey, Dad, I have a favor to ask of you," Pilar said, trying not to smile too wide. "My beautiful friend here was drinking one of the wines someone brought, and she thought it was juice," she said.

Levi raised his eyebrows.

"I know how it sounds, but it is true," Pilar said, stifling her laughter. "She had one and a half cups of sweet wine and now look at her." Pilar unwound her arms from Ruth, and Ruth began to sway.

Ruth decided to interject. "I normally would not consume so much juice, but I haven't eaten today."

"I believe you," Levi said, smiling. "Let me give you some bread and water. That will get you back to normal in no time."

"Make it quick, Dad. If her brother or husband find out, I will be in trouble. I was the one supposed to be watching her," Pilar said with feigned urgency.

"Here you go. This will help," Levi said, setting down a glass of water from the basin and two large rolls stuffed with pieces of meat and seasoning.

Ruth quickly grabbed one of the pastries and took a bite. She chewed a few times and swallowed it down with a large drink of water. "Thank you," she said in between bites. "I didn't realize how hungry I was."

Levi looked at Pilar. "Who forgets to eat?" he asked.

"This one does. I think we will have to put her on our weekly route of food deliveries. She is way too skinny for my taste," Pilar said.

Ruth ate both pastries quickly and drank the entire cup of water. "Can I have one more cup of water?" she asked.

Levi took the cup and filled it. "Here you go."

Ruth gulped the water down. The swimming in her head began to subside. "I need to use the restroom," she said.

"Come on. I'll take you to the portables that we set up," Pilar said.

Ruth didn't hide her disgust. "Is there not another place I can go? I really do not like using the holes in the ground."

"Well, you're going to have to get used to it. That is all you will have from now on," Pilar said, smiling. "I doubt if Bear knows what he's gotten himself into. He now has a princess living with him."

"I'm not a princess," Ruth said. "I'm an Elite Efficientist, but I'm not that anymore. I'm only a seamstress."

Pilar eyed her father and turned back to Ruth. "Wow, Ruth. The honesty is coming out. I may have to ask you a bunch of questions on the way to the restroom."

Pilar grabbed Ruth's hand and pulled her through the crowd toward the wooded area where the portables were set up. "Okay, we are here. How do you feel? Can you walk?"

"I'm better now," Ruth said, standing up straight. "The food and water helped a lot. Tell your father that I'm sorry."

"Oh, Ruth, you worry too much. Believe me, my father has seen a lot worse than a woman who accidentally drank a little too much wine. I'm going to wait right here at this tree.

The portable is right there, and I don't see anyone around. Once you are done, come back here and we will go back to the party. No one will know what happened," Pilar said.

"Thank you, Pilar. You have been a wonderful friend to me," Ruth said.

"I know I am. Now hurry up before Bear starts asking questions. The portable for the woman's restroom is behind that group of trees over there," Pilar said, pointing to a large cluster of trees.

Ruth made her way to the trees. She was feeling better. She knew she needed to be more vigilant at taking care of herself. She couldn't forget to eat. What if she was stranded from home for a long period of time? She would starve to death in only a few days. Pilar was right. She was married to Bear who was a Colonial. She could no longer act like an Efficientist Princess.

She walked around the cluster of trees and grimaced. Several large wooden boards were nailed together to make a small encasement over what she knew was a hole in the ground. She opened the door that was hinged onto the wooden structure in two places. The smell wasn't too bad. She would have to hurry and get the deed over with. She stepped into the wood structure and let the door close behind her.

When she finished, she opened the door and stepped out. She was thankful no one was waiting in line behind her. She hated seeing the faces of those who would use the restroom after her. It all seemed too intimate for her. When she would go to PR events, she never used the restroom. She only stayed long enough to make an appearance and leave.

She walked around the small cluster of trees, but did not see Pilar. She began to walk toward the tree that she last saw her when a man stepped out of the woods in front of her. She recognized him right away as one of the fighters who was at the fighting camp. His baldhead was painted white. He wasn't able to fight because of a knee injury that was initially caused by Bear. Zach didn't go into the details, but he did say that the Bald Eagle was not to be trusted.

315

"Your friend left you," he said.

The man towered over Ruth, and he held some kind of hammer in his hand. It was obvious to her that he was under the influence of some sort of drug. His eyes were dilated and his breathing was rapid.

Ruth screamed out, but he slapped her across the face.

"You better keep your trap shut," he hissed. "I see that the Shaman has taken an interest to you. I owe him something for what he did to my knee. I would like to repay him personally, but I was suckered into another fight. Now I'll have to use you instead."

The man presented the hammer and began to lift it with his right hand and catch it in his left hand. "I can tell the Shaman likes you. He sang that song, and he couldn't keep his eyes off of you."

He stared at Ruth. "I can see why he likes you, but I'm a bit surprised. The Shaman used to like his women a little more womanly, if you know what I mean."

Ruth tried to run, but the man caught onto her hair. "This will only hurt for a minute. If you stay still, you might even be able to walk again. That will teach your boyfriend never to mess with the Bald Eagle again!"

Ruth screamed as the man pulled her up by the hair and slammed her body against a tree. He lifted the hammer above her knee.

CHAPTER FORTY

Bear walked up to where Levi was putting up the last of the food. "Have you seen Ruth?" Bear asked. "I can't seem to find her or Pilar."

Levi smiled and began to laugh. "Now, if I tell you, you can't be mad at Pilar. It wasn't her fault."

Bear smiled, trying to suppress the anxiety he was feeling. He had sung the song for the wedding, but he hoped that Ruth would see it was written for her. When he was done, he helped the band finish setting up. He went back to where Ruth was sitting, but she was gone. He looked through the crowd, but he couldn't find her. Thankfully, Pilar was gone too, so he figured that they were together. There were a lot of fighters at the wedding, and he wouldn't trust them with any woman, let alone his new wife.

"What happened?" he asked.

"Apparently, your new bride forgot to eat today. And she drank a few glasses of sweet wine, thinking it was grape juice. I had to give her some food and water to sober her up a little," Levi said, not hiding his amusement.

Bear clenched his mouth. Had she not eaten that day? He ate while she was getting ready for their wedding, but he didn't see her eat. "I need to be better getting on her about eating," Bear said.

"No harm done," Levi said. "Pilar took good care of her, and I gave her some food and water. She felt better right away. Ruth needed to use the restroom. They should be back any minute now," Levi said.

"Where did you set up the women's portable?" Bear asked. "I'll go check on them now."

Levi pointed. "Right through the woods over there behind that big grouping of trees. Pretend that I didn't send you. I don't want Pilar lecturing me. You know how she gets."

Bear nodded and walked briskly toward the woods. He shouldn't have left Ruth alone. A lot of the fighters stayed for the wedding, and one in particular had a vendetta against him. This was not the place to leave his new bride alone. Pilar was strong, but even she would have trouble defending herself if one of those fighters got a hold of her.

Bear made his way past the tree line. Everything got dark and his eyes quickly adjusted. Suddenly, he heard a scream. He knew right away who had made it. Ruth was in trouble. He ran toward the tree cluster, but he couldn't see Ruth at first. Finally, he saw a flash of white, and he knew who it was. The Bald Eagle had found a way to hurt him. He had Ruth pinned against the tree, and he was holding a hammer above her.

Bear lunged toward the figure and ripped him away from the tree. Ruth fell to her knees. He saw her crumpled form on the ground and rage filled him. He grabbed the hammer and threw it into the woods. Then he reached for the man on the ground. The smear of white paint was all over his face. Bear's fist pummeled the man's face.

"You coward! Fighting a woman with a weapon!" Bear yelled.

"I'm doing to her what you did to me!" the man yelled back.

Bear's fist planted another forceful blow into the man's jaw. "She's my wife!"

Bear could no longer control his body. He mounted the man and began wielding both fists into his ribs and face. The man became limp, but Bear's fist kept hammering. "Don't you dare touch her again!"

Zach and Pilar ran past the cluster of trees. Zach fell to his knees and grabbed one of Bear's fists, trying to protect his own face from receiving the blow. "Bear, he's out! Stop! You'll kill him!"

"I want him to die!" Bear said, pulling his arm away from Zach.

Pilar ran to Bear and grabbed hold of his other fist. "Stop, Bear! Ruth is watching you!" she yelled.

Bear stopped. His chest was heaving and blood covered his fist. He looked back at the tree that Ruth was leaning on for support.

"Did he hurt you?" he asked, looking at her knees.

"I'm bruised," she said, placing her palm to her mouth. "But you stopped him before he hit me with the hammer."

Pilar and Zach let go of his fist. He got up and walked toward Ruth, grabbing her with his bloody hands and taking her into his arms.

Zach knelt next to the man and placed his hand on his chest. "He's still alive. He won't feel very good in the morning," Zach said, turning to Pilar. "Thank you for coming to get me."

Pilar got up and walked to Ruth. "I'm sorry I left you, Ruth. I saw him coming, and I knew exactly who he was. He was carrying a weapon, but I couldn't see what it was. I knew I couldn't beat him. I ran as fast as I could to get help before he came to you," Pilar said, sweeping Ruth's hair away from her face.

"You did the right thing," Bear said. "He would have only hurt you to get to her."

"How did you get here so quickly?" Pilar asked. "I was looking for you, but Zach found me first."

"I was talking with Levi and he told me about the wine, so I wanted to make sure everything was okay," he said. "I heard Ruth scream and—" Bear stopped. He hadn't felt this desperate since he watched his mother die. He saw Ruth's body fall to the ground, and all he could envision was the worse.

Bear turned to Zach. "Thank you for coming. You saved me from killing this man." Bear looked at the man unconscious on the ground. "But I still want to hurt him," he said, his body became tense once more.

Ruth embraced him harder. "Take me home, Bear. I'm getting cold," she whispered.

"Get her to the truck, Bear. I'll take care of the Bald Eagle. Some of his men are still here. I'll have them pick him up and take him," Zach said.

"Thank you," Bear said.

"Consider it my wedding present," Zach said. He got up and walked toward Bear and his sister. "You need to take Ruth home and not let this incident ruin your wedding night. You were able to protect her. She will be fine."

"Yes, I was," Bear said, as he held Ruth tightly. "I thank God for leading me to her."

Zach nodded. "The weather is turning. The cold front is coming in," Zach said. "Go home before the snow begins to fall."

"You are right, my friend. Thank you for everything," Bear said. He reached his bloody fist around his new wife's body and picked her up, bringing her close to his chest. "Come with me. I have a surprise for you in the truck. Let me take you to our home."

Ruth smiled. The night shielded her bruised face. "Will that something happen to be new tub?" she asked.

Bear smiled. "You'll have to wait and see."

Pilar watched as Bear carried Ruth away into the woods. She could feel the intensity of their emotions for each other. Once they were gone, the energy that pulled them together left with them. An icy breeze pierced through the woods, separating her from Zach. She looked toward where he knelt next to the painted man, beaten on the ground. His concern for the man was obvious. She had prayed that Zach would change for so many years, and now she realized that he had. Except his change brought him closer to God and further from the relationship she wanted from him. She didn't know if they could ever find their way back to each other.

"You want me to watch him while you get his friends?" Pilar asked.

"Yes, I remember them sitting by the band. They didn't seem like they were in any rush to leave," Zack said, getting up. He looked at Pilar. "Are you cold?"

"I am, but I'll be fine," Pilar whispered.

She looked at Zach. "I want to let you know that I know who Ruth is. I don't want you to have to hide it from me. I know how terrible you are at lying," she said.

Zach stared into Pilar's eyes for a long moment. "How did you find out?"

"I put together the clues. Remember when I first saw Ruth? I was riding my brother's bike, and when I asked you who she was you said *Eve* first. When we visited Pastor Tom, you both kept having these private conversations, so I knew something was up. And yesterday when Bear proposed to her, he said something about her bodyguard. Then tonight when I was talking to Ruth, I mentioned Eve Pallue and her tone stiffened a bit. Then just as we headed to the portables, she mentioned being an Elite Efficientist. That's when I realized who she was. I didn't say anything because I didn't want to make her uncomfortable," Pilar finished.

"I'm sorry we didn't tell you earlier. It's not something people will understand or even believe," he said.

"Just remember that I'm on your side, and my family and I will help you and Bear in every way possible to keep her safe," Pilar said.

"Thank you, Pilar. Your support means a lot."

CHAPTER FORTY-ONE

Bear slowly rolled his truck into the grassy area of his yard right when the snow began to fall. He was glad they made it home safely. Normally, the snow would have halted his drive, but they made it home in time. He looked toward his bride. She was the most innocent woman he had ever met. God had saved her for him. He didn't deserve her, but he would not reject the gift that he had been given. The light of his truck flickered on. Her expanded pupils caused her to squeeze her eyelids together in the light. He could now see the bruises on her face. One particular area on her lip looked swollen, but not too much. She would feel and look better in a few days. Her lavender dress was stained red by the blood of another man.

"We need to get you out of the dress," he said. He got out of the front seat and walked around the truck. He opened the truck door, and moved Ruth's legs toward him. He gathered the fabric of her skirt, and pulled the dress over her head. He threw the material on the ground. She wore only a simple white slip under her dress. He saw that she was unashamed to be wearing next to nothing before him, and he liked that.

"I am cold," she whispered.

He lifted her small frame and pressed her toward his chest. He closed the truck door with his foot and walked to his house. He noticed that light was coming from the windows. He opened the door and was thankful for the fire in the stove. He looked around. His grandfather had prepared the home for them. Ruth's old door was tightly closed. The old man must have switched rooms while they were gone. He would no longer be sharing a room with his grandfather. He would now share his bed with this precious creature in his arms. Bear sat Ruth next to the fire.

"Warm up while I wash my hands," he said in a husky voice.

Ruth sat down on the chair, allowing the fire to warm her. She watched Bear as he walked to the kitchen, but she said not a word.

Bear went to the basin in the kitchen and rinsed the caked blood off of his hands. He would not let a foolish kid ruin his wedding night. He had bided his time. He had been gracious and sung for Reyna and Javier's wedding, but the entire time all he could think about was Ruth. The image of her lying on the table in the front yard wearing her white nightgown was seared into his memory. The image of her at the river, washing clothes with the scrubbing board between her legs ate at him every moment. The stories she told him from the *Bible* resonated with him. She was everything he could want in a woman and more. In all his dreams, he would have never envisioned a woman like Ruth being his wife. God had blessed him abundantly, and he would never take that gift for granted.

He dried his hands on his pants and turned back to Ruth. She was staring at him still with the womanly innocence that he had grown to love. He pulled his shirt over his head and flung it on the floor. He had some bruises from the spars and fighting lessons he conducted during the fighting camp, but they were nothing like Ruth's bruises. He walked slowly up to her and gently grasped her hand and placed it on his chest. "I am yours," he whispered before kissing her.

He felt Ruth finger the small pearl around his neck. He knew it held meaning to her and because of that he valued the pearl even more. The pearl represented many things, but most of all, it showed that Ruth was no longer searching for a home. She was staying in his home with him. He knew that loving her came with a risk. The World Government would look for her if they discovered she was alive, but he was more than willing to take that risk. In fact, that risk gave his life renewed purpose. He would protect Ruth with every last fight he had in him.

He gently stroked the swollen portion of her mouth with his thumb. "He struck you hard," he said.

"Yes," she whispered. "He wanted to hurt you, so he hurt me. I tried to fight him off, but he was too strong."

"No, he is weak and a coward. He couldn't attack me, so he attacked the one I love. He must have been watching us. I will be more careful in the future," he said, feeling his heart rate rise again.

"It is over," she said. She took his hand from her face and placed it on her chest. "I am here, and I am yours. Keep your attention on me."

Bear felt the smoothness of her skin. "That won't be hard," he whispered. Her body had warmed from the fireplace. Now he wanted to warm her himself. He picked her up and carried her to his room. He closed the door behind him. The cold front swarmed around them outside, but he knew the heat inside would last the cold, winter night.

It had been two days since their wedding, and Ruth still felt a tingling sensation in her body when she looked at Bear. They were barricaded in the house. The cold front dropped several inches of snow. It was more snow than Bear had ever seen in that area. They stayed tucked into their bed, talking, reading and sharing their love whenever they wanted. Ruth hadn't expected love to feel like this. She knew now why her father frowned on it. Marriage was nothing short of a supernatural miracle in her mind.

She had taken several heated baths with the tub that Bear bought her. He gathered snow and warmed the water on the stovetop. Thankfully, he had chopped wood to last the entire season. Bear's grandfather stayed in his room or he wandered out to his stump for a while until the cold drove him back in. He kept his distance from the newlyweds, and Ruth appreciated his consideration. He had even cooked the new couple meals a few times. Today he left bowls of grain and dried berries out for them. Ruth sat at the table with Bear and ate her breakfast. She eyed the LPS, wondering about the articles that she had been writing. Did people actually read them? Should she continue writing them?

She didn't know what was next for her, but she did know that after thirty-two years of life, she had finally found her way home. She would enjoy her time with Bear for as long as the snow prolonged their honeymoon time. They would find their way together. Their lives were both on the verge of change, and God would be their constant center on the journey they would take together.

"What are you thinking?" Bear asked between bites.

Ruth smiled. "My life as Eve Pallue was an illusion. I worked so hard to add to the facade that my father had created. But my life with you is so real. I feel more alive than I have ever felt. When I saw you sing at my mother's funeral, I felt a glimpse of what I'm feeling now. That is why I began to like you. That is why I had to research who you were."

Bear looked down at his food. "My past almost killed me. I had many demons in my spirit from the drugs. I welcomed them into me. But Naomi helped me fight them. When Zach's father died, I stayed here to help him through it. I thought I owed him that, but Naomi got a hold of me. She loved me without judging me. My father was always distant from me, but she showed me how God was a Father who would never leave me."

Ruth nodded and stared at her new husband. She felt no need to fill up the air with more words. She enjoyed being silent before him.

"God kept me here for almost five years. He took me out of the fighting circuit and, besides my grandfather and my young fighters, I have been alone. If I would have known that I was waiting for you, I would have never complained about the days of waiting. I would wait a lifetime for you, Ruth," he said. "It feels like I have waited a lifetime for you."

Ruth smiled. "And I have waited a lifetime for you," she agreed.

He reached over and grabbed her hand. "Thank you for being patient with me. I can sometimes be so blind."

"Thank you for being patient with me," she said, smiling. "I can sometimes be picky."

"Don't I know it," he laughed. "I've filled that tub up with hot water for you many times in the past few days."

Suddenly, they heard the sound of a motor in the front yard. Bear got out of his seat and looked out the kitchen window. "It's your brother," he said.

Bear waited by the door until Zach reached the porch and he opened it quickly. "Come inside. It is freezing out there."

"Thank you, I almost didn't make it," Zach said. "I didn't want to bother you, but I had something important I needed to ask of you both and the time is limited."

"Come sit down," Ruth said. "Here have something to eat." She handed him her bowl of dried nuts and berries.

"No thank you," he said. "Levi has been keeping me well fed. He wanted me to bring you this bag of sweet bread." He sat down and set a stack of papers and the bag of sweet bread on the table.

Instantly, they heard the door to Ruth's old room open. Bear's grandfather popped out and walked toward the table. He nodded to Zach, took the bag of bread and headed back to his room. He closed the door behind him.

The three of them laughed.

"He deserves those sweets," Bear said. "He's been keeping his distance here these last few days."

"Will you be coming back home?" Ruth asked. She knew that Zach had been staying with Levi and his family, but she didn't know how long that arrangement would last.

"Actually, Levi has given me Reyna's old room for now, since she has moved in with Javier. Also, Tom has given me a room at the trading center, so I will be going back and forth."

"How is Pastor Tom doing?" Bear asked. "I didn't get to talk with him as much as I wanted while he was here. I guess I was too busy with my new bride," he said reaching out for Ruth's hand.

"He is doing okay. He is the reason why I am here. I mentioned to you both about the changes the World Government will be implementing soon."

"Yes, we know about the mandatory HMS connection and that that the World Government will try to move everyone to government housing," Bear said.

"It's going to get worse than that. The World Government wants to make all bartering illegal. Pretty much they are trying to force all Colonials to become citizens, so they can use us as a workforce," Zach said.

"Why does that bring you here?" Ruth said. She knew her brother would not bother them unless he had good reason.

"You know that we have a—well a kind of a mole—inside of the World Government. He has sent us a plan to prepare the Colonials for the changes that the World Government is implementing. But the plan involves a great risk."

"What is the plan?" Bear asked.

Zach looked at Bear and Ruth. "I'm not for this plan, but I wanted to bring it to you, so you could have the choice. It will involve Ruth coming out as Eve Pallue again."

Ruth thought about the bank key card that she had kept for almost one year. "Is it about my jewels at the World Bank?" she asked.

Zach nodded, "Yes, I know you still have the key card. And your account will not be closed until a full year since your death, which is not far away."

"There is no way Ruth is exposing her identity," Bear said. "She will have to live her life in hiding. Not only will her old bodyguard be after her, but the entire World Government will want her dead."

"I know, I know. I agree with you, but our resource from the World Government is adamant that I tell you," Zach said.

"Are we any closer to knowing who this mole is?" Ruth asked. "How can I trust someone that I don't know?"

"All I know is that he would make sure that we would be able to get into your vault. And we would be able to take as much out as we could carry," Zach said.

"Why do you say, *we?*" Ruth asked.

Zach stared at the table. "Because Li and I would be going with you. We would be on the run from the World Government for the rest of our lives."

"We don't need whatever you have in the vaults," Bear said. "I have plenty, and your sewing has brought us much. We will always have enough."

Ruth looked at Bear. She loved how much he loved her. He loved her to the point that he would ignore the greater good of God's people. "We have enough, but what about all the other people who don't want to be assimilated into the World Government? My jewels could possibly fund an entire movement against the World Government."

"That is why I have to bring the plan to you. Tom has collected over a dozen of those old-style computers and passed them to different leaders in the area, but he wants to reach beyond Old Texas where we live. There are many people being affected by the World Government, but we are unable to connect with them. Tom believes that we need to be united in order to resist the World Government. He wants to be able to fund a well-organized revolt with leaders willing to stand up for their religious freedom. He also believes that many people will turn to Jesus during this time, so he wants to prepare resources for seekers."

"Are we to trust this man who claims to be on our side? What if he is a spy *for* the World Government? What if Randall is disguising himself as the spy to gain access to Ruth?" Bear asked. "I will not put my wife's life at risk on speculation."

"There is no way we will know for sure, but he did warn us about the *Unum Vernum* and many other things. Look, I don't want to persuade you either way. I came to bring you the facts," Zach said.

328

"And why wouldn't I go with Ruth? I am the one who needs to protect her," Bear said, aggravated by the entire conversation.

"That's the reason why you can't go with her. You can't protect her if you get yourself on the World Government's Radar too. You have a high profile in the Colonies. If you become a target, you won't be able to hide yourself, let alone Ruth," Zach said.

"There is no use arguing about the details until we know for sure we are going to do it. What are those printouts that you brought in?" Ruth asked, pointing to the stack of papers on the table that Zach set on the table.

"These are some articles that the mole highlighted. We can't make heads or tails of them, so I brought them to see what you thought," Zach said, spreading the printouts on the table.

Ruth looked at the papers, and one image in particular stood out to her. "There was an attempted murder?" she asked.

Zach looked at the printout. "Yes, a lower ranked Efficientist tried to stab Neil Elder, but a man from Randall's team stopped him and was stabbed instead. Randall ultimately took the man down. No one died."

"Can I see the printout?" Ruth asked.

Zach handed her the page.

She saw an image of Randall wearing his typical suit. Her life with him seemed so distant now—almost like a dream.

"Here are a few more articles of the incident," Zach said, laying a few pages on the table in front of Ruth.

Ruth let her eyes linger over the pages. Suddenly, her heart began to race. She snatched one page in particular up and brought it to her face. It wasn't Randall she stared at, but the man behind him. He was a large, dark-skinned man wearing a suit in the bodyguard fashion.

"Who is this man?" Ruth asked, pointing to the man.

"That is Matt Coughlin. He's the man on Randall's team who saved Neil's life. Why?" Zach asked.

Ruth put the paper down. "That man is Jonah," she said.

"The man who saved you from the fire?" Bear asked, staring at the image.

"Yes," Ruth said. Tears began to stream down her face. "He is alive."

Zach picked up the paper and examined it. "Well, I think we found our mole."

Onoma Series:
Eve of Awakening: Book 1
Bear into Redemption: Book 2
Mark within Salvation: Book 3
Hunt for Understanding: Book 4
Straight to Eternity: Prequel Novella

I hope you enjoyed this fiction series. If you like this book, please write a quick review on Amazon. Also, if you enjoy my writing, check out my other non-fiction and fiction works on my website, www.alisahopewagner.com.